See My Smile

Michael Herd

First published in the United Kingdom in 2016

For further information on this and other works by Michael Herd contact michael@herd.uk.net

ISBN: 1535289341
ISBN-13: 978-1535289344

Book cover art work by Matthew Herd

DEDICATION

To my wife Marita and sons Matthew and Jonathan who make each day worth living.

ACKNOWLEDGMENTS

My thanks to the many hundreds of entrepreneurs with whom I've worked and whose stories have provided the inspiration, but not the subject, for these stories.

CHAPTER ONE

It was dark and it was early, only a pale glimmer of moonlight passed through the curtains. John twisted his torso beneath the duvet, careful not to disturb the warm sleeping body next to him. Drowsily, he reached out towards the small alarm clock on the bedside table. He tried to visualise the route, under the lamp shade, past the cold mug of half-drunk tea, over the cheap spy thriller that had remained unread for weeks. Nearly there. Just as he stretched out his fingers, his thumb knocked the precariously balanced watch. He silently cursed as it clattered to the floor, to him the noise was deafening in the silence of the bedroom. He paused for a moment, Lucy, his wife, stirred, but she seemed undisturbed by the cacophony, the rhythm of her breathing returned. He moved again, more carefully this time, more awake now, and grasped the tiny timepiece. Activating the small backlight, he brought the simple face of the clock up close to his night-blurred eyes. Four a.m., he sighed, he knew he would not be getting back to sleep tonight.

His side of the bed was damp with his sweat, making it an uncomfortable nest. He longed for the deep, unconscious sleep his wife enjoyed next to him. As he lay, his bladder, confused by the early activity, ached. Too much coffee last night. Nothing for it, might as well get up, he thought to himself.

He eased his long, though no longer athletic, frame from under the covers and sat, body slumped on the edge of the bed. As his eyes became more accustomed to the half-light, he stood, a little unsteadily, and started the treacherous barefoot trek across the bedroom, careful to avoid the assorted detritus of life that littered the floor. He had just reached the door, congratulating himself on a silent passage, when his wife's soft sleepy voice brought him to a halt.

"John?"

"It's early love, go back to sleep." As he reached again for the door handle, she spoke again.

"I've been thinking. If you really want to do this, then do it, we'll manage somehow," she said sleepily. She paused long enough that John thought she had returned to sleep, but as he turned she said drowsily, "But, John."

"Yes, love?"

"Don't …" she paused.

"Don't what?"

"Don't ever, ever risk our home."

He half smiled in the darkness, trust Lucy to be supportive, "Of course love," he said gently, "not the house."

John stepped through the bedroom door, his bare feet sensing the smooth, cool wood floor of the landing, he quietly pulled the door closed behind him. There was a glow from the cheap plug-in nightlight by the bookcase. Walking close to the wall, to avoid creaking boards, he made his way across the landing towards the stairs. He paused as he passed Daniel's bedroom door, but there was no sound from his son, just the steady ticking from the carved wooden clock, a present from a doting grandmother. As he reached the stairs, he curled his toes over the edge of the top step, like a diver preparing on the high board. Once sure of his footing he looked down to the hall in darkness below. Using the banister as a guide and with his feet feeling their way for each step, he made his way downstairs, careful not to step on any abandoned toys or a comatose cat. He only relaxed when he had made it across the hall and into the kitchen and closed the door behind him.

He switched on the light, the bright spots blinding him for a moment. Next the kettle, his bladder would have to wait. He moved to the breakfast table where the abandoned paper pad and pen from last night's brainstorming were still lying. As the comforting sound of the boiling water pushed back the early morning quiet, he looked again at his first attempts to put a form to his idea.

> ***EarStream - Business Plan***
> *This new business will seek to exploit a new, patented technology that uses advanced electronics to enable the focusing of sound for medical, military and gaming applications.*

He sighed, after four hours all he had managed to achieve last night was three pages of barely intelligible scribbles, a company name, a roughly sketched logo and the first three lines of a business plan. But, he mused, at least he had a company name now, EarStream did sound like a business, or at least a product. But who was he kidding, he knew nothing of starting, let alone running a business. How could he take this risk?

Why not go back to his old life, a safe income, a job that he had been good at and sort of enjoyed and allowed him to support the family that meant the world to him.

But this business idea wasn't like that. He couldn't just turn it off. It had become an obsession, a 'what if' that gnawed at him, keeping him awake at night with a mixture of trepidation and excitement. Was he an entrepreneur or just a naïve dreamer? There was only one way to find out.

He could manage the risk, couldn't he?

In the end it would be worth it, wouldn't it?

It hadn't started out like this. He had had no plans, no intention of starting a business, but somehow it seemed like the only way to take the idea forward. He couldn't just leave it, the prospect of doing something that could possibly help Daniel meant so much more to him than just doing a job.

That meant he had to try, didn't it?

CHAPTER TWO

It had started three months earlier; the early autumn wind was swirling the fallen leaves as he made his way up to their house. It was a late fifties brick semi, solid looking, built to last through the generations. Like most of the street, the once colourful front garden had lost its lawn, trees and flowers and was now a concrete hard-standing for cars. The street had been shabby chic in the seventies and eighties when young professionals had taken the properties on, knocking down interior walls and installing bijou kitchens. Now, builders' skips were a rarer sight on the streets. Many of the bigger properties had been converted into flats, fuelled by the buy-to-let investors. A few of the smaller semis, perhaps now with less chic, still served as good sized family homes for the couples early in their parenthood, like John and Lucy.

His fingers fumbled for the front door key. John was rushing, he was running late for dinner. In jeans and open neck shirt he looked exactly what he was, a computer programmer. Like many young graduates from Brighton, he had been swept up into the tech career dreams of IT and had thrown himself into the world of C++ and JavaScript. When he had graduated, good programming jobs had been easy to come-by, especially up in London. But as the boom in the City had passed and the financial crisis began to kick-in, the banks and consulting houses had cut back on their software teams and commuting had become an expensive way of wasting three hours a day. Now, several years on, he found himself working at Enterprise IT, a small software company along the coast in Worthing, developing and maintaining CRM systems for local clients. His unfashionably long hair and beard was all that remained of the applications idealist who had believed that good software could free the people of drudgery and give everyone new opportunities. Now disillusioned, programming was a job. It paid the bills and he could get home at a reasonable time each night. His code was good, but pedestrian, there were no new ideas, no revolutionary designs, no spark.

As he opened the front door the welcoming warmth and smell of a bubbling Bolognese greeted him.

"Hi," he called to the kitchen. He shook off his coat in the small, cramped hall and dumped his bag amongst the clutter. "Something smells good."

Lucy gave a thin smile as she came from the steamy kitchen, she looked weary and a little troubled. In her early thirties now, some of the vibrant energy of the dedicated teacher had left her. She had adopted the uniform and manner of the young harassed mum, bare feet, serviceable faded jeans and a cheap cream t-shirt, items that washed well and definitely didn't need the iron. Her kind and intelligent face, showed a few more lines round the eyes than John remembered. Was she laughing more now? He didn't think so. Her beauty had matured, perhaps even faded a little, but you could see when she smiled that it wasn't far below the surface.

"Hello," she replied. "Did you remember the parmesan?" On seeing John's blank look, she sighed, "Never mind, we'll have cheddar. Get yourself washed up, the pasta will be ready in five."

John grimaced, "Sorry. Clean forgot. Where's Daniel?"

"The usual, he's hardly moved from the lounge today," Lucy sounded tense, and John realised that perhaps this hadn't been such a great day in the Miller household. He turned and made his way towards the lounge, fixing an exaggerated smile on his face. As he entered, he called out, "Daniel. DANIEL! Where's my favourite boy?"

Daniel, was small for his three years. His auburn hair sat slightly awkwardly on his broad head, as if it was a size too big. He was a sturdy child, but with delicate hands and features. He was seated cross-legged on the lounge floor in front of the television. He had his back to the door. His dark blue tracksuit was a little small for him, leaving a glimpse of pink bare back between his top and his trousers. The TV was on. A pair of manically cheerful presenters singing happy songs on a children's show, but Daniel did not appear to be watching it. He had a small red plastic car in his hand that he was holding close to his face, squinting and turning it slowly to look at its moulded lines. More cars were lined up in an orderly fashion on the coffee table beside him. Daniel liked cars and he liked them lined up.

"Daniel, what have you been doing today?

"Heh, that's a great looking car.

"Is it a sports car?

"Red's my favourite colour for sports cars.

"Can I see?"

John didn't really know why he spoke like this to Daniel. His son didn't respond to it. Perhaps John believed this was how you were supposed to talk to your children. Was he pretending to be a parent, a father? A father should be able to communicate with his son. Have a special father-son bond? Why couldn't he?

And Daniel didn't respond today. It could sometimes take hours for him to fully recognise his father's presence. John tried again, making sure that his voice didn't convey any of the frustration or sadness that this nightly routine produced.

"Daniel, DANIEL, daddy's home." He reached for the remote and switched off the television, still no reaction. He leaned down and scooped up Daniel in his arms. The child squirmed, trying to see his car and even more concerned with keeping his face turned away from his father's. John kept moving his head, trying to make eye contact, gently saying his son's name in an attempt to get a look of recognition.

After a minute or two, his son's obvious discomfort got to him, he gently returned him to his place on the rug and stepped away. Daniel resumed his examination of the car. John's heart ached. What would he give to be able to step into his son's closed world, stare into his eyes and make him understand how much he loved him? But not today. Today Daniel was in Daniel's world. A world like an impenetrable bubble that kept all others out.

He switched the television back on, bent down and stroked Daniel's hair away from his eyes, "I'm going to talk to mummy now. You can show me the car later," no response, he stood up and walked slowly from the room. Maybe later Daniel would see him, show him his car, maybe later.

***

It had been about six months since Daniel had been diagnosed as being on the autistic spectrum. Nobody said autistic anymore. Though John and Lucy had strongly suspected it, it was a still a shock hearing an expert confirm it. At first their GP had thought it may have been a hearing problem, but after hours spent in the audiology clinic, this had been discounted. Daniel could hear OK; he just didn't always respond. They had read the books and researched the latest findings on the Internet, but still the diagnosis seemed detached from their child. It wasn't denial. It was just that Daniel's symptoms seemed so much more personal than the characteristics of autism as outlined in the literature.

Yes, Daniel's language development had been slow compared to other children of the same age and yes he was a little odd in social situations, but all kids develop at different rates didn't they?

And, yes, Daniel liked to line things up, and to do the same routines again and again, but heh, none of us really likes change. Was his behaviour really doing anybody any harm?

One book had said that an autistic child may recognise your face but not be able to read or interpret the expression, the emotion. In other words, they couldn't tell if you were happy or sad by looking at your face. John and Lucy couldn't accept that Daniel couldn't see them smile. It broke their hearts to think of it. Daniel was their son and he must see how much they loved him.

So *as* his parents, they wouldn't give up. They had seen the development of their child before the decline. When he was two, he had been such a happy, *normal*, child. They understood the diagnosis, they weren't delusional, but that didn't mean you stopped believing that things could change. There had been plenty of stories in the press of miracle improvements, though never cures for autism. They would continue to search for ways to help their child, to try and break down the wall and let their son see them smile.

CHAPTER THREE

The dinner party had been in the diary for weeks. It was just Jake and Jane from two doors down having an informal supper, but for Lucy it was like Cinderella going to the ball. She and John didn't get out much together. Where do you get a baby sitter for an autistic child? It was not that Daniel was difficult. But occasionally he reacted irrationally to something and once upset he was difficult to settle. Anyway, potential sitters, and even friends, got nervous and anxious about looking after him. So it was a real treat that Lucy's mother was staying over and had offered to give them a night off.

As John entered the bedroom, Lucy was standing at the mirror checking her seldom worn make-up. She was wearing newly bought and slightly risqué underwear. It suited her figure perfectly. She was quietly singing an old Bee Gees number to herself and her body swayed as she jived to her own rhythm. She loved the old disco classics, she even kept her mum's original record player in the bedroom like a guilty pleasure. John approached from behind and put his arms around her. The scent of her musky perfume drew his lips to her neck. She closed her eyes and leant back in his arms, as his hands moved up her body, she murmured.

"Down boy, or I'll never get my clothes on."

"Suits me," whispered John as he moved his lips up her neck towards the earlobe, "we could be fashionably late."

With a long sensual sigh, she pulled away and tried to compose herself as she turned, "Mum's downstairs, it's nearly eight and Jane likes to eat early. I've not had a decent glass of red and a sensible adult conversation for months. And that includes talking to you."

As John smiled and started to move away, she reached for him and murmured teasingly, "But hold the thought, later I'm all yours."

John kissed her gently on the lips and snapped the elastic of her silky panties, "Till tonight then." As he walked away John took up the song that Lucy was singing, tried, but failed with a John Travolta move, they both laughed and badly sang a chorus together.

"Go and make Daniel's supper," she said, "or I'll never be ready."

God, it was great to see her happy like this, John thought, it made him remember why he had married her. He couldn't recall the last time she had worn her make-up, she usually preferred the clean, fresh natural look that she had cultivated at University, so it created a real contrast when she applied the full eye-shadow, blusher and lipstick, especially the bright red lipstick she was wearing tonight.

***

In the years after university John and Lucy had had the ideal work-life balance. They had stayed on living in Brighton, not quite wanting to give up the student life. John got a job in London, Lucy at a local primary school, but even with his commute, they seemed to move effortlessly between their work and social life's. Both had retained many of their friends from college. This was a City that held on to its graduates like a social magnet. Their two groups of friends operated in parallel worlds of work, sport, shopping and then came together in the pub on a Friday night. It was easy-going and fun. They lived for now, not realising that they would probably never have this level of leisure time and disposable income again, until they retired, and then they might not have the energy.

As the group reached their late twenties things began to change. Couples, once loosely aligned, started firming up their relationships with rings and mortgages and vows. The Friday night sessions became a couple of pints and then just a swift half before leaving the diehard singles to their imagined world of nightclubs and parties. The first children were cute, a novelty, something to coo over. But soon the groups started to divide into the 'haves', having partners and children, and the 'have nots', not having sleepless nights and responsibilities. There was some resentment, some jealousy and many mistakes. But then the social crowd quickly became more like a reunion than the norm. New mums made new friends at the toddler groups, PTAs, kids clubs, a shared cycle of activities. Common interests. Weekend diaries were filled by children's birthday parties and family outings. No time for five-a-side football or club nights. House parties were tamed by carry cots and baby sitters. Stag and hen nights seemed to be marking the end of friendships as well as the start of couples.

And then they had moved. Only a few miles, but it might as well have been a different country. John had got this new job in Worthing, so there was now no need to live a walkable distance from a commuter station, it gave them an opportunity to get a bigger house, more space for Daniel, a small garden. Space to entertain, but nobody came. The easily promised meet-ups at the cocktail bars quickly dried up for Lucy. She was no longer part of the 'cc' list for socialising. John would meet his old university pals at techie networking events but rarely socially. It was a drive away now with all the baby stuff rather than a late-night cab. Then Daniel didn't get on at the local toddler groups, he was different, didn't fit in, so Lucy kept him and herself away. So there was no gathering of the mums at the play-school gates, no coffee mornings or 'ladies that lunch'. For them their home-life became an endless stream of medical, social and educational specialists, social workers, and finally each other.

God she so needed this dinner party.

***

Jake worked at the University of Sussex and Jane with the local council, so their parties were always an interesting mix of town and gown. They had no children and perhaps that helped in their relationship with John and Lucy. Autism, or any mental disability seemed to have a polemic effect on other parents with children of the same age. It either made them overly sympathetic, not wanting to offend by discussing the achievements of their own offspring. Or worse, they could almost ostracise you with their continuous talk of toddler groups and birthday parties to which you were never invited. With Jane and Jake, it was different, Lucy could be what she was, an intelligent, sociable, beautiful, funny and confident woman that had other topics of conversation beyond children and autism.

When John and Lucy arrived at the party, they were a little late and the conversation was already humming. Lucy was quickly in her element. A room full of potentially interesting people she didn't know. But John stood back. As he had got older John had felt his social confidence wane. He was comfortable on his own, or with Lucy or even with small groups. But he found the small talk with strangers a bit of a trial. He would find himself either getting too engrossed in a conversation and so monopolising one person all night, or flitting from the edge of one group to the edge of the next, failing to mask his indifference.

While John helped Jake with the drinks in the kitchen, Jane took Lucy round and introduced her to new faces. When John returned to the lounge, he stood awhile and watched. God she was beautiful. As the evening progressed they hardly spoke to each other, but as if through a sixth sense they always knew where the other was and they would catch each other's eye with a smile and a flirtatious glance. Would that it could always be like this.

At dinner, Lucy alternated between talking animatedly or being engrossed, the perfect listener, but always gorgeous. In contrast, John, at the other end of the table struggled as he sat between Sophie and David, two very intense academics discussing an interface between psychology and engineering. Just as John started looking around for someone, anyone, to rescue him, he realised that the academics were staring at him, obviously waiting for his response.

"Sorry," said John, rather flustered, "I didn't catch that, I was distracted by something Jake was saying to Lucy." John looked down to the far end of the table to where his wife was sat.

"Exactly," said David triumphantly, "a perfect example of the 'Cocktail Party Effect'."

"What?" John was even more confused, "the what effect?"

"Ah! I'm glad you asked," said David, and looking towards Sophie, "it's my latest area of research and I'd be fascinated by a psychologist's input," he said, before adding as an afterthought, "and, of course, yours, John."

John groaned inwardly, what had he started.

With obvious pleasure at finding a captive, and seemingly interested, audience, David started his explanation with gusto. "The 'Cocktail Party Effect' describes the human brain's innate ability to focus on one type of sound to the exclusion of others. This involves recognising the specific attributes of say tone, frequency and volume in a voice and then separating this from the background noise. This sounds simple but of course the ambient sound is infinitely variable.

"Think for example of the way in which you can apparently hear a voice better if you look at the speaker, just as John did just now. Think what's involved in concentrating on the sound coming from one source. It's fascinating. Do you see what I mean?"

At this point, before John could reply, Sophie, the psychologist, broke in with her own thoughts on the phenomena, relating it also to the dog's ability to focus on a particular scent or an eagle's visual prowess. John was losing it a bit. His degree and current work in computing meant he kept a reasonable general knowledge of most areas of science. But this was quite a specialist area. However, as he listened, and even though much of the technical jargon they were using went way over his head, there was something in David's theory that intrigued him and he wanted to know more. While it was difficult to interrupt their flow, he waited for a pause in their debate and interjected his own high level input, "You mean if I concentrated really hard I could hear if Pascal over there is hitting on my wife?"

They all turned and stared at Pascal, a young, handsome and very intense French professor on secondment from Paris, who was getting very friendly and turning quite tactile with Lucy. She was loving it, her eyes gleamed and her cheeks were slightly flushed, but John was confident that she was only playing. Sensing an audience, Lucy looked over, smiled a smile of smiles at John and leant over and whispered in Pascal's ear that they were being observed. Pascal immediately withdrew, a shocked look on his face as his ardour paled, his cheeks reddened.

“I don’t think we need to hear that to get the meaning,” John laughed and returned to his own academic.

"OK, so I get the principle, but where’s your research going?” Sophie said.

“Well, that’s simple,” replied David, “we are developing intelligent and evolving software and hardware to replicate this brain feature in electronics.”

As the discussion intensified John was pulled deeper and deeper into the theory of the ‘Cocktail Party Effect’. He was struck by the many potential uses: improved security surveillance; sharper microphones; better hearing aids. But for John a different application was forming in his mind. Could this new technology help Daniel?

John waited again for a chance to break into the conversation. “Wow, this sounds amazing. So how do you take these applications forward?”

This drew a blank look from David, who replied unenthusiastically, “Who knows? I guess you'd have to look at patents and all that stuff.”

“So!” interjected Sophie, keen to get back to more academic matters, “Do you think you can get this into Nature?”

“That's the plan,” replied David, smugly. “This should push up my Research Assessment rating, and hasten my professorship.”

“Wooah,” Sophie looked impressed, “you'd be one of the youngest Professors in the Department.”

“But wait,” broke in John again, “what about the applications, patents, you must —?”

“Just as long as it doesn't delay publishing,” interrupted David.

“But …” his voice trailed off as he felt a hand on his shoulder. It was Lucy.

“John, I think it's time we headed home. We've got an early start tomorrow.” Lucy smiled, but firmly squeezed his shoulder again, to cut out any argument, adding in a husky whisper, “And I believe I’ve got a promise to keep.”

John looked around and realised that some of the other dinner guests were readying to leave. He rose and put his arm round Lucy. As they eased away, he looked back at the two academics, already lost back in their intense conversation. “I'd really like to talk about this further," he said towards David, but he wasn't sure if either of them heard him.

***

Wired, was that the word for it? John couldn't concentrate on Lucy as they left the party. As she linked arms and walked dreamily back to their house, the perfect couple, John's head was spinning. He hardly noticed as Lucy fussed over her mother, Joan, when they got home.

"Did you have a nice evening dear?" Lucy's mother tried hard to be a perfect grandparent, there when you needed her, but never intrusive. In her late sixties, she had had Lucy late, and so always regarded her as her miracle baby. When Daniel came along, the last in a long line of grandchildren, he felt even more special because he was Lucy's. But while she doted on Daniel, she found it hard to accept that he didn't react in the same way to her cuddles and kisses as her other grandchildren. In a typical northern way, her solution was just to love more and talk less.

"Oh mum it was a lovely evening, thank you so much for coming over. The food was yummy; you would have loved it. It was chicken I think. And the wine, well that was never Jake's strong point, but by the fourth glass I was definitely getting used to it. But just to be out, to be talking, to be meeting, to be discussing real things. It was wonderful."

"That sounds lovely dear. Was that nice young man from number —?"

But Lucy cut her off, "*Mum*, it was a lovely evening and now John and I would just like to *relax.*"

"Oh, I see, I'm sure I never meant to get in the way of your *relaxing*!"

"Come on mum. I'm sure you and dad must have done some *relaxing* in your time?" As her mother made flustered protestations, Lucy bundled her up the stairs towards the spare bedroom.

"Good night John!" Joan called out, then added mischievously, "Don't get too relaxed!" There was a grunt from John in the kitchen, and then she was gone.

Lucy kicked off her shoes and was humming gently, busying herself with creating the right atmosphere in the lounge. Low lighting, soft music, Adele she thought. A last glass of wine would be nice, or maybe port, or didn't she have a pre-made Pina Colada in the fridge. She thought they had some left from last Christmas, she was sure it didn't go off.

"John. Does port go off?" There was no reply, "John?" Perhaps he was getting things ready as well. Whiskey, she decided, whiskey on ice. That would build on the inner warmth that she was certainly feeling. Yes, whiskey. Perfect. She danced her way to the kitchen.

"I could offer you a warm embrace," she sang as she entered. John was at the kitchen table, laptop out, eyes fixed to the screen, as Lucy danced round him, hands on his shoulder, in his hair, touching his arms, his cheek.

"To make you feel my love."

"Lucy, you've got to look at this," his voice was serious, sober. Certainly not *relaxed.*

She gave up on the flirtatious dancing touches, "So much for cocktails," Lucy said to herself, this was looking more like a 'Bloody Mary' than a 'Slow Comfortable Screw', she thought. He didn't even respond when she tried to wriggle onto his lap and pretend, playfully, to obscure the laptop. He just tried craned his neck to see the screen round her. She was in the way.

Later. Very sober. Black coffee rather than whiskey. She had managed to move him to the lounge, where he sat with laptop on lap. She curled up next to him, trying to stay awake and sound interested.

"Look," said John, "it's all here online." John turned the laptop screen towards Lucy, who read, sleepily:

"The 'Cocktail Party Effect' describes the ability to focus one's listening attention on a single talker among a mixture of conversations and background noises, ignoring other conversations," she tried to stifle a yawn, then continued with little interest.

"The effect enables most people to talk in a noisy place. For example, when conversing in a noisy crowded party, most people can still listen and understand the person they are talking with,

and can simultaneously ignore background noise and conversations ..." Lucy trailed off, finding it hard to concentrate on the unfamiliar text.

But John hardly noticed, "It's just an idea," he said excitedly, "but maybe it could work. Could Daniel's autism be treated like mental noise, could a development of the 'Cocktail Party Effect', be a way to reach Daniel?" He didn't know, but he knew he had to find out.

"Lucy? Lucy what do you think?" But Lucy had left for bed. John hadn't even noticed her go.

CHAPTER FOUR

The following week, Lucy was out shopping with Daniel at the local Waitrose. Daniel enjoyed sitting in the trolley, not in the seat, but in the trolley. He liked being surrounded by the boxes, tins and packages. He was fine as long they weren't actually touching him, unless he chose to hold them. Too many times she had had to leave a trolley full of food as she carried a distraught Daniel from the shop. Lucy often wondered how long the trolley would be left, abandoned in an aisle. So Lucy would carefully place the items around Daniel so that they wouldn't inadvertently roll or fall onto him as she pushed the trolley round. She did it subconsciously now; this was just how you shopped.

Daniel was examining a jar of chicken stock, there must be something about the shape of the lid or the jar that held his attention. Or perhaps it was the colour, or the way that the granules moved in the jar as you turned it upside down. Or the sound, it made a very slight sound as you moved it. Lucy didn't know. She just accepted that Daniel would sit in the trolley turning the jar in his hands, holding it up at different angles and squinting his eyes to catch an angle, or a reflection or the light. She tried to ignore the looks that some people gave him, and her, as they passed the trolley. Except that she *didn't* really, they angered her, she resented their embarrassed looks, their pity. Sometimes she even resented their perfect families, their less complicated lives. But most of the time, she just shopped and Daniel sat and examined.

She was reaching the last few aisles, just the frozen and cereals to go, and was so engrossed in keeping the shopping away from Daniel, that she didn't notice when Jake and Jane walked up. They were hand-in-hand, relaxed, Jake holding a small basket, perhaps a few special ingredients for their meal together. Jake liked to experiment with the cooking, make his own pasta, sauces, that sort of thing. Lucy couldn't imagine having that sort of couples' night any more, let alone John cooking anything.

"Lucy! How lovely to see you." Jane gave her a friendly hug and a peck. "And Daniel. You look like you're having fun with that jar." Daniel didn't look up. But Jane being Jane just moved on matter-of-factly. She turned back to Lucy, "How are you? It was lovely to see you on Saturday. Isn't Pascal gorgeous?"

Lucy felt herself blush slightly.

"And John," Jane continued. "I saw the way you dragged him home. Early night was it?" She laughed, "All I got was 2 hours of washing up and Jake asleep in the chair."

"It had been a heavy week," protested Jake, sheepishly.

"Actually," said Lucy, "it was odd, I was feeling very mellow after all the good wine and company, but John was all wound up, completely obsessed with something one of your university mates was talking about. By the time he came to bed, I was long gone. Cocktail effect or something?"

"Oh that must have been David Lowe," said Jake. "'He's doing some interesting stuff. Too much maths for me. What was John's interest?"

"I'm not sure really. Seems to think he's found a cure for Daniel, or something. God knows, but I can't get him away from his laptop. Desk research he says he's doing. He's so engrossed I almost wish he'd discovered porn," she laughed. She looked to Jake, "I don't suppose you could talk to him. I don't want him building this up into another huge disappointment." There had been so many, so called, 'miracle cures' in the papers and on the Internet, Lucy had stopped looking.

"Sure, why not?" replied Jake, "I'll grab him for a beer and let's see what's got him so excited." Then he added with a mischievous smile, "Plus I'm sure I can find some interesting girlie sites, if you'd prefer it."

"That would be great," said Lucy with relief, "well, not the girlie bit". With a strained smile she added, "He's in most nights. To be honest we're in every night. Thanks Jake."

***

John hadn't had much time for pubs over the last few years. What with Lucy's pregnancy, then Daniel's problems and now his own obsession with this new business idea, it had stopped him feeling that it was all right to go out on his own. He encouraged Lucy to go out with friends, whenever the opportunity came up. He himself had let most of his friendships lapse and he had found that he no longer felt compelled to initiate social nights, so he had got out of the habit. He honestly couldn't remember the last time he had gone into a pub in the town centre. Or anywhere for that matter.

He pushed through the glazed front door. The 'Weasels Return', now there was a name. He wondered what the history was behind it, or was this some 'twenty something's' idea of novel branding. He was struck by the clean air. God, it must have been a long time, he still associated pubs with smoke and beer fumes. At least there were still regulars in here, drinking beer without food, playing pool, watching football. He made his way to the bar. Again, not the jostle he remembered. Most people were sitting in a civilised way at neatly distributed tables. He checked out the beer pumps, Green King, at least they still did a proper beer. He had never got used to the insipid British lagers. As the barman pulled the pint, John heard the door open and turning saw Jake enter the pub. He seemed far more at home in these surroundings than John felt. Perhaps the University still had a pub culture. He acknowledged Jake with a wave, but didn't speak until Jake was close to him. "Good to see you Jake. What are you having?"

Jake started looking more closely behind the bar. "What blonde beers have you got?" he addressed the barman, who stood aside from the chiller cabinet so that Jake could see the contents.

"The Brigand is popular sir, but not if you're driving," he said with a warning look, "It's nine percent."

"No, I'll go for something lighter, how about a bottle of Triumph, and some nuts please."

"Good idea, I'll get some plain crisps as well," John added.

John's pint glass looked somewhat old fashioned on the bar towel (at least they still had bar towels), next to Jake's bottle, he had eschewed the glass. John felt even more out of touch when he offered the barman a tenner, expecting change, only to have to go back to his wallet to find a twenty.

They took their drinks and snacks to a table by the window and away from the TV. "God I haven't been here for years," said Jake. "Not since my misspent youth. I think it must have changed name. What was it? The Thieves Kitchen I think. And now it's something to do with weasels of all things.

"There are professors in our English department who would refuse to enter this place, just as an apostrophe protest! Perhaps they had a misspelt youth." Jake quipped, enjoying his own wit. "Do you come here oft...?" He stopped and laughed, "I didn't mean that as a chat up line." He puts on a posh accent, "Do you frequent these local hostelries regularly, dear boy?"

John laughed, "No, to be honest I hardly get inside a pub at all these days. Prices have jumped."

"Ah, that'll be me with the fancy bottled beers, sorry about that. Guess I'm too used to the prices in the student bars." Now settled, Jake moved the conversation on. While he and John had met many times over the years that they had been neighbours, they had never been close. Lucy was more Jane's friend, and the husbands, well the husbands 'got on'.

"Good to see you at the weekend."

"Thanks for the invite. It was good to get out. Lucy especially misses the social life, now that we've got Daniel."

"Sorry if you got stuck with some of our professors. If you get some of them onto their research, they can bore for England."

"I know what you mean, but actually this time I found it really fascinating."

"Yes. Lucy said that something had got you stirred up. They can sometimes be a little insensitive."

"Nothing like that. Just the research that David, Dr Lowe is it, is doing, made me think of possible medical applications?"

"Medical? Didn't think that was your thing. Computers isn't it?"

"Yeah, software. I know very little about general medicine as such, but over the years I have learnt a fair bit about autism. And well, this 'Cocktail Party' idea, well maybe it could have applications."

"'Cocktail Party'? I'm not with you. I haven't really followed David's work. Jane does one of her classes with his wife, Abby. He's probably told me about it, but it all tends to go over my head. What exactly has it got to do with autism?"

And so again, John had to try and explain his thoughts. Which he found hard as they weren't clear to him. Plus, he didn't have the real technical or medical knowledge to express it.

"When I come home from work, I go and see Daniel, but it's as if he doesn't see or hear me. We know that his sight and hearing are fine, very good actually, but it's as if we're blurred or something, he can't distinguish us. I don't really know how to describe it and Daniel can't explain it. But, I think that my voice gets lost in a fog of other sounds, but not real sounds, just noise, sort of interference, in his brain. The thing is, sometimes it doesn't matter if it's quiet or not, he still doesn't hear me." John's voice cracked slightly with emotion, "It's the same with his sight, he can see, but he doesn't always see me."

"Christ John. That sounds awful, but how does David fit in?"

"Well, to be honest, I don't know if he does. His theory is based on how the brain can distinguish selected sounds from the noise of a crowd. Maybe, the same approach can help the brain distinguish my voice from the noise or interference that's in his head. Oh I don't know, it's probably stupid, what do I know?"

"No, hang on," said Jake encouraging John, "it makes some sense to me. Not the science of course. But intuitively it could be the same. It's certainly worth a conversation. I think David's away at the moment. Conference somewhere. But I can fix up a meeting when he gets back. In the meantime, maybe it's worth talking to the University's Intellectual Property guys, there must be easy ways of doing this. They keep telling us academics we should find more practical uses for our research. I can find a name. Not someone that we usually find in the English department."

John brightened, "If you could, that would be great. Thanks."

The conversation moved onto lighter matters, but they found they had little in common. They roamed around sport, John rugby; Jake cycling, music, John classic rock; Jake jazz, and their mutual friends, turned out they were their wife's mutual friends. After an hour they were definitely flagging, both with one eye on the TV looking for an excuse to leave.

Jake cracked first, looking at his phone, "Well, I've got an early lecture tomorrow, so better do some prep. I would use the excuse that leaving it to the last minute keeps it topical, but that doesn't really work when you're teaching nineteenth century poetry."

"Right," said John laughing. "But seriously, thanks for meeting me. And if you could get me that contact that would be great."

"Sure, will do. And thanks for the beer, it was good to get out of the house." With that Jake rushed to get out of the pub. John sat contemplating the dregs in his glass. Going to the pub definitely used to be more fun than this. He looked around. Groups of two or three men leaning together round the small tables near the bar, their shoulders almost touching, conspiratorial, pints in hands, eruptions of laughter. The couples, clustered round the edges of the room, like they had been flung out on a centrifuge, most sitting side-by-side, hardly looking at each other, phones on the table or in hand, distracted. Only one couple, sitting opposite each other, eyes focused on eyes, hands close on the table, but not yet touching, drinks forgotten, phones forgotten. First date, John thought. He got up and wandered over to the bar and got himself another pint. It was only eight thirty, he couldn't go home yet. As he returned to the table, he saw another lone man in the corner, pint half drunk, reading a book. Better than sitting in a hotel room, John thought, but only just.

He pulled out a small notebook from his jacket pocket. He had written 'New Business Notes and Actions' in thick pen on the cover. It had felt entrepreneurial and dynamic when he had started it, ready to capture his ideas, never let an opportunity pass without making a note for future reference. He had kept it by the side of his bed. But after his initial flurry of web research into the 'Cocktail Party Effect', and listing possible names for the company, his last action list had consisted of 'Contact David' and more recently, 'Contact Jake'. He neatly ticked off the second point and added underneath, 'Contact University IP'. He looked again at his list of possible names: 'Audiotech'; 'Hear & Far'; 'EarStream'; and 'TecHeard', but none of them leaped of the page.

He and Lucy had had fun playing word games with the business names, his favourite had been 'Shaken Not Heard', but somehow puns didn't fit with the seriousness of the project. He stared again for a full minute at the list of four names and then with a sigh added a question mark next to 'EarStream'.

Exhausted by his actions, he closed the notebook and leant back. Lifting his pint glass, he took a sip. Even beer didn't taste the same. He looked at his watch, eight thirty-four, looked at his phone, nothing new, no emergency messages from Lucy. He sighed, got up, put his notebook back in his pocket, and left the pub.

CHAPTER FIVE

As John now worked locally and Lucy had not returned to teaching, they had decided that they could, or would have to, manage with just the one car. Lucy was taking Daniel to his special needs pre-school group that morning, so John was having to plan his visit to the University by train. Whilst in no way complicated, just one service from Worthing to Brighton and then another out towards the campus, it felt so different from his previous commuting days to London Bridge, that he decided it needed some further research. John enjoyed checking the local services, stations he had never heard of, let alone alighted from. The train for the University went to stations where the platforms were too short for the trains, sounding more like the age of steam in deepest rural England than on the edge of a modern city.

He arrived at the station mid-morning, well ahead of time for his appointment at the University. The train to the campus only took twelve minutes from Brighton so he had a good hour to kill. He probably could have fitted this meeting into his lunch-break, rather than taking the whole day off, but he felt that this meeting was seminal in deciding his future and so it shouldn't be rushed. He wanted time to consider, to cogitate, to dwell on his future plans.

At eleven o'clock, the early frantic commuter bustle of the station, as John remembered it, was long gone. It was actually quite pleasant travelling at this time, it gave him the chance to calmly consider this opportunity and his other responsibilities. He had decided to get the earlier train rather than grabbing a coffee at the station. It would be good, almost therapeutic, to have a wander round the campus before his meeting. Like many cities there were two Universities in Brighton, the University of Sussex was the more *research focused*, and was concentrated on a single leafy campus on the outskirts of the city. The other, the University of Brighton was more *applied*, historically it was an amalgam of smaller technical and teacher training colleges, and was spread across several sites in and around the city centre.

It was odd, even though he had studied here, John had rarely visited the other campus. It hadn't been a conscious decision, he hadn't avoided the Sussex students, but the two groups rarely mixed. The student pubs and housing districts for both universities were in the same areas of town. The students looked the same, sounded the same and in many ways acted the same, but somehow managed to remain distant from each-other, with each maintaining an air of superiority, but for their own reasons.

Now, looking back, there had been a bit of an aura for him about going to university. None of his family had been. It wasn't just that you had to have higher exam grades to go to a university like Sussex, at eighteen, he had focused his choices on the cities he wanted to live in and the degree courses that offered a clear path to a career, so Applied Computer Science at Brighton had certainly fitted the bill, and he hadn't been disappointed. He'd enjoyed his time, made good friends, he'd met Lucy, got a good degree and that had led to gainful employment. But he'd always felt that he may have missed out on something, something more intellectual, less practical. If he had gone somewhere else, would he have spent his student days in a different, more ethereal world, discussing philosophy and poetry with the intellectual elite, rather than getting hammered on cheap beer in the student union bar after his practical coding workshops? He would never know, but now as he arrived at the campus and surveyed the sixties architecture and green spaces, he wondered if they would have inspired him in a different way, or to a different life.

The sign at the entrance of the campus reminded him of a puzzle where the signposts are there to confuse and misdirect rather than aid. There were the different Schools, arts buildings, gyms, laboratories, institutes, lecture theatres, workshops, bars, halls of residence. Phew, he thought, as he stood before it, it was like entering a small town.

It was nearing lunchtime and it was a beautiful late summer day. The pathways were congested with a seemingly endless stream of young things. It was good to see that the student dress sense hadn't changed since his day. T-shirts and shorts and backpacks were still the standard uniform, just the logos and the names of the bands emblazoned on the shirts had changed. The lawns were crowded with students sprawled around in small groups. But the groups were strangely quiet, almost calm, preoccupied with their mobile phones rather than their friends.

Following the signs that hopefully led to the Science Block, the pathway wound in and out of the red brick and grey concrete buildings, which possibly had a greater architectural impact from afar rather than close up. The only other splashes of colour came from the large notice boards. It was good to see that mobiles and social media hadn't completely replaced student notice boards. A colourful collage of A4 sheets pinned haphazardly on the board, fought for attention as they shouted out their concerts, bar nights, union elections, pub crawls, sports clubs, political rallies and cinema listings. It seemed that at least some students hadn't lost their desire to be radical, there was no shortage of opportunities for them to take affirmative action on any number of causes.

He made his way, via three wrong turns and direction consultations, to the main engineering building. He entered a maze of dated sixties style stairwells and corridors. It took him back to his own student days, trudging to lectures in soulless high rise buildings. Somehow he never envisaged a *research* university to feel like this. Despite the lawns and the impressive campus architecture, once you got inside the buildings the institutional corridors and offices were much the same wherever you went. It wasn't all dreaming spires, he supposed. That was somewhat comforting, gave him some reassurance that he shouldn't be overawed by being there.

Finally, he found room 3.2, strangely next to room 3.8, and knocked on the cheap blue panel door. A rather plain white sign declared the occupant as 'Dr Ian Billing – Intellectual Property Office'.

“Come!” A booming voice resonated through the door. With images of the Wizard of Oz in his mind, John tentatively turned the handle wondering if he would find a giant or a midget on the other side. Contrary to his expectations, it was a rather normal, though noticeably harassed, bearded chap in his forties that rose from his cluttered desk, hand outstretched in welcome.

“Dr Billing,” he announced, introducing himself. “Glad you could stop by.”

“John,” replied John, unsure whether to add the Mr, or maybe add some letters after his name, “John Miller.”

“Good, good,” muttered the good doctor, as he returned to his seat. “Sit, sit. And you're interested in the micro RNA models for diabetes? Yes?”

“Err, No,” replied John. “‘The Cocktail Party Effect’. Dr David Lowe's work.”

“Oh yes, of course, thought you didn't look like a biochemist. Now where are the papers?” He rummaged through the precarious piles of papers and files on his desk. Sometimes there was order in such seeming chaos, but not here, Dr Billing clearly wasn’t sure what he was looking for and when he remembered, had no idea where it was located. Eventually, he pulled out a thin file, containing just a couple of sheets of paper, in a simple green cardboard folder.

“Right now, what have we got here...?

"No Invention Disclosure.

"No NDA.

"No patent search.

"No IP route map.

"No commercialisation plan.

"No defence warrants.

"No impact statement.

"No heads of terms.

"No licence documentation ... Oh dear, oh dear, this doesn't seem to have progressed at all. What is it *exactly* that you want to do with Dr Lowe’s research?”

John felt rather bewildered. “Well, erm, I was chatting with David, erm, I mean, Dr David Lowe, at a Dinner party with Jane and Jake Stevens. You may know them; Jake works at the University ....”

John realised that his host wasn't listening, he was back rummaging on his desk through piles of contract-like documents. He kept quiet until the silence drew Dr Billing's attention. Then he continued, slowly and clearly.

"Dr Lowe's 'Cocktail Party Effect' algorithm, I want to try and use it."

There was a long pause, while Dr Billing seemed to reappraise the situation and more explicitly John. John felt like the suitor meeting his girlfriend's father for the first time. Did he have decent prospects? John kept silent, waiting for the inspection to finish. Were his intentions honourable?

"What *exactly* do you want to use it for?"

"Well, I'm not absolutely sure. But I think —"

"— You're not sure? You think? We have to have something more concrete than that. How will we know how to value the licence?"

John felt the conversation was getting away from him. Clearly he needed to show more dynamism. Be confident. Be specific.

"I want my son to see my smile!" he blurted back. As soon as it was out he realised how absurd it sounded.

Dr Billing fixed him with a stare for a long moment. "I beg your pardon. You want to do what?"

"Sorry. That probably sounded a bit odd. I have an autistic son, Daniel, and I believe that Professor Lowe's work could help us break through his social isolation."

"I see. A medical application. We may need to involve the ethics committee. Clinical trials. Have you considered the MRC or the TSB or maybe even the Welcome Trust?"

"I'm sorry, the what? I haven't considered anything or anybody. I'm just interested in the technology." John's frustration was starting to get the better of him.

"I think I understand, Mr ... err."

"Miller. Mr John Miller."

"Well, Mr Miller. Let me get one of our Business Development Managers. I'm more IP and legal. Please wait here, while I call. She's just down the corridor."

Compared to Dr Billing, Laura seemed encouragingly human. She had breezed into the room. Taking one look at Dr Billing and

John, she gauged the frosty atmosphere and whisked John out of the science building and across the road to a surprisingly normal looking cafe. She had such a light and easy manner that John started to feel more comfortable. The coffees were bought. Latte for her, Americano for him. The pastries, muffins, cakes, biscuits and tray bakes were declined. And finally, they were sat in a couple of easy chairs squeezed into the corner of the room. Their knees almost touching.

"Right. Now what's this all about?" Laura asked gently.

John recounted his story. Dr Lowe's research. Daniel's autism. His ideas. His conversation with Dr Billing.

"OK," said Laura, "What Ian, I mean Dr Billing, meant was, there are various funding bodies and charities that can help fund universities or companies to develop new technologies. The TSB, is the Technology Strategy Board, they do a whole range of technology development grants, anything from a few thousand to do some market research to a quarter of a million for creating a proof of concept. The key thing is that most of the grants need a sizeable contribution from the person or company applying. Some of the grants are designed specifically for working with a university...."

John tried to listen, but she was losing him, especially when he noticed a striking, arty poster on the wall behind her head, it was promoting a pub crawl around the North Laines in Brighton and John was transported back to his student days and the time he had first met Lucy. He had noticed her from afar, but she had always seemed unattainable, part of the cool, arty set, that didn't normally associate with geeky computer guys. But that night was different. It had been a three-legged pub crawl, and staggering around hog-tied and half-cut was a great social leveller. Lucy and her pal were hopeless, they had fallen way behind their group and when John and his mate Will had come across them they were sprawled across a low wall by a small park, they were giggling uncontrollably. John and Will had helped them to their feet but they seemed to have lost complete control of their lower limbs. Ever gallant, the lads had offered to see them back to Student Union bar. They had split the girls and John had ended up tied to Lucy for a thirty minute, blissful, arm-in-arm, laugh-filled, wobbly walk back to the

Uni. John was her hero and she bought him a drink and pecked him on the cheek in thanks. John was stunned, couldn't believe his luck, but then she was gone, subsumed back into her group and apart from fleeting glimpses during that nights' post-crawl disco, he hadn't managed to catch her alone again.

Laura had stopped her spiel as she had seen that John's eyes were wandering and his mind was obviously elsewhere. John noticed the silence and reluctantly tried to snap out of his happy memories. With difficulty he refocused his attention. Laura started again with renewed vigour. "Where was I? The MRC, is the Medical Research Council, there's also the EPSRC for engineering and physics and BBSRC for biotech and biological sciences. These are the main funding bodies for university research, where a company may be a partner, but won't receive funding. Finally, you get medical charities, like the Welcome Trust, that will also fund medical research. There's loads of other types of business funding schemes, like the KTPs and Innovation Vouchers, but the TSB is probably the main source. What you definitely do need is a credible business plan to attract funders and to get the University to work with you and ideally, the direct support of the academic."

Even though Laura's words washed over him, they were a relief. They were words that made sense, if only because Laura gave them sense. He still didn't have a clue what a KTP was or a TSB, wasn't one of them a bank, but it didn't matter, Laura knew. He leaned back and watched her, not taking notes and not taking anything in. She wasn't particularly attractive, at least not in a classic beauty sort of a way. She had a slight schoolmarmy air, her dark hair worn long, but pulled back and tailed at the back. Black rimmed glasses that framed soft brown eyes. She obviously knew her stuff and enjoyed her work. She leaned forward as she spoke, quite animated and intense. This was obviously advice she had given out before, but she had a way of making it seem personal. But most importantly, John knew that if he listened, he would understand her as she seemed to understand him. She could be a bridge and interpreter between this strange university world of academic research and intellectual property, and him. But he guessed that he had still better listen to some of what she was telling him.

"So if you put in an initial EOI, I mean, Expression of Interest, form into the TSB, I can get the full economic costing data for the lab work and we can go from there." She sat back. Satisfied that she had provided a comprehensive summary of the business and academic actions to take forward to an attentive audience.

"So that means *you* will help me then, right?"

"Yes, John," she smiled, "I will help you. Here's my card, contact me by email or phone. I work most mornings. But I'd get in before the holidays start, it can be a nightmare getting things done otherwise." She got up. The meeting over. Her job done. She put out her hand, but John hadn't stood.

"Oh thank you," he said reaching his own hand up to hers. "I think I'll will stay here for a while, if that's OK. Let things sink in."

"Sure," she replied, looking a little nonplussed. She liked to escort the externals off the University premises after her meetings. Academics in many ways were more predictable, more manageable. When normal people came in off the street you never knew what to expect. "I'll leave you to it," and with that she was gone. Just an empty styrene coffee cup to show she'd been there at all.

John just sat there. He had no real idea of whether that had gone well or badly. While he had never supposed that this would be easy, he had assumed that he would at least be able to understand if he was going forwards or backwards, or even to be on the right road. At least he had Laura now. Hopefully that would be a start.

***

'Historical Intellectual Property costs', 'Minimum Royalty Payments', 'Licence Assignments', 'Fields of Use'.... It was like another language, but worse, you felt like you needed a lawyer to translate it. Strange, how little you knew about the law, just that vague notion that everything was at least five hundred dollars an hour. Or was that just in the Grisham novels?

In the world of computing, there was always a manual or a help file or at least some FAQs (Frequently Asked Questions). But where do you start in the world of intellectual property and patents. John trawled his memory for past episodes of 'Dragon's Den' for inspiration, but somehow Theo's and Duncan's interrogations of poor dispirited would-be entrepreneurs didn't provide the answer.

As far as he could work out from the University's dense policy web pages, the University owned all the ideas dreamed up by the academics, which they referred to as Intellectual Property or IP. This didn't seem right at first, surely if it was the academic's work? It was something to do with 'paid to invent', and when he thought about it more seriously most companies kept or owned the ideas their employees came up with. You would just think that with Universities it would be a bit different. But he supposed at least it gave an office to talk to, rather than chasing down the individual professors. The University then shared any proceeds with the inventor. OK sounded simple, but how do you get to proceeds. It all seemed to be to do with licensing. Again, John could relate to that, he'd read those stories of the millionaire inventor making one penny for every 'cat's-eye' that was produced. But he didn't have a product. And certainly didn't have any income to pay licence fees. And anyway, the university didn't have a patent, so was that good or bad? If it wasn't protected, who owned it? Anyone? The Dragons liked patents, protection, IP. So how did you protect something if you didn't own it? Where do you start?

And so the hunt for information started. Patent office, business support sites, inventor forms, celebrity entrepreneurs, investors, tech transfer offices, self-help books, accelerators, business nurseries, incubators. The list seemed to be endless and seemingly more focused on selling you something than telling you what to do next.

***

John sat back and rubbed his eyes, strained from hours staring at the screen. Some of these so called business support sites seemed more designed to put you off than help, he thought. He was currently looking at EU funds, but getting completely lost in the various frameworks, protocols, calls and programmes. Was his idea a medical device, new electronics or a computing project? And where was he supposed to find all these European partners, he was finding it hard enough to find out who to talk to locally.

"John, JOHN! Are you with us?"

John had been so engrossed he hadn't noticed Steve, his current project leader, come to the open door of his office. He was now leaning casually against the door frame. "Oh. Sorry Steve, didn't see you there. Lost in the moment, so to speak."

John pushed his chair away from his desk and made to stand up, attempting to keep Steve's attention away from his screen. His eye glanced up at the clock above the door. Christ, he must have been on this funding site for almost two hours.

"What's up?"

"Hey, didn't mean to disturb your *moment*," said Steve sarcastically. "Just need a quick heads-up on the GK project, I'll be sending in the project update tonight."

"GK, yes of course. Pretty much on track I reckon, let's say seventy-five percent complete?"

"Seventy-five? You were at eighty percent two weeks ago. Have we got a problem here? Steve looked to John for a response, when nothing was forthcoming, he said, "You know that the various project streams have to come together at the beginning of next month, any delays on your part will create downtime across the whole project. That's a lot of non-billable time, you know how Phil will react to that? He'll really be busting your chops."

Phil was the MD of the company. He was from a finance rather than a technical background and all he seemed to care about was billable time. Each member of staff had to complete time-sheets showing how they had spent each fifteen minutes against a complex array of project codes allocated to each task within the project. These 'hours spent' were then compared the budgeted hours and progress achieved against each task. Every week Phil sent out charts and summaries of each member of staff's time management performance, if you dropped below ninety percent billable there would be a review with management. John had clocked plenty of project time, well so his time-sheet said, the problem was he had got so locked into his own research, that he hadn't actually written any code. You could get away with this for a couple of days. There was always a bit of 'thinking time' built into these projects, but he was now, way behind.

"Oh sorry Steve. Getting mixed up with the Starburst project."

"The Starburst project got pulled last month! Come on John, what's going on here? Is there a problem with GK or not?"

"No, of course not Steve. Just had to go back over the resourcing sub-routines. Bit of I/O interference. Let me check back against the schedules and I'll give you an accurate progress figure this afternoon."

"Are you shitting me here John? This isn't like you, thought you were mister reliable? Have you noticed all the *suits* in with Phil? It's never a good sign when the *suits* are in, lawyers, accountants, they always mean trouble."

Seeing the worried look on John's face, he tried to re-assure him. "OK John, give me a figure by two this afternoon. But it had better be higher than eighty percent!"

As Steve left, John logged back into the project system, he had better show some pretence of working. "Shit," he said to himself, "suits." He hadn't even noticed the suits, he wondered what Phil was up to.

CHAPTER SIX

There are six lifts, four escalators and two automatic doors in the shops in the town centre and John and Lucy knew them all. It was their Saturday ritual. A strange, inefficient shopping route for them, but the highlight of the weekend for Daniel. It had taken them a while to understand the particular attraction for Daniel. All kids like escalators, right? But not in the same way as Daniel. For Daniel there was a real intense fascination. This wasn't a bit of fun? Lifts, escalators and automatic doors for Daniel were a serious business, requiring his full attention. To understand you had to try and rethink things from his point of view and getting into the mind-set of an autistic child was never an easy thing to do.

The breakthrough was achieved one busy Saturday lunchtime with the automatic doors at M&S. A much deserved, but unplanned lie-in meant that they were late leaving the house. The town was busier at this time. Couples holding hands. Families with children running amok. And a seeming whole Grand Prix of mobility scooters. But a routine was a routine. And you didn't mess with a routine with Daniel. They'd done the lifts in Top Shop and Debenhams and the up escalator in Boots, they'd come down by the stairs to save the down escalator for later. So fourth on the list was the M&S automatic doors, this was one of Daniel's favourites.

Daniel had run up to the door, it had duly opened, he had stepped through and then turned quickly to watch the doors close behind him. But not this time. An elderly couple followed him through the doors. Daniel dissolved into tears and screamed. John scooped him up into his arms while apologising to the alarmed couple, but Daniel wriggled and squirmed to be put down. Once free, he pushed his way through a standard door at the side and retook his position outside the automatic doors waiting for them to close. Tears still streaming, he walked steadfastly towards the doors, but a young mother with a pram was coming the other way. She cheerfully thanked Daniel for opening the doors for her, but hurried off when he again wailed in anguish. It took a while. With John on the inside stopping customers coming out and Lucy outside stopping then coming in, Daniel finally made it through the doors.

John and Lucy knew that it would take a while for Daniel to calm, and in this mood there would be no peace if they tried to complete their shopping trip together as a family. As Daniel sobbed in John's arms, John shared a look with Lucy. She nodded, the message unspoken. "I'll come and find you," Lucy said with a gentle smile, "I won't be long, I've just got a few bits to get." With that she tousled Daniel's hair and touched John's cheek affectionately. "See you later boys," she said as she turned and left for the shops as John and Daniel started to walk towards the beach.

There was something special about the sound of the sea on pebbles, it had a way of calming everything down. John walked along the edge of the surf with Daniel in his arms, the sound of the sea washed over them. The regular rhythm of the waves helped to slow Daniel's breathing and his racing heart. As he held him close, John could feel Daniel's heart thumping against his own chest, but he could sense the waves worked their magic. Daniel was gulping in air as he wept. Calming, calming as the tide slowly came in and settled on the stones. When Daniel seemed more settled, John gently set him down, encouraging him to stand on his own. John knew that if he continued to hold him, Daniel would fall asleep, and then their day-out would be over. Daniel stood there for a moment, holding onto his father's trouser leg with one tightly clenched hand. They both looked out to sea. There was nothing really to see. Just a freight ship far away on the horizon. The kite surfers, a regular sight on this part of the coast, were too far off to the east to be visible from here. There were no swimmers, bathers or even paddlers. The pier was to their right, but all they could really see were the many fishing rods protruding from the wooden balustrade. It was quiet, apart from the sea, the coast-road, while not far away, was silenced by the bank of pebbles that had been pushed into place to form a flood defence. They just stared out to sea. The vast greyness seemed to dwarf their thoughts and emotions, to neutralise them into calmness.

After a further five minutes watching the sea, the spell had been cast. Daniel let go of John's leg and bent down to pick up a stone that had caught his eye. Unlike most of the pebbles that had been smoothed out by the perpetual weathering of the sea, this one was still angular and fractured. Daniel held it up to his eyes, turning it slowly and while studying it he walked unsteadily back to where the hill of stones started to rise and he sat down, keeping his eyes all the time on the pebble.

John, rolled the shoulders, feeling the last of the immediate tension leave his body, at least for a little while. He bent down, searching for a good skimming stone. He found one, dark almost black, a good size to sit within the crook of his index finger. A good skimmer was difficult to find. It had to have the requisite roundness, smoothness, and be of the perfect size and weight for your own hand. When you found one, you almost felt reluctant to just throw it away into the sea. He remembered when he was a child he would always collect the perfect skimmers in a beach bucket and take them home. They were too precious to waste on the sea. Every year his dad would wait a few months, and then add the stones to the rockery.

John held the perfect skimmer in his right hand, his index finger curled around the smooth sides. The leading edge of the stone had been thinned by the sea and was now like a blade ready to cut through the wind and conquer the waves with its bounce. He relaxed his knees. You needed to get low, almost down to wave height to get the right spin, the right skim. As he bent down John felt again the weight, felt the smooth surface, perfectly fitting his hand. He rose again and slipped the stone into his pocket. Too good for the sea.

Half turning, he reached down again and picked another stone, this time without careful selection. It was too heavy, too square, too big, too rough. He turned back to the sea, crouched and skimmed the stone. It caught the slight breeze which ruined the flat trajectory, it hit the sea, too hard and too near to an oncoming wave. It bounced once, bobbled up, it had lost too much speed. It hit the water again and was gulped down by the sea. Gone forever. John was disappointed, but glad that he hadn't wasted his perfect skimmer. He touched the outside of the pocket in his jeans. It was there, saved for another day, a perfect skimming day. It would join the beach bucket of perfect skimmers outside the back door at home.

Just then Lucy appeared above them walking across the stones from the direction of the pier. She was carrying two '99' ice creams and an empty cone containing a flake. She called down. "I thought I might find you here."

Daniel didn't respond to her call, even when she joined them and sat down beside them, Daniel in the middle, on the stones. He reluctantly gave up his stone for the ice cream cone. Daniel didn't like the coldness of the ice cream, but he liked the cone and the flake. They sat in silence and ate.

"It must be the sequence," Lucy said to John later, when they had finished their ice creams. "He has to see the complete sequence, it's the same with the lifts. You get in, press a button, the doors shut, you go up or down, then the doors open again, and you get out. Predictable, routine, repeatable, foreseeable. It gives him certainty, knowing what's going to happen next."

"That's all right, until some pesky person comes along who just wants to use it as a door, or a lift," John replied.

Lucy seemed so much more comfortable with Daniel's autism. She had a calm and rational approach that she could apply to each circumstance, something that John could apply easily within the impersonal world of software code, but struggled with in his personal life.

***

"Predictable. Foreseeable. That would be nice," John mused. But how could you *foresee* and write a business plan and *predict* the income stream for a business and even a technology that didn't exist yet.

‘What's your forecast revenue and gross margin in year two’, the voice of the TV Dragons haunted him.

He had been trying to understand the financial planning side off and on for days now, but seemed to be getting nowhere. You started by thinking about the big items, rent and product development, but then got bogged down in what his ‘sundry office costs’ might be. Why? Why, because that was what it said in the 'Business Planning for Dummies' book he had bought. Strange, they hadn't had one for ‘How to Write a Business Plan for a new Audio Technology Company’. All the examples were for *normal* companies, like plumbers or web designers, the types of companies that already existed. Companies where you could *foresee* the costs and *predict* the revenues, not like his.

Still, it had to be done. No one was going to invest or lend on the basis that he thought he had a good idea. They all wanted market research, competitor analysis, SWOT analysis, or so the books said. Maybe his meeting later that week would help. He had been referred to another part of the University, a TECHub, whatever that was. But it sounded vaguely promising.

***

It had been a long week for Lucy. It felt like she hadn't had an adult conversation for days. Sure she'd had texts and the occasional call from friends and her mum, but always it had been the banalities of life. She was fine, they were fine, John and Daniel were fine. Life was fine. But life wasn't fine. She found it hard to admit it to herself, but she was lonely. Daniel had brought her and John closer together. They had built a wall around themselves to protect the family. A wall of *fineness* where they wouldn't admit their feelings and their anxieties to those outside. But now with John focused on his new business, she felt trapped inside the walls, found herself alone. To admit to those outside that their life really wasn't fine, would reveal their life as a lie. She wasn't ready to do that yet, was she?

At first wine seemed to help. The glass or two to celebrate the weekend with a special meal with John, had become a nightly pick-me-up, more often than not drunk alone, in front of the telly. But heh, it was only a glass.

Well, tonight was a Friday wasn't it? Daniel seemed content with his toast and his DVD and his cars. And John was here, albeit slumped on the sofa with his laptop, but at least he was here. As she entered the lounge, she put a smile on her face and enthusiasm in her voice.

"They've got that new legal thriller film tonight on the box. You know the street lawyer one that we wanted to see at the cinema. Shall we order out and sink a bottle of wine with it for a change?"

"Sure, sounds good," mumbled John, still engrossed in his laptop. He had found a website with case studies of successful academic entrepreneurs in the States. For them the passage from lab to Lamborghini seemed so straight forward, they never had their doubts or their wrong turns. Maybe that was just twenty-twenty hindsight. It was odd, John thought, so much was made of the Americans positive attitude to failure as being one of the main drivers of their commercial success, but in all the entrepreneurial stories that he had read, they never put a foot wrong.

"Hmm," thought Lucy, under-whelmed by John's lack of enthusiasm, "do I order the Chinese and open the wine in the full knowledge that the odds are high that greater disappointment will follow later, or do I cut my losses and have something from the freezer with a repeated TV period drama and ignore him. I can still have the wine."

It was some hours later, about the same time that the battery in John's laptop started to fade, that John noticed Lucy munching through a 'low-fat chicken lasagne for one' watching an old episode of Upstairs Downstairs.

"Heh, what happened to the take-away and the film?" he enquired distractedly.

CHAPTER SEVEN

There seemed to be so many types of business centres, innovation centres, enterprise units, hubs, workspaces, incubators, even a Technopole, but what was the difference? Their websites all showed pictures of fancy new buildings and talk of ecosystems and environments. Was that what he needed? He didn't think he wanted and certainly couldn't afford an office yet, who would work in it? What he really wanted was to be told if his idea was a good idea, and if it would work and that everything would turn out all right and would it all be worth it. Where would you find that?

The phone rang. God he hoped it wasn't the client, he hadn't worked on the GK project all week. Reluctantly he picked it up.

"John? It's Phil. Can you come through to my office?"

It sounded like a question, thought John.

"Oh, hi Phil. Just in the middle of something, how about this afternoon?" That would give some time to at least get up to speed on the various projects.

"No. Now, please John."

The phone went dead. Phil had been polite, but firm. He hated it when Phil was polite, but firm, meant he was being serious. He grabbed a few project files, well any files really, just to look busy, and left his office.

Phil's office was one floor up. Not exactly a 'management floor', but slightly more mixed that John's area, where it was all coders. The stairs led onto the southern end of a dark central corridor that ran the length of the offices. The light from open office doorways spilled out onto the corridor, followed by the noise of office bustle. He walked down the corridor, barely conscious of the project charts, health and safety notices and faded posters adorning the walls. Phil didn't go in for much office decor. John's pace was slowing. He sensed people looking at him through the open doorways. Strange, he hadn't really spoken to many people round the office for the last few weeks, he'd been distracted. He felt foreboding. Were people talking about him? Did they know something he didn't?

He was nearing the end of the corridor, where it opened out onto a small reception area. Gail, Phil's PA was at her desk. She looked up at him and smiled. She had a nice smile, but was this a sympathetic smile?

"Hi John. Go straight in."

She hadn't even offered him a coffee. None of their usual slightly flirtatious banter. She wasn't his type, too tall, too blond, too archetypal smart secretary, and he didn't reckon that he would be hers, but they enjoyed their gentle exchanges. Perhaps it was only going to be a quick chat. But she looked so serious. At least she hadn't offered him 'a last meal'. Was he being paranoid, or was it just his nerves, he hadn't been sleeping well. Too much on his mind. Maybe a bit of a guilty conscience. He hadn't been putting in the project hours he normally did for the last few days, or was it weeks?

He pushed at the half open, half glazed door, knocking gently. He didn't normally knock. Pull yourself together, he told himself. It's probably just one of the clients having a moan. He should take the initiative?

"Phil. Hi, I'm glad you called me in. Gives me a chance to go through some of the issues on the GK account ..." He was stopped by Phil's raised hand, held up flat and straight like a traffic policeman.

"Just come in and sit down," Phil sounded quite terse. He indicated to the two chairs positioned in front of his desk. As John turned and looked, he realised for the first time that Phil wasn't alone. An austere looking woman, probably late forties, black suit, plain white blouse, she looked up at him from the chair and smiled politely. She looked polite, but firm. She didn't *fit-in* in this casual software environment, she looked regal, actually no, she looked legal. John pulled the chair back away from the desk. He wanted to keep them both in his line of sight, nobody sneaking up on him.

No ambushes. He sat and tamely put the project folders on his knees. He looked from one to the other. They had coffees, he hadn't been offered a coffee, not a good sign. Warning bells were ringing in John's head. He shouldn't back down. He needed to regain the initiative. But looking again at the two polite, but firm, faces he knew the game was up. His shoulders sagged.

"John, this is Hermione. Hermione is from Thomas HR; they provide us with employee advice from time to time."

John and Hermione nodded, politely to each other. Introductions complete, Phil looked to Hermione as if waiting for a prompt. She nodded again and Phil resumed.

"John, I'm not sure quite what's up, but you don't seem to have had your mind on the job for some weeks now. The projects are backing up and it's really beginning to affect critical timelines. And as you know, we pride ourselves on meeting those timelines."

"Honestly Phil, I can explain about the GK project —"

"— Really John, it's too late for that, I handed that one over to a subcontractor last week, you didn't even notice."

John was staggered, someone had been working his code for the last week! That knocked any last bit of resolve out of him.

Phil continued. "From what I can see you are working on your own projects and that is clearly a breach of your employment contract." He looked towards Hermione.

"Yes," she added, "This would appear to be a clear misuse of company time and resources. Certainly a disciplinary issue —"

"— Which is something I would like to avoid with you John, and why we called this meeting now. John, you have been a loyal and productive employee for the last few years, really up until last month, I value that. But we run a tight ship here and I just can't have deadlines being missed." John sat sullenly, feeling like a naughty schoolboy, but he had no answer to the charges.

Phil looked over to John, almost paternally, "You know John, when this is all over I would be genuinely interested to know what it is that has got you so distracted. You were always one of my best coders, I would really like to know what it is you are working on." John looked up, encouraged by the positive words, but as he made to speak, Phil held up his hand again to stop him.

"But obviously not right now, maybe in a month or so, when all this is sorted. Right now, I need you to leave —"

"— Phil," broke in Hermione, "you can't —"

"— Hermione. I promise you that I can and I will. I know what we talked about, but I know John and I think we can understand each other's positions here." He turned to John, and said gently, "John. I want you to leave. I want you to pursue whatever it is that's driving you. I will pay you your three months' notice, on the provision that," Phil, held up a single finger. He looked at Hermione, but she avoided his eyes. This was obviously not her advice. "One, you sign what's called a 'Compromise Agreement', which basically says that we have reached this conclusion amicably."

Hermione nodded, at least he got the name of the procedure right, even if he hadn't broached the subject in correct way. Phil, rather unnecessarily replaced his one finger, with two.

"And two, you agree to provide some consultancy time, at no further charge to the company, or the client, to support the project team in taking over your code. What do you say?"

"You're firing me?" said John quietly.

Hermione made to intervene, but Phil stops her and answered himself. "I'm probably not supposed to say this, but yes. Let's say I'm letting you go to pursue your other interests."

"I've never been fired before," said John quite abjectly, his eyes looking down at his knees. "Can I think about it?"

This time Hermione jumped in before Phil can do any more damage. She hated it when owners thought they could *manage* situations themselves. They should leave it to the professionals.

"John. Listen. Phil has made a very fair offer, which avoids any unpleasantness and lets us all get on with our lives as painlessly as possible. But, we need to settle this now. Right now. And then you can go home." She picked up a document from Phil's desk and passed it to John with a pen. "Why don't you take a few minutes to read it through?"

John took the document and opened it. The words and sentences and clauses and numbered paragraphs didn't really register. He knew he probably didn't have a leg to stand on. He had been spending most of his work time, well, all of his time, on EarStream. He thought Phil was probably trying to be fair. Certainly fairer than he needed to be. Probably fairer than Hermione would have wanted him to be. But he was still shell-shocked. Phil even seemed to be interested in his project. But fired! He had never thought he would ever be fired. He thought of what this would mean. How would he tell Lucy? God, how would be tell his mother! Phil was offering a way out. Save face. Leave on good professional terms. People would accept that, well maybe not his mother. She would never understand why anyone would give up a decent job for a totally uncertain future. And Lucy, would she understand. At least this way he would have a bit of cash and some time to dedicate to the project. He could get the company started, talk properly again with the University. There was a cough and John realised that Phil and Hermione were staring at him as he sat, with the document in his hands, still on page one, but he was staring unseeing into the middle distance.

"John?" prompted Hermione.

"I accept, thank you." John said, but this time with more confidence. He'd been given the push, but perhaps this was just the push he needed.

***

Lucy sat on the stairs, one eye on Daniel sorting his cars on the table in the lounge.

"At first it was quite fun, a new interest, something to talk about, something that was exciting, but unlinked to the real world. We would sit over a glass of wine and try and think up good names for the business, or have fun sketching a logo, but now ..." Lucy was starting to well-up, she was glad that they were on the phone and that her mum couldn't see her.

"Come-on now love, it's probably just a phase. Most men go through it you know, I guess it's a control thing. Even your dad, he didn't like taking orders from the boss. Not that he ever did anything about it." Joan's voice was warm and calming, she didn't like to think of her daughter being unhappy, but struggled to understand her life, maybe if they lived nearer it would help. She tried to sound supportive, "He'll probably get over it soon."

"It's not really like that mum, there hadn't been any problems at work. It's not even really the business stuff, it's this new technology thing, he's becoming obsessive about it, searching the internet, finding out about patents and stuff."

"Patents, you don't want to be getting involved with patents, I was reading something in the paper only the other day about the amount of money wasted on patents. Some con-man, or something, millions wasted ..."

"Oh, it's not a con mum, it's research from the University, so I'm not worried about that."

"I thought he had a good job?"

"He does mum, a very good job. I just wish he would concentrate on it and forget all this new technology stuff, so we can get back to normal."

"I know love, perhaps he just needs a night out with his friends."

If only, Lucy thought, if only it were that simple, if only John had some friends. "I've got to go now mum, got to go and take Daniel out."

"Oh bless him, how is he. Does he still like his cars?"

"Yes mum, I think he'll always like his cars."

***

An hour after his meeting with Phil, John was sat at his desk, half-heatedly sorting through his drawers, dividing the contents between a cardboard box - keep, and a metal box - bin. It felt rather sad, the last couple of years of his life reduced to a half dozen company biros and assorted promotional USB sticks. He still had the unopened box he had brought from his last employer. What was he going to tell Lucy, would she understand if he didn't immediately look for another job? Would she understand that for the last month he hadn't been doing this one?

A text message pinged on his phone. It was Phil, he said he was serious about hearing more about the idea in a few weeks, and giving his personal mobile number. Plus, there was a web link for something called the TECHub. He still wasn't too sure what that was, but now at least two people had mentioned it.

Maybe he should pick up the local paper on the way home, look for the job adverts. Did they still have job adverts in the local paper? It had been a long time since he had looked. No, he had to take this opportunity. Make this three months' work for him. He would tell Lucy tonight. She'd understand, realise it was worth it.

***

"You've done what?" Lucy said in complete shock.

"Left. I've left Enterprise IT, it wasn't working out and I thought that if I left I would be able to concentrate more on EarStream."

"Oh, it's got a name now has it?"

"Yes, EarStream, it was one of your ideas I think, I quite liked AudioTech, but when I checked on Google —"

"—- Hang on, forget the bloody name John, I really don't care what it's called - you *really* mean you've left? What now, today, just like that? Don't you have to give notice or something?"

"No. They just let me go with three months' money in lieu of notice. Very generous of them. Phil seemed quite intrigued by my, our plans."

"You've left? But what about your salary? What are we going to live off? How are we going to buy food? How are we going to pay the mortgage?"

"As I said, Phil has given me have three months' money, that plus our savings —"

"— That was our holiday John. I was really looking forward to that holiday."

"There'll be other holidays love. I need to do this."

"Oh, 'you need to do this', that's all right then," she said sarcastically, I wasn't just looking forward to a holiday John, I need a bloody holiday John."

"Look love, I'll, we'll, make it work out. Look at this as an opportunity —"

"— An opportunity to be broke," Lucy still looked stunned by the news. "And you didn't think to talk this over with me first?" She had her head in her hands. John wondered if she was going to cry or scream at him.

"No." John paused, and tried to think of a believable answer to that one. This conversation had gone much better in his head when he'd sat in the supermarket cafe building up the courage to come home and tell her. "It just sort of came to a head, made me decide there and then."

"Wait a minute." John didn't like the look in her eyes as Lucy raised her head and stared at him. "Wait a minute. You haven't quit have you? You've been fired. What the hell did you do?" She was definitely angry now.

"I didn't do anything," John replied plaintively.

"Have you been working on this ..." she struggled to remember the name, "... while you've been in the office? Is that it?"

"EarStream," he reminded her, unhelpfully.

"You've been working on this *EarStream* when you should have been programming, or whatever it is that you do?"

"Well ..."

"Oh you bloody fool. It's one thing being obsessed at home; I'm getting used to being ignored. And Daniel, well Daniel probably hasn't noticed if you're there or not."

"I've never let it affect Daniel," John protested.

"You think losing your job doesn't affect Daniel! Are you mad? We live in a house John, we wear clothes, we eat food. All of us. You may be prepared to make these sacrifices. But it would be nice if you considered the rest of us before you get yourself fired.

"You'll have to go back in. Go and see Phil, tell him it's all been a big mistake. Tell him you want your job back. Beg if necessary. Tell him you've been stupid concentrating on this daft idea, that can't possibly work. Tell him you're sorry and that you'll work hard now ..." She stood up from the kitchen chair and stormed out of the room, clearly crying now. John heard her running up the stairs.

This is not going well, thought John. He looked around and saw that Lucy had been part-way through making Daniel's evening meal when they had started this disaster of a conversation. He had wanted to try and explain the passion he felt for the idea, how he believed that making EarStream work was his destiny, something that he had to do, or at least try. But he had just come across as weak and incapable of holding down his job. He stood and went over to the work surface and picked-up where Lucy had left off.

"Daniel," John called out, "Daniel. I'm doing your tea, what shall we do with your vegetables?"

There was no reply from Daniel or Lucy.

Two hours later, it was dark. John had sat with Daniel while he had eaten his meal, John himself wasn't hungry. The conversation had been a little one-sided. John had described his day and the big events that had taken place. Daniel had watched an episode of Teletubbies, his eyes fixed on the screen while he mechanically forked his food to his mouth. While his attention seemed rapt, Daniel didn't seem to respond directly to the action in the programme and John wondered what, if anything, of the surreal programme, Daniel took in.

At one point Daniel's concentration was broken when he inadvertently dropped his fork. As he looked down at his plate, confused, John took the opportunity to gain his attention as he held out the fork to him.

"Daniel. Here it is, here's your fork." Daniel held out his hand for the fork, without taking his eyes off his food.

"Look at me Daniel. Here's the fork." Daniel took the fork, without acknowledging his father and returned into his trance-like state and resumed eating. John sighed, sat back and watched his son with love, fascination and frustration. He let him eat his tea in peace, his mind drifting back on the last article he had read about the 'Cocktail Party Effect', could it really work, could it help him to break through to into Daniel's world.

Later, it was dark now, John had bathed Daniel and got him settled in bed with a favourite audiotape. Lucy hadn't returned so John made his way quietly up the stairs to their bedroom. His wife was curled up, almost foetal on the bed, still fully clothed, though John could not tell if she was asleep. There was no sound. He sat in the pine rocking chair that they bought when Daniel first came home from the hospital. Daniel had been a difficult feeder and the gentle rocking motion had acted to calm both mother and child. John leaned back and closed his eyes and spoke quietly and gently to Lucy's curled back.

"You're right love, I didn't quit, I was fired. I would never have made such an important decision on my own, without involving you, but it was forced on me and I tried to hide that, to my shame. I'm sorry I did that." He paused to see if there was any reaction from Lucy, but apart from perhaps a slight deepening of her breathing, there was none. He continued.

"I have been obsessing, I know that. And it has taken over my life both at home and at work. I have not been supporting you at home and I was definitely not pulling my weight at work, they were right to sack me and you were right to be angry with me.

"When I watch Daniel I feel so helpless. I want so much for him to be happy and it tears me apart that I don't know if he is. When he is locked away in his own mind, is he content? Or is there another little boy, our son, who is silently screaming to be let out. I know that we shouldn't always measure Daniel against our own expectations of life, but it's so hard thinking that he might not have the satisfaction of finding independence, making friends, finding love in others, all the things that have made our life worthwhile. I find this so hard. I love and admire you so much for the life that you are giving Daniel. I know only a tiny fraction of the frustration, pain and emotional turmoil that you must go through every day. Your resilience and resolve to give Daniel the best of you is one of the many things that I adore about you. But I have to find my own way of helping him.

"When we went to that party and I talked to the University Professor, something clicked. The way he described his scientific work, there seemed such a strong connection in my own mind with how Daniel is, that I couldn't ignore it. I had to follow it up, to see if there was something there that could help Daniel. When I went to the University, they only seemed interested in the science and the publishing, not the application. I realised then that if *I* didn't do something to try and see if this technology could help Daniel, then I couldn't be sure if anybody else would.

"This isn't a pipe-dream love, I'm under no illusion that suddenly I'm going to become a great entrepreneur, the more I read and research the more terrified I become. I know I'm taking a risk and perhaps I'm being selfish, but I have to follow this through. I can't walk away from an idea that might help Daniel, that might make his life better, might give him an opportunity to make more decisions for himself. I'm sorry that by my doing this it might make our life more difficult financially and certainly it wasn't the sort of insecurity that you signed up to when we got married. It would mean a lot to me to have your support, I have no right to demand it or even to expect it, because I know this will be hard on all of us.

"But I hope at the very least you will accept why I must try and make this work."

There was still no reaction from Lucy. John stood and left the bedroom, closing the door gently behind him. He checked in at Daniel's bedroom door, he was fast in a dreamless asleep. Then he returned downstairs to the kitchen, he got out a pad of paper and a pen from his work-bag and started to try and frame his ideas into a plan, a Business Plan.

***

"John?"

"I've been thinking. If you really want to do this, then do it, we'll manage somehow," she said sleepily. She paused long enough that John thought she had returned to sleep, but as he turned she said drowsily, "But, John."

"Yes, love?"

"Don't," she paused.

"Don't what?"

"Don't ever, ever risk our home."

He half smiled in the darkness, trust Lucy to be supportive, "Of course love," he said gently, "not the house."

CHAPTER EIGHT

He was not sure what to expect as he had made his way back to the University and to their TECHub. When he had made the call to arrange an appointment, the voice that answered sounded like a human, so nothing innovative there, he thought.

The walk up from the station had been all up hill, and now that he had reached the top of the steps he was rewarded with a fine view over the campus and to the rolling green hills of the Downs beyond. The TECHub building itself with its modern glass frontage stood apart from the red brick architecture of the rest of the University.

John opened the heavy glass door and entered the bright modern interior, it was dominated by a large futuristic, chrome and glass reception desk. Even though the reception space was spacious and hardly crowded with people, he was conscious of an energy about the place. An irregular stream appeared from the cafe, corridors and stairs feeding into the reception. There were lots of informal greetings and short conversations as people crossed paths, John felt a casual intensity, a sense of purpose in the atmosphere.

The surroundings felt comfortable, not at all intimidating. John approached the reception desk and was welcomed with the bright smile of the young girl behind the desk. Definitely not an avatar.

"Can I help?" she asked pleasantly.

"Sure," John replied, "I'm John Miller and I'm here to see Simon Robinson."

"Of course," she checked her screen, "Simon is expecting you. Please take a seat and I'll let him know you're here." She indicated some trendy armless visitor seats clustered around a low table. John thanked her and walked over to the seats. He noticed a large in-out board on the wall, it was full of names, company names, John assumed. The large TV on the wall was showing a slide-show announcing future events and business news stories of recent awards and contract wins. Were all these companies based here, he wondered? The building didn't seem big enough. He looked back up at the list of companies on the board, daft he thought, as he realised that he had automatically checked to see if EarStream was listed. He smiled to himself, maybe one day.

He had just got himself settled reading a local business magazine when he sensed somebody standing over him. He looked up, he recognised Simon from the photos that had he had seen on the TECHub website. Simon was certainly a little older, maybe late forties, than most of the people that John had seen passing through the reception. And a little smarter, blue pinstripe suit trousers, rather than the tech uniform jeans. But he also stood out for the quiet intensity there was about him. He was here for a purpose.

"You must be, John?" He said with an outstretched hand and an open smile. "Don't worry I'm not clairvoyant, Claire called to say you'd arrived and," he looked around the reception, "you're the only one here. I'm Simon."

John struggled to get up cleanly from the leather stool. "Hello, thanks, it was good of you to fit me in."

"Of course, no problem. Shall we grab a coffee?"

They walked through into the cafe where there were scattered individuals focused on their laptops and at least three meetings ongoing, this was clearly a part of the work environment rather than a social area. In one of the meeting groups the attention was focused on a man in a suit, client or professional advisor, John assumed. Simon quietly acknowledged people at tables as he passed, not wanting to interrupt the flow of their conversations. John got the feeling, just from seeing the way that the people in the cafe reacted to him, that Simon was both liked and respected.

When they had got their coffees, Simon checked that John was comfortable having their initial conversation in the cafe, "I'm happy to move us through into my office if you'd rather, but sometimes it's good just to start with a more informal chat for a first meeting."

"No, I'm fine here," John was delighted, he felt comfortable and relaxed here. This would be a conversation around his idea rather than an intense examination. "If we need to get into the detail ..."

"Then we can move through, absolutely, and sort out a non-disclosure agreement if we need one."

There was a pause as they both sipped their coffees before Simon continued, "I understand that you are working with the University on something?"

"Hoping to," replied John hesitantly, "I've had an initial conversation with their Intellectual Property people …" John checked his notes, "a Dr Billing ..."

"I know that whole side of research commercialisation can seem pretty daunting if you're not used to it. It would be good for you to meet one of their Business Managers, Laura ..."

"Oh, I did meet Laura, she was really helpful," John said more brightly.

Simon smiled at John's reaction, "Yes, Laura is a pleasure to work with." He shifted in his seat and leaned forward as he looked more intently at John. "Good, so the conversation with the University has begun, perhaps we can start with you telling me a little more about the business idea."

"OK, well, I met Dr David Lowe socially, and he told me about his research into the 'Cocktail Party Effect', which is where the brain can distinguish individual voices from a crowd. Do you know of his research?"

"Yes, I'm aware of it, but not the detail. Tell me what you have in mind."

So John told his story again, but this time careful to keep it business focused, not mentioning Daniel at all.

"So what's the motivation for your business? Why are you doing it?" Simon's comfortable casual manner had put John at ease, but while it was straightforward to talk about the 'what' of his business, the 'why' was another thing entirely.

John paused and then sighed before he launched into a stock answer using jargon he'd picked up from the copious business books he'd been reading. “I want to create a high growth, knowledge based business, with an anticipated exit in three years via a trade sale.”

“Really?” Simon smiled. “Forgive me, but it looks to me that there is something more personal behind this.”

John looked up into Simon's face. It had been a while since he had shared with anyone the real reasons why he was doing this. It was so easy to get lost in the process, rather than the objective. Would Simon really understand? Perhaps it was some type of psychometric test. Would revealing the emotional roots to the business show a vulnerability, make him look weak? Was he weak? Was he kidding himself?

But John wasn't ready yet to let his defences drop, he replied, “I see a real growth opportunity around this technology across a wide range of markets.”

“OK,” replied Simon, seeing that perhaps this wasn't the time to delve deeper, “let’s take a look at those markets and what sort of development capital you might need?”

***

His mobile phone was ringing. An old fashioned ring tone, 'Classic', he thought they called it, unsurprisingly, 'boring' was Lucy's more judgmental opinion. To John, it made perfect sense, it sounded like a phone, he thought.

His head jerked up, as if from a trance, his mind had been elsewhere, but for the moment he couldn't think where. His hand automatically reached for the phone to switch it off. That was the protocol here, the etiquette of 'hot-desking'. An eclectic group of would-be entrepreneurs sharing their work-space, each locked on to their individual laptop screens searching for the killer idea that would launch them from these humble beginnings to start-up stardom. How many of them would make it, he wondered? The odds weren't that great according to the statistics, well over half fail in the first couple of years. And that's why they come here, success rates were definitely better inside a business incubator, but there was no certainty. When John had had the tour around the TECHub, he had known then that he wanted, maybe needed, to base himself there and the 'hot-desks' was a logical first step. To be amongst others striving to do the same as what he wanted to do. To be part of something bigger not just on your own. To be within a community but without the permanence or cost of an office, a place to 'pitch-up, perch and prepare your pitch', was how Simon had described it. So he had joined the other business hopefuls, as they gathered, scattered across the individual workstations in this the 'hot-desk room'. They may be on their own, but they shared a common home and a common dream.

He needn't have worried about the phone, he realised, the room was empty. It was dark outside. He looked again at his phone to check the time, three missed messages from Lucy. Shit! How could he have missed her texts, he had been sitting right here, he hadn't left the room and his phone hadn't left his side? Why couldn't she just let him get on with it? He didn't need this guilt trip as well. He knew he'd lost his job. Knew he wasn't providing for his family. Knew he was being a bad father, a bad husband. Pull yourself together, he told himself, feeling sorry for yourself wasn't going to solve anything, the quicker he could determine whether this EarStream idea had legs, the sooner they could make sense of this situation.

He looked around the room, during the day it had been busy, but not distracting, it was like sitting in a pub, convivial to have people around you, meeting, chatting, going about their normal life, but not entering yours. Then after a few sessions, you started recognising the faces, you saw them in the cafe or elsewhere around the Hub or the Campus. Greetings started as a nod, but quickly moved to speech. This was after all why you were here, to gain confidence and support from your fellow travellers. Everyone working here was doing something interesting, creating something new, so why wouldn't you want to talk to them, get to know their stories, learn from their experiences. Lucy would never understand. Why would you pay to sit a table in another building using your laptop, when there was a perfectly good table at home, especially when you didn't have any money? She didn't see the need for camaraderie, for having like minds around you. John had found that the longer he sat on his own in the spare bedroom, or at the kitchen table, staring at his laptop, the more alone and desolate he felt. It had all seemed so hopeless, his efforts pointless, how did he expect to achieve this on his own. But at the Hub, he met others that were achieving things, people that didn't seem that special, people no different from him. Different experience, different ideas, different motivations of course, but basically people that wanted, or were driven, to try and make something out of their idea. And so, just sitting with people with similar ambitions, in a place where people did achieve success, gave renewed momentum and confidence to his venture.

But now it was dark, and it was late and he was alone. Now he wasn't drawing a buzz from others, like adrenaline shared, now he wanted to go home but was afraid of going home, because he had chosen to be here rather than to be at home.

He turned back to his laptop screen and the umpteenth version of his business plan. He'd just have another hour, he thought, maybe by then Lucy would have calmed down, if he left it even longer, maybe she'd be in bed by the time he got home. He switched off his phone ignoring the messages from Lucy and turned back to the keyboard. How would he describe his 'Unique Selling Point'?

***

God, where was he! She had phoned and texted, but nothing from him. She didn't know whether to worry about him having had an accident or just be fed up with him for ignoring her and the family. But tonight, why couldn't he just have come home tonight. He knew that she had arranged to go out. For goodness sake, it didn't happen very often. But when her old friend Charlotte had invited her out to meet up with their old group of college pals, it seemed too good an opportunity to miss. These were friends from before she had become defined as the mother of an autistic child. These were friends who knew nothing of social services and special needs. These were just friends that knew and liked Lucy, for the person she was, not her as a reflection of the people she cared for.

But no, he didn't care did he, or maybe he did, maybe he cared enough to want to hurt her? He wouldn't even have spent the evening with her, God knows he went to such great lengths to not be with her during the day. What was the point of forking out good money to sit at a desk in some business centre miles away?

He should be saving his money, their money. Think of the travel costs.

The sooner he came to his senses the better. Just who did he think he was risking everything on *his dream*? What about her dreams?

Well sod him. This wasn't the first time he'd let her down in the last few weeks, but it wouldn't be long before it would be the last.

***

"Yes mum, yes, I've left my job. No of course not, everything is fine. Yes, I'm doing my own thing, got this idea for a new business. Yes, I'm sure, never been so sure of anything in all my life. Lucy? Absolutely, Lucy's backing me all the way. Yes, we're fine for money, I've been saving. Yes, it was a good job. And local, no travelling. Yes, I was lucky to have found such a good job. Look mum, I had to do this, had to give it a ... Yes, mum, I'll let you know if we need some help."

As John finished the call, standing in the hall, he saw Lucy watching him from the kitchen and the look didn't say, 'I'm backing you all the way'.

CHAPTER NINE

John's first 'customer insight' meeting took place in one of the well-appointed meeting rooms at the TECHub. As well as John and Simon, they were joined by Anne, a technology commercialisation specialist that John had found online. In contrast to the people John had met at the Hub, Anne presented a cold and impersonal attitude. Simon had warned him about this, "Many consultants believe that they have to appear superior to justify themselves and their fees." Her presentation was a lecture rather than an engagement. John immediately felt he was being spoken down to and sold to.

"The key to many of these markets," Anne was explaining, "is the TRL, or Technology Readiness Level. This scale was developed by NASA and provides a means to assess the maturity of the subsystem building blocks in a new system. First developed for the space industry it has now been applied to many other industrial sectors as a standard terminology for describing how close to market readiness a technology is."

While John tried to concentrate, he sensed Simon's growing impatience with Anne's presentation. Was it her style or the content?

"For military and security you really need to have got the technology to TRL 6 or above to interest the big boys, but for many media applications you can progress quite a long way on a POC or Proof of Concept model."

"And how do I know where I am?" asked John, a little irritated by the patronising way that the Technology Specialist was addressing him.

"My company provides a seventy-six-point questionnaire to help determine your position. But if you really don't know, I'd assume a TRL of two or maybe three."

"But what about all the academic research, the conference papers —," John protested.

"Oh academics. They rarely get the idea beyond TRL 2. They're in a different world."

"Oh God," said John under his breath, "we're going backwards."

Simon, seeing the conversation going nowhere interjected. "Anne. I'm a not a defence specialist, but don't the MOD run a special scheme for novel technology ideas?"

"Ah yes, the CDE, Centre for Defence Enterprise," Anne accepted. "But that's not where the big money goes."

"Well, we're not necessarily after big money here, are we John? At least not yet. Just a bit of a steer. Perhaps this CDE could help. What do you reckon John, worth a shot, see if they bring the big guns out?"

John could see that Simon was trying to lighten the mood and move things on, even though Anne looked less impressed. "Sure, let's run it up the flag pole and see who salutes," he said with a slight smile, joining in.

"The CDE is not just for the military applications," Anne trying to keep it serious, "they also make introductions for the intelligence services and GCHQ."

"Perfect." replied Simon. "*They* definitely need to hear better! Let's see what we can do."

Following the meeting and over coffee, Simon cautioned John about being too put off by the consultant.

"It's a consultant's job to make it look difficult, otherwise you might think that you don't need them. At this stage it may be all about how to access the right sector experience. How do you get to find out if an idea is worth pursuing? There is only so far that you can go with desk research, you can get so much more if you can talk directly to the people in the know.

"People get caught up in the adage, 'cheaper, faster, lighter', without necessarily following it through with, 'which one matters most'? And 'who does it matter to'? There is little point in producing something that is faster, when speed isn't the problem. And it doesn't matter how good your marketing is at shouting just how *fast* you are, if your customers want something that is *lighter*."

Simon paused to sip his coffee and to let the idea sink in with John, before he continued, "Sure it can be different when the technology is fundamentally new, where it's not an incremental change, but you still have to find a problem that other people think is worth solving."

"But how do I find out what the problem is?"

"A more fundamental question can be, 'whose problem is it?' Take for example a new type of wound dressing, you might assume that the most important factor is, 'is it better for the patient?', but the patients don't make the buying decisions, do they? And in many cases, it's not even the doctor. So you can see that understanding what the NHS manager thinks is important. Which one of his many targets will the product help him meet?"

"But surely in the end it's about the patients, isn't it?"

"Well patients, and waiting lists, and budget deficits, and health outcome surveys, and training budgets, and nursing unions, and ..."

"OK. OK, I get it," protested John laughing.

Simon continued. "Well it's the same with EarStream, we think that it should be wanted by the security industry because the technology is good for picking out a particular voice from a crowd. But we don't know if MI5 think they have that problem, maybe they think what they have now is good enough. Why should they change?"

John looked confused, "But surely if it's better ...?"

"Yes, but better for who? If you talk to the man in the field, the spy I guess, they might say that the key issue is the range of the sensor, that's because being further away from the target and less conspicuous is a great advantage if you're the one at risk. It's their safety so they don't care about the cost."

"Sounds fair," agreed John.

"But, like the patient in the NHS, the spy doesn't make the buying decision. For the buyer that's just one factor amongst many. We need to understand how they value different factors. Will the government pay ten percent more say for the equipment with a ten percent better range?

"But even that's too simplistic. Even if the technology is cheaper and better than what they currently use, there can be a cost in making a change. It could be an increase in the cost of training or restocking or the cost of changing the software they use. None of these things are covered in your pricing, but they may have a big impact on the buying decision."

"So it's all about how they compare things?"

"Yes, you're right, it's all about how they rank and compare products. At least it is when you are replacing an existing product."

"Oh no," said John. "I sense a 'but' coming."

"Yes. But what if you can deliver something new, something that they couldn't do before? So now we are talking about the art of the possible, not just comparing alternatives. The problem then becomes deciding what the pricing point should be?"

John's head was spinning. "Christ Simon, I thought you were supposed to be simplifying the issue, not making it even more complicated."

Simon nodded sagely, "I know John, but unless you admit that you don't the answer, you won't ask the question. If you can work out who is making the buying decision, and what criteria they are using, then you have a much better chance of creating a product that the customer really wants."

Simon checked his watch, "Gotta go," he said, his light manner returning as he stood up and headed off for another meeting, waving to a couple of groups at the other tables as he passed. John was left wiser but not necessarily any clearer about what he needed to do next. Simon had set his mind reeling about who he was supposed to be selling EarStream to.

One problem though was that when he had first joined the TECHub, John had been clear, in his own mind, that he had no interest in the security applications of the technology. For him it was merely a means to an end, but the more he worked on the project, the more the means became the end. What had started as a pragmatic diversion now wasn't returning to the original destination. The security application was more interesting as a business proposition to everybody else, even though it wasn't where John had intended to go. He couldn't help but get caught up in it, to be excited by the security market, because everyone else saw it as the key business opportunity.

But did it move him closer to a solution for Daniel?

***

The following day, John was still feeling fired up with the prospect of working with Simon. At last, someone who seemed to understand and have the resources to help. Such a relief. He wanted to share his experience with Lucy.

"So, this TECHub, it really is this great place at the University. Loads of people like me, with ideas, ordinary people," said John animatedly as they sat at home at the cluttered kitchen table.

"You mean people giving up perfectly good jobs and a career to *follow their dream.*" Lucy wasn't in the best of moods, but even so, her last phrase came out with more bitter sarcasm than she had intended.

John looked hurt, "Oh you know what I mean. Not your typical, 'TV Apprentice' like, loud mouthed entrepreneurs. These were real people, real engineers, software guys, games designers. People that are trying to create something new, to make a real difference."

"I know. I'm sorry John. It's just that the car's knackered, it sounded like an old tractor coming up the hill last night. And we can't afford to replace it, or even get it fixed. It feels like life has been put on hold for EarStream —"

"For Daniel," interrupted John, "it's *all* for Daniel."

"But *is it* though?" Lucy came back. "It may have started that way, but now it seems like the whole *start your own business* thing has taken over. You're not the same John. *We* used to be the most important thing in your life. We, Daniel and I. Us, your family. Not EarStream. Not the University and patents. Not the fucking TECHub." Lucy put down her coffee cup with such force that the coffee spilt, splashing the table and the papers that John had been working on.

"Lucy!" John shouted as he tried to push the coffee away with one hand and lift up his papers with other. "Watch out! These are important."

Lucy gave John a withering look as he clumsily tried to mop up the spilled coffee to protect his work, she stormed out, swerving past Daniel who, attracted by the ruckus, had come in and was stood in the doorway watching.

Daniel entered the kitchen and looked at John in his rather detached way, "Juice," he asked simply.

"Not now Daniel," John snapped, "can't you see daddy's busy."

***

"Oh I know he *thinks* he's doing it for us. But we want him *actually* doing things for us, with us, now, not in some make-believe future, when he's found a *cure* for Daniel". Lucy was tired, and she sounded uncharacteristically bitter.

Lucy had met John's mother, Patsy, for a coffee in town. Patsy, who had been recently widowed, had moved into the area to be closer to her John, Lucy and Daniel. Patsy was as elegant as she was fiercely intelligent, of that generation of women who had not had the educational and career opportunities to fully realise their potential. As a result, she lived her ambitions through John and Lucy, but was terrified of alienating them through too much interference. So she feigned indifference.

While Lucy and Patsy got on OK, the relationship had never been exactly warm between them. Lucy always felt she was being judged, and she felt, judged not that highly. Patsy was so unlike her own mother, whose uncomplicated love and support was unconditional. Whereas with Patsy, Lucy she felt the continued need to prove herself.

Dressed in Jaeger from top to toe, Patsy looked a little out of place in the simple, utilitarian cafe where Lucy had arranged to meet. Its unmatched crockery and furniture gave it a *thrown together* feel, as if the owners had just woken up that morning and decided to open up. But the food was good, though plain, the coffee excellent and the staff friendly and accommodating. It was one of the few cafes where Daniel felt comfortable, and that made a sensible conversation more likely.

"A *cure* dear? I didn't think you could cure autism." With that she continued to fuss over Daniel, who was concentrating very hard on the triangular pieces of toast that Lucy had carefully cut for him. “Is it always triangles? How strange. But why not? I've always been rather partial to pentagons myself.” She tried to stroke Daniel's hair, but he wriggled away from her. “You just don't like the fuss, do you Daniel. A bit like your Grand-dad.”

“Oh you know what I mean,” Lucy said with a sigh, “and yes it's been triangles for quite a few months now.” She looked sadly at the carefully cut, geometrically perfect triangles of toast.

“Count your blessings,” said Patsy, “they're certainly a lot easier to cut than pentagons. And so much easier to nibble,” she said towards Daniel with a smile.

Lucy couldn't help but share the moment and smiled gently as well. Looking at Daniel, but referring to John, “If only he could find someone to help him. An investor. Angels, I think they call them. Someone to share the burden, the challenges.” She paused and then added with more of an edge to her voice, “and the expenses.” She was getting upset again, “All those bloody costs, lawyers, patents, accountants ... and no income. I can try and support him emotionally, but who’s going to support the family financially?”

“Chin-up dear,” said Patsy wistfully, “drink your tea before it goes cold. Come-on now Daniel, let's put four triangles together to make a square.” But she withdrew as Daniel moved his plate away from her. She sat back with a sigh, but with a thoughtful look on her face, “That's OK, my angel. Nana won't fuss”.

CHAPTER TEN

The kitchen had never been exactly tidy. The pine breakfast table acted as a dumping ground for newspapers, post and pamphlets. But now it seemed to have become John's office. They had already given up the spare bedroom to EarStream. Got the IKEA utility desk, chair and filing cabinet. But John felt cut-off up there. Too solitary. Couldn't concentrate. Too lonely. And so every day, John and his papers and laptop appeared in the kitchen and Lucy felt she had to tiptoe around him, or offer countless cups of tea. And then there was Daniel. He needed his own space, but needed to be encouraged in social interaction, so needed to be close to the rest of the family. That meant that Daniel got the lounge. So that left the bedroom, the hall or the loo for Lucy, if she wanted to be alone.

Lucy needed some space to herself. She loved Daniel dearly, but love and patience only took you so far. She had to get out of the house now. Just to walk. To hear nothing but her own thoughts.

"I'm going out for a bit," she called out to John as she gathered her keys and bag. "Look out for Daniel. He's in the lounge, but will probably need a drink soon."

"What!" John gasped, looking up from his pad of paper, "I'm working."

Looking over his shoulder at John's scribbles. "Looks more like doodling to me. Dan will be no trouble and I've got to get out of here for a bit."

"Look. No! This is important. I've got to present this in a few days to get into their *quarterly decision cycle*." Seeing Lucy's face, John cringed, where had *quarterly decision cycle* come from? What was happening to him? Perhaps he was reading too many business books. He waited for a deserved sarcastic reply from Lucy.

"When it starts generating some income, then it will enter *my* decision cycle," she replied, knowing she was probably being a little unfair. "We can't live like this. We're on top of each other all the time, I need a break, to have my own space, especially when all we've got to talk about is our lack of money." She opened the door. "I'll see you later. Don't forget his drink. DAN," she called out. "I'm popping out for a bit." There was no answer from the lounge. "Daddy will get your juice." Without looking back, she left.

***

She didn't normally read the local paper, The Herald, but this morning she couldn't face the nationals, which were full of the latest Middle East crisis, celebrity gossip and alleged sexual predators from the seventies. So she turned the pages, hardly taking in the fetes, weddings and local shop openings. Past the letters - not too angry today; the horoscope - no tall dark stranger; and the crossword, too cryptic.

She came to what used to be called 'The Women's Pages', she hadn't realised that they still had them, mind you it had been a long time that she had delved this deep in the local paper. A new diet she saw, something to do with a super-fruit, 'eat less and do more' she heard her mother say, never one for fads. Apparently cardigans were coming back, she looked around at a group of lady pensioners at the next table - obviously no one had told *them* that cardigans had ever gone out of fashion. Down the right hand side of the page was 'Lynda's Column', the photo showed a well coiffured, confident looking woman who proclaimed to be a 'Life Coach'. Where did these people get off doling out their advice? But she read on.

> ***What's stopping you?*** *It is the things around us that create our insecurities, especially for women. Too many voices, usually men's, tell us that we can't do it, I'm telling you that*

you need to shout back "Yes I can." You are a capable, intelligent woman, you don't need to be tied to a job, a relationship, a life that you didn't choose. Stand-up, feel your strength and confidence, look life in the eye and scream, "Yes I can."

Who reads this rubbish, she thought to herself with a smile? She turned to the 'Jobs Page'. As she scanned it, one particular advert seemed to draw her attention. There was no colour or graphic, nothing to create an obvious visual impact. Maybe it was the font that was different, she didn't know but something caught her eye?

'Digital Media Magic', was it the name that drew her attention? You didn't often see the word 'magic' used in that way, not in the Internet age. Now companies seemed to be more intent on devising new words or relying on little known language derivations to create a distinctive brand name. Apparently, she'd read somewhere that 'Google' originated from the word 'googol', the number one followed by a hundred noughts, but now it was probably one of the most used verbs in the dictionary. But 'Digital Media Magic' appeared to say something simpler about the business. They did something with Digital Media, and they did it well - what they did, she had no idea.

She read on:

Digital Media Magic

An award winning Digital Marketing Agency, is looking to recruit an

Office Manager and Administrator.

The successful applicant will be a good team player, computer literate with strong organisational skills, a positive personality and a sense of humour.

She read through the advert more carefully, 'Digital marketing', she wasn't quite sure what that was, but she could look it up. 'Office Manager and Administration', well if she could organise and manage *their* house and *their* life, she could organise an office. And admin was admin, no-one really knew what that meant. 'Computer Literate', well she was fine, as long as they didn't ask her to type. 'Positive Personality and a Sense of Humour', described her perfectly, she thought to herself.

She sat back thoughtfully. That was it, the answer to being crowded out at home, the lack of income, feeling worthless and undervalued, loneliness. She'd get a job. She could do this, she was a 'capable, intelligent woman', who had run classrooms and families. Whatever Digital Marketing was, she could run that. Surreptitiously she tore the advert out of the cafe paper and resolved that she would apply today, when John was out of the way. Why she felt she had to hide it from John, she had no idea, but easier to tell him when she had got a job. If she got a job. Better to ask for forgiveness than permission, isn't that what they said.

She checked the advert again, hoping that they didn't want to see a CV. How would she describe the last three years of her life looking after Daniel? No, just a phone number, and it was local. Perhaps she should do some research, look them up. No, phone them now, she thought, this is 'of the moment'. She checked the number again, pulled out her mobile, no longer the latest model, and dialled. As the phone rang, she composed herself. Expecting to speak to a receptionist, she was taken off guard when the phone was answered by a suave, deep, un-accented voice.

"Digital Media Magic, Jason here."

Jason? Wasn't that the name given on the advert? Why would he be answering the phone? "Oh hello. I'm calling about the job advert in the Herald. Can I speak to, erm, Jason?"

"Speaking." the deep voice replied, "what's your name?"

He certainly had a directness about him. "Lucy," she replied, a little tentatively, "Lucy Miller."

"You sound perfect Lucy. Where are you now?"

"I'm in a cafe on the High Street, I just happened to be looking through the Herald and saw your advert, it just seemed —"

"— Come over now. We're just round the corner. Past the chemist, red door, you can't miss it."

"No, I couldn't possibly. I haven't changed, prepared, anything."

"Come just as you are." Jason's voice carried an intensity, a confidence that was compelling. "Come now. It's better like this. Let me meet the *real* you."

Despite her misgivings, Lucy felt herself being drawn in. If she said 'no now, what did that say about her? She was presentable. Well just, if she kept her coat on. She still had some of the residue of Daniel's breakfast toast near the bottom of her t-shirt. Maybe if she tucked it in. It was only as she stood up to look down at her jeans she realised she was still holding the phone. Worse, she realised that Jason was still holding on at the other end. She hoped to God she hadn't been talking to herself out loud.

"OK. Yes, all right Jason, I'll come now. Give me ten minutes and I'll be there. The red door you say. I'll be there."

"Perfect," was all he said.

Lucy stood, looking at the phone as it clicked off. She couldn't believe that Jason had just hung up, but more than that, she couldn't believe that she had just agreed to go to her first job interview for eight years at ten minutes' notice wearing her *scruffy mummy* gear. Oh god what would John think? What would her mother think? But now most importantly for her, what would Jason think? She was intrigued by his voice, his directness, his intensity. She couldn't get the image of Jason King out of her mind, but surely he wouldn't have a seventies droop moustache. Get a grip girl, she told herself. This was a job interview, not a blind date.

Ten minutes later. She had done her best with the limited supplies she had had with her in her handbag and the cafe's loo. Her hair at least combed, though hardly styled. A little mascara and lip gloss, she had no proper makeup with her. But, what the hell. She was now feeling good about this. She didn't need to hide behind eyeliner and pencil skirts. She was a 'strong, confident woman', the words from the Women's Page stuck in her head. She had the skills and experience of a teacher and a mother. What couldn't she do?

She left the cafe and walked down the street confidently, she reached the red door and looked up at an array of intercom buttons, she assumed that DMM must be Digital Media Magic. Suddenly her self-confidence drained away. As she stood there wavering on the door-step, she felt a presence behind her, like a shadow looming. Her body gave an involuntary shudder, as she turned she realised it was a man, a boy really, dressed almost entirely in black. Black shirt, with some type of skull motif, partly obscured by a black waistcoat. Black cargo style trousers, very baggy, with lots of bulging pockets and loops of silver chains hanging from the waistband. He was topped with long dank black, obviously dyed, hair, crowned with a black bandana and tailed by black Dock Martin boots. He would have appeared threatening but for a very gentle clean shaven face. He was obviously waiting, politely, to enter after her.

"Can I help you?" he grunted, with surprising good manners. "Are you here to see Jason?"

"Err, well, yes," Lucy blustered. Then trying to compose herself. "Yes, I'm Lucy and I have an appointment with Jason."

The black figure eased past her, entered some numbers on a key pad, opened the door, and then stood aside to let Lucy through. The courtesy was so unexpected, that Lucy was unsure quite how to react. Should she perhaps bow or curtesy, or maybe tip? She reprimanded herself. Why shouldn't a Goth have manners? Or was in 'Emo', she had lost track of the fashion trends. They all have mothers don't they? What it did do was provide Lucy with a distraction and took her mind off her nerves.

"Thank you," she said more breezily as she stepped inside. "Do you work with Jason?"

"Yeah," he replied, "SEO and PPC accounts."

"Oh, fascinating." She managed as she started up the stairs, following the upward pointing arrows leading DMM visitors to the third floor. Then added, conspiratorially to the boy as he clumped up the stairs behind her. "This is a bit embarrassing; could you tell me what DMM do? SEO and PPC just sounds like gibberish to me."

He sighed. Clearly manners and small talk weren't interchangeable. "It's digital marketing. How you promote things on the web. PPC, that's Pay per Click, Google Adwords, and SEO is Search Engine Optimisation. You know?" The effort of such a long sentence seemed to exhaust him. He swallowed hard, and put his head down as he continued up the stairs, discouraging more conversation.

"Right, got it. Digital Marketing. That makes sense. Thank you."

They had now reached the third floor, having past fairly nondescript doors on the first and second that announced that they belonged to a recruitment agency and a firm of solicitors. The door was a deeper blue and the DMM logo more garish with its gold lettering. Again Lucy had to step aside as the Goth or was it Emo worked the pin pad. As soon as the door opened he disappeared through an internal door on the left leaving her on her own in small reception seating area.

The furniture was very smart and modern. Brightly coloured squashy seats, smoked glass tables, up-lights. A complex looking micro-music system played soft jazz, an even more complex looking coffee machine promised anything from jasmine tea, to espresso to cafe macchiato. A deliberately haphazard pile of designer magazines created a splash of colour on the table. She searched for a company brochure, or any literature to give her more background on the company. But to no avail. In a separate smoked glass display case there were some small statuettes and plaques - awards. As Lucy tried to get into a position to be able to read the inscriptions she became aware of another person in the room watching her intently.

"Lucy I presume." He wasn't tall, but his dark features and impeccable but casual clothes made him striking. Everything about him oozed confidence, but not arrogance. He wasn't over-dressed, she couldn't imagine *him* torturing himself in front of the mirror deciding what to wear, he just had a natural style.

He looked at Lucy with a slightly amused expression. "Gary told me you were here."

"Gary?" Lucy at first looked bemused, but then realising that this must be her congenial Goth doorman, she couldn't help a smile. "Of course, *Gary,*" she paused, waiting for him to speak, but when he didn't, she felt she had to fill the silence. "You must be Jason?" She put her hand out straight in front of her. Far too formal for the occasion, so she quickly let it drop. "Good to meet you. Great looking office."

"He does prefer to be called Merle, means the black haired one apparently in some ancient Elfin script, but I can't get used to it. Once a Gary, always a Gary in my book. But Lucy, that's a good name, an honest name."

Lucy had no idea how to respond to that. So she gathered her bag close to her chest and looked at Jason expectantly. "The job?" she said.

"Of course. Come. Come through. Coffee? I'd get someone to get it, but I have no one...."

"No, I'm good, maybe just some water."

Jason led Lucy through the door into the main office. "This is it," Jason announced, "welcome to my world."

Around a dozen desks were laid out in small but very distinct groups around the open plan room. The different desk groupings seemed to have adopted the persona of their users. In one area, in the darkest corner of the room, Lucy saw Gary sitting in what was clearly the techie corner. His colleagues, all male, dressed in what she presumed was the grunge style, black t-shirts with mysterious messages, long dark combat trousers or shorts with a surfeit of pockets and heavy black boots. Whatever skin was on show was pale and hairless. Lucy recalled her mother remarking that lads like this could do with a good boil wash. But the more Lucy looked, the more she realised that the 'unwashed' look had been more carefully cultivated. This was *clean* grunge. There was no chatting or social interaction at these tables. Each head was encased in large headphones and eyes were fixed on the screens. Their fingers worked in a blur across the keyboards. Following her eyes, Jason remarked. "Our tech team."

In the middle of the room, separated only by a few feet from the techies but a complete cultural divide, was a second grouping. Two girls, colourful in primary Primark, seemingly very young, all hair and nails. The desks were covered in small plants, photos, and the paraphernalia of the teenage girl. They worked the phones. "Tina and Jules, our beautiful sales team," Jason kept up the commentary. The two girls looked up simultaneously and beamed.

The remaining desks were more individual, though Lucy was taken by the simple stereotypes. Their workstations were lined up along the outside wall, like flowers that needed the sun. Jason went through them in turn. "Charlie, graphics." Sun bleached blond, surfer look, tanned legs below Oakley shorts and shirt, relaxed posture as he leant back in his chair surveying his extra-large screen. "Becky does the copy, but not the coffee." She looked up at Jason with a thin grim grin, obviously it was a joke many times made and worn thin. She looked booky, somewhat more studious than the others, dark framed glasses, straight dark hair falling over her face. Clothes more austere, older looking, but Lucy presumed she wasn't. "Finally, Anne our resident chef, she cooks the books." Older, looking stern in her examination of the spreadsheet on her screen. She seemed out of place with her sensible and comfortable blouse, loose fitting trousers and shoes. Lucy was almost taken aback when she looked up pleasantly and smiled a welcome.

"And now the *management* suite." A whole corner of the office had been partitioned off with book shelves and display cases. Inside she could see a very modern, shiny and tidy, black desk, dominated by the latest and largest Apple IMac computer. Extending from the desk was a conference table with 4 matching chairs, a glass water jug and glasses clustered in the middle. A separate informal seating area had been created to the side, with two leather chairs facing each other. It seemed like an entirely different world. An empty, cleared desk sat at the entrance to the office. "That will be your desk," Jason added with a confident smile. "You'll fit in perfectly."

"Wait," protested Lucy, "I don't know what the job is. The hours? What the company does? The benefits? I don't know anything, and you know nothing about me. I might be a right troublemaker."

"You're not are you?" He did look slightly worried.

"Well no. But I might be. We should have an interview. I could fill out a form, do a psychometric test. You should take up references."

"Spare me the suspense, what would they say?"

"Obviously they would be good," she laughed. "Conscientious. Good with people. Excellent attention to detail."

"There we are then. You sound perfect."

"No!" Lucy was getting frustrated, but wasn't sure why. He just wanted to give her a job. What was the problem? "You haven't even seen my CV."

"Alright, I give up," said Jason with a resigned smile. "Let's do this your way." He gestured to the easy chairs. "Please take a seat and prepare to tell me about your school days. But first I'll get the coffees. I have no assistant you see."

She felt lost in their conversation, it seemed to last for hours, though in reality it was little more than twenty minutes. The hum of the computer servers, clatter of keyboards and chatter of the sales girls was cancelled out by the intensity of their talk. Perhaps it was his voice. Deep, yes, but it was the calmness, it had a soothing melodious quality, like talking to a late night radio show host. The rest of the office faded into the background. These two chairs were their world, for these few minutes nothing else existed. She couldn't remember much of the detail of what they discussed, it ranged around her life, her teaching, her parents, her dreams and aspirations. It was his interest in her that gripped her. His questions gently probed her, got her to say things, personal things, which she didn't normally talk about. He talked with a smile, but his questions weren't in any way mocking. It was certainly not like any interview she had ever experienced before. In some ways it was like that first kiss on a dance floor at a teenage disco. She was lost in the moment, baffled by the intensity of the feeling. But it wasn't sexual or emotional. Sure Jason was good looking and charming. But there was nothing in this meeting that made her want to rip his or her clothes off. He wore nice clothes. She felt opened up, gently and kindly, but still opened up. What struck her most was the way that he got her to talk about her past in a way that made her proud of it. Nothing was dismissed, positives that even she hadn't seen, were drawn out of every element of her life. Every element that was except her family. She hadn't talked about Daniel or John. Was it that Jason hadn't asked? Had she denied them? Was she hiding them?

Now she was outside on the street, leaning against the brick wall by the side of the red front door of the DMM office. She didn't really remember leaving. She did remember him shaking her hand. It was one of those handshakes where he shook with his right hand but placed his left hand on her forearm. Usually she hated these faux sincere gestures, that she usually associated with the over familiar salesman, but here, with Jason, it seemed right, showed that they shared a moment of significance. She remembered looking at his hands as they shook. He had nice wrists. A semi casual, but crisp dark blue butcher striped shirt. Good quality. Watch and cuff links gold, not flashy, but classy. Funny, she wouldn't have expected cuff links. Slightly tanned skin, the right amount of hair, clean, strong fingers. But no, while they suited him, she wouldn't have expected him to wear cuff links. John never wore cuff links.

She tried to remember how they had left it. She had insisted that she email him a CV and a letter of application. He had laughed at her need to keep to the formalities. He had a nice laugh, one that laughed with you, included you, not at you. Email, did she have his email address. Panic. Then she realised she was holding something in her hand. His business card. Thick, good quality, well designed. He would then write to her, with an offer. Or a rejection. Could he reject her now?

Get a grip girl. It was just a job interview. Wasn't it? Was that all it was? Was that how he saw it? How he saw her? Should she ask him? Call him? No, they had met, had some form of interview and had agreed next steps. She should wait to see what happens next.

She looked at her watch. Christ had she been out that long.

She rushed home. Key in the door. Excited by what had happened. Something unusual. Something for her, about her. Now she could share it with John. As she walked through the door she called, "John. You'll never believe what —"

"WHERE THE HELL HAVE YOU BEEN?"

CHAPTER ELEVEN

It had been a long time since Lucy had waited for the post to arrive. The joy of birthday cards. Trepidation of exam results. The emotional turmoil of Valentine's Day. She smiled fondly when she thought of John's letters, it had been much earlier in their relationship, when they were living apart for periods, living in different parts of the country. He had been such an accomplished letter writer. Funny and serious. A strange mixture of banal observation with such a straightforward approach to affection and tenderness that it could sometimes take her breath away. Unlike her, he didn't pre-plan his thoughts, or re-read his words, he had just written what he felt and sent it. Where was that man now? Where was that sensitivity, that honesty of emotion? Was it all down to the digital age? The texts, the emails. Was that what cut the heart out of the message? Was that why John could no longer communicate with her? She sighed, maybe she should write him a poem?

So it had seemed strange that at the end of the job interview Jason had said he would *write* and let her know about the job. Not a call or an email. He actually wanted to send her a letter. What did that say about the company or about him? Traditional or maybe backward? Jason hadn't seemed like a technophobe. Plenty of evidence of computers and mobiles on his desk. It was a *techie* company after all. But Jason had certainly been different.

Seeing Lucy's quizzical expression, Jason had said, "I really appreciate the time and consideration you will have given to apply to us for this position. I feel that you deserve a professional and personal reply. Your talent is clear; you've sold yourself well to me. Now it's up to me to make *you* want to work for *us*." It should have sounded pompous, but something in Jason's manner made his words seem very personal to her, made her feel special. Was he just a flirt? Did he say this to everyone? Lucy didn't know the answer, she did know that he had made her feel special and she did know that she enjoyed his attention.

The strange circumstances of the interview had blurred a little now, she could not quite believe that it had happened the way it had. She had never told John what had happened. His anger and annoyance at her being out and his having to look after Daniel seemed so unreasonable to her, it heightened her need to do something for herself. He had said that she had made him miss an important phone call, because Daniel wouldn't settle, kept bothering him, because she wasn't there. And so, after that, she hadn't volunteered where she had been and in their sulky silence, he hadn't asked.

The next time John was out she had got on to the computer and searched back in her personal files for a CV. It had been years since she had updated it. It was all GCE grades, college courses and work experience. Nothing about the five years teaching and three as Daniel's mother. How can you capture that experience in a few lines of text? But then she realised she didn't have to, Jason had explored her life in the way he had talked with her. He now knew her more intimately than a CV could ever present. So she added the bare basics, just positions, dates and places, and printed it off. She tried four or five times to start a letter. But couldn't decide how formal to make it. Odd, she had insisted on having a letter and now she couldn't write it. Even an email seemed inappropriate. In the end, trying to match the spirit of their meeting, she decided to send a card. They had a good selection in Smiths. So with Daniel in tow, he liked looking at the racks of cards, especially the rotating ones, and Smiths had a lift - they headed out to town.

It was always better to promise the lift as a reward at the end of their shopping rather than as a treat at the beginning. Luckily the card section was quiet, so Daniel didn't annoy anybody by continuously turning the display rack. Strange, so many cards, but they didn't have a dedicated section for 'Thanks for the Weird Interview. Here's my CV' cards. Luckily not having any idea what she was looking for helped her find the right card. It was a modern French café scene, a very smart couple sitting together at an outside table enjoying the sun - him reading the paper, she talking on her phone. Together, but apart. 'Digital Media', she thought. Magic. First pay, then Daniel can have the lift.

After the third ride up and down one floor, the shop manager looked like she might be losing her patience. Lucy took Daniel firmly by the hand to limit any protest, gave a weak smile of apology to the manager and left the shop. Back on the pedestrian precinct she and Daniel walked past three smart cafés to get to the one that did marmite on toast and a passable coffee. Different worlds she thought, but life was less complicated if she chose places where Daniel felt comfortable.

Seated in the window seats. Daniel focused on the traffic outside, he had his three toy cars, lined up on the table while he munched his toast. Lucy had asked for a cloth and had carefully wiped and dried the table. Marmite wouldn't have been the best addition to her CV. She unwrapped the cellophane from the card. What to write? Keep it simple, she thought. No innuendos. Nothing too personal. It's a job! She sat back and let her mind drift. Finally, it came to her. She wrote the short note inside the card. Carefully folded her CV, squeezed both into the envelope that came with the card, good job her CV only ran to two pages. She had decided to hand deliver, so she just wrote Jason Collins, Digital Media Magic on the front. Daniel was a little perturbed by the diversion on their walk home, but was placated by posting the letter through the big red door. Lucy was surprised she had done it, but the fact that she found it easy reinforced in her mind that she needed to do this for herself.

And so for the last few days she had found herself waiting, expectantly, but feeling a little foolish because of that expectation, for the postman. She checked the time again on the kitchen wall clock, eight o'clock. Was the post late? It had been so long since it had mattered that she had no firm idea what time the post usually came. Despite being poised for it, she was still startled when she heard the rattle of the letterbox and then the comforting sound of the letters coming through the door and falling to the worn hall carpet that they had planned to replace this year. She tried to remain calm as she rose from the table, smiling at Daniel, "Mummy's just going to get the letters sweetheart". Daniel stared at his toast. He liked toast.

Perhaps she should have told John about the job, or the interview or even that she was considering going back to work. But there had never seemed to be the right time. Once the moment had passed, when she had come back from the interview, and that was his fault after all, it had seemed difficult to bring it up. She definitely didn't want to appear as if she was hiding something. Having job interviews was perfectly natural, loads of people had job interview every day. Well, maybe not quite like the job interview that she had had. But that was Jason wasn't it. Had to be different didn't he? And Jason, he *definitely* wasn't the reason why she hadn't mentioned it, why would she be nervous about mentioning him to John? Anyway, as the days passed, why start a potential argument before she knew if she had definitely got the job? And did she have the job? Where was his letter? Maybe he wasn't serious, just teasing her, he didn't seem the type, but who knows? No, she was sure that she and Jason had made a real connection. And maybe this was the day when the letter would come, and she would have to have the conversation with John.

Returning to the table with a little bundle of mail, she forced herself to sit down before investigating the collection of envelopes. A flyer for a Chinese takeaway, bank balance transfers, a credit card statement. Nothing unusual, special. But, what's that at the bottom? Good quality envelope, handwritten. But then she recognised the handwriting. She scowled in disappointment. She started to open it with a knife from the table but then slammed all the letters onto the table in annoyance. This wasn't the letter she wanted.

"John, what the hell is this?" Lucy shouted from the kitchen with an edge to her voice. There was a long silent pause. John was still in bed, god knows what time he'd come to bed, she thought. They not only seemed to be living separate lives, they were now living in different time-zones. She called again, "John! I mean it. What the hell is this?"

"What the ... What's what?" He shouted from the bedroom, his voice was muffled by the duvet still wrapped round his body.

"Your mother. She's up to something." She could hear his heavy footsteps as John lumbered down the stairs. But she waited until she heard him reach the bottom of the stairs before she shouted again, "Why can't she stop interfering?"

"What are you talking about?" John entered the kitchen, his hair tousled, his face still a little misshapen from sleep. "What's she done now?"

Lucy handed him the smart, Basildon Bond blue envelope with their address elegantly written on the front in a neat, un-flamboyant script. The envelope had been roughly opened with a table knife. Judging by the butter smears on the envelope, probably the same knife that Lucy was using aggressively to cut up a piece of toast for Daniel. Would Daniel notice that these weren't quite the usual uniform equilateral triangles? John placed the envelope on the table, propped up against the margarine tub, while he pulled the kitchen chair out and, leaning heavily on the back of the chair, sank down unceremoniously into the chair.

"Well! What is it?" Lucy insisted, "What is she up to?"

"I don't know. Give me a chance. Don't suppose there's a chance of a cup of ..." Lucy's glare cut him off. "Well no, maybe I'll check this letter first."

It was a problem with his mother. She always made you feel under-dressed, maybe a little unclean, even when she wasn't there. He could never think of her as anything less than 'well turned out'. Even her gardening and decorating clothes were ironed. Should he wait until he was washed and dressed before he opened the letter? How could a letter make you feel under-dressed? But then she always did, her presence would always be enough to make you feel slightly unkempt, or like this morning, a bloody mess.

He had been at it until late again, till around three he thought. His head was heavy and his mouth tasted foul from the four or five too many coffees he had had. All evening and half the night spent at the kitchen table. Only separated by a thin wall, but still completely away from Lucy, Daniel, his family. But no matter how much he stared at the papers, he still couldn't make sense of it. Two piles. The first: quotes for engineering development costs, office costs, patent costs, legal fees, marketing costs. Tens, no hundreds, of thousands of pounds. The second: mortgage, telephone bill, credits cards. And on top a quote for their car, mere hundreds of pounds, but still seemingly unattainable. How could you ever make the big plans work when life kept getting in the way? Perhaps if he were single, no dependents, no mortgage. Perhaps then it would be easy. But then who would he be doing it for?

He stared at the envelope. God forbid his mother would ever use mismatching paper with the envelope. But no, as he pulled the single sheet of crisp, neatly folded blue paper from the envelope he saw it was Basildon Bond as well.

"Well read it then!" Lucy's patience was running thin.

John unfolded the letter slowly, as he did so a second smaller piece of paper, a cheque, fell to the table. He glanced down, five hundred pounds, he sighed, but smiled. Sadly, five hundred pounds was a significant amount of money at the moment. Not enough to make a real long-term difference, maybe not enough to warrant Lucy's ire, but plenty to pay a few bills and to get their car fixed. "She's sent a cheque. Obviously realised things are a little tight at the moment," he paused, "that's nice,"

"Oh no John. You read it. There's bound to be more to it. It's never as simple as - 'a little helping hand'."

John returned to the letter. He unfolded it, sat back in the chair and seemed to spend too long reading what Lucy could see were only a few lines of text.

"Well!"

"Well, she wants us to go away, have a holiday, just the two of us, a weekend away. Says we should have time to talk. That's nice."

"Nice?" Lucy erupted. "We don't have the money or the time for weekends away, for holidays, especially without Daniel, you hardly see him as it is. What about the bills, the mortgage, the car? I don't need to be told when to speak to my husband, I need a husband who listens and talks back. Your mother, she just doesn't understand ...." The last sentence was lost as she burst into tears. She turned, trying to hide her upset from Daniel, she ran out of the kitchen and up the stairs to the bedroom.

"She's suggested that hotel we like on the Isle of Wight, the Farringdon. She'll have Daniel for a few days. That'll be nice." He paused, conscious that he was only talking to Daniel, who looked at him quizzically. "That's really nice, isn't it Daniel" He let the letter fall to the table and groaned as he put his head in his hands.

Daniel after examining the roughly cut triangles of toast pushed the plate away in disgust. John knew there would be no pleasing his family this morning.

Upstairs Lucy sat on the bed, tears streaming. She wiped her eyes roughly, forcing herself to stop crying. She was cross with John, how had they let the relationship get to this level of bickering? She was cross with John's mother, what right did she have to interfere, to try and help? She was cross with herself, how could she be thinking about jobs, life outside the family, her own selfish needs, when her family needed her? And she was cross with Jason. Where the hell was his letter?

CHAPTER TWELVE

A week later. John had cashed the cheque and booked the hotel and ferry (something he would never normally do himself, Lucy was the one with the organisation skills). He had packed the bags himself, packed Daniel off to his mother's, with more effusive thanks. He had prepared the car and now stood outside the house holding the car door open, waiting for her.

The letter had come. It was everything that Lucy had hoped for. Personal, witty and positive. She had phoned to accept as soon as she could find an excuse to get out of the house. Jason was away, the States she thought they said, back in a couple of weeks, but he had left word to arrange a start date with her when he returned. It seemed odd to Lucy that Jason would allow others into their relationship, but she agreed to start on a Monday in three weeks. So she had plenty of time to tell John, to wait for the right moment. There would never be a right moment. And now this weekend away. Creating more of the wrong moments. Or maybe not. His mother wanted to give them time to talk. Well they could talk about this, couldn't they? But first she must try and make an effort.

She came out of the house, purposely leaving the front door open. This was his idea, or rather his mother's, he could lock the door. She got into the car, not acknowledging his over-formal curtesy, and settled herself. John sighed. Gently closed the door, not a moment to slam. He returned to the house to shut and lock the door and then walked back to the car. Lucy was deliberately not meeting his eyes. God, thought John, no-one in this family will look me the eye. All set. He thought about a rendition of 'We're all going on a summer holiday.' Maybe not. He pulled away from the kerb. They were off. He staring at the road straight ahead. She staring out of the passenger window.

The two-hour drive south along the South Coast was hardly undertaken in a holiday spirit. "I can't believe you said yes," seethed Lucy, yet again, "and don't you dare say it's *nice*!"

"It's a weekend away. What's not *nice* about that?"

"We can't afford it, that's what. The whole time there I'll be thinking about how we can't afford it. Every time we have a drink, I'll be thinking, we can't afford it. Each meal in the restaurant, I'll be thinking, we can't afford it. Each night alone in the hotel, without Daniel, I'll be thinking we really can't afford this."

John, felt the tension ease a little. "I know what you mean," he chanced his arm, "every leisurely breakfast with the papers, I'll be thinking. Every round of golf, I'll be —"

"Every swim in the pool."

"Afternoon tea in the lounge."

"Walk on the beach."

"Nightcap in the bar."

They started to smile now, then, as they looked at each other, John joined in as Lucy said, "Every coffee on the terrace, we'll be thinking, "we can't afford this"."

"That's nice," concluded John with a sigh. He switched some light pop music onto the car radio and they sang along, the tension gone. That's one of the things he loved about Lucy, she couldn't hold a bad mood for long.

***

The Farringdon had become a favourite place for John and Lucy. They had first come here some years before, when Lucy was pregnant with Daniel. One advantage of living on the South Coast was that a relatively short drive could be rewarded with quite a different type of resort. Hastings, Eastbourne, Brighton, Worthing, Portsmouth; they ranged from party town to retirement home. Each had its own style and culture, driven by both its resident and holiday community. The Isle of Wight was different again. It was as if the short ferry trip took you back in time, not just across the sea.

Even the idea of a ferry, now seemed of a bygone age. Holidays these days nearly always involved a flight to and from a nondescript airport. The clothes that had seemed sensible for the four am outward journey, were revealed to be totally inappropriate by the creases and sweat stains when you arrived six hours and fifteen degrees hotter later. And that was why you went, it was hotter. But when you got there you complained about the heat. The hours of the carefully coveted holiday time spent smothering yourself in greasy lotions to either protect you from or recover from, the sun. If you were really lucky, you slept late, then the entire afternoon would be too hot to do anything. But in most holiday countries there was no contingency for anything to do when it was too hot to do anything. In Britain we had cinemas, museums, indoor amusements, heated swimming pools, end of the pier shows for the wet days. Sometimes you prayed for rain, just to fit all the wet day activities all in. But on a hot holiday, you just prayed that your holiday finished before you ran out of sun cream or books.

Lucy had discovered the Farringdon on one of her internet trawls trying to find a good way to spend John's small, but much anticipated, bonus on something frivolous. They hadn't wanted a city-break or the more conventional resort hotel. The Farringdon sounded perfect. The ex-home of a long dead English writer, the hotel had made few concessions to modern times to cater for the occasional tourist that had searched hard enough to find it. But mainly it served its reliable regulars. Those who liked the old world, slightly faded, charm. The chef that still recognised that Britain had seasons and that a kitchen garden could dictate a simple but delicious menu. Management that saw good service as a mark of a proud profession, not of subservience. And that it was the little personal touches that made a hotel stay memorable.

And so John and Lucy had found their refuge. Everything they loved about the hotel was exemplified by their favourite moments there, after dinner coffees on the terrace. No harsh outdoor lights or children's play area. Just a terrace looking out onto a moonlit sea. Coffee was ordered, then served rather than delivered, by a trusty old retainer (probably much younger than the impression conveyed). Beverages were served in slightly battered silver pots. One for the fine coffee. One for the hot, foamy, milk. Sugar lumps in a bowl, with tongs. Bliss. A place to unwind, to relax and yes, to talk. “Nice,” thought John.

***

They hadn't so much *dressed* for dinner as *changed.* It was their way of rewarding and respecting any quality evening time together, rather than conforming to somebody else's rules. Dinner at the hotel was simple. No starters. Just an excellent rib-eye for him and sea bass for her, fresh veg from the hotel garden and buttered baby new potatoes. And, of course, one good glass of wine each, a light Sauvignon for her a heavier Merlot for him. They couldn't afford it, they remembered.

Their conversation had remained light. Memories of previous visits. Anecdotes from work and friends. The requisite conversation about Daniel, what they'd read, heard and watched. Autism seemed to be the perpetually in the news at the moment. But nothing heavy.

The waiter approached their table, “Desert madam?”

John interjected, “No, I think we'll just have —”

“Coffee on the terrace, sir, of course.”

They made themselves comfortable outside on the old, but sturdy, oak garden furniture with its deep blue cushions. They relaxed back into the chairs and looked out as the moon shone down over the calm sea creating what looked like a silver, gleaming pathway. Their hands automatically reached for each-other. They let out a mutual sigh, “Nice.”

The waiter came slowly through the slightly peeling French windows and made his way to their table. Methodically he laid the two saucers and two unmatched cups, “Large, as requested.” The sugar bowl, “Brown Demerara, as requested.” The first dented, but gleaming silver coffee pot, “Coffee sir, Columbian as requested.” The second, silver pot, this one with a slightly ill-fitting lid, “Hot milk sir, steamed, as requested.” Then finally, as John smiled and nodded his grateful thanks to the waiter, and as he leant forward ready to pour, the waiter added, "And this sir," he laid a large, thick manila envelope on the table between them.

"Thank you. But I didn't, haven't, don't know what —" stammered John.

"Special instruction from reception sir." As if this somehow explained everything.

John and Lucy stared, transfixed, at the envelope. It looked formal, A4 with an addressee label 'John and Lucy Miller', and then below their names 'Care of the Farringdon Hotel'. It was thick, certainly containing more than a few sheets of paper. And in the top left hand corner, handwritten, 'Private and Confidential, to be delivered with evening coffee,' and then that day's date.

"What the hell?" Said John incredulously.

"Don't open it," said Lucy sternly, "it's got your mothers' hand all over it.

"But it's typed."

"Don't be ... You know exactly what I mean."

They sat in silence for a few minutes, staring at the envelope. Lucy started fidgeting, "Well open it then!"

"But you said ... Oh what the hell." John realised it wasn't worth arguing, he reached over a picked it up, testing the weight in his hands and checking the package for lumps like he was trying to guess the contents of a birthday present. He held it to his ear and shook it. "I don't think it's a football." But this was no time for flippancy.

"Oh for heaven's sake, give it here." She reached across him and grabbed it impatiently. She hardly paused before tearing open the envelope and tipping out the thick sheaf of papers. They looked very official and legal and she could see from the crested header sheet, they were clearly addressed to John. "Oh God," she panicked, dumping the papers into John's lap, "what's she done now? Is she suing us?"

"Hang on," said John after he'd had a chance to read the cover letter, "she's not suing us. She's *investing* in us, or in EarStream, to be exact. I think this is what they call a 'Term Sheet'. Jesus! She's investing one hundred thousand pounds."

"Investing! Investing in what? You've done nothing yet."

John looked a little hurt at that. "Investing in me I guess. My idea. The potential of the business. But heh, who cares? It's a hundred grand, our troubles are over." A huge smile on his face, this day was going perfectly, he leant forward again to pour the coffee. "Now *we can* afford this."

"No!" said Lucy, all serious now, "we can't. What does she want? She wants to control you. She always wants to control everything!" She was close to tears.

"Wait, no," John wasn't really listening as he read on. "This is good, she's doing it properly, a proper business investment, it's going to be OK. Oh mum, you angel."

As they got back to their room, John was the happiest he had been for months. Now he could plan, rather than just worrying. He felt the pressure easing from his shoulders. He wanted to share this new positive feeling with Lucy. Now they could build this together rather than pulling themselves apart. He could look again at grants, to leverage his mum's investment. He could talk again with the university, the patent agents, the design engineers. But not tonight, tonight they could relax, enjoy a night when they weren't engulfed in worry. He had reached for Lucy's hand as they had walked back to their room.

Lucy knew she should share John's happiness. He had worked so hard to get to this point, given up so much. Now, thanks to his mother, he had a way forward. They had only drunk a glass of wine each, but John seemed almost drunk with relief. She must share this with him. She was his wife; they should share everything.

As they entered the room, John spun Lucy gently round so that her back was to the door as John eased it shut. "God I love you Lucy," he spoke gently as he took her in his arms and leant down to kiss her.

"I've got a job," she delivered it like a bucket of cold water to his face.

CHAPTER THIRTEEN

John was up early after a fitful sleep. He was torn between the excitement and trepidation of taking the next steps on the EarStream project, working with his mother, and then trying to understand what was going on in his relationship with Lucy. They hadn't really talked last night. She had said something about a dream job with a digital marketing company, which as far as he could tell, she knew nothing about. But as soon as he tried to ask questions she had become overly defensive. He knew that pursuing his dreams of developing the technology had put strains on their marriage and family life. He knew that Lucy was frustrated about being at home with Daniel all the time and having no money didn't help.

It had been a joint decision for Lucy to not return to work after the maternity leave, especially when they started having problems with Daniel's development. Of course situations and feelings change, but surely Lucy getting a job was something that they should have discussed? Was she just hitting out at him for taking the decision about the new business without consulting her? Even so, they did need to work this out, if she went back to work, who was going to look after Daniel?

But he couldn't see that Lucy getting a job really solved anything, especially now that his mother was putting in some cash. She didn't have to work. And who was this Jason guy?

But for now he felt it would be easier to try to be supportive, to focus on the practicalities. How could they provide effective care for Daniel while he pursued his new business and Lucy started a new job? Perhaps then Lucy would open up a bit, talk about what she wanted. She had seemed very distant the last few months. But at least he didn't have to worry about money, just for now.

He looked down on Lucy sleeping. It was too easy to forget how beautiful she looked when she slept. She was on her side, her shoulder length hair lying across the pillow, framing her face. She looked peaceful. It had been a long time since they had made love. So many things between them had been put on hold. As he watched her sleep, he felt himself getting aroused. They were on holiday after all. He wanted to show her how much he loved her. How much she meant to him. How important it was that they worked this out together. How good they were together.

He slipped back into bed, back under the heavy hotel duvet. Tentatively in slid across the mattress and cuddled into her back. Perfect. He reached over and started to caress her full breasts through her nightshirt. Feeling the nipples start to respond to his touch, he moved his hand down to her thighs, her stomach, her bum then back to her breast. Rhythmic caressing, growing firmer, more intense. As her body warmed to his touch and moved to the rhythm of his hands, he pushed up her nightshirt, gently touching, stroking, caressing her soft skin. He found her warm sleepy body truly exciting, every curve and crease was like a new discovery. As she and her body became awake, he kissed her neck and drew her body back towards his own. She groaned as his hand pushed aside her panties and his fingers eased between her legs. He knew she was his. She reached back behind her and slipped her hand inside his shorts, her fingers curled around him, they both groaned. There were no words. They both needed this. Needed to share each other. Needed to be one.

***

There are few things better after morning love making than a hotel buffet breakfast. They had slept curled together until nine, showered and dressed in quiet happy harmony. There was no need for words this morning, no explanations, no apologies, nothing to break the moment. Just a glance and a smile, they were one. They didn’t really speak until they were seated at the table for two by the window in the hotel dining room.

"So when do you start?" John said with a gentle smile as he dipped his finest local sausage in the perfectly fried egg.

"Fifteenth," she replied, uncertainly. They were both tip-toeing round the subject. "But I'm sure there's some flexibility, depending on what you've got on that week."

"No, don't worry. It's important that you create the right impression when you start. We'll work it out. It will no doubt be a while before the new funding kicks in, so Daniel and I will manage." We'll have to, he thought to himself. But tried to be positive. "It will be good to have some extra cash coming in."

"OK. Thanks," she smiled warmly, and reaching across the toast rack, placed her hand on his, "we'll work this through. It'll best for all of us."

"Oh course," said John, though he couldn't help thinking, how it was going to be better for Daniel?

They went back to the important task of eating their way through the buffet. "Why do you say there'll be a delay with the money? Surely your mum will just hand it over?"

"I'm sure she would, though there will inevitably be lots of legal paperwork. But, I was thinking it through earlier, if we're clever we can use my mum's money to help match some government grants. There seems to be some good schemes out there, especially for research and development projects, but you have to have some of your own money to match it. There's something called a Smart Grant, where the Government will match the money you spend on developing a new product. It's competitive, but Simon reckoned that with the university involvement we should stand a good chance. But the thing is you have to be able to show you have the money in the bank."

"So you have to hold on to it then? I can't get my car fixed?" She was sounding a little peeved.

John was trying not to get irritated, when did *their* car become *her's*? "Not all of it. We'll just need to plan a bit, sort out the urgent things, like *our* car, and then see what the expenses are like. It will be easier now you're earning."

"The job is not just about the money John."

"I know, I know. You need it for yourself." He was trying desperately not to sound trite or sarcastic. Must avoid pretentious phrases like, 'finding yourself', 'creating your own space', and 'recalibrating your chi'. He tried to take a practical approach. "Even so, the extra cash will help. By the way, how much are they paying you?"

"Well, I'm not sure, I haven't actually asked."

"What? You don't know? What type of job is this?" His voice was rising now and he could see Lucy starting to bristle in self-defence. He wanted to ask about how they were going to pay for the child-care for Daniel, there was a good reason why she hadn't returned to work before now - but he desperately wanted to keep up their good mood. "Never mind. I'm sure it will all work out, you haven't even started yet. They sound like an interesting company."

"Yes, sure." Don't snap back, she told herself, so she remained restrained.

"I think I'll try the smoked salmon," he said rising to make his third trip back to the buffet. "Can't let good salmon go to waste. Can I get you anything? Then we can work out what we are going to do today. Hire bikes or back to bed?" He added with a grin as he set off with plate in hand.

"I'll try the salmon as well," she called after him, with a smile, the mood regained, "and then I'll consider the options."

***

The meeting room at Pearce, Pearce and Monmouth was plush. The legal firm was based in the professional district of Chichester, which as the County Town of West Sussex had that Private Client feel of dealing with old money, rather than the Corporate City firms. Pearce, Pearce and Monmouth was set-up for conveyancing, wills and wealth management for its clients. But for John it was like entering a different world. He was seated at a light oak board table, feeling lonely amongst the fourteen chairs. He had been provided with a coffee and a biscuit, which he sipped and nibbled, it might be considered uncouth to dunk in this environment. He stared at the blank pad of Pearce, Pearce and Monmouth headed note paper that was laid out in front of him, along with the Pearce, Pearce and Monmouth embossed pencil. This was a strange environment to meet your mother.

Then she entered, with a bustle, accompanied by a very tall besuited, clean shaven man in his fifties. It was obvious that they had been having a pre-meeting as they seemed halfway through a conversation that John wasn't a part of. They sat, side-by-side across the table from him. Adversarial. Should John have brought his own legal counsel? Surely not? This was a mother supporting her son, wasn't it?

The tall, thin, angular man, took the lead, introducing himself as Martyn, 'with a y', Pearce-Monmouth, a senior partner at Pearce, Pearce and Monmouth. He started to introduce his mother, but then stopped as John stared at him. Was this a joke, thought John, she's my mother.

"I'll take it the counter parties know each other," Martyn, 'with a y', said with great seriousness. John and his mother didn't respond, but when Martyn looked directly at them in turn, they felt compelled to nod.

"Mrs. Patricia Miller, henceforth referred to as Party One or 'The Investor', has made an initial offer to invest a sum of one hundred thousand pounds, into the company EarStream, henceforth referred to as 'The Company', in consideration of twenty percent of the ordinary shares. Mr John Miller, henceforth known as Party Two, is the nominated Managing Director of the 'The Company' and currently owns one hundred percent of the shares, there being no other shareholders."

John raised his hand, like a school boy, interrupting Martyn's, henceforth known as 'The Lawyer's', flow, "I do want to give my wife some shares in the company."

The Lawyer nodded, appearing to acknowledge John's contribution, then carried on, dismissing it. "Party Two *currently* owns one hundred percent of the shares in 'The Company'." He looked around the table, as if twenty faces were looking back. "Is that a fair summation of the situation?"

Patsy was clearly starting to lose patience, "For goodness sake Martyn, get on with it, we all know why we're here."

Two hours later, John was again seated across the table from his mother, but this time ensconced in an over-stuffed armchair in nearby hotel lounge. They were having or rather *taking* tea. This seemed to consist of a multitude of containers and implements to hold and handle the leaves, the water, the sugar, the milk, and then tiny versions of sandwiches and cakes. For once John was showing little interest in the food. A thick pack of papers sat on the antique table in front of him, all neatly packed with a Pearce, Pearce and Monmouth document folder. John had been very quiet since the end of the meeting with the lawyer, still a little shell-shocked.

Martyn had run through a whole series of legal documents related to the new business and his mother's investment. Company formation, Articles of Association, Shareholder's Agreement, Management Service Agreement, in the end, John's head was swimming with the clauses, warrants, terms and conditions. John found it hard to see how a business that didn't own any assets and wasn't buying or selling anything could have so much paperwork attached. His mother had sat impassively throughout, without questioning or commenting, which was pretty unusual for her. This was a standard process, Martyn explained, pro forma documents, nothing special. It was as if John and his mother were just an audience to a fine legal performance, it seemed to have so little to do with them.

"Mum," John said while his mother continued to fuss with the tea paraphernalia. "Mother!" She looked up at that. He continued more quietly, "Mum, why are you doing this? Or more importantly, why are you doing it *like* this?"

She stopped pouring and sat back in the over-stuffed chair. "Well John, in part it's because I can. Your father left me well provided for, mainly, perversely, by dying too early. So I received the benefits of a substantial death in service on top of the more than adequate pension pot. He would be proud of you striking out on your own, even though I think you are mad to give up a good job and take this type of risk. And that is the other reason. Your father had a longing to start his own business, a passion to 'do his own thing', he even had his management team and backers lined up. They all *believed* in him, but no, not me, I said no. And your father, being the kind of kind man that he was, god damn it, listened to me and buried his own ambition for the sake of our marriage."

John has never heard his mother speak this way before about his father, he made to interrupt, to ask a question, but his mother raised her hand to stop him and continued her story.

"But it didn't help our marriage," she looked away into the distance, "I never forgave him for giving in to me, for not following his dream. And, while he never said it, I believe that he never forgave me for stopping him.

"And now it's you. As I said, personally, I think it's a stupid idea. But maybe I would think of any idea like this as a stupid idea. I believe in order, of finding and knowing one's place, of not believing that you should strive to be something that is outside the normal expected progression in your life. Whether you succeed or fail in starting your own business, you are challenging the norm. To me that is irrational. It's a risk you don't have to take; it threatens your place in society.

"So I can never agree with what you are doing. But having seen how much it hurt your father to bury that dream, I don't want to see that happen to you. Your father died before I could say I was sorry for taking away his chance to express himself in business. He was a success, but a success at making somebody else's dream come true. He thought that someone was me, but no, it was some faceless business executive. I have lived with the guilt that I held him back, made him suppress his ambition. I can't put that right for him, but I can help *you*."

It was the most emotional statement he had ever heard his mother make. He had had no idea of his father's unfulfilled dreams and his mother's guilt. It explained a lot of the unspoken tension. "But why all this?" He gestured at the pile of legal documents on the table, "why not just help?"

"Oh it's because I can be such an interfering old busybody. And you don't want me naysaying all the time. It was Martyn's idea. Making it less personal, taking it away from the family. Keeping it so formal allows me to remain as a silent partner, absolutely no reason for me to be involved. Who knows, I might even make a profit. So I'm not risking that much and really you're just getting your inheritance early. If you lose the money, well, it's *your* money. You're not beholden to me in any way. I may even have a proxy Director to represent me."

"But mum —," started John.

"— No buts John," she interrupted firmly, "I've made up my mind. I want to give you the opportunity that I took away from your father. But remember dear, this won't be easy on Lucy or Daniel. It may have been wrong for me to have said no before, but there was a good reason for it. This may be your dream, but you must share it with your family, otherwise it could drive a wedge between you."

John was silent. This wasn't the type of *moment* he was used to having with his mother.

"Now let's have this tea before it goes cold and get you back to your family. I've taken up quite enough of your day."

"Thanks mum," was all he could say.

CHAPTER FOURTEEN

"OK," said Simon as he and John sat together in the TECHub cafe. "We've got the legals sorted with the Shareholder Agreement and Articles of Association for EarStream, the company. We're waiting for the tax status to be confirmed so that your mother, sorry investor, can finalise the funds transfer into the company accounts. Just checking you have set up the company bank account?"

John had been nodding and checking off his to-do list. "All done. Deposit and Current Accounts. They won't agree an overdraft through until the investment funds have been deposited. Typical they won't lend until you definitely don't need it!"

"Now, now, that's a very cynical view of banks within an entrepreneurial society. What about the grants? What's the thinking there?"

"Well, I'm quite interested in getting a grant, either to help the business side or to pay for the research. I think I'd prefer to leave any further equity investment at the moment. What I really want to do is to get on and do something, rather than spending all my time deciding which form to fill in. If I can use my mum's investment money to help me get a grant, then that would be great."

Simon nodded, "I think you're right. You can create problems for yourself if you try and bring in equity funds alongside a friend or family investor. A professional investor will probably value the business quite differently, and usually lower than what you've already agreed with your mother. That then raises a question mark over whether your mother might ask for additional shares in the company."

"Hmm. Given the way mum's brought in the lawyers, I wouldn't want to do anything which re-opens that conversation. Maybe best to leave well alone for now."

"You're probably right, plus you will hopefully get a higher valuation later on and maybe attract some more smart money."

John looked puzzled, "Smart money?"

"Sure. 'Dumb money' is just money, valuable, but no added value if you know what I mean. Smart money, it might come with contacts, market access or management experience. In many ways the 'added' value can be far more important than the money itself. All investment money is looking for a return, but smart money can potentially have more impact in helping to achieve it, as it gives greater credibility to the idea."

John still wasn't looking sure. Seeing this Simon carried on. "OK. Say for example you're setting up a new online product and you're faced with two potential investors, both of whom is showing interest. The first is a friend of a friend, who has inherited some money and is looking for some future tax efficient revenue. The second, well let's exaggerate for effect, the second is Sergey Brin. Who would you choose?"

"Sergey? ... Oh you mean the Google guy. Well, him of course."

"Of course. But why, specifically?"

"He's Mister Google, isn't he? If he thinks you're worth backing, it must be a good idea."

"And so ...?"

"And so, other people will take the company more seriously. You'd get more publicity etc."

"Exactly. You'd find getting investors, employees and customers much easier because they're buying into Sergey."

"Do you know Sergey? Do you think he'd be interested?"

"Well, no. He's just an example. But what you can do is target that type of investor. Find ways to make them aware of the company. The important thing as you start to build the company, is finding investors or non-execs or advisors that give that added credibility. For example, like that meeting we had with Anne from the Defence Consultancy."

"Don't remind me," John grimaced.

"Yeah, I know. But say you were targeting the defence industry. Having an investor with retail experience wouldn't be as much value say as a, 'General Somebody - retired', home from active stints in Afghanistan and Iraq. Someone that can phone his ex-colleagues and has instant credibility. Someone that can give you industry relevant advice, knows and can explain buying patterns. Understand the operating conditions of the market, what standards the product has to meet. Attract other advisors and investors that would back his judgement."

"I get it. But where do I find them, and how do I decide which market to even aim for with EarStream?"

"In many ways, that's the next step. Let's go back to our original conversation. You've got your mum's investment, so let's agree that for now you want to focus on grants and loans to increase the pot, but that we would like to attract some 'smart money' later on."

"Sure. And I'd rather avoid taking on more debt at this stage. I've got no security."

"Really? What no assets? What about your property, don't you own it?"

"Best not to go there at the moment. Lucy and I are tolerating each other's plans at the moment, there's no way I can bring up risking the house."

"OK. Hopefully we can avoid that. So let's look at the grants. The key is to find the right grant at the right time. For example, there are general business grants that are focused on job creation, and others that are purely about creating new products. Also worth looking into tax credits when you are doing R&D."

Simon saw the bemused expression growing on John's face. "Don't worry, we'll walk you through it."

"Thanks, that's a relief," John sighed?

"Best to try and keep it simple," said Simon. "Concentrate on making the most out of your mum's investment."

"Yeah, a hundred grand doesn't go very far these days," he laughed as he said it, but Simon could see he wasn't really joking.

"OK, let's get started. From where I think you are, you need to build some credibility with the University in order to get access to their IP. Getting a Government grant will help with that."

"Fantastic!" John said more brightly, "let's get one of those - what's the catch? There's always a catch."

"Not really. But it does have to be a good project, with genuinely new technology and market potential. It's a competitive process, so you have to make a good case."

"Market size, market potential. Everyone seems to want to know that. But how can you know when the product doesn't exist?"

"I know what you mean, but there are ways. Hang on, I there might even be some grant help available for that as well." Simon, flipped open his laptop and spent a couple of minutes searching. "Got it," he reads from the screen, "'this grant enables companies to assess commercial viability, through: market research, market testing and competitor analysis, intellectual property position and initial commercialisation planning.' Perfect."

"And I can get this market research grant and the one for R&D?" John sounded a little more hopeful.

"Sure. Even better, these government schemes like it when businesses go through their schemes in a logical fashion. It's part of the so-called 'Funding Escalator'. The government, like you, wants to hedge their risk, so best to invest a relatively small amount in say checking that there really is a market for a new product, before they invest a bigger amount in developing it."

"You mean like doing focus groups?"

"That's one way, but market research is much wider than that."

"What was it Steve Jobs said about focus groups? Don't trust them, customers don't know what they want," John was impressed with himself for dragging that one out of a part read autobiography.

Simon smiled at that. It was amazing how many new inventors declare that they knew better than their customers. "Absolutely, and when you're the head of Apple, you can make those calls too," he retorted light-heartedly. "In most cases, people tend to use focus groups to choose between design variants, rather than looking at the introduction of a whole new type of product. Plus, at Apple, he didn't have to convince somebody from government that they should invest their money when you've got little or no track record."

"But I wouldn't want to spend too much on market research, I need most of the money to move the technology forward, and to live off."

"No problem. As long as you do get enough data to strengthen the case for your next grant proposal." Then Simon added flatly, "Or it tells you not to waste your money."

"What do you mean waste?" John sounded offended.

"Nothing specifically. Just making the point that it's better to invest a little to find out where there's no market for your product before you spend a fortune developing it. You'd be amazed how many people treat customers as an afterthought. And the way they've set up the grant system, encourages people to check the market. "It's a bit like the patent system, when you first apply for a patent no one looks at your application for a year, they just confirm the date they've received it. It's called the 'priority date', and it is the official date that is used in any patent disputes, that is if someone else has filed, it is the priority dates that decide who filed first. Anyway it's the date that is important. You get a years' worth of 'pat pending' protection, when you can tell people about your idea and see if there is enough interest in it to justify the cost of continuing the patent process."

"Oh right, so 'pat pending' doesn't mean that much then?" All John could think about was 'Wacky Races'.

"It means you've filed for a patent. Not that it's been granted or even that anyone has checked that the idea doesn't already exist. But importantly, it means you have some protection."

"But which market and how? EarStream could potentially be used in medicine, in defence, in espionage, plus any number of areas I haven't even thought of yet."

"What you can do is to start looking at what the criteria are for a 'good market' for EarStream and then start comparing how the different sectors measure up. There will be lots of facts that you don't know and lots of assumptions that you have to make, and that will guide your market research. I'm not saying it's easy, but it's a process and the more you work at it, the better your market knowledge becomes and the better your future decisions will be."

"And the government will give you money to do this?" John was warming to the idea.

"Yes. You've got to sell it well and meet the funding requirements. But yes, they want to encourage people to develop their inventions into real businesses."

"OK, where do I get the form?" John sounded more convinced.

CHAPTER FIFTEEN

Lucy had always felt she was a confident person, comfortable in new situations. Sure the interview with Jason had thrown her a little, but that was understandable given the unusual circumstances, plus she thought she had recovered herself quickly. Growing up she hadn't been particularly fazed by new experiences, on her *first-days* at school, university, teaching practices, she had breezed in, taken the initiative, started conversations, made herself belong.

But sitting here, in front of her dressing table mirror in her underwear, she felt anything but confident. Every part of her, from her down cast face, to her fidgeting feet, showed her nervousness and the lack of her usual self-confidence. She hadn't meant to be irritable and snappy this morning, but in the end John had given up and taken Daniel out to the cafe for breakfast, just to give her some space.

John was trying to be supportive, Lucy knew that. Indeed, she was trying to be supportive to him. Unfortunately, their mutual support had become little more than banal encouragement. They were avoiding all the difficult questions between them.

Why had she taken this job?

How had John lost his?

What did taking John's mother's investment mean?

Who was going to look after Daniel?

Who was Jason?

No, now they just focused on the short-term, the here, the now. Making sure household chores were done, parenting duties shared. Recognising each other's moods and pressures and compensating for them. Organising their diaries so that his business meetings and her new work days were aligned and didn't require Daniel to be passed around too much. But they didn't talk about how they were feeling. How the prospect of their new challenges made each of them nervous, excited or even nauseous. They didn't share their uncertainty, their fears for the future, their real need for each other. And so Lucy sat there nervous, anxious, lonely, a little queasy, needing reassurance, definitely needing a supportive hug from her husband. And John had thought it best to take Daniel out and leave her alone. Oh well, she told herself, she had put herself in this position, she had better get on with it.

She had half her wardrobe laid out on their double bed. Clothes were arranged into outfits according to degrees of formality, a business suit to the left, his side, she hadn't worn this since her last teaching interview which was years ago now, before Daniel. She didn't even know if she could still get into it. Formal didn't seem right for Jason, she thought. Next an array of summer dresses, or should they be termed frocks, in the middle, bright colours, bold patterns, assorted lengths from mini to maxi. Did they make her appear frivolous, not taking the job seriously enough? More Pimms and strawberries than business calls and appointments. Then there were the smart-casuals, laid out to the right side of the bed, her side, the better quality jeans, no rips or adornments, no blue denim, tops more muted in colour, no logos and not too figure hugging. The problem was the mix of people she had met at DMM, there wasn't really a *type* that she could fit in with. She couldn't grunge with the 'techies', or 'Primark' with sales or 'Board' with graphics, there was no role model for her. She knew it didn't matter. Jason wasn't employing here for her dress-sense. It was all a symptom of her lack of self-confidence. Why was Jason employing her? She'd never been a PA, she knew nothing of digital marketing, she'd never even written business emails. What was she doing? Why was she going to make a fool of herself?

It was eight-thirty in the morning. Jason had suggested she come in for nine-thirty on her first day, to get settled in before their regular staff meeting at ten. That would be a good way of introducing her and for her to get a feel of what was going on in the company. Better get going girl or he'll be introducing you to the team in your pants, Lucy told herself sternly.

***

While he wouldn't necessarily admit it to Lucy, John was starting to enjoy taking Daniel out in the mornings. The freshness of a new day was usually matched by Daniel's mood and attentiveness, so mornings were his best time of day. Daniel always seemed to regress and become *more* autistic when he was tired or ill or hungry. He would become more withdrawn, less able to maintain eye contact, more isolated. Working at home John had become more attuned to Daniel's moods and his daily cycle. Through this he had realised that in a normal working week he was always coming home just when Daniel was at his least receptive to him, or for that matter, with anyone. Seeing Daniel in the mornings, especially over breakfast, he had appreciated far more the highs and lows of Daniel's autism and his emotional swings. This was the time when, if only in very small bursts, you could interact more with him, encourage him to try new things. At first he was quite resentful that Lucy hadn't discussed this with him, found more ways of involving him when Daniel was more receptive. But, he realised that it wasn't intentional, just the practical result of him being at work and she at home. Lucy wasn't keeping Daniel's best times to herself, or excluding him, they were just part of his daily routine.

John found it very poignant that when they went out as a family, to local special needs or autistic support groups, that he was one of the only fathers that attended. Yes, of course, he knew from the news reports that there were far more single mothers these days, but this was quite extreme, he would often be the only dad in a group of fifteen to twenty families. He could feel quite intimidated, like having a mum and a dad in a family was somehow now the exception. The talk amongst the other mums was often of the *bastard* dads, the focus either on the father's access (too little or too much), or maintenance payments (always too little). John couldn't believe that he was the only father that actually loved his wife and cared about his child.

He and Lucy had talked about this. Was there something about the family dynamic in a 'special needs' household that created more break-ups? Was there something in the male psyche that made it harder to cope with special needs? Did mothers in that situation become more absorbed than normal with the needs of their child to the exclusion of everything else, and everyone else, including their husbands? Was it that the mother was usually the one with more direct contact with the child, and so could then resent the part-time involvement of the father? Could it sometimes be as simple as John only usually saw Daniel when he was tired and hungry and so unreceptive, so that John felt more isolated from his son?

Whether the EarStream project actually worked out or not, he was glad that he had been able to have a little more quality time with Daniel and to get to know him a little better. He felt that he could now be a better father and a better husband, if only his relationship with Lucy could get back to normal. It was all too strained, too *trying to be nice*, that it felt false, pushing too many things beneath the surface.

John and Daniel arrived at their local cafe. Daniel rushed to find his favourite seats by the window overlooking the road, which fortunately were free today, sat down and started to get his toy cars out and arrange them on the table. John ordered an Americano, a glass of milk and toast, always toast, and remembered to ask them not to cut it. John was becoming more familiar with those small elements of Daniel's routine than made life flow more easily and he was also becoming better known around the cafes and shops in town as he took Daniel out.

As the drinks and toast arrived, the two of them settled in quite comfortably. Dad cut the toast carefully, obeying all the necessary geometric principles, and Daniel acknowledged, if not quite openly appreciated, it. Daniel got on with the important task of eating and arranging his cars, while John got the paper out. He probably ought to be sorting through his 'to do list' for today, but what the hell, let's have some father and son quality time he thought. He read the paper.

***

Lucy arrived at the office at nine fifteen, not too rushed, not too flustered, but only because she hadn't taken any time to have breakfast. She had settled on smart casual and was comfortable that her cropped *smartish* light blue chinos and sensible white shirt, with minimal jewellery and makeup, allowed her to fit-in but not stand-out. It was a good balanced look in an office of many looks. The welcome from the DMM team was similarly mixed. Grunts from tech, hugs from sales, a cool hand flourish from graphics and the request to fill out a form from accounts. Jason wasn't in yet.

Lucy made her way to her desk, which was strategically placed between Jason's management area and the rest of the office. She was pleasantly surprised to find it clear and clean, with a decent looking PC and even a small bunch of flowers in a simple vase - though no indication of who had put them there. She sat down in the highly functional, but surprisingly comfortable computer chair and heaved a relieved sigh. So far so good.

As she sat, trying to look busy, but with absolutely nothing to do, Jason arrived. He created quite a kerfuffle as he struggled through the door with a large box of assorted fruit juices and carrier bags of cakes and pastries. He gave a very broad and very welcoming smile to Lucy. "Got to celebrate the arrival of our new employee," he said warmly, "especially as now she's here I won't have to get the breakfasts anymore." He laughed, well everyone laughed. Lucy realised that the office and the company only came alive when he was there. Without him it was just a disparate group of ill-fitting individuals, but with him it seemed like a team united in a purpose.

The girls from sales, Tina and Jules, rushed to help Jason with the bags. Lucy realised too late that she probably should have been the one to help him, but heh she was just finding her feet. They bustled through a door that Lucy hadn't even noticed in the corner, Lucy got up and followed them through into what turned out to be a quite spacious meeting room, well equipped and furnished to seat twelve with a big screen and fancy looking conference phone in the middle of the light oak table. It wasn't an opulent boardroom, but it was smart, modern, professional and a little surprising, rather like Jason himself, thought Lucy.

Lucy helped Tina and Jules to lay-out a breakfast spread on the table, she caught Jason's eye, she smiled and mouthed a thank you. It had been several weeks since the interview, but she felt like they were old friends. He grinned as he turned and left them to it. As he stepped back into the main office, he called out, "OK troops, let's get this done, and no mess in the Board Room, we've got Davies and Jackson Solicitors in at eleven. Lucy you'll need to join us and take some notes for that one."

And that was it, she was in, part of the team, back in gainful employment.

***

Back at the house, Daniel was in the lounge playing, a much watched CBeebies DVD played on the TV. Daniel seemed to prefer to re-watch programmes that he knew well rather than have something new. John was in the kitchen at his laptop. He wondered what Lucy was doing, how she was getting on, on her first day. He thought of phoning her, but didn't want to, one, disturb her in the office, or two, appear as if he was checking up on her. He decided that a text would work better, he got out his mobile.

'To my working girl. Hope all's going well on your first day, proud of you. Love J xx'

His mobile rang. He found that it always took him by surprise when it rang when he was texting. He didn't recognise the number, so answered quite formally.

"John Miller."

"Ah, John, its Nancy here from the University. I work with Dr Billing. Ian forwarded me your email and asked me to fix up an appointment to talk about your potential use of University technology. I don't suppose you are available this afternoon, around three?"

"Three, this afternoon?" Repeated John, as he desperately tried to think through the logistics. "Yes, of course. I can be there. Would this be with Dr Billing, at his office?"

"Yes, that's right. I believe that Dr Billing wants to go through some licence terms."

"Oh, OK, that's good."

"Great, that's confirmed for three then. Thank you. Good bye."

"Good bye."

As John finished the call. He sat back in chair. He suddenly felt exhausted. It was the mix of excitement at moving the business forward, he had been waiting for weeks for this meeting, frustration at the need to quickly find someone to look after Daniel, and trepidation at going into a legal discussion where he was unsure of his ground.

***

It felt like the first day at school. She had a new pad of paper and three new sharp pencils laid out at what she thought would be her place at the table for the meeting. She was ready to capture somebody else's wisdom. After the staff meeting, which had started jokey and welcoming and then turned into a long list of project updates which meant nothing to her, she had cleared the table and tidied up the board room. She found the kitchen area and prepared some water and glasses for the next meeting. She still hadn't had a chance to talk to Jason on her own and when she returned to her desk he was deep in a video conversation on his Mac.

With eleven o'clock looming she looked over to the sales girls and whispered, she had no idea why she whispered, "How can I find out the names of Jason's visitors."

Trudy smiled and made her way across the office, she seemed pleased to be seen as a source of advice. She leant over Lucy's desk and with a blur of keystrokes switched the screen between files and programmes. Lucy couldn't possibly follow what she was doing, and she was relieved when the tapping stopped and the screen was left on a calendar screen showing that day's date.

"There you go, nothing to it," she said, a little patronisingly, thought Lucy. "It's a Gerry Jackson and Liz Bolshaw. She's the managing partner and he does the marketing, according to this. Potential new client."

"Oh great, thanks," replied Lucy helplessly, none the wiser about how you accessed the system. She made a note of the names and kept an eye on the external door to the office, she had no idea who answered the intercom on the door to the street or who was supposed to let them in. At least that question was answered a few moments later when a buzzer went off on *her* desk. Clearly it was her. She was supposed to be the doorman. Thankfully the unit of her desk only had two buttons, one that said, 'Intercom' and a second labelled 'Entry'. She pressed the former and spoke in her best BBC Announcers voice, "Hello, DMM?" There was a muffled response over the intercom, she thought she could distinguish a man's voice, and perhaps the words Hancock and Davies. She took the chance.

"Thank you, please come up to the third floor." She pressed the entry button, and sat waiting hopefully that they would find their way in.

As she waited, Trudy leaned over and again in a stage whisper said, "You will need to let them in."

Lucy cursed silently to herself. "Of course, thanks," she managed to say to Trudy as she got up, made her way over to the reception area and opened the door. She could hear the heavy tread of her visitors making their way up the stairs to the third floor.

***

John had used their list of emergency contacts for Daniel and struck gold with his third attempt, Debbie from just down the road could pop over for a few hours that afternoon, but needed to be away by five thirty, when her own children were due to be picked up from their various after-school clubs. John thanked her profusely, went and informed Daniel that he would need to go out after lunch, but it was all right because he liked Debbie. He prepared a quick platter of toast and an apple for Daniel. When at last he had him settled, he was able to sit down in the kitchen and give himself a few hours to prepare himself for what he expected to be a key meeting with the University.

***

Lucy thought that the meeting with Davies and Jackson had gone well, though looking at the scribbled meeting notes you couldn't tell. It was very hard to make sense of a discussion that was filled with buzzwords and jargon, especially as the less you knew, the more copious the notes you had to make, as you didn't know what was important. However, Jason had seemed pleased and the potential clients had seemed happy. There was talk of retainers and success fees and KPIs and SLAs, so Lucy was pleased. She had not said a word for the whole hour and a half, her right wrist was numb from writing, she realised that you seldom had a need to write anything long-hand any more. Jason had presented well and Liz and Gerry nodded and laughed in all the right places. She had shaken their hands when they had got up to leave, but Jason had shown them out, all warm handshakes and smiles. Now she remained seated at the meeting table, feeling a little shell shocked.

Jason breezed back in, he seemed energised by the meeting.

"So, Lucy," he sat down next to her, watching her face closely, "what did you make of that then? Another client in the bag?"

"Me? Oh I don't know; they did seem impressed with your presentation. But if I'm honest —"

"— I know," Jason broke in, "you had no idea what I was talking about. I'm afraid that was perhaps a little unfair of me, especially as I hadn't had a proper chance to introduce you to the business. But, I thought that you could cope with being dropped in at the deep end. Which you did."

"All I did was to keep schtum!"

"In my book, that was coping well. Let's go through your notes."

For the next hour, Jason painstakingly went through the entire meeting, using Lucy's rather verbose notes as a guide. He went through the digital marketing challenge as presented by the client, essentially how to make a firm of solicitors, which do the same thing as every other firm of solicitors, be the first choice for people searching locally for legal help. He described in detail the techniques that his team would use to evaluate the web presence and digital marketing profile of Davies & Jackson Solicitors and their immediate competitors. To understand how their potential customers were searching, what search engines and what search terms they used, what proportion clicked through on a link when they got the results of searches.

Professional firms generally used sponsored links, banner ads and blogs in their digital marketing. The end result of their research project, as Jason described it, would be to establish what Davies & Jackson Solicitors would need to do to get on the first page of search results for selected search terms locally. They were currently only on the first page for one out of their top twenty. In an ideal world they would get Davies & Jackson to be number one on Google, but these days that was increasingly difficult and certainly very expensive for generic search terms. He explained that there was little value in being number one for people searching for 'Davies & Jackson Solicitors'. The real value was being on the first screen for people searching for 'Conveyancing Sussex'.

Lucy's head was buzzing, but she realised that by doing it this way, at the end of the meeting, she got to understand what DMM did from a client perspective, rather than from an internal DMM viewpoint, which would probably be dominated by *what* individual team members did technically, rather than *why*. As Lucy's job was to be more client facing, but not sales, then this perspective was far more valuable. In many ways Lucy could relate it back to her teaching. For example, it was much easier to teach young children Maths within a real world context like shopping, rather than the more theoretical list of sums.

When Jason had finished going through the detail of the meeting sequence, he answered Lucy's many questions, they moved from the nonsensical to the rational as her understanding and confidence grew. He stood up, obviously ready to move on, but happy to continue if needed.

"Does it make a little more sense now?" he asked patiently.

"Absolutely. I appreciate the time you've spent." And Lucy meant it, she really felt that she had gained a good grasp of the industry and the business. Amazing what an intelligent approach to teaching and coaching could do.

"You're worth the investment," Jason added with a smile.

And there it was again, thought Lucy, was he a flirt, a tease or a genuinely good people manager? She held up her copious meeting notes.

"I'll type these up," she said, "but it may take a while." She laughed as she flicked through the numerous pages of scribbled text. "Not sure if my ten words-per-minute typing is up to this."

"No need," Jason smiled again, "they were entirely for your benefit. I'll send Davies & Jackson a brief summary proposal now. When you've got a few more under your belt, I'll hand that job over to you." He turned, and as he walked through the door, said back over his shoulder, "Good work today Lucy. I knew you'd be right for us." He smiled again, "Well right for me."

***

John considered again what he had learnt about IP licensing deals, he had spent a long time researching on the Web and had talked his findings through with Simon at the TECHub. He tried to think through what his position should be if the University raised them with him. He knew that he wasn't in a very strong position as he didn't have the cash or even the immediate prospect of a revenue stream to pay for licence fees or royalty costs – let alone any patent costs. Even so, he knew that if he were to raise investment he would need the technology to be protected and to have some 'Exclusivity' over the use of it for a reasonable time period.

As far as John knew the University hadn't patented anything on EarStream yet, and without a patent they couldn't licence it. So in his mind the priority had to be to show enough interest and potential that the University would go forward with filing a patent on the understanding that John would soon be in a position to sponsor research and to look seriously for commercial opportunities.

John was so engrossed in his thoughts that it took him a moment to notice the dull pain in his leg, he looked down, Daniel was standing next to impatiently banging his thigh. He was bored, "Out, out," he repeated robotically.

"OK Daniel, we'll be off to Debbie's in a minute, you go and pick your favourite cars to take, while I get ready."

John sighed and tried to refocus his mind on the University and licensing terms.

It seemed too early to make any commitments on 'Royalty Structures' and 'Minimum Royalty Payments', but these were bound to come up in the discussions. Simon had suggested that he try and put off any final decision on these aspects of the agreement until some funding was secured. John hoped that the University would be up for this, as he really couldn't commit to any future costs at this stage. On his side was that the University didn't have anybody else looking to take this particular technology forward, plus Simon had told him that the University was under pressure to do some deals.

While there was a lot of the detail around IP licensing that John didn't understand, at least he felt better prepared than the last time and so would hopefully be less intimidated. Plus, he had something to offer this time, he had some money that could go to Dr David Lowe, to further his research. That must be good?

Although it hadn't been *that* long since the original dinner party, where John had met David, it seemed a distant memory now. He had read all David's publications, plus many other articles around the subject, and nothing had indicated that the idea wouldn't work, but that wasn't the same as proving that it would. The one thing he hadn't done was to meet David again, he wasn't sure why, maybe he needed a plan, a way forward to offer David, to prove his credibility. To show him that this was more than a dinner-party pipe-dream. He felt he was nearly there. And he felt he was as ready as he would ever be for meeting the Dr Billing at the University.

***

The rest of Lucy's first day was a bit of an anti-climax. Jason had disappeared off to London. When it came to lunch, all the DMM team remained at their desks with assorted microwave re-heats for the girls from sales, rolls, crisps and coke for the 'techies' and sushi for graphics. Accounts just worked through, never taking her eyes off the screen. Lucy hadn't thought to bring lunch, too used to the school lunches from her past. So she slipped out into the Town to find a sandwich. She was quietly elated from her morning with Jason, she had successfully stepped up to new challenges and increased her technical understanding. She also felt that she had strengthened her connection with Jason after he had shared his business thoughts with her. What made that connection more intense, but also slightly furtive, was that she had no-one to talk to about it, no-one else to share it with. She had tried to call John, to check on Daniel, but his phone was off and she'd had no voicemail or text messages. She sighed and kept her elation to herself.

***

If he could whistle he would have been whistling to himself in that self-satisfied way that whistlers' whistle. The meeting with the University had gone well. He had met Simon from the TECHub first and that had really helped to confirm the strategy for the meeting, understanding what were good outcomes for the University so that he could make sure that, even if the University didn't get an immediate financial return they got publicity and commercial links, plus the promise of future returns. The lovely Laura from the University Business Office joined his meeting with Dr Billing and in the end she had led the discussion and made sure that he had enough in terms of an agreement that he could apply for grant funds. So now he could meet with David Lowe, again with Laura, to create a technical scope of work. Instead of taking one step forward, he felt like he had bounded ahead four. He felt like celebrating.

He was on his way now to pick up Daniel. As he parked the car, he got out his mobile, which had been off all afternoon, he immediately saw two missed calls from Lucy, and then he saw his unsent text to her, somehow he hadn’t got around to pressing send. Damn, he thought, maybe they wouldn't be celebrating tonight. He'd have to gauge the mood when they both got home.

***

As celebrations went, fish and chips and a shared bottle of beer was quite restrained, reflecting their current relationship rather than their current moods. Neither felt they could share their day's success as neither her job nor his new business belonged to them as a couple, what was new was separating them rather than drawing them together. If you celebrated the things that separated you, it could push you further apart.

CHAPTER SIXTEEN

The first EarStream Company meeting was held in the Board Room at the TECHub. Simon said that it was often useful to invite academic colleagues away from their labs and into a business space, it gave a better focus to the discussions as it took the academics out of their comfort zone and made them more willing to accept input. Simon would lead the meeting along with Laura, David Lowe would be accompanied by Björn, a young post-doctoral student, who would probably do most of the actual work.

Simon brought the meeting to order, "Good morning everybody, let's get started. John, do you want to bring everybody up to date with where we are?"

As all eyes turned to him, John had that realisation that not only were they looking at him, they were looking for him to lead this project. He was supposed to be the thrusting entrepreneur bringing technology out of the labs and into the market place. He had never been much of a leader, never had to be, always a capable team player, perhaps a strong number two, but never the actual leader. He sat a little taller in his seat, held his head a little higher, well if that's what it takes, so be it.

"Thanks to you all for being here. While we have only just started, I feel that we have already come a long way. We obviously have some interesting technology." All eyes shifted to David, who acknowledged with a nod. "We have some initial ideas of the potential market areas and Simon has offered that his team can back this up with some market research." Again eyes moved and were acknowledged with a nod.

John continued, "The University has agreed to an initial no-fee R&D licence, contingent on us getting some grant funding and a committed research spend with the Engineering School."

Laura smiled, she felt very pleased with herself for getting Dr Billing to allow this agreement with so few strings attached. All too often universities asked for too many financial guarantees on what are risky start-up projects meaning that nothing actually got started. She knew that John and his new company wouldn't pass any form of due diligence, but she had felt a strength of commitment with John that gave her some confidence. And anyway, Dr Lowe had been working on this idea for the last five years and nobody else had shown any interest. So what did the University really have to lose?

"The next step," John stood at this point, in his now commanding way and went over to a flip chart grabbing a pen, "in order to make the grant application we need to specify the product, a market, a technical scope of work, an IP strategy, financial cash flows and wrap these up in a credible business plan," John added each point to the bullet list on the flip chart. He felt important standing at the front writing things down, as if by merely being able to list then, it proved that he understood them and so could deliver them. It was all about confidence and credibility. As he moved away, he saw how the writing sloped down to the right, he felt less in command. Perhaps Lucy could show him how to write in a straight line.

In many ways the list hadn't changed since John had first sat down at the breakfast table all those months ago, but now he was reasonably confident that this team could manage to pull all the necessary aspects together.

Simon interjected, "One key thing with the grant proposal is that we are not going to focus on the potential autism application. While I know that was the original driver, it's a hard market as far as commercial outcomes go. We can focus the R&D on other applications, for example security and defence, where the IP position and potential customers are clearer and then cross apply back to medical applications. It's all the same technology after all."

John wasn't altogether comfortable with this, but he was prepared to accept the logic of the argument from Simon, and also

Laura, if that would help get the grant. But he knew that he would need to fight to keep autism as the priority application.

Simon continued, "Right the next thing is the actual technical work. David do you want to come in here?"

David looked a little uncertain. "Ahhamm," he cleared his throat, "well, our current research programme is focused on the translation of snail models. The fascinating thing about snail's brains is that —"

"— David," interrupted Simon, "I think we might be talking more about more empirical experiments around actual applications of the algorithms here, rather than the basic research, fascinating though that sounds."

David resumed, a little flustered, "I suppose what we could do, and by 'we' I mean Björn, is to take the electronics to the next level. Create some more robust embedded systems where we can take the theory outside the lab and apply it to some real-time situations."

Simon looked pleased, "That sounds perfect David. Björn can you prepare a work plan to develop a proof of concept model? Then I can work with Laura on the costings and with John on which market applications we should focus on.

"It's important that the project includes market engagement." As he saw blank faces around the table, Simon added, "I mean talking to customers, or at least potential users. These type of projects are about proving that you can do something novel and that people need it or want it in sufficient numbers to make it work as a business."

There was a lot more nodding at this. They went round the table several more times to make sure that everyone agreed on what was needed and when it was needed by. As people started looking at their watches or their phones, Simon reckoned he had held their collective attention for about as long as he could. So he called the meeting to a close. The two doctors were first out of the room, rushing to return to the safety of their academic offices. Björn hung back, either he was interested in more information about EarStream or the TECHub or he was just interested in Laura. As Simon and John looked at him, Björn edged towards Laura, it was clearly the latter. With a smile Simon stepped back to let

Björn pass. Björn tagged along behind Laura as she swept out of the room, she waved cheerily, clearly enjoying the attention.

"Young love," remarked Simon, "I suspect soon to be thwarted." Seeing that John was not tuned in to the people around him, he returned to the main subject of conversation. "So how do you think that went? Happy?"

"I guess so. Everything seems to be moving forward. I just hope we can pull everything together. I've heard that the academic side can sometimes hold things up."

"Oh don't worry about that. Laura's on the case and I think that she won't have a problem getting anything she wants from Björn." Simon laughed and started to hum 'The Power of Love' as he gathered his papers together. "Coffee before you go?"

John had no idea what he was talking about with the Björn references, so looked a little confused, but he shook it off. "Yes, thank you, I have got a few questions about the market analysis." They headed downstairs to the Innovation Cafe.

The cafe was crowded, being lunchtime. This was a different crowd from elsewhere on campus. Most of the younger entrepreneurs looked like they were five years out from university, there was also a smattering of *suits* - funders, lawyers, accountants, customers. There was a real buzz to the conversation, which seemed oddly intense for a coffee shop. These were serious people talking business but in an informal setting. Sort of summed up the TECHub to John.

As they took their seats and settled in over their coffees Simon again caught John off guard with his question.

"So how are you holding up?"

"OK I think. I'm sure we can put the application together."

"Sure, the application. But I was wondering more about you personally, you and your family. How's your son, Daniel isn't it?"

"Yes, Daniel, he's fine. Lucy's got him today. Her boss has been very reasonable in letting her work flexibly," John sounded wary.

"Look," said Simon, "I'm really not trying to pry. This doesn't have to be part of what I do. But I am very conscious that you and all of your family are going through some big changes and face a lot of uncertainty at the moment. That can put a strain on the family just at the time when you need their support. Let me see," he started to count them off on his fingers.

"You've started a new business.

"You've lost your job.

"Your income is uncertain.

"Your mother is now your major shareholder.

"You're doing a different job in a completely different environment.

"You're working from home, with no regular hours or structure.

"You're now a part-time house-husband.

"Your wife has just decided to start work again, changing the home dynamic.

"You have the stress of an autistic son.

"You feel you need to find a cure for autism.

"So, I feel justified in asking how you are holding up, it will have a major impact on whether you can make this project and this business work."

"Before I thought I was fine, but now I'm not so sure."

"Look it's not just you, I have seen it so often here, when someone starts a new business it can have a big effect on their personal life. They can't help it, they're not meaning to ignore their family and friends, but they're busy, maybe feeling out of their depth, and there's nothing to stop them working all hours, and when they're not working, they're thinking or worrying about the business. It's too easy to forget that they need people around them for support."

"Yeah, but I decided to do this, not them, I don't want Lucy to have to worry about it. She's got enough on her plate." John protested.

"You may think that you're protecting her, but be careful that she doesn't feel that you're excluding her. I know you're doing this for them, but they need to believe it."

"What do you mean? Lucy knows why I'm doing this."

"Then let her be a part of it. Don't shut her out."

It was a conversation that Simon had had many times before, but knew from long experience that it may not sink in with John straight away. He sensed that he had said enough for now. He would just need to keep an eye on John. He changed the subject, "What did you think of the market analysis that we did with you?"

"Actually very illuminating," said John, more brightly, "I enjoyed the brainstorming with the student team, they certainly came up with some novel applications for EarStream. I'd definitely never have thought of using it for sheep dog training, but there you go, maybe not the biggest market. The student mind works in mysterious ways," he laughed.

"That's the beauty of the brainstorming sessions, nothing is ruled out, sheep dogs may not be a priority, but thinking about them may actually lead you to an entirely different but linked application idea. I don't know, like umm, helping a blind person hear a warning bark through the traffic noise. Again, not a huge market, but that gets you thinking, what other situations would, 'being able to hear a warning signal in a noisy environment', be useful? What about cyclists wearing noise-cancelling headphones?"

"No, I do get it. The brainstorming creates a long list of ideas, but you need a way to deciding which to do first."

"Excellent, a new technique well learnt. It's all too easy to go straight for what looks like the biggest market, without thinking where the 'early adopters' might be."

"Absolutely, and I guess it gives us framework to look at any other applications we come up with."

"Oh yes, with new technologies like this, you'll keep coming up with applications. The trick is having a way of deciding which ones are *not* worth doing."

"I like that. Good to have a process, a structure to work with. It's a bit like the good software projects I've worked on, you start with a specification, but there always a way of assessing new ideas as the project moves forward." John added confidently, back on the solid ground of software development.

Simon recognised John's increasing confidence in talking about the business. "That's good work," he said, "I bet it also showed up gaps in the market knowledge?"

"Too right! It's easy making assumptions on how big your market might be, but quite different when someone asks you to actually put a figure to it."

"If only one percent ..."

"Yep, I fell for that one," laughed John, "if only one percent of people with a social communication disorder had one —"

"— Then we'd all be rich!" laughed Simon.

PART TWO

6 Months Later

CHAPTER SEVENTEEN

Six months on and the Miller household had more of a feel of business efficiency about it. Lucy had found that she had a talent for managing people and was becoming indispensable to DMM in general, and Jason in particular. John had been awarded a decent sized technology grant to match his mother's investment, so EarStream had money to spend with the University on the technology development. He now had his own desk within the 'Start-Up' Suite at the TECHub, Björn was working away in David Lowe's lab producing the first working prototypes of the EarStream product. John and Lucy were both careful to limit the time they were working away from the house, minimising the time that Daniel had to spend with friends and child-minders. They had enrolled Daniel at a 'special needs' playgroup, so that would provide some additional support, if he settled in all right.

They had both discovered a new-found confidence and satisfaction in their new roles at work, but they lived separate lives. Everything got done, responsibilities were shared, Daniel was fed, watered and entertained, when he let them in. Food was bought and prepared, but rarely eaten together. The house had never been cleaner, but was emotionally sterile.

***

John was at his desk when his phone rang. He had moved on from the 'hot desks' at the TECHub, while this arrangement had solved the initial problem of having a credible business address and access to Simon, now that he had real technical work going on at the University, he felt that needed a more serious presence. So he had upgraded to having *his* own desk within an office shared with other companies on the ground floor of the Hub. Even though he now had a permanent base, he had had neither the time nor the money to *create his space*, and so nothing adorned the walls and the cheap IKEA furniture provided by the Hub remained spartan and impersonal, with no pictures, knick-knacks, lucky charms or memories. The personal effects box he had filled at his last employer sat, unopened, in the corner. He viewed with some envy the decor and feel of the offices of the more established companies around the Hub. As far as the offices go, apart from in this the *collaborative workspace* area the TECHub provided nothing but the space, a blank canvas for the individual companies to paint their individual personality and character. For some the influence was Google, all bright colours, deck-chairs, fancy coffee machines, AstroTurf and space, lots of space. There were the professorial studies, poorly lit by up-lighters, arty posters on the walls, cluttered desks and shelves bulging with books, lots of books. There were the geek caves, dark with the blinds permanently down, tables covered with dismembered computer carcasses, like the leftovers from a digital buzzard's feast and leads, lots of leads. There are labs, white coats, hard floors, sinks and bottles, lots of bottles. Then finally there were those like John, who just worked with the bare minimum to make a practical space, not intentionally minimalist, just not a priority minimal, like a new divorcé's bedsit.

"Hello." John answered the phone rather distractedly. He was in the middle of researching websites to try and find information on the security services. It was, not surprisingly, difficult to find public information about a secret service.

"John. It is Björn. I am glad that I grabbed you. Can you come now to the lab? I have something good to show you."

"Björn. Good. How are you? Are you in the lab? Haven't seen you all week. What is it?" Stereotypically British, when talking to foreigners, John would confuse Björn, who was from Norway, by answering his questions with a mix of superfluous statements, more questions, with the answer buried somewhere in the middle. Björn had learnt to ignore most of what John said at first and then just repeat the question.

"So John, you come to the lab now?"

“Right Björn, I'm on my way. I've been doing some interesting ...” he realised that Björn had rung off.

***

Lucy was at her desk when her phone rang. The desk, once timidly hidden in the corner of Jason's management area, had moved. She now sat more boldly, more central to the room and to the organisation, from here she could keep watch over Jason's flock whilst always protecting the man himself. She wouldn't say that she had become part of the team, she hadn't really tried to fit in. She was there for Jason.

Her desk shouted efficiency with minimal personal items, save for one family photo. It was a picture from last spring, in the park, John pushing a giggling Daniel on the swing. He liked swings.

She answered the phone, it was Debs, she was the Personal Assistant for Monica, the Sales Director from Southern Sun Holidays. Southern was Lucy's first client where she was the Account Manager. She had been nervous when Jason had first asked her to take it on, but his confidence in her had really helped. He had given her an 'industry briefing' before the first client meeting, so that she had gone in armed with lots of facts and figures. Based on these, coming up with the first scope of work had seemed pretty simple.

"That's the hook,” Jason had explained, “effectively a loss-leader. The trick is to build on the early results, let them see the benefits of our approach, and then to gradually increase their spend."

So the account had started small, but through close working with Monica, Lucy had created a good understanding of the client, their customers and their digital marketing needs and, as importantly, a good relationship with Monica. Lucy had been rewarded with a steadily increasing client revenue stream from Southern, within three months it was one of DMM’s top twenty clients. But more than that, Lucy could see that the digital marketing was working well for Southern's business, there had been a thirty percent increase in their customer enquiries. This was so satisfying, she was not only achieving good business results for DMM, for Jason, but also for the client. The next meeting with

Monica, she knew, would be critical, it would be to look at the 'customer conversion rates'. "It's one thing getting the customer to the client's website, but it's still up to them to close the deal," Jason had coached her.

"Debs, how are you? Good to hear from you. How's that gorgeous daughter of yours?" Lucy was proud of herself for remembering that personal detail, Debs was a proud working mum, as was she, Lucy reminded herself.

"Oh you know, she really is fabulous, just starting to crawl, it's difficult to tear myself away from her every day."

There was a pause, Lucy was worried that she may have inadvertently nudged Debs into a melancholic 'missing your kids while you work' diatribe. But no, Debs was back, all professional.

"Thanks for asking. Monica is keen to get a date in the diary to go through the next phase of the campaign. How are you fixed for next week?"

Yes! Lucy allowed herself a silent fist pump. Jason would be delighted. She was delighted. She was delighted that Jason would be delighted.

"Next week is good for me," she said calmly, reigning it in.

***

Dr David Lowe's lab at the University was everything you would expect it to be. After walking through a maze of institutional corridors, lots of blue doors and nameplates, John entered the cluttered five hundred square foot space that sat at one end of the second floor of the engineering block. There was electronics equipment everywhere. Every surface seemed to be covered with boxes of parts, bits of computers, oscilloscopes, screens of various sizes, test switches, synthesisers, signal chasers, scanners of every conceivable type and leads, so many leads. But no people. John craned his neck to try and locate Björn through the industrial shelving racks. He knew he, or someone, must be there, because he could hear a buzz of conversation. He kept walking diagonally across the lab, towards the far corner, where he knew the desks were located. As he got closer, the voices got louder, he didn't recognise them, in fact it seemed like a whole crowd of people, too many for this small space. And then he saw

Björn, sitting alone at a table with a laptop a microphone and a tangle of wires and circuit boards in front of him. He was beaming, but motioned to John to stay quiet. John moved round the table to be behind where Björn was sitting, he could see the laptop screen which was full of audio signal traces. The voices, that John could now see were emanating from an array of speakers at the far end of the lab, about thirty feet away, were a cacophony of unintelligible speech. John thought he could differentiate about ten different voices. And then they stopped. Björn looked up at John, still smiling.

"John, great that you made it. Have I got something to show you?" He refocused his attention back on the screen and started pounding the keys.

"Twelve voices. You hear?" He looked up at John, who nodded agreement, ten or twelve he couldn't have been sure. "Now listen again." He clicked the enter button and sat back in satisfaction. The cacophony started again. John tried to pull out individuals, but it was impossible, unlike a normal conversation, they were all talking at once. As Björn typed a few more commands, the mass of sounds faded slightly and as he clicked on an individual trace you could hear one of the voices, a lady with slightly northern accent, become clear, she was talking about music. Björn moved his mouse and selected another trace. The volume of the lady's voice reduced and merged with the babble, while another voice, this time a deep American man's came to the fore, he was discussing the merits of rib steak over sirloin. Björn started laughing, clicking different traces and one by one each of the twelve voices became clear and distinct and then were subsumed into the melee of noise as he clicked another.

"I've done it. I've done it," he kept saying as he laughed. John gradually cottoned on and began laughing too.

***

Lucy was delighted when she saw Jason enter the office, it was gone four, but he'd been in London today and she hadn't really expected him to make it in. He looked tired, she thought, and more than just the *tired, I've been to London* look. To be honest he looked weary and maybe a little worried.

"Jason!" she called, "good news ..." She stopped as she saw that he wasn't his usual self-assured self. He looked across at Lucy as he walked through the office, and forced a smile onto his face.

"Lucy, how's it going? Give me a mo., I've just got to check something." He weaved past Lucy's desk to his Apple Mac and sat down.

Lucy felt unreasonably frustrated. She had bottled up her excitement from the Southern Sun call all afternoon, not wanting to share it with anyone else in the office until she had had a chance to give Jason the good news. Now, he was back, but still she had to wait. She scolded herself for acting like a petulant teenager. She tried to get back to the proposal she was preparing for Monica, but found it hard to concentrate. She looked across at Jason. He was hunched at the computer. Hunched? Jason didn't hunch. Something must really be wrong.

As if he sensed her looking, Jason turned, he gave her a small smile and summoned her over with his hand. As she left her desk and started to walk over, he got up and moved to the casual chairs in the far corner of his office area. Keeping it informal, thought Lucy, or keeping something from the rest of the staff? He sat and motioned her to join him. He leant towards her. It felt slightly conspiratorial, what was the big secret? But his first words surprised her.

"So what's *your* good news?" He said with a half-smile, "I could do with some."

How am I supposed to respond to that? Thought Lucy. Should she be giddy with excitement at her latest client break-through or should she downplay it to mirror his mood? How importance was her tiny success put against his woes of the world?

"Oh just Monica from Southern Sun. She wants to meet to go through the next phase of the project," she kept it low-key, matter-of-fact. "I'm meeting her next week." But she couldn't help a slight, self-congratulatory smile as she finished.

"That's fabulous," Jason gushed, obviously making the effort. He placed his hand over hers, "That really is great, good job, they could become one of our best clients. I'm proud of you."

Lucy was a little taken aback by his over-reaction, and quickly withdrew her hand, but gave him a concerned look. "Thanks

Jason. Is there something wrong? You don't seem your usual self."

"Me, no. Just the usual rough and tumble of business. Nothing to worry the team about."

"But Jason, this is me. I don't just feel like one of the team."

"Sure. Thanks, I appreciate it. Let's just see how things play out ..." Sensing that the conversation was over and that Jason was lost in his own thoughts Lucy got up to leave, but Jason looked back up at her, "But seriously, great work with Monica, we need good clients like them and good employees like you."

Employee? How could he think of her as a mere employee? Lucy returned to her desk. She was troubled by the conversation and the effect that Jason's subdued mood could have on the team. She looked around, but each seemed to be locked into their screens. No-one had noticed.

***

"Let me make sure I've got this right," John said. After the lab test John and Björn had gone over to the Engineering cafe to celebrate, David Lowe was also due to meet them there. "It's fantastic the extra speed you've got through the circuits and the ease with which the tuned-up algorithm picks out the speech patterns in real time."

"That's right," Björn replied grinning, "I've cut the digital recognition time down by eighty percent. It's virtually instantaneous."

"Wow. And the confidence levels?" John knew that there was little point being fast if the reliability wasn't there. This was why voice recognition software had taken so long to become accepted.

"Tests so far are at ninety-five percent, and with the self-learning system it will improve further."

At this point David Lowe arrived. Ignoring John, he looked straight to Björn. "So the new algorithm worked then?" he asked before he sat down, obviously excited by the developments in the lab.

"A dream," replied Björn, "ran the B2.3 test without a hitch and the G5.4 with a ninety-eight point five percent veracity."

David smiled. He had designed a series of random signal processing tests with an increasing level of sound complexity. Achieving over ninety percent was almost unprecedented. The important thing was that the lab work showed that the algorithms generated repeatable results in a wide range of conditions, not just performing well in defined tests. He asked a few more highly specific technical questions of Björn and then, seemingly satisfied, he sat down, only then acknowledging John's presence.

"So John, did you witness our little breakthrough?"

"I did David, very exciting, hopefully we can incorporate this into our planned application prototypes."

"Well, there are more tests to do and Björn will need to focus on creating data for publication for the next three months. I think we have enough for a decent paper now."

There was a pause as John let this sink in. "Err, no. The funding is for the application development, not for publications. I want us to start looking at a prototype I can try out with Daniel." John felt a sense of foreboding. He had been warned by Simon that he may have to fight over priorities with the academic, but had assumed that this would come later in the process.

"It's important that Björn achieves his publication targets if he is to progress his research career," insisted Dr Lowe.

“No! The prototypes take priority," John surprised himself with the firmness of his response. It was partly his money after all, but more than that, the lab demonstration had reaffirmed to John why he was doing this and so his response was emotional as well as practical. Seeing the software cut through the background noise and focus on the sound of one voice was a revelation to him. Could this really work? Could he make something that would break through Daniel's isolation and hear *his* voice? Dr Lowe looked quite taken aback by John’s harsh tone, but he didn't argue, just turned away mumbling about academic integrity. John made a mental note to follow up with Björn, he didn’t think this would be the end of the matter. Perhaps he should mention it to Simon, and maybe Laura as well, they would know how best to handle Dr Lowe’s academic integrity.

CHAPTER EIGHTEEN

John and Lucy dreaded going for tea with John's mother. It was always tense. Lucy felt perpetually on-guard, as if she was being judged all the time. And they could never predict how Daniel would react. Not that he ever really did anything wrong. But sometimes Lucy felt that there was an expectation that he should in some way *perform*, to show Nana how he had progressed, to read, to recite, to do a dance. That's what *normal* grandchildren did. So Lucy piled pressure on herself, but if she pushed Daniel too hard to do something, then his negative reaction could be extreme. And now there was a new dynamic, what would Patsy the shareholder be like?

They pulled up outside Patsy's tasteful Sussex cottage, the garden immaculate. Hedges clipped, grass mown, paths swept. Unpacking the car, John and Lucy felt that there was nothing in their life that was as organised as Patsy's garden. They looked at each-other, sharing a weak smile.

"Well, here goes," said John grimly, "once more unto the breach. I wish it was once more onto the beach!"

"Heh, you've given up a good steady career to follow an impossible dream, risking her money in the process and I've abandoned her son, her grandson and all maternal responsibilities for blatant self-gratification. I can't think why this shouldn't go well."

John laughed, "At least it can only be better than we expect." He reached into the back seat and started the complex exercise of extricating Daniel from the straps, harnesses and buckles of the child seat. "Come along big Dan, let's go and see Nana. She's sure to have nice cake for you." Daniel didn't respond, he was mentally locked on to one of his cars, a new one that John had found earlier at the toy shop, a yellow Porsche.

A Porsche, Lucy had said that John was letting his entrepreneurial spirit get ahead of itself, he hadn't even made his first million yet. John lifted Daniel out and made to put him on the pavement, but Daniel wriggled and kicked in protest, so John lifted him back into his arms.

"And don't call him *Dan* when your mothers around. You know she hates it."

With John carrying Daniel and Lucy struggling with two bags, plus flowers, that were definitely not from the garage, they made their way up the path to the front door.

The door opened before they reached it. "Oh, you made it then? Come along Daniel, let's go and see what Nana had got for you." Without another word to John and Lucy, Patsy reached in and took Daniel in both her hands and lifted him clear of John's hold. "Come along big chap. Oomph, you are getting heavy."

John made to help, but Patsy gave him a look, he lowered Daniel to the floor and then Patsy took him by the hand and led him off down the hall. John and Lucy were left standing on the doorstep. While this had happened before, Lucy would never get used to it, it was so different from the gushing welcomes she, and the family, got from her own mother.

"Well, it's lovely to see you too. Come on in and make yourself at home." Lucy said sarcastically, to no-one in particular. She dropped the bags and the flowers where she stood and though tempted to turn around and return to the car, she trudged off after Daniel, who she could hear laughing from the kitchen. Hard as she was with Lucy, Patsy was great with Daniel, she just ignored his autism, took him as she found him and found simple ways to connect with him. Patsy would often say that he just had 'Danielitus'. Lucy envied her simple approach, it was fine for the here and now, it kept Daniel happy but there was no progression, no expectation of helping Daniel to achieve more, to find out what his potential was and then to help him realise it.

John was left standing on the doorstep. The bags and flowers cluttered around his feet. "That could have gone better," he said to himself. Why was his mother always like this? He could cope with her having a go at him, he was used to it, a lifetime's practice. And Daniel, she was always great with Daniel, but why couldn't she make the effort for Lucy? In the early years it had been fine, his mother had treated Lucy as just another girlfriend, plus his dad had been there to gently jolly things along. But after they had got married and his dad had died, it was almost as if his mother resented other people being part of her family. That the shock of losing her husband meant that she had to draw John closer to her. Why? To protect him, to protect her? John didn't know. He just felt Lucy's hurt and frustration. He had always hoped that she and his mother would become friends, to support each other. But while Lucy had tried, she was a warm and loving person, who was so easy to be friends with, his mother continued to put up the shields and to treat her with such an offhand coolness that it made John not just sad, but angry. Could his mother not see what a great couple they were, what a great mother Lucy was, how happy he was? Or maybe that was it. Maybe she didn't want him to be happy, John thought, did his own mother want him back, to come home and fill the void in her own life. Well, thought John, there's absolutely no way that's going to happen.

When John got to the kitchen he placed the bags in the corner and stood there awkwardly holding the flowers. Daniel was propped up in an old fashioned, spindle backed oak kitchen chair with sturdy arms that held the assorted cushions in place behind him, keeping him comfortable and secure. Patsy was fussing around him, but making him laugh by deliberately making a mess of cutting up his toast, ending up with squares and crooked circles and even an octagon, but not the required triangle.

"Well, is that a triangle Daniel? Surely this must be a triangle?" As she carefully created a pentagon in the now cold and rubbery toast.

Daniel could hardly contain himself as he shouted, "Noooo!"

Somehow, Patsy always managed to get away with teasing Daniel where with anyone else, even John, there would be a danger of Daniel getting upset. Lucy was sitting at the far end of the table. Careful to give Patsy and Daniel their space. She was perched on the edge of her chair, legs entwined, her body tense. But above the table she rested her elbows on the table and with her chin in her hands she smiled serenely as she watched their game. John smiled at her as he walked to the kitchen sink and placed the flowers on the drainer. He turned and kissed his mother lightly on the head, she reached back and squeezed his arm without interrupting her game with Daniel. John took the chair next to Lucy and took her hand, neither spoke, not wanting to interfere with a moment of simple and companionable happiness for Daniel - he didn't have enough of them.

Tea was over. Daniel was happily ensconced in Patsy's lounge with a selection of his cars (John was secretly pleased that the Porsche still seemed to be a new favourite), and a DVD that Lucy had brought from home. Daniel often didn't watch the programmes on the DVD, they just seemed to provide a comfortable background noise that eased him into his self-contained world and allowed him to relax. There were therapy books that maintained that you should keep autistic children mentally stimulated at all times, to keep them continuously engaged with the people around them. But John and Lucy felt that you couldn't live like that, not and have anything like a normal family life. And in the end what was the harm in letting Daniel have his moments of self-absorption? He wasn't hurting himself or anybody else, and during them he seemed at peace. Sure the books and the magazine articles did their best to make you feel guilty, make you feel that in some way you were depriving your child if you didn't devote every waking moment to provide constant attention. But in the end they decided that they really did know what was best for Daniel. So especially at times like this, when Daniel needed to calm down from the excitement of the visit to his Nana's, they could see nothing wrong with letting him cocoon himself in a much-watched DVD and line up and examine his cars.

Back in the kitchen Patsy was at the sink sorting out the flowers, while the kettle boiled for the umpteenth time. Patsy always complained about them bringing her flowers, claimed it created yet another job for her to do in cutting them and arranging them in a vase. But John suspected that the complaint would be even more vociferous if they arrived empty handed. You just couldn't win. John and Lucy sat quietly watching her back as she worked. The earlier tension had been dissipated by the cheeky game that Patsy and Daniel had played. But now they were preparing themselves for the inevitable inquisition and, they suspected, a not uncritical appraisal of their circumstances.

Patsy completed her task and placed the sumptuous looking floral display in the centre of the table. "I would have preferred some simple cut daffs from the garden. Such a waste of money these bouquets," she said, not overly appreciatively. But John at least knew that the care she had taken in the display revealed her appreciation.

She turned to Lucy, "So my dear, I hear you have a job?" This threw them, as they had expected that she would start by focusing on John.

"Yes," answered Lucy, not sure quite what to expect from her mother-in-law. "I really feel I've got the hang of the business now, starting to make a real contribution, only last week —"

"— And who is looking after Daniel, while you're *making your contribution.* Is he being passed from pillar to post, like a lost parcel?"

Lucy bristled, "No, it's all well organised. We try to have as much continuity of care as possible for Daniel."

"'Continuity of Care'. What on earth does that mean? It makes you sound like a social worker. *Who* is looking after Daniel while *you* are at *work*?" She made Lucy's *work* sound not just insignificant, but something almost tawdry.

John intervened, "Lucy is only working part-time mum, and I'm working some of the time at home. So there's only a couple of days a week that Daniel is either at the play school or at a friend's and they reckon that that's good for developing his socialisation skills."

"It's not puppy training you know," she said disparagingly. She turned on John, "So *you're* looking after him at home now as well are you?" While her voice was still quiet and steady, as she, there was a definite edge to it, "I thought you were too busy with the new business, that's why you had to give up your proper job? But now you have time to look after Daniel, that's nice."

"Look mum," John was trying to keep calm, but there was something in his mother's voice that always wound him up, "we're just trying to make things work as best we can."

Why couldn't she see and accept that they didn't have all the answers yet, that this was hard for them as a family and would take time to settle down. That while their change in circumstances had been disruptive for Daniel, they were doing their best to give him plenty of quality time, shared between the two of them, not just Lucy.

"I'm really enjoying having more time with Daniel. I never used to see him, he was always going to bed when I was coming home. I still get plenty of time on the new business."

"I see," there was something mocking and sarcastic in her voice, "as long as you think you are making the best use of *your* time and *my* money." She turned back to the sink.

John could feel the knot of anger growing in his stomach. He looked at Lucy who mimed screaming, which made John want to laugh, and helped to lighten his mood. Thank God for Lucy, she had warned him that he would pay in 'oh so many ways' for taking his mother's money, and he was only just starting to find out just how many ways there could be.

"OK, probably time to get our young man back home." Lucy started bustling up Daniel's things. John headed off to the lounge to get Daniel.

"Yes, I'm sure you two young business people have got important meetings to prepare for, I'll return to my simple lonely existence."

"Oh come on now mum, you have a pretty full life now, what with your charity work and your art courses." But Patsy ignored him as she fussed around Daniel.

"And when will I get to see my favourite young man again, heh, now that his parents are so busy?"

"We'll be over again in a few weeks." John noticed Lucy silently shouting 'Noooo!', behind his mother, as she gathered Daniel's plate and cutlery from the sink.

They were ready, Daniel was back in his car seat. The bags were in the boot and Lucy was in the driver's seat waiting impatiently for John who was still at the door with his mother.

"Thanks for everything mum. We are working it out you know." He leaned forward to give her a kiss goodbye, but she bent forward so that he can only peck the top of her head on her greying hair.

"I just can't understand why you won't let me look after Daniel some of the time. It would be so nice for me to have more time with him."

"What *you*? We never thought you wanted to," John was quite taken aback. "Of course, I'll talk with Lucy."

They pulled away in the car, a forced smile and wave from Lucy. "She offered what? Why the hell couldn't she just mention that at the beginning, rather than trying to pile the guilt on you first? Now it feels like if we accept and use her, we've failed somehow, but if we don't, we're being callous. God that woman!"

Lucy acted out a scream again, which tickled Daniel and he whooped with laughter, which was so infectious that it set them all off laughing as they drove away.

CHAPTER NINETEEN

Gino's was deserted mid-afternoon on a Thursday. Like eighty percent of all the local restaurants, Gino's served pizza and pasta, but this was the quiet time and the pseudo Italian staff, mainly Romanian, were re-laying tables and polishing glasses. Jason had suggested that they have a chat outside the office, and Gino's was far enough away that they wouldn't be casually spotted by staff, but near enough to be an easy walk for Lucy. Jason had been out in London that morning, so he was coming straight from the station. Lucy arrived first and took a table by the window, looking over a windswept beach. She appreciated the silence and became quite contemplative as she stared out of the window. Why had Jason wanted to see her outside the office? The sea today was grey and uninviting; paddlers were limited to the seagulls. A lone father walked past the window slowly pushing a pushchair, the child so wrapped up against the cold that all you could see were her eyes, and only the surfeit of pink clothes gave it away that there was a girl inside the bundle. The father looked sad, a little lost. Lucy thought of John and Daniel. They would be both at home at the moment, she wondered what they were doing. Were they happy? Did Daniel miss her? Should she be at home? The waiter ambled over and distractedly brought out his pad and pen awaiting her order.

She looked up at him, “Just a Cappuccino please."

He looked disappointed, was it really worth relaying the table for this? "Pastry, cake, ice-cream?" he offered (he'd clearly been on the up-selling course).

"Nothing thanks. Just the Cappuccino. My friend is coming, maybe he will want more."

The waiter turned on his heel, without a smile. He was better than this.

Lucy returned to the view. The father and child had moved on, replaced by a harassed looking mum trying to control two young children racing their scooters. Would Daniel ever ride a scooter? Lucy mused. His physical development had been delayed at every stage. Late crawling, late standing and late walking. Was there a documented *right* age for scootering? Lucy smiled to herself, would she and John have to start searching for a tandem scooter, just as they had with the special seat for the bike. That's what had made it all possible, she and John doing it together, suffering the pain and the worry together, but that had been tempered by shared moments of tenderness, and even humour at their situation. It helped that their personalities balanced each other, she the pessimist fearing the worst, John looking for the positive in every situation. One thing that they had definitely learned was not to look too far into the future. Would Daniel ever live on his own? Have a job? Get married? Have children? They couldn't know. They couldn't envisage how Daniel would develop. And it was wrong to measure his development against other people's norms. There was no such thing as typical autism. All they could do was provide a warm loving home and help him reach his potential whatever that might be. And they both knew that the best way of doing that was together. But they weren't doing it together, were they?

She heard the restaurant door open and looked up. In her quiet thoughtfulness she had almost forgotten she was here to meet Jason. It was him. He looked distracted as he bustled through the door, but smiled as he saw her. His arrival was interrupted by the waiter returning with her coffee.

"Hi Lucy," he said as he weaved through the set tables in the small restaurant, "thanks for coming —."

"Your Cappuccino Madam. You will wish for sugar, chocolate —?" The waiter butted in.

"Oh, you're having coffee. I was thinking of wine. *I need* a wine. White or —?"

"Yes, chocolate, please," she said looking towards the waiter. She turned to Jason. "Hi. No problem and thanks, but no, I'm fine with coffee just at the moment."

She looked at her watch, it was just after 4pm, then realised that he might read that as her thinking that he was late arriving or drinking too early.

"Oh go on then, maybe a white."

"White sugar, madam?" The waiter proffered a jar of assorted sweeteners.

"No white wine. A small glass."

"Wine madam? You want wine not coffee?" He reached for her cup.

"No, the coffee's fine!" She laughed as he reached out to protect her cup. "I'd like a small glass of dry white wine as well."

The waiter looked perplexed. He turned to Jason. "Coffee, wine, white, red, tea, all?"

Jason looked similarity confused. "Just a very large red please." There was a pause while the waiter put pen to paper. "That's red wine, not sugar." The waiter paused for a moment, but didn't look up. Jason deposited his briefcase on a spare chair, added his coat, and then dropped heavily into the seat opposite Lucy. As the waiter walked away shaking his head, he added, "What was all that about?"

"Who knows?" said Lucy, "I think it's fifty-fifty whether we get the wine. How was London?"

"You know, London was London. Always changing, always the same."

"Oh dear, you sound down. What's up?"

"That story definitely needs wine, so let's wait. First you can tell me about *your* week, to cheer me up."

"Me. Nothing interesting there. Just the usual humdrum chaos of living with an autistic child and mad scientist," she laughed.

"Of course, remind me, which one is your husband?" He laughed with her. "How is Daniel? Has he settled with his new child-minder?"

"Who knows? He's settled, but does that mean he's happy? He's getting less sociable and more uncommunicative, but we don't know if that is his natural regression or a reaction to his change in circumstances. Oh god, you're getting me depressed now." She looked away. She couldn't help it, she welled up whenever she tried to talk about Daniel honestly.

"Sorry, I didn't mean to upset you."

"No. God no, it is good to talk about it. There's been so much disruption at home, you can't help but feel so guilty."

"Guilty? Why? You've got to make time for your own life as well." They paused as Lucy sipped her coffee. Jason smiled affectionately at the milk moustache left on her upper lip and offered her a serviette. "Speaking of dedicating your life to something, how's John getting on with the *big idea*?"

"Oh good, I think. We don't talk as much as we used to, but he did say that he had some big meetings coming up with key potential customers on both the military and the medical sides. I think his frustration is that the amount of interest he's generating is great for the business, but doesn't necessarily move the autism project forward. Problem is, he needs the money they might offer."

"Fascinating," Jason responded enthusiastically, John's progress seemed to have sparked his interest. "Fascinating. I'd love to meet him sometime."

"What! You and John?" Lucy was alarmed. This was something that she knew might happen sometime socially, but definitely hadn't planned on it happening anytime soon. And she had thought it might be a fleeting introduction at a social occasion, not a full-on conversation. She felt strangely panicky, but knew that rationally there was nothing to be ashamed of. She tried to hide it, put it off. "Sure, that would be lovely, when he's got more ...." She trailed off as she saw the waiter coming over with two very large glasses of wine. "... Ah. The wine. Now that it's here, I feel that I need it!"

Lucy was relieved. The arrival of the wine created a natural break in the conversation. Hopefully they could leave the subject of her other life. Jason and John were like two parallel worlds for her, ones that she hoped would never collide. Not that she had done anything wrong, nothing that she should feel guilty about. Nothing had happened. Nothing was going to happen. She knew that. She only hoped that Jason knew that. Not that she was arrogant enough to think that Jason would want her, especially not with all the baggage she carried. But there was something reassuring to her that she could step from one world to the other, leaving Daniel and John behind, just for a few hours, be able to think about other things, do other things - normal things.

Once they were settled with their wine, the waiter returned with green and black olives. He also brought the habitual wine bottle candle for their table, and despite Lucy's jokey protestation, that this 'wasn't a date', lit it. Jason clinked her glass with his. They both sat quietly and sipped, letting the new warmth of the good wine and the restaurant atmosphere envelop them.

"So, London?" Lucy broached.

"Hmm, London," Jason seemed to mentally drag himself back from a better place, "definitely could have gone better. But it's a long story."

"Well, I'm not going anywhere," Lucy smiled. Much more comfortable being the concerned listener than the one sharing her troubles. "Perhaps it would help to talk it through."

Jason sighed deeply and drained his glass. He looked up and signalled to the waiter for another glass of wine. He glanced at Lucy's glass, but she had barely touched it and she put her hand over the top to indicate that she was fine. An evening for pacing herself, she thought.

"It all started last year," he began. "We'd had a good year, a couple of the accounts had grown significantly and it looked like the right time to expand, grow the business and increase the size of the team. Before that I'd pretty much done the sales and most of the tech delivery myself, which was fine for staying still, but no one survives by staying still. Or so the business books say." The waiter arrived with his second large glass of wine, but it didn't interrupt his flow.

"I guess it all started with the new office. I was stuck in the classic entrepreneur's dilemma. To grow I needed more sales. To get more sales I needed someone selling other than me, or at least someone taking some of the admin or tech off me. That needs more equipment and more space. Most of all it needs cash and that was in very short supply. I was looking around for a cheap new office, and that's when I met Maria. She was managing a property portfolio for her daddy. He seemed to own vast chunks of Sussex.

Maria, she was, how do I put it ..." Jason got the young love, faraway look.

"I think I get the picture," Lucy felt a pang of jealousy, "so the lovely Maria?" She was sure that Jason blushed.

"Yes, Maria. She showed me the office, and well we got talking, went for a drink, I told her about my business. I guess, I *bigged* it up a bit. Jason the great entrepreneur," he laughed self-mockingly. "Anyway she bought it. The whole thing. And suddenly I had a girl, an office and an investor!"

"Heh, hang on a minute," interrupted Lucy, "that's a bit of leap, from drinks to investor."

"Yeah, tell me about it," Said Jason bitterly, "it all started so innocently. Lovely girl, wants to help me out so she tries to persuade her daddy to cut me a deal on the rent for the office. No problem, I thought. What's the harm in that? So after a couple of weeks she arranges for me to meet her daddy, Ricardo Benni. By this time, she's angling to move in to my apartment, I'm getting my commitment-phobia, but I want the office," he paused, drained his glass and started looking around for the waiter. Lucy, took another sip from her glass, she had been rapt as Jason talked and she had not touched her wine. Eventually he got the waiter's attention and reassured that there was more wine on its way he resumed his story.

"So it's off to her father's house, big place, showy, just off the coast road in Brighton. Did I mention that she's Italian? So when I get there it's like the whole *Godfather* thing. She becomes daddy's little girl and I get the full interrogation. Not just me, my background, family, business, prospects, the whole works. Maria sits pretty next to me, holding my hand and fluttering her eyelids at her father. Honestly it was like a bad Mafia movie." The waiter arrived again and replaced Jason's glass, paused for a moment to see if there were any more orders, then glided silently away.

"So you and the godfather and the goddaughter. What happened next? Did he make you an *offer you couldn't refuse*?"

"Well, you might laugh, but essentially yes. He wanted more and more details of my business and then he said he could offer me a deal on the office rent if I gave him shares in the business. I said no, he said why. I tried to be clever and say that I was talking to the Venture Capitalists. He said, OK maybe he and his partners could invest. How much did I want, and what deal were they offering? This was all moving so fast and all the time Maria keeps squeezing my hand and looking between me and her daddy with those doey eyes. I tried to pull out or divert the conversation, but he was all over it.

"He made me an offer of a couple of hundred thousand for sixty percent of the company. I said no, it was too much equity. He said how much then? I thought, if I counter with a low percentage, it will put him off. I really should have told him then that I wasn't interested. But no, I said forty percent. I thought, there's no way he'd accept a one and a quarter million-pound valuation. But he looked at me very hard. I thought he's definitely going to pull out. Then he looked again at Maria and her beautiful but imploring eyes and said what the hell, fine, his lawyers would be in touch to work something up. Only one further condition, I give Maria a job."

"Wow. Two hundred thousand quid. That's quite a dowry. She must be one hell of a girl, this Maria. Hang on, Maria, is the that Events Coordinator that never comes in?"

"Yeah," Jason looked a little sheepish, "she likes organising client parties. Only trouble is, no client has ever asked us to organise their party. So that didn't really work out."

"But why do you keep her on then," Lucy complained, "She's just an overhead, maybe even a liability."

"I know, I know, but how do you sack the backer's daughter?"

"So you're a couple then. I always thought that there must be a little lady at home."

"There is, but sadly not my home. That didn't really work out either."

"But you kept her on the payroll?"

"As I said, you don't want upset daddy."

"Hmm. At least you got the half million. That must be some consolation."

"You'd think so wouldn't you? But no daddy's lawyer got the contracts wrapped up so tight that even though it's in the bank, I can't access it without his permission over spending plans."

"So you've got a sleeping business partner that you're sleeping with and his daughter that you're not. Unusual I'll grant, but what's the problem now."

"He's getting impatient. He says his money isn't working for him. No real growth in the business, no likelihood of selling the business. His investment agreement enables him to take more equity, I mean increase his share in the business if I don't meet the growth targets, which I haven't."

"But if you haven't met the targets, why would he want to increase his share?"

"To get me out of the way. Probably put Maria in charge."

"Oh god. That would be awful."

"Precisely, I couldn't inflict that on the team."

"So what happened to the money, his investment, I mean? Has it all gone?"

"No, that's just it. The money is still sitting in a separate bank account. I can't access it without him approving a business plan. And he just won't approve anything that I've put in. The thing is that while digital marketing is still a growth sector in terms of clients, the profit margins have been sucked out of it by the huge increase in the number of new digital marketing agencies that have been set-up. The competition is killing the market. Specialist skills that we used to charge at a decent rate, are now offered from Indian companies at a quarter of our prices.

"Don't get me wrong, it's still a nice business, and if you perform well for your clients, like you have with Southern Sun, and you deliver the extra web traffic and sales, then you can charge sensible money and make a decent profit. But it's not the high growth business that this guy thought he was investing in. But unless my business plans show that level of exponential growth, he won't agree them and release the money." Jason delivered this with a desperate shrug of his shoulders. His whole body was deflated from his usual confidence. Lucy was genuinely upset by his visible demise.

"Can't you just give him the high growth plan that he wants, just to get him off your back."

"If only. An overly ambitious plan just gives me and the company even more impossible targets to meet and so hastens his take-over. The more I fail to meet sales projections, the quicker he can take control. The funny thing is, this doesn't seem to be about the money for him - I haven't lost his money and the company is still profitable, just about."

"Can't you just give it back then?"

"It's not that simple. The money now belongs to the company. It isn't a loan that can just be paid back and we didn't allow for any of this in the 'Shareholder's Agreement' when he invested. The only way he can get his money back is if we close the company or the company buys back his shares, and of course now he wants a higher valuation on the shares than when he invested, plus he wants money for the back rent. Either way it will destroy the business that I have worked so hard to build. For Christ's sake it's like dealing with a loan shark.

Lucy could feel his frustration. She tried to replay it, just to make sure she understood. "So if I've understood this right it sounds like a Catch-22. You can't give the money back without closing the business, but you can't use the investment because if it doesn't deliver the unrealistic high growth that he expects, you will lose the business to him. Sounds impossible. Surely there must be a reasonable, pragmatic way out?"

"Maybe, if I was dealing with a reasonable, pragmatic man. But to him this seems to be more about honour, I haven't delivered on my promise to him or to his daughter. He isn't just walking away."

"And you?"

"Everything I have is tied into the business through loans and guarantees. Plus, this business is a part of me, it *is* me. Why should I give it up? I just have to find a way of delivering an investment return back to him, and try and get him off my case."

Jason's last comments were said with such frustration and bitterness that their conversation was silenced and they sat and nursed their drinks in an awkward silence. To ease the tension Lucy excused herself to go to the loo. When she returned a few minutes later, Jason looked more relaxed, two fresh glasses of wine were on the table.

"Sorry," he ventured, "that sort of killed the mood. As my mother used to say, 'a problem shared is a problem doubled', let's talk about something else. Has your husband changed the world yet?"

While Lucy felt a little uncomfortable discussing John with Jason, it was a welcome departure in the conversation.

"Actually he seems to be doing pretty well. Apparently there was quite a breakthrough in the lab last week and they now believe that they have something serious to show investors and industry people."

"Sounds good. I'd love to know more about it. Is this still purely related to the autism idea?"

"No, that's just it. The main interest seems to be from the military, police and security services, which is not an area that John knows at all, but that's what the potential investors are interested in."

"Wow, heavy stuff. I might have some contacts that could be interested. Is it OK if I mention it to them?"

Lucy was quite taken aback; she hadn't expected the conversation to go in this direction at all. "Oh," she paused, "I'd need to check. There's patents and stuff and all sorts of confidentiality agreements. I hope I haven't said too much already."

It was now Jason's turn to look embarrassed, "Heh, I really didn't mean to put you in an awkward position. Obviously, any introduction needs to be handled professionally. I was only trying to help."

Lucy looked equally uncomfortable, "Oh I know. It's just that John gets a bit paranoid and obviously anything in the security sector has extra ..." She paused looking for a word. "Well security," she laughed, lightening the mood, "let me mention it to John, I'm sure he'd welcome your input. And I really appreciate it."

After two fairly awkward conversations, they both seemed nervous about broaching any more topics, so after another half an hour idly talking about the weather and TV shows, it was clear that the evening was winding down.

Lucy left the cafe around six. She felt a little heady from the wine on an empty stomach and thought she had better walk in the fresh air before heading home. She had been surprised by her conversation with Jason, firstly by the serious nature of his business problems, but more by his willingness to open up to her. He must feel secure in his relationship with her to reveal that level of personal vulnerability. She had been slightly annoyed by his interest in John's business, but she realised that he was just changing the subject after an awkward moment, she just didn't want him to be interested in John. While loathe to admit it, even to herself, she was jealous, she wanted all his attention on her. A light rain was falling, but she didn't notice, she decided to walk down to the seafront and let the sea air clear her head.

Jason watched her go as he sipped the last of his wine. He felt drained, both from his confrontation with his investor and the intensity of the exchange with Lucy. He hadn't meant to open up like that, there was something about her that just got him talking. As he sat doodling on a serviette his mind wandered over their conversation. What would he give to be starting again like John? A big idea, a dream, optimism, confidence, a supportive wife, a purpose, hope.

Jason's pen stopped in mid-air over the serviette. He stared at the paper, four names that he had unconsciously drawn: Benni; Lucy; John and his own in the middle, lines and arrows connected them. Strong arrows connected his name to Benni and Lucy to John. A fainter, more uncertain line connected Lucy to him. He put down the pen and just stared at the drawing for a long few minutes. Then his eyes cleared and face hardened, he picked up the pen and carefully drew a line between Benni and John. Again, he paused staring at the paper, then having seemingly made up his mind he pulled out his mobile phone. He stood and looked around the restaurant, it was still virtually empty, he walked towards the door as he started to punch in the numbers then held the phone to his ear. After a few moments, he stopped walking and his body tensed.

"Mr Benni, it's Jason, I think I may have found a way out of our little problem."

CHAPTER TWENTY

"So they call it an 'elevator pitch', but essentially it means describing your business idea in a few sentences, which is supposed to be the time it takes to ride a couple of floors in a lift if you happened to bump into a potential investor."

"Do investors often ride elevators looking for investment propositions?" John was getting a little bolshie with Simon as his confidence grew.

"No but they do have notoriously short attention spans," Simon sighed, "and it's definitely better to catch them when you're on your way up rather than coming down."

Simon knew it was always difficult to judge when a new entrepreneur was ready to be put up in front of investors. Too often they believed too much in the encouragement they got from their friends and family, but these were usually the uncritical comments from people who didn't want to be the ones to poop on a new business idea. While Simon always looked for ways to increase the confidence of the entrepreneurs by helping them to understand how to plan and run their business, he knew that this confidence had to be built on a solid business proposition, not false promises that an investor or a customer could easily see through.

John was starting to get an appreciation of his business opportunity, he had worked on market research, customer engagement, licensing and business models. He had written his product and market development plans, but now he needed to be able to show that he had gained a real all-round understanding of the business. One way of doing that was putting him in front of real life investors to see if he could convince them that he could deliver on a business opportunity. Investors would rarely back an entrepreneur on the simple basis that they had got a good idea, even if the potential market was big, it was all about backing the person or the management team to be able to deliver on that idea.

So by introducing investors (John's mother didn't count), Simon was testing John's ability to convince a highly critical audience. Not only must the investors believe that the technology represented a good business opportunity, but also that John could build a team and manage the delivery of first a product, then sales, profit and finally value to the investor. You couldn't blame the investors, they would only and should only put their money where they thought the reward was worth the risk. The entrepreneur himself was often one of the biggest risks.

John was at a delicate stage, his growing confidence was being bolstered by market knowledge and understanding, but he needed to be aware of how much he still needed to learn. But also, importantly, he didn't need someone who would intimidate or bully him. Simon needed to find someone that would be a good match for John, irrespective of whether he invested or not. Simon smiled to himself, he enjoyed playing Cupid and watching the early courtship was always fascinating.

"So, this elevator pitch, is it a presentation, a document, what?" John still hadn't really got the idea.

"In some ways it's everything. If you can create a really effective pitch, then it will start to form the basis of all your documentation. It needs to be short, simple, compelling and clearly understandable," said Simon, making an elevator pitch for an elevator pitch.

"Ah short. I like short." John had been looking at too many examples of long detailed business plans.

"As a wise man once said, 'the shorter the speech, the longer the preparation', it's surprisingly difficult to sum up a complex idea in a few sentences."

John started to reply, but then thought better of it as his brain kicked in. How would he describe EarStream in just a few sentences? Perhaps it did need more thought. "OK, let me sketch out some ideas of the pitch over the next few days. Then it would be great to get some feedback from you, and maybe even try them out on a friendly investor?"

Great, he's learning, thought Simon, he's not just jumping in with his first reaction, he's keen to this as an opportunity to properly test out ideas with a constructively critical audience, before he's got to do it for real.

"Anytime, John, anytime"

CHAPTER TWENTY-ONE

Bliss, thought Lucy as she turned over under the duvet away from the light, and buried herself deeper into the cocoon's warmth. She was having an unscheduled day off. Jason was away and all her client work was under control, so a chance to have a day all to herself. John was scheduled to take Daniel to the playgroup and then to travel on into London, so that gave a whole morning on her own and then time with Daniel this afternoon.

As she lay, half dozing, the sounds of John showering washed over her. What could have been an annoyance, keeping her awake, was actually a joy, reinforcing that she didn't have to get up yet. He was humming, he was actually humming. She couldn't make out the tune over the sound of the shower, but there was definitely notes there. She couldn't remember when she had last noticed John humming. Things must be going well with the company, she *should* know, she was his wife she should know why he was happy. She could feel a knot of annoyance deep in her stomach, she would know if he had spoken to her about it, if he hadn't bottled it all up. But no. She reprimanded herself, she didn't know because she hadn't asked, just as he hadn't asked about her work. It was fine 'keeping the peace', and 'letting sleeping dogs lie', it kept life at home civil, calm, controlled, but it wasn't what she had signed up for, it wasn't sharing their lives. She didn't resent his happiness this morning, she just missed sharing it. Something had to change. She kicked off the duvet and walked towards the bathroom, undoing the buttons of her pyjama jacket as she went and pulling the drawstring so that the baggy bottoms fell to the tiled bathroom floor. Naked, she entered the steamy bathroom and stepped into the shower reaching for her husband. The humming stopped.

Daniel sat at the breakfast table looking from his smiling mum to his grinning dad and back again. Did he sense the difference in the atmosphere, Lucy mused, the doctors had said that autistic children couldn't always read the emotion on people's faces, but looking at him now, she couldn't, wouldn't, believe that. She knew that Daniel understood far more than people said, and that he was always happier when his parents were being nice to each other. She leant over and rearranged the triangles of toast on Daniel's plate. She smiled at Daniel, she smiled at John. It wasn't just the shower, afterwards as they had dressed, they had both gushed out news from their individual lives that they had not shared with each other. There was no time for reflective reactions, for considered responses, that could come later, but they were both sharing and that was a big start.

John had decided to make scrambled eggs on toast to celebrate their breakfast together as a family. Even Daniel had tried some in the spirit of collective happiness, though he had quickly reverted to the toast, he liked toast. But at least he had tried. John announced that he would cancel his trip to London. He had planned to spend the day researching the security and surveillance markets at the British Library, but that could wait and he was happy to put it off for another day. They were also running late for Daniel's playgroup, but they'd be fine. Better to share this time together and more time with Lucy.

"Wow, so you're actually going to meet real spooks." Lucy's eyes gleamed, her mind on Daniel Craig, her favourite James Bond, the prospects at EarStream had really moved on while they had been living their separate lives. Hopefully not *because* they had been leading separate lives. "Do you get to go to MI5? It's that cool building on the Thames isn't it? The one that looks like an unfinished pyramid?"

John laughed. Lucy's renewed enthusiasm was infectious. "Eventually yes, but for the first meeting they've got people coming down to the TECHub. Simon's arranged for them to see a few companies. But they've certainly shown an interest in us. It would be great to get you into the TECHub sometime. Meet the team."

As Lucy paused before replying, John worried that he may have pushed things too far, too quickly. But no, Lucy smiled and said, "Are you in need of a glamorous assistant then, your own Miss Moneypenny?"

"Always keen to show off the company's assets, well your assets definitely."

"Not sure I'd pass the security clearance. My dodgy past!"

"They probably haven't caught up on the last hour's steamy goings on. So we should be all right."

"They always turn on the taps in the bathroom when they want to fool the 'buggers' in the movies."

"We're safe then, but mind your language in front of the children," John smiled, part at their flirty, dirty wordplay, part at the memory of their shared morning shower.

"But seriously, you must come down to the TECHub so I can show you round and show you off. You should meet Simon, the Hub Director, apparently he plays a mean 'marriage counsellor' as well as everything else."

"Hopefully we won't be needing his skills in that area."

"Sure. But I know he would like to meet you. He says that even if you're not working in the company, you're a key part of the team."

There was a natural pause in their conversation. John cleared the plates, while Lucy fussed over Daniel. He was quiet this morning, but seemed at peace. Lucy guessed that the happy banter between mum and dad calmed him. In fact, everything was better when she and John shared.

Lucy felt emboldened by the good mood. "Jason, my boss, also said that he'd like to meet you. He said he's fascinated by your project, would love to know more."

"Oh, he knows about me, does he?" John regretted this as soon as he said it. He didn't mean to sound suspicious or jealous, but it came out wrong.

Lucy was a little flustered, "Of course he knows about you, I talk about you all the time." That was quite an exaggeration, but she was on the defensive. "Only last week he was asking about the progress of your experiments and the interest you're getting from investors."

"This is supposed to be pretty confidential Lucy. What exactly did you tell him?" There was an edge to his voice now.

"Nothing John. Nothing important, he was showing an interest, that's all. Being nice, being a friend. Not every one's trying to steal your idea John."

John walked over behind where she sat and leaned down resting his hands on her shoulders. "Oh, I'm sorry love. I'm being a paranoid prat. I've had so many people drumming confidentiality clauses and non-disclosure agreements into me that it gets into a habit.

"I'd love to meet Jason. He sounds nice and that digital marketing sector is fascinating. Let's fix it up over the next few weeks. Dinner, drinks, whatever you like. He can bring his partner, make it a foursome."

"Oh I don't think he has a partner, he separated from his girlfriend - and well that's another story, he could give you horror stories about the investor he's had in his business."

There was a pause in the conversation where John looked hard at Lucy and Lucy kicked herself, why on earth had she said that?

"A threesome then. We can take it in turns to play gooseberry," John quipped, maintaining his good humour.

Lucy replied dubiously, "Gooseberry?"

"Well, you and I are married, so Jason plays gooseberry. But then Jason and I can talk about investment and you can go and powder your nose and then you and Jason can chat digital marketing or whatever it is you get up to, while I get the drinks in. Sounds like a fun night."

Lucy couldn't tell if John was annoyed, teasing her, making a pointed remark or just trying to be funny - and not succeeding. She felt it best to assume the latter. She decided to change the subject quickly.

"What the hell, it's a lovely day," (it was pouring with rain), "let's both play hooky, drop Daniel off and go and be busy doing nothing."

"Sounds perfect. The spooks can wait. We can go and play I-spy, all by ourselves," John laughed. They were back on the same wavelength, all antagonism, maybe not lost, but at least eased aside by good humour and a real desire to enjoy each other's company. "What do you think...?" He looked out of the window, "… Picnic?"

Lucy laughed, "Let's go for spontaneity. See what our fine town has to offer."

"Pizza or pasta then, or we could —"

"— No. We're not having a KFC, this is supposed to be a day for us with country-air and culture and pure middle class indulgences. Scones. We need scones and jam and cream, lashings of cream, clotted cream. Where do you think we get an afternoon tea?"

CHAPTER TWENTY-TWO

John was sure he would never get used to meeting his mother as an investor. Why did it need a formal summons from the lawyer? Why did they have to meet at a 'neutral location', usually the lawyer's? And why did it always have to involve middle-aged men in suits? But always, without fail, his mother wouldn't let him know what the meeting was about. And John, who still had a childlike awe of his mother, never dared to ask her.

Today they were meeting in London at the City offices of Pearce, Pearce and Mountford, his mother's solicitors. Once again he was led through to a plush but impersonal conference room, with highly polished dark wood furniture and twelve leather upholstered chairs placed around the oval table. The room was empty of people, but he was getting used to that. Was it a part of the tactical game? He had always found it quite intimidating entering a meeting room when the other participants were there seated waiting for you, it made you feel small, guilty, answerable. There was just something about a seated group looking up at you that made them appear judgmental. So much easier when people remained standing until you joined, or stood as you entered. How much more welcoming, encouraging you to be part of the group.

Coffee was laid out on a side-table. A cafetière, un-plunged, china cups and saucers, real milk in a jug and sugar cubes, brown and white, with tongs. Should he help himself? John thought probably not. In the centre of the table there was a water bottles surrounded by cut-glasses tumblers. Surely helping yourself to water was OK. He reached for a glass. The bottle was tall with a long thin neck. It had one of those complicated flip top seals with wires that looked like a metal puzzle you get to untangle at Christmas. John had always struggled with the puzzles, but this was just a stopper on a bottle, easy.

He held the bottle firmly round the neck with his left hand, he knew these stoppers could sometimes be very stiff, he took hold of the metal clasp on the stopper and started to prise the sprung metal away from the glass. He was expecting stiff, maybe even a pop when the seal was broken, but no, it slid easily way from the bottle. The tension in his left hand was too great, expecting to balance the stiffness of the opener, as the seal opened his left hand pushed forward tipping the bottle.

They say that a little water goes a long way. John remembered something to do with surface tension and smooth surfaces from his school science lessons, and this gleaming table was definitely smooth. The water leapt from the confines of the green bottle, its long narrow neck seemed to arch in an effort to fling the water as far as possible. Reaching the polished surface of the dark wood it spread rapidly and inexorably across the table, engulfing the carefully placed pads of paper and company pencils. John looked around frantically for something to stem the tide, "Damn, dam!" He said out loud. If only, he thought. There were some flimsy tissues in a box on the side table, but they did little more but add papier-mâché to the disaster scene. He looked around desperately for something to stem the tide. There was a low storage cabinet by the door, he flung open the doors and scanned the shelves, ahah paper towels and serviettes. He grabbed a pile and headed back to the table. His first task, he saw, was to protect the electronics, the plugs and leads designed to hook up computers to the projection facilities, good he was starting to think strategically, two serviettes made an adequate flood defence. He took a moment to step back and survey the scene - should he mop or sweep? His gaze took in the main doorway and the layout of the conference room. If he mopped he would potentially be left with a pile of wet tissues and serviettes, too many for the absurdly small bin in the corner, plus it would be a time consuming process. Alternatively, he could sweep towards the far corner, where hopefully people wouldn't immediately spot the wet carpet. He swept, using the edge of one of the writing pads creating a small tsunami across the table, the water cascading off the corner, furthest from the door, and water-falling onto the leather chair (he really should have moved that) and then onto the deep pile carpet. Three more sweeps and most of the liquid evidence was gone. A minimal drying sweep with paper towels, here the shiny surface worked for him, the sodden towels were then deposited onto the wet chair which he pushed under the table and he was there. Finally, he hid the empty bottle down the side of the bin and allowed himself a deep breath. Crisis averted. He had perhaps only been in the room less than five minutes, but he felt he had aged five years. He sat down as he heard the door handle, he stood as the party of three entered the room - he didn't want *them* to feel intimidated by him.

"Johnnnn." The tall lawyer had a strange way of elongating the final syllable of names, so it came out more like a purr, maybe for him this showed familiarity. John remembered Martyn Pearce-Mountford, of Pearce, Pearce and Pearce-Mountford from their previous meeting. "Good to see you again. Let me introduce —," he turned to John's mother.

"— She's my mother!" John said, trying to keep the irritation out of his voice. He moved towards her. Was a familial hug appropriate in these circumstances? He saw her face. Clearly not, she was all business today.

"Mother," he nodded towards her.

"John," she replied.

Martyn Pearce-Mountford stepped forward again, his tall frame awkward around his much smaller mother. "John, let me introduce Giles Lansbury. I've asked Giles to join us as he has particular experience in the security services and military sectors."

John shifted his gaze towards Giles, who stepped forward and shook John's hand. Certainly a military bearing, though not as old as John had first thought. Late forties, perhaps early fifties. Short, very neat hair, he moved easily, looked fit, but not overly muscular, more like a distance runner, definitely the clean cut military look, John thought. Very firm handshake, John tried not to wince as his fingers were crushed.

"Good to meet you," opened Giles, "from the little that Martyn has told me it sounds like a fascinating technology area you're developing."

John realised again that there had been a pre-conversation that he hadn't been party to. He looked from Martyn to his mother. "Thanks, it would be good to get your input. I don't know how much you've been told and what your specific area of knowledge is?"

Martyn stepped in, "Let's not get ahead of ourselves. Let us make ourselves comfortable, please sit down, can I get you coffee or maybe some water. Oh we seem to be missing the sparkling, let me get some." Martyn left the room, searching for assistants, leaving Giles, Patricia and John to rather awkwardly gather themselves around the table.

As John moved to sit he noticed a pool of water that he had missed at the far edge of the table, he felt himself blush, he had almost forgotten about the incident with the water bottle. He moved to place himself in the best position to hide the wet chair and the damp carpet, and sat down. His mother still hadn't really acknowledged him. Had he done something wrong, or was this just her being aloof and business-like?

"How've you been mum?" he ventured.

"I'm fine," she replied curtly, "we can talk after the meeting."

"OK. By the way Lucy sends her —"

"— Later John," she cut him off.

Martyn bustled back in, this time with a harassed assistant carrying water bottles and biscuits. She fussed around them, passing out glasses and coffee cups. As she re-dressed the table, she moved one of the headed pads of paper and was surprised to discover a puddle of water gathered beneath it, she looked up, but John couldn't meet her eye. She worked with that harried bustle that made John think that Martyn must have had harsh words with her. It stung him that she had been probably been reprimanded for something that was *his* fault, but that feeling was swept away when he looked at Martyn, there he stood, tall and overbearing, supervising rather than helping, the stance and look of a bully. At that moment John despised him. Was that a protective instinct for the young girl, or was it just a way of covering his own embarrassment? John stood and lifted some of the other pads of paper, so that the girl could wipe underneath.

"Here," he said, "let me help you."

She looked up gratefully. She stole a look sideways to see that Martyn wasn't looking and then mouthed a thanks to John. John hated himself for his own deception, especially as he now had that warm glow of having performed a simple act of kindness. She finished, and with the table now back to its pristine best, she left, head down, not looking at Martyn. But Martyn had noticed John's eyes following her out of the room.

As they finally all gathered around the table, Martyn focused on John with a knowing look, as if he had found John's Achilles Heel. A line from a Superman film came to his mind, 'That's his weakness, he cares for these humans'.

Oh, the complexities of life.

As they sat around the table, John realised that once again it was him alone on one side of the table, with his mother, Martyn and Giles railed against him on the other. He was getting paranoid. Drinks were served and then they all settled down looking around expectantly.

As usual Martyn kicked off proceedings, "John, Giles, thank you for joining us today. When Patricia and I met the other week ..." John bristled as he saw Martyn's sycophantic smile to his mother, surely there was nothing going on between Martyn and his mother. "She explained that John's research and development work had been progressing well and that the company ..." he checked his notes, "... EarStream, is attracting some interest from the defence industry. And we wondered if some input from an industry veteran might be helpful, and I straight away thought of Giles. Giles, would you mind giving a brief resume of your illustrious career."

With such an introduction, it was unlikely that Giles' career would be anything less than illustrious, but John found it difficult to concentrate as Giles went through his regiments, commissions and postings over a twenty-five-year career that spanned both specialist forces and the intelligence services. John's interest was however piqued when Giles spoke of his time at Portland Down. He had worked in the defence research labs and then been transferred into QinetiQ, the defence technology transfer arm, where he had worked for five years. Recently he had taken early retirement to concentrate on family and writing, but still took key consulting roles to keep his hand in and his contacts fresh. He said his interest was in non-exec roles that would fitted with his expertise and where he felt he could add real value.

John appraised the man more closely. He had initially written him off as another Martyn, preening in his own self-importance and ingratiating where he saw the potential for a fee. But Giles, perhaps because of his field training, had a quiet self-assurance about him. He returned John's look, not as a challenge, he didn't care who blinked first (he knew it wouldn't be him). John blinked. Giles smiled. "Any questions about my background John?" he asked looking intently at John.

"Err, no," replied John. How did you respond to a CV like that? But then thought again, "What do you think of the idea, is it a winner?"

"Early days, John, early days. But definitely worth a further look. It's not as if there aren't lots of competing surveillance technologies out there, what we have to look at is whether EarStream has an edge. The key is not just about what it can do, but that it can do something that is needed, better than the other options.

"It's definitely good that you have a range of possible applications, more strings to your bow, so to speak. Also if you can get an early win in one sector, then it gives much added credibility in the harder to enter markets. I understand there is a potential medical application?" Giles's reply was smooth, polished by real experience, and echoed much of what Simon and others had said about these technology markets.

"Yes, I'm hoping that it might help in breaking through cognitive barriers with autistic children." The more John said it, the more believable it sounded - he thought.

"Hmm, medical devices and security applications, you're not going for the low hanging fruit are you?"

"I'm afraid not - not unless you can think of another application that's hanging more within reach."

Giles laughed, "Maybe, maybe, I'll have to put my thinking cap on."

"So what exactly would your role be in the business?" asked John, sounding quite formal and business-like, looking in turn at Martyn and Giles, "And what is it going to cost me?"

"Well, umm, err, that's really ...," stammered Martyn, before Giles stepped in.

"John. No-one is trying to fleece you. We're here to help. Your mother needs someone to represent her interests, while not getting too personally involved herself. She thought that if such a person could provide relevant industry experience and a few grey hairs, then so much the better. My initial proposal to your mother is that I would do this pro bono, as a friend, maybe just expenses, until such time as the company has either raised more money or has developed a decent revenue stream. At which time it's up to you whether you want to employ me directly."

Giles looked a little sheepish, "To be honest, I get bored and my wife wants me out from under her feet. Projects like this keep my contact book current and often opens the door to other opportunities - I do make the occasional small investment myself. I like working with enthusiastic people and I like the challenge of bringing new ideas into the market. I'm happy to use my name and my influence to get EarStream in front of the right people. More than that, I hope that you will feel you can use me as an old head, that has seen some deals and worked through the system. What do you say, shall we give it a go? If we don't get on, you can always go back to your mum and have me fired," he laughed at that one, Patsy and Martyn joined in.

John joined in too. But he still didn't feel he should agree too quickly. He had read how important it was to have the right *mentor*, and while this Giles seemed ideal on paper, was he? How did you tell? Was he staring at the choppers of the proverbial gift-horse? How could he possibly know? In many ways he didn't really have a choice, he had no real reason to doubt Giles' experience and he was right, he could always go back to his mother. He wished Lucy or Simon were here, they were good at reading people.

"OK. I agree," he proclaimed.

There were smiles and handshakes all around. EarStream as a company was starting to take shape.

CHAPTER TWENTY-THREE

Lucy had been putting it off for some weeks. What had started as a seemingly casual suggestion from Jason for the three of them to have a meal, had now become a persistent request. Surely he could sense her reluctance? She couldn't just come out and tell Jason that she didn't want him to meet John, that it would be like the two separate parts of her life colliding. It wasn't that Jason posed any threat to her marriage, but she wanted to maintain this separate life, with its hint on latent romance, not open it up to inspection, force her to choose. But Jason just wouldn't let it drop.

"How about Thursday night," he pressed. "We could try that new tapas bar down in the town centre. Does John like tapas?"

No of course John doesn't like tapas, he was a straight steak and chips man, Lucy thought. But naturally Jason would, more cosmopolitan, more travelled. Another demonstration of her two worlds and that pleasure of being a different woman in each.

"Not a great fan," she replied, dismissively. "He never knows what to order. Too much choice." She didn't add that she was equally as ignorant in these matters. In her mind this just presented another opportunity to lay her innocence in front of Jason and plead that he chose for her. Or was it for him to choose her? She couldn't do that with John there could she?

"Heh, I could choose for all of us, lay on a feast."

He just didn't get it, screamed Lucy in her head, she didn't want him to choose for me. She wanted him to choose *me*.

"I think just a pub meal, would be best," she had given in.

"Pub. I'll go one better. How about that new gastro-pub out on the coast road? I've heard it's good. Thursday? Shall we say eight o'clock? Does that work with Daniel?"

No way out now, thought Lucy, maybe she could come up with an excuse and cancel on the day. But the considerate swine, he had already thought of Daniel. "Sure, can't wait," she said, without conviction, "my friend Pam owes me a few hours. Will you be bringing your latest squeeze? A foursome would be fun." She hadn't heard Jason mention a girl for weeks.

"No, just me I should think. Can't seem to keep the girls tied down these days."

"You should try reading '50 Shades', get a few tips."

Jason looked blank for a moment, then as his eyes showed recognition, he smiled. "Of course, sorry, I'm being a bit slow. Too much on my mind."

"Ah, concentrating on your own grey matter," she paused, waiting for a reaction to the pun. But gave up, his mind was obviously not on their conversation. He seemed distracted, it was almost as if that as soon as she had agreed to the dinner, he had checked out and moved on. What was going on in his mind?

***

She hadn't seen much of Jason during the week, but when he did he had made sure to confirm their dinner date. He was being so insistent that she decided not to put off the inevitable. It was just a pub meal after all.

John wasn't keen. He'd had a long day trying to put together the figures for the business plan and the last thing he needed now was Lucy to announce they were going out for dinner in a couple of hours. He was all for being supportive of Lucy's new found career, but wasn't sure about it becoming part of their social life. Lucy assured him that it was just a casual meal, no need to get dressed up. He grumbled, but the thought of a good steak got him moving towards the shower. It's wasn't just the heart that could be reached through a man's stomach.

Lucy sat on the edge of the bed in her dressing gown considering her wardrobe. Who was she dressing for tonight?

Both her men seemed preoccupied at the moment. Jason had been more distant since their night in the ristorante, wouldn't engage with her in the same way, not their usual casual, flirty chit chat, he was more formal, more like a boss. John, well John was John, locked in his own world of business, she knew he was grappling with lots of new stuff, trying to get his head round the technology, the finances and the marketing side, but even so. Funny, she thought, John now seemed as locked away from her as Daniel. Would either of them ever break free?

In the end she dressed for herself, what the hell, she didn't get out much anymore. She knew the skirt was too short, the heels too high and the 'T' too tight but she wanted to express herself, to be noticed. Noticed by someone, anyone.

She sashayed down the stairs, humming a Beyoncé number.

"Mum."

See, Daniel noticed her. She smiled as she got to the bottom of the stairs and bent down to Daniel, teetering a little on the high heels.

"Yes my Darling. What is it?" she said, with her hands on his shoulders and looked directly into his face, thrilled that he had noticed and responded to her.

"Juice," he said simply, and handed her his glass, and then squirmed to be released.

"Daniel. What do we say?" There was a constant need to reaffirm social behaviour with Daniel. Introduce the rules and then reinforce them consistently. Strangers often remarked on Daniel's politeness, but this was definitely learned behaviour, rather than innate social skills.

He turned back, though didn't look into her face. "Juice please," he said without any intonation, just a conditioned response.

"Of course Daniel, thank you." But he was gone. She rose unsteadily, the glass in her hand, her mood broken, tears forming in her eyes.

John walked through to the hallway, he was dressed in the same jeans and an over-worn polo shirt that had seen better days. Not scruffy in any way, but just no effort made. He stopped when he saw Lucy, giving her an appraising look, "Wow," he said, "am I missing something? I thought this was a quick pub meal?" He completely missed the tears in her eyes.

Lucy pulled herself together, forced a smile on her face, and with hand on hip and chest pushed out, took on a provocative Mae West pose. "Girl's gotta make an effort sometimes, ain't she?" She strutted off to the kitchen to get Daniel's snacks ready for their new sitter, Pam, who would be arriving soon.

Hmm, thought John, what was all that about?

John and Lucy arrived at the pub a few minutes late. While John was still outwardly resentful at being summoned to this meal, it was a night out and they didn't get many of those at the moment, and Lucy did look gorgeous. He'd held her hand as they walked from the car and she'd leaned into his arm and laughed at his jokes. It was almost like being a couple again.

Jason was at the bar watching them enter.

When she saw him, Lucy felt herself drawing away from John, as if he was the guilty secret. Sensing this, John looked around, saw the good looking man at the bar and pulled Lucy in closer, protectively. As they made their way to the bar Jason stepped out confidently, smiled and extended his hand to John.

"John. How great to meet you at last, I've heard so much about you." He turned to Lucy, "Lucy, you look fabulous." He leaned in for a social cheek kiss. "What can I get you guys to drink?" He turned back to the bar to get a bartender's attention.

John was feeling his initial animosity fall away, taken in by Jason's easy charm. He looked at Lucy and smiled, "OK," he mouthed, she nodded. It was odd, she thought, she had expected to be the one in control here, but she was feeling really unsure and nervous.

Successful in his task, Jason, turned back to them, "Lucy, white wine is it? Sauvignon Blanc?"

Lucy nodded, "Please. A large one I think."

John bristled a little that Jason knew his wife's drinking habits, but then shook it off. Jason had probably seen more of his wife than he had in recent weeks, and whose fault was that? Jason looked enquiringly at him. "Pint please Jason, bitter, a pint of bitter, thanks."

Jason nodded and turned back to the bar. "So that's a large Sauvignon, pint of best and a Peroni for me and perhaps some olives. Can you start a table tab?"

John noted an easiness to him, he was obviously very comfortable in these surroundings, not just like a regular, but someone that was used to playing the host, used to using the *good service* of an establishment to enhance his own position. It was as if he got the staff working just for him, offering him special treatment, when all he was really doing was expecting or demanding their best level of service. It was a clever social device, John thought, impressed, maybe even jealous, rather than annoyed by it. John looked over at Lucy, interested to see if she was drawn to the performance, but he saw that her early brash confidence had receded, she had pulled her jacket close around her, seemingly embarrassed by the party clothes underneath.

They collected their drinks and since the bar area was quite crowded decided to go straight to their table. Like most of the hostelries around town these days, the *gastro* had rather taken over from *pub* and the majority of the tables were reserved and given over to diners. While the buildings still tried to maintain the old feel of the *snug*, with horse brasses and pictures of local beauty spots, the meals were more like twenty-five quid a head and there was more wine drunk than beer.

As soon as they were seated, Lucy made an excuse and headed off to the ladies. She wished she had a girl-friend there to help diffuse the situation. But seeing Jason and John getting on, she wondered if it was just her that was feeling the tension.

John and Jason were sat opposite each other and it seemed as if the only point of common interest had just left the room. It should have been an awkward silence, but Jason used Lucy's departure to focus the conversation on John's business. "How are things going working with the University?" he asked with genuine interest. "I've always imagined that that must be quite a different environment, *Town versus Gown* and all that."

"I guess it would be if they didn't have their own *business focused* people on the inside to help us," replied John honestly, "it's like them having their own intermediaries, that can help to manage the relationship with the academics, a bit like translators. I guess if you barged in and tried to negotiate hard directly with an academic then you would nowhere fast. Not because they are trying to rip you off, or anything like that, it's just that they may have a different way of looking at success."

"Isn't it obvious what success looks like?"

"Not really. The University is not there to make money and the academics are often more driven by their research interests, so selling their research is not that high on their agenda."

"That must make it better for you, if they're not interested in the money."

"Again, it's not as simple as that. It's about understanding their motivations. If the research is all neatly packaged up in a patent, then it can be relatively simple to buy the technology from the university, they've got lawyers who negotiate these deals. As I say, that's the easy bit. It gets more complicated when the Professor is still involved and the research is still active. You need them to continue working on the technology, but you want them to focus on your stuff rather than concentrating on their research. And if that wasn't hard enough, they still have to fit in some teaching."

"Can't you just offer more money?"

"Sure, I guess that might work with some, but you'd be surprised how many are not purely motivated by cash. You have to find other incentives: it could be the opportunity to publish; or the chance to go to a conference; or maybe just convincing them that their research will make a real difference."

"Are all academics so high-minded?" Jason sounded bewildered.

"No, of course not. I've not experienced that many, but you will see the odd professor in an Aston Martin and suspect that that's not because they're an inspirational teacher. But in many ways they seem to be the exception rather than the rule. I've heard it said that many academics claim that they would have been millionaires if they'd gone into business, but they chose a higher calling. I suppose it's another form of reverse snobbery. So the key is not making assumptions about the academic's motivations, you have to get to know them and work with them to find out what makes them tick."

"And that's what you've done is it?" Jason still looked confused by this uncommercial academic world. "Got to know them, the academics, understood their motivations?"

"To be honest no. I started with the same cynicism that you have, but luckily I've found some good people to work with and they manage the university side and stop me from blowing the relationship. I didn't have the knowledge or the patience, but over time I've got to know them much better, and we sort of rub along, we know that we don't have the same goals, but at least we are travelling in the same direction."

"Jesus. It sounds like doing business while walking on egg shells!"

"It certainly helps if you have a good reason to do it. And I have. Ah here's Lucy back."

They both looked up and smiled as Lucy returned to the table. She looked different than when she left. She was standing straighter, filling her clothes, rather than hiding in them, she had re-fixed her make-up and hair, she looked like a girl on a mission.

She sat down, determined now to be the centre of attention. "So have you two guys set the world to rights? It looked like a serious discussion." She was sitting right up at the table, forcing herself to be in the eye-line of both men, there's no way that they were having a conversation around her. She downed her remaining wine, with a slight wince. "Whatza girl gotta do to get a drink round here?" She said with a laugh.

Both John and Jason reacted, looking round to spot a waiter, seeing none in the area, John surprised Lucy by being the first up, "Another wine?" he said. "Another beer for you Jason?"

Jason nodded and raised his bottle, "Cheers, put it on the tab." John headed back to bar. Jason turned to Lucy. "You look amazing," he said with a glint in his eye, "you'd better not come into work like that, our tech boys couldn't cope."

Lucy laughed, "Oh I think I'm a little old for them."

"I'm not sure they're used to seeing that much skin in the flesh so to speak, less threatening on the screen. Plus, for some of them I don't think their own skin has seen the sun for many a long year."

"So you've got me down as having the screen porn look, have you?" Lucy pouted, pretending to look annoyed.

"No. I've got you down as having the *real woman* look, that's the one that scares most men...," he paused. "Seriously, you look great, but tonight I just want a chance to meet John and to get to know you a little better, the real you."

John returned from the bar carrying the drinks, with menus under his arm. He noticed Jason and Lucy draw apart as he neared the table, conspiratorial or guilty, he wondered?

"Shall we get our order in before that big group at the bar takes over the kitchen?" He handed out the menus. "I like this place, haven't been here for years, I'm sure they only did burgers last time."

"Yes, it changed hands a few years back," replied Jason. "I know the guy that runs its. I think he's still trying to get the menu right for the local crowd, but it's getting there."

Why wasn't John surprised that Jason would know the proprietor and probably acted as a local food connoisseur? "Well he's got my vote, they've got some great looking steaks."

"Mmmm, that seafood pasta sounds yummy, what are you going to have Jason?" Lucy was lapping it up.

"Oh I think the ricotta and truffle ravioli in lobster bisque sounds good." John thought Jason sounded like a restaurant critic, 'Does that come with fries', he mused to himself.

Over the meal Lucy held court, playing to her audience as if they were a couple of suitors. She flirted, she teased, she shared *in-jokes* with each, which would leave the other cold. Was she disappointed that neither man rose to the bait? She had expected John to be more protective, Jason to be more forward, but both seemed to be content to sit back and watch as her performance played out. Whenever there was a lull in her conversation they went back to their earnest talk of their businesses, and their experience with investors, bankers, lawyers and staff. When she returned from one of her frequent trips to the loo, that Sauvignon seemed to be going down, and through, all too easily, she must be on her fourth glass by now, she caught Jason in full fawn.

"What I really respect about you," Jason was looking intently at John, maybe they had had more beers than Lucy had realised, "is that you are doing something really innovative, creating something new that hasn't existed before, something that could make a difference. My business is fine, I may even be good at it, but really it's just a *me-too* digital marketing company trying to second guess Google better than the next man."

"No you must be good at it ...." John's concentration was drifting, "... it's a very competitive industry. Got to be good to survive."

"But you, you've got physicists working for you, and you don't even understand what they are doing. You've got Intellectual Property for God's sake. What I've got could be found in lost property."

"Oh I'd say you've created something more than that Jason," interjected Lucy, trying to stop this becoming a business love in. "You've built a team and clients that are loyal to you —"

"But for how long Lucy, for how long ..." He turned back to John, "I'm jealous of you John. Jealous of your passion, jealous of your patents, jealous of your potential."

But not jealous of your partner, thought Lucy.

As the meal finished and Jason insisted on picking up the bill, it was John that Jason embraced rather than Lucy. It was John that suggested they do this again. Was Lucy even to be invited, she wondered? It was Lucy that fought to bring her emotions under control. She hadn't wanted this evening to happen, but now it had she couldn't understand how bad she felt about it having gone so well.

"Nice guy," said John reasonably, as they started their walk home. Lucy wanted to scream.

CHAPTER TWENTY-FOUR

There was something about having your own front door, even in business, an Englishman's castle.

When he started, John had needed the TECHub to give a sense of reality to his business. When he was working from the kitchen table, it had seemed unreal, like he was playing at it. Working here at the Hub placed him in a community of other entrepreneurs, people who were like him, working in their own businesses. Sure having the address was important, but the sense of belonging to something bigger, was vital to building his confidence.

John had been happy working from the hot-desks, but he very much viewed it as temporary. John saw the Hub as a place to build his business, to lay down roots, to draw every ounce of confidence, support and expertise from the other members in the TECHub. And now he had reached the point where he felt ready to take the next step, it was time to move into his own office.

In most practical aspects it made no difference. He would park in the same car park, EarStream would be listed in the business directory the same way, he would nod to the same reception staff, chat to the same people in the cafe, use the same meeting rooms. But having your own space, your own front door felt so different. It was like becoming a grown up, getting your own place. Now he had a business of substance, with his own furniture, shelves, filing cabinets. It didn't matter that it was the smallest office in the Hub, it was his, theirs, the company's - and it was where the company would grow. John knew that his company needed its own space, its own identity, and now he had it he could grow within it, and then to outgrow it, secure in the knowledge that a bigger space was waiting for him, on the same terms, but with minimum hassle.

John was growing more comfortable in his position as an entrepreneur. In many ways the evening out with Jason had had the opposite effect than he had expected. He had resented being told that he had to go out with his own wife. He was suspicious of Lucy's relationship with this Jason bloke. He hadn't had the time, or certainly hadn't made the time, to talk to Lucy about her new job, to understand the dynamics of her new life. He realised from the very change in her that this was more than a simple job for her. This was becoming a very important part of her life, but a part that didn't include him. And so he had gone to the meal expecting it to be confrontational, expecting to be watching Lucy for signs of sexual interest in Jason, for infidelity, expecting to have to compete for Lucy's attention. So he had been surprised that Jason seemed to be more interested in him than in Lucy. He had shown genuine interest in EarStream and had been impressed by what he had achieved so far. Jason had shown far more interest in his business than Lucy ever had. If Jason had been an investor, then John would have felt that he had made an effective pitch and that was an important confidence boost for John.

The call had come out of the blue, through the TECHub switchboard, which was odd in itself as so few people had that number.

"Hello, EarStream, John Miller speaking." John still felt odd answering the phone this way.

"Ah hello, did you say you are John Miller."

"Err yes, and you are?"

"Ah, Mr Miller, could you confirm your position with EarStream?"

"Look no, is this a sales call or something, what is it that you want?"

"I can assure you that this isn't a sales call, I'm calling from the law firm Byall, Byall and Woods, could you please confirm your position with EarStream."

"What is this ..?"

"Mr Miller, please, I cannot continue unless we can complete this simple confirmation of your identity."

"Yes, I am John Miller, and yes I am the Managing Director of EarStream. Now can you tell me what you want?" John was getting exasperated.

"Mr Miller we have been tracking your company as a potential EIS investment opportunity for our clients, a Mr Riccardo Benni, would like to arrange a visit to meet you and discuss your business."

"Potential investor?" John hadn't realised that this was how investment meetings happened, he had always assumed that you had to approach them. Maybe Simon had set this up. "Sure, OK, that's fine, when would he like to meet?"

John had a good feeling about this.

Things were not quite so rosy at DMM. Since their evening out Lucy had started to notice differences in Jason's behaviour. He was less predictable in his comings and goings to the office. It would normally take a crisis for him to miss the Monday morning meetings, but he had been absent for two out of the last three, and even more surprising, there was no warning or apology to the troops. Each time they had sat gathered in the Board Room waiting for him to hustle into the office and bring the company to life. She had tried to jolly them along, to run through the projects as best she could, but it was no good, she was like skimmed milk to his full-fat, a pale imitation, a poor substitute for Jason, who was the lifeblood of the business.

But now, when he was there, it was little better. His moods had become more erratic; he was less conscientious in the attention that he normally lavished on his staff. That was what they craved, a quiet word of encouragement or simple recognition of a piece of work well done. Jason had been a master of this positive management style, his staff didn't just work for him, they worked *for* him. It was personal. The salary at the end of the month, the commissions, they were a bonus sure, but really they worked to make Jason proud of them. And Lucy could understand it, she felt the force of his personality, she knew that she worked *for* him. But loyalty built on such a personality trait could soon start to fall away if the praise, the encouragement, the personal attention faded. It was like a drug that the staff were hooked on; they needed their fix of Jason, and at the moment he wasn't there enough to give it to them.

Another change in Jason was his generosity at work. Not in the big things. Jason had always excelled in finding small thoughtful personal gifts or treats for his staff that truly motivated them. These came across as natural acts of kindness, not premeditated, not planned, just that's the way Jason was. Lucy was convinced that he must have some sort of a Smart App on his phone that prompted him to say or buy the right little things that made people warm to him. But now, he was what could only be described as penny-pinching. He had made the bookkeeper, Anne and Lucy sit and go through the office expenses and petty cash receipts to find savings and cut-backs. Cheaper coffee, no free biscuits, no donuts for the staff meetings, no fresh flowers ... A few quid here and there, that couldn't possibly make a difference to the finances of the business, but would change the feeling within the office, would make it feel like any other office, whereas his team had always felt that their place of work was *special*.

They started stretching the payment terms on their invoices as well. Each week, Jason would go through the list of creditors and give instruction as to who should be paid. Jason had always been so self-righteous about paying his invoices, he had been stung so many times by big clients spinning out the payment terms from thirty days, to sixty and often ninety days. It had infuriated him, and even though it had often made DMM the cash buffer in the middle, he had paid his suppliers on time. But no longer, and Lucy had the unexpected and uncomfortable role of fending off the calls from the suppliers' accountants and directors first enquiring after and then quickly, demanding payment. Lucy soon became aware of how quickly a company's reputation could be damaged within the local business community. More and more often suppliers, that a few months earlier would have happily offered credit terms, would now demand payment before delivery. If they weren't careful they would enter a downward credit spiral, where the less cash they had, the less credit they would be offered.

Strange though, despite Jason's lack of attention to his staff, whenever he was in and even when he spoke to Lucy by phone, he never neglected to ask after John. He said that he had been inspired by meeting him, seeing his passion and commitment for his new business. Lucy was at first gratified by his interest, it seemed such an unexpected outcome of their meal out. But as the questions kept coming she began to tire of his pestering. Life at work was becoming more difficult for Lucy and one day it just snapped, Jason had disappeared unexpectedly for a day, leaving Lucy with disgruntled clients, when she finally tracked him down Jason's first question was "How's John?"

"What do you mean, 'how's John?'," she blurted out, "how about, 'sorry Lucy for leaving you in the shit with the Penfold account'; or 'sorry team for missing the morning meeting again'; or maybe just, 'how's my bloody company?'. That would be nice. But no you just want to know about my bloody husband, God knows why. He's just peachy thank you. Doesn't really talk to me much, but I'm getting used to that as now nobody talks to me at work either. But don't you worry, John's fine, he's talking to an investor so maybe he won't sell out my home from underneath me. So yes, John's fine, thank you for bloody well asking."

Strange he didn't ask again.

Lucy didn't have a good feeling about this.

CHAPTER TWENTY-FIVE

"So just what the fuck do you think you were doing?"

There was a shocked silence in the DMM offices. No one had heard Jason raise his voice before, let alone swear at one of the team. Everyone stared at Tina who was in her usual seat with the sales team in the centre of the office. Jason was standing behind her, leaning over intimidating, he had a sheet of printout pinned to her desk with his outstretched finger. His whole body was shaking, his face white. The girl's face collapsed into tears.

Lucy felt she had to intervene. They were her team now and she needed to be the buffer between them and Jason.

"Jason," she said calmly, as she stood, "can I see you in the Board Room."

Jason remained still, looming over the weeping girl.

"Jason, now!" There was some advantage being a teacher and a mother. She knew how to be firm. Jason's shoulders sagged and he picked up the paper, turned on his heel and started walking towards the boardroom. He didn't speak. Didn't look around at the other team members, but stared hard at Lucy, then nodded as he passed her. She followed him in and shut the door behind her.

"What on earth is going on?" she almost hissed, "I've never seen you like this."

"Oh that stupid girl."

"What? What can she possibly have done to cause that reaction from you?"

"It was our last decent client, Klinco Partners. The only one paying decent rates. Tina sent them our new promotional offer. The email was only supposed to go to new prospects."

"So now they think they can get a better rate?"

"Oh, I wish. I've been properly reamed out, torn a new arsehole, so to speak. 'It's all about loyalty', they say. They believe we've been shafting them."

"But surely they realise that for the new rates, they don't get the same level of service, they don't get *you* designing their campaign."

"Nobody believes in the quality anymore. Digital marketing is bought and sold like a commodity now. As far as they see it - we're using our long-term relationship to screw them."

"So what do we offer them?"

"Too late. They're gone. We've been fired. I can't believe it. Fired by Klinco! They're just a fucking two-bit e-tailer. Wouldn't even have made our top ten client list last year. And now *they* get to fire *us*. And I care, it really matters to the bottom line."

"Things can't be that bad," she said unbelievingly.

"Oh, you don't know the half of it, if the investor calls in his ...." He trailed off, not wanting to put the worst case scenario into words. "... Yes, it's bad. And I don't have a 'plan b', 'c' or whatever." He put his head in his hands, his whole body was shaking with emotion.

"Surely there's something we can do." She was taken aback by the physical reaction he was having, it was almost as if the realisation of the seriousness of the situation hadn't been there before. "Let me call the accountant, see what she suggests?"

"I've fired the accountant, she had no solutions, only different ways of measuring the problem. She doesn't seem to realise that it doesn't matter whether it's a hundred pounds or hundred thousand pounds, if you haven't got it, you haven't got it."

"Right. You've fired the accountant. That's helpful," she couldn't keep the sarcasm out of her voice. He glared at her. But someone needed to take charge. "Look, you hitting out isn't helping anybody. Why don't you go home, or at least get out of the office? I'll talk to the people and see where we are and what we can do next. I'll call Janet, I'm sure she'll still give me some ideas about what to do, despite you firing her, this is supposed to be when you need the professional help."

Jason just grunted and got up to leave. "You talk to who you want," he said as he walked to the door, "I say we're fucked. And I'm going to drown my sorrows."

Lucy watched as Jason grabbed his jacket from the back of his chair and made his way across the office floor. With his head down, he didn't meet the eye of any of his staff. Didn't notice the weeping Tina being comforted by Loo. There was an eerie silence as he left. As the main door shut behind him, there was a chatter amongst the staff. They had not seen Jason like this before, they didn't look like they would be getting back to work today. Lucy wanted to run after him, but was held back by her new loyalty to the team. She got up and closed the door, leaving her alone, she needed ten minutes to clear her mind and prepare herself to *face the troops*. She could see now that Jason wasn't in the right headspace to deal with the inevitable fallout from the downturn in their business.

She pulled out her mobile from her bag and located the number for their *'ex'* accountant Janet. Hopefully Jason hadn't alienated her so much that she wouldn't help out. Lucy put the phone down. She needed to think this through, utilise her friendships and build allies. Maybe an initial text to Janet would work, more a personal plea for help from, maybe not a friend, but certainly someone more than just a client. She picked up the phone again and started to text.

> *'Hi Janet, I guess you realise that we've got a few financial problems here at DMM at the moment. Jason is finding it difficult to communicate, I wondered if we could have a chat. I could really do with a steer on what actions I need to take. Best wishes - Lucy.'*

Lucy sat back and sighed, it wasn't much but at least she felt better having done something. She didn't have long to wait as her phone rang less than a minute after her text. She looked quickly at the screen, the display confirmed it as Janet, thank God. She didn't want to talk to anyone else at the moment.

"Janet, thank you so much for calling me back."

"Lucy. I was surprised to get your text," her reply was rather curt.

"Janet, I'm sorry for whatever Jason said to you, he's not himself at the moment. But I know you and him have worked together a long time."

"He was particularly rude," she said, Lucy thought she could detect a hint of a smile behind the comment, "I haven't been called a 'money grasping capitalist whore' before - I might put it on my business card."

"Oh god, he didn't did he?" Lucy felt a giggle rising in her throat, "he seems to have been shouting at people all day. He's just hitting out, you know it's not personal, he's just like a toddler having a tantrum."

"But with a more extensive vocabulary," Janet laughed, "look Lucy, of course I'll help, but it'll have to be outside the office. Jason talked to the Managing Partner after me, and he may not be quite so forgiving. Plus, you are down on our *payment at risk* list at the moment, which means no billable hours until we're sure that you are solvent.

"Why don't we grab a bit of lunch away from the office and we'll try and come up with a plan, how about 'Joe's' down on the seafront?"

"Oh thank you so much Janet, you're a lifesaver. I'll be there at twelve. Is there anything I should do before me meet?"

"A good start is to get a list of live projects and see where you are with them both in terms of the work programme and the invoicing. I've still got a pretty much up-to-date cash flow report and debtors and creditors list, so between us we should be able to see where the company really is. I'll also bring along a list of local insolvency practitioners. See you at twelve."

"See you there." Lucy terminated the call. 'Insolvency practitioners', the words made her feel quite sick.

***

John's hands were sweaty. What should he do? If he went and washed them now and Mr Benni arrived while he was in the toilet, then he would be caught in one of those hand-shake with wet hands moments, where all the other person can think is, 'Had he had a wee or a poo', or was that just how *he* thought? Great first impressions. ‘Calm down’, he told himself. He resorted to wiping his palms on the back of his suit trousers.

That had been an issue as well. What do you wear? He knew it didn't matter, but of course it did. Do you go for the hip Google look, expensively casual jeans and shades? Thing was he didn't dress like that normally. Wasn't it more ridiculous to pretend to dress in designer casual than it was to wear a suit? What would the investor expect? He'd even asked Simon, and got a rather enigmatic response, 'There is no right answer', had been his reply, well that's really bloody helpful. Simon often said that sort of thing, apparently it's the difference between coaching and commanding, mentoring and meddling. But to be fair, he had gone on to say, 'You either dress for yourself or dress for your visitor. The fact that you're thinking so much about it probably means that you're more bothered about the impression you give, than they are by the impression they take'.

Well that was a bit deep. But at least it made him think about the decision rationally, rather than fret about it. He wanted to give a good impression and he wanted this Mr Benni to know that this meeting was important to him and that he took his interest seriously. He had been brought up to expect to get dressed up for important events. His mother had insisted that they should all dress for Christmas lunch, even when it was just the family, that you couldn't possibly go in to take an exam in un-ironed clothes. So what he wore was more about impressions than expectations. What the investor expected him to wear was irrelevant, the investor would know that he had made the effort to make a good impression, and that was good. It was times like this that he could really do with asking Lucy, but she was even more distant at the moment. He'd wear his suit. Now what about a tie?

***

Lucy stood at the closed door preparing herself. This was very different from going out in front of a classroom of seven year-olds. To her this was Churchill on the beaches, this was her Alex Ferguson half-time talk. These were real people, real jobs, real lives. This wasn't missing a night out, people on the other side of that door, people she knew, wouldn't be able to have a holiday, wouldn't be able to pay their rent next month. And her job was to keep them onside while they tried to save the business. Could she rise to the occasion? Strange, she thought probably most business leaders would prefer to do this than to face a classroom of seven year olds. But as a teacher she couldn't have imagined herself having the confidence to do this even a few months ago.

Deep breath, she opened the door and walked through. The chatter stopped and she felt all eyes turn towards her.

"OK guys, listen up," as she looked at the expectant faces, she felt a surge of adrenalin go through her body, "you've probably realised that something is going on with the business. You've all been here a while. Most of you longer than I have. You know Jason, you know his loyalty to you. You know that he would do anything for you. Well, now I'm going to ask you to do something for him. I'm going to ask you to work with me to try and save his business, save our business."

She paused. There was silence in the room. All eyes on her. She had them. They would work with her, for her. The situation was bad, but this felt good.

***

And there they were, signing in at the front desk. An investor, a real investor. Well, at least one of them was. There were two of them. Two suits. Was he expecting two? Do they hunt in pairs? They were wearing suits, he was glad he had worn his suit, despite the fact that everyone else in the TECHub reception area and cafe were dressed in jeans. He strode across the reception area with what he hoped came across as confidence.

"Mr Benni," he held out his hand noncommittally towards the two men, he didn't know which was Mr Benni and didn't want to choose the wrong one, "I'm John Miller, MD of EarStream. Thanks for coming out to the TECHub, I hope you found it all right?"

The shorter, but bulkier, of the two men turned and shook his hand. He had a dark Mediterranean look, Italian, John assumed, it could have been Sicily or Crete or Cyprus, but probably Italian. His clothes were of high quality, but understated, dark blues. In his fifties, probably, physically well past his prime, tired looking eyes that had seen too much in life. It didn't look he expected this meeting was the highlight of his day.

"Thank you John. I am Riccardo Benni, but please call me Benni. This is my lawyer, Charles Downey, he has a particular knowledge of intellectual property matters." Charles was certainly the sharper of the two, louder pinstripes on the suit. Younger, blond hair, fashionably long, well groomed, all business.

"Great, good to meet you Charles. Are you from a local firm?" John offered his hand.

Charles looked positively affronted. "Byall, Byall and Woods, we're in the City," he spat it out, as if the law hadn't yet reached the South Coast. The handshake was limp and damp, and definitely not friendly. Benni laughed, "Charles does not normally venture outside the M25. He's unsure about you country folk."

John warmed to Benni as he cooled to Charles. But more importantly it lightened the tone and created a connection. "Coffee?" offered John, as he guided Benni into the cafe. Charles lurked behind.

Simon was ensconced at his usual table. He looked up and smiled, offering encouragement with his eyes, he was on call to join the meeting if John wanted him for support. The café manager, Jenny served them cheerfully, recognising the situation as she so often did and offering to bring their order over. John knew then he would get the real cups, rather than the takeaways, without asking. It felt like everyone at the Hub was rooting for him.

"Shall we have our coffee here, before we go through?"

"Certainly," Benni said, "an interesting place. Are there many companies like you here?" Charles was wiping crumbs off the chair with a serviette before he would risk his pinstriped backside.

"Would you like to meet the Director of the Hub, Simon, he's just over there?"

"Sure, it would be my honour."

Simon responded immediately to John's wave and came over, introduced himself and sat down. It was a good way to lead in to the meeting, give John a chance to calm down. Simon was also very good at referring to EarStream as 'full of potential' and 'one of the rising stars at the Hub'. John just hoped he could live up to the hype.

***

Janet was already there at 'Joe's'. She was a little younger than Lucy had expected, early thirties she thought, well turned out and really quite good looking under her business-like bob of blond hair, she had warm brown eyes and a ready smile. Lucy could see why Jason had liked working with her. She felt an absurd twinge of jealousy. Janet had selected one of the bigger tables at the side, away from the window, and already had her papers spread out. She smiled reassuringly at Lucy as she settled herself at the table.

"Hi, how are we holding together? Has he showed up yet?"

"No, he's gone AWOL. I'm starting to worry about him, he's really not acting like himself." Lucy sighed and there was a shared concerned look between them. Lucy had a feeling there was more than an accountant-client relationship between Janet and Jason. She pulled herself back to the business in hand, "Thanks so much for meeting me. I've got the team pulling together, but God knows if we're going in the right direction. At least only one person, Tina from the sales team, has left, and to be honest I couldn't blame her after what Jason said to her. She and Jules are pretty tight, so I'm not that confident that she'll be there when I get back."

"Sounds like you're doing just fine. Sales isn't your priority right now; you need to get cash in quickly from the projects that you've done or are doing. Jason should never have walked out on you like this, but you never know how people will react. Look let's have a coffee, maybe share a cake and chat a bit before we get into the numbers. You look like you could do with a moment to take a breath."

"Thanks yes. It has been a bit full on." She realised that she knew nothing about Janet, but here she was acting like a real friend. "I hear they do a mean carrot cake here; I've been meaning to come with my son."

"Oh, does he like cake? How old is he now?"

"Oh, no. He only really likes toast. It's me that goes for the cake. Daniel, he's coming up to four now."

"Yes, of course. Jason did mention it. Autism isn't it? Jason does talk a lot about you."

Lucy was quite taken aback. Why was Jason talking about her to Janet? She and John had always been very private about Daniel. It was one of the reasons she had drifted away from many of her friends, she didn't like to think of them discussing Daniel behind her back. The waitress taking their order prevented Lucy from responding, but Janet recognised her reaction. "Sorry, I should explain. My own son, Richard, he's ten now, has Asperger's, so that's probably why Jason told me. Since my Terry walked out five years ago Jason has been very supportive, and we've got close, as friends that is, so we have more than accountant - client conversations."

"I had no idea," replied Lucy, it seemed that at every turn she found out something else about Jason she didn't know, "he's quite the dark horse, isn't he? But if you were so close, I can't understand how he could —."

"— What, fire me? Well to be fair, he fired me as an accountant, not as a friend. We can be both you know. And I guess that's why I'm here, friend first, accountant second."

"I guess I'm the same, hopefully a friend first, PA second."

"The way he's behaved; he doesn't deserve either of us. The bastard - how could he fire me?" they both laughed at the incongruity of the situation.

"Right," said Janet, "cake break over, let's get down to work, how deep in the shit is this company?"

"Crumbs!" said Lucy and they both laughed before they got down to serious work.

***

After all the introductions and background over coffee, Simon had wished them a productive discussion and excused himself, though John knew he would be available if needed. John had moved the party through to one of the well-appointed meeting rooms. Simon was right, using the Hub's facilities as if they were his own boosted his confidence, it felt professional, he didn't have to apologise for anything. The investors were here because he had a credible technology and business opportunity, all they had was money. They had to sell themselves to him as much as him selling

EarStream to them. The room was comfortable, laptop was on, the screen fired up, presentation ready. Now to pitch.

***

The table at 'Joe's' was now well covered with neat piles of paper. They had gone through all the ongoing projects and listed the work-in-progress and when it was likely that they could invoice the client (Lucy was pleased to have spent the time with each of the techie guys getting this information). Anne, the bookkeeper, had provided the list of outstanding invoices, and based upon their payment history, when they were likely to receive the money. Anne had also provided a list of what bills were outstanding. Of particular importance, according to Janet, was keeping the taxman sweet with VAT and PAYE returns – "It's amazing what proportion of failing businesses are taken into liquidation by their own government", Janet had explained.

"OK, good job," said Janet leaning back in her chair and stretching. "It looks to me that as long as Jason doesn't take any drawings, then we can just about keep the business solvent for a few months."

"Sounds good," Lucy didn't sound convinced, "Solvent sounds good, but what are Jason's drawings? Isn't that his salary? What does he live off?"

"That's the other side of being an entrepreneur. He's the one taking the risks and so gets the benefits when things are going well. Jason can't pay himself through dividends if the business isn't making a profit."

"God, poor Jason. What will he live off?"

"Don't worry about Jason, he's taken enough out of the business in the past. If he hasn't put something away for a rainy day, that's his lookout."

"Yes, but surely, he can ..."

"Seriously Lucy, we've got more deserving people and more serious things to think about than Jason's sushi bill." They sat in silence for a moment.

"Now for the hard stuff. What costs can we cut?"

"It's mainly salaries I suppose, but who do we cut?"

"At this stage we need to concentrate on immediate revenue generation. So that would be - who do we need to complete the projects that we have and get an invoice out? That takes precedence over broader marketing and developing sales leads."

"OK, so we lose the sales team, if we haven't lost them already. But to be honest that won't save that much, the telesales are pretty much minimum wage, they get most of their pay through commissions."

"Yes, well it's a start. What about the graphic designer, is he on active projects?"

"Charlie likes to get involved in all the projects, add the design twist, as he calls it."

"To be harsh, that's not the same as being *billable*. We need to work out what billable work he has and then decide whether it's worth keeping him on, or whether we lay him off and then use him, or another freelancer, on a sub-contract basis."

"Can we do that? I mean lay him off and then re-employ him?"

"Sure, that's common practice, you just have to be careful not compromise any of his employment rights. What we want is the flexibility and to reduce the ongoing overhead spend. If Charlie becomes a project cost, rather than a salary cost then that affects how solvent we are."

"And what about the other tech guys, they've each got their own projects."

"In general we can treat them in the same way. Though of course we have to expect them to go and try and get work elsewhere."

"Then aren't we at risk of cutting out the very technical skills that makes DMM a business. Isn't this just death by a thousand cuts?"

"Yes, difficult to get around that. If there are one or two key technical guys who could keep all the main projects going, so that we can keep them on staff and let the rest go, that may be a better solution."

"Oh I hate this," cried Lucy, "it's like playing God. Who stays and who goes?"

"You just have to be dispassionate about it Lucy. You're making rational, objective decisions on the basis of the skills needed to complete the jobs. In the end the guys will respect you for that. Try not to think about the personalities."

"But that's just it, they are personalities, real people."

"You have to be objective. That's the only way to make decisions that you can justify to yourself and if necessary, to others. This is about deciding which of your staff the company needs most, rather than which employees need their job most."

Lucy dropped her head into her hands. She hadn't signed up for this. Where was Jason, this was his company, it should be him making these decisions?

***

"And so in summary, we are seeing commercial interest in multiple applications from multiple markets for this technology. Our next step is to strengthen our IP position and to produce demonstrators suitable for each market application. This and market assessments is how we will use the investment we are raising now. From there we see that there could be potential opportunities for both IP licensing and producing our own products, these strategic decisions will determine our future investment needs and the selection of our strategic partners to take the technology into the priority markets."

John sat down, feeling exhausted, even though it was only mid-morning. The pitch seemed to have gone well. The technical bits had been covered by a demonstration video that Björn had made in the lab. He had kept the jargon down to a minimum and Dr Lowe had, thankfully, remained a mysterious blurry white coated figure in the background. As Simon had predicted it was the opinions from future potential customers that had made Benni sit up and take notice, the IP aspects were hardly discussed, Charles seemed comfortable that the University had handled IP, rather than John.

"So Mr Miller, a very interesting presentation." While Benni's accent was very pronounced (Italian John thought), his English was good, "I like this business and I have heard good things about you."

This confused John who could think of no connection he could have had with Benni where he could have left an impression good or bad. Perhaps this was someone that Giles knew, John made a mental note to check.

But for now, it was time to keep it smooth. "We certainly see the *scalable* opportunities in developing such a *platform technology*, are you an active investor in this *space*?" John inwardly cringed at his own vocabulary, he was starting to sound like the type of tech fund manager that Simon had advised him to avoid.

"Me? No. Not hardware. Mainly property, some digital. Digital marketing."

"Ah interesting. My wife works in digital marketing, an exciting sector."

"Bene, good, but always difficult to back the right, how do you say it here, horse?" Everybody laughed at that, sympathising with the poor investor. "But with EarStream, maybe the same problem, so many uses, how do we pick the right market?"

John was gratified with Benni's use of *we*, clearly his investment was nearly in the bag, this allowed him to open up more, he didn't have the non-disclosure agreement (NDA) in place yet, as Simon and Laura had strongly advised him to do, but what the hell, Benni seemed a nice guy and it must be safe if there was a lawyer present, even if he was Benni's man.

"The background IP covers all the application areas ..."

"... But this hasn't been granted as yet? The Patent Office could dispute your claims?" interjected Charles.

"Of course, as I made clear, the University filed the patent a few months ago, so we have 'pat pending' protection. We've had a professional patent search done, which looked good. But as you IP lawyers say, 'nothing's certain till it's certain'."

"I have never said that," Charles responded tetchily. John was definitely not warming to Charles.

"No maybe not, it doesn't matter. What I was going on to say is that we believe that there is an opportunity for further application specific patents, which will be particularly valuable if we decide to licence."

"Is the patent so important?" Benni queried. He had managed to make and lose several fortunes without ever having a patent.

"We believe so yes, for this technology. Some of the applications will undoubtedly need significant additional investment to develop the technology into useable products. The exclusivity and protection provided by the patent is needed to encourage that investment, to give the market protection against the competition. It protects our *first mover* advantage and creates *barriers to entry* for the competition." John was pleased he had done so much background reading so that he could spout these things off at will.

"But patents are expensive and I hear defending them even more so. Is this not just a game for the big boys?" Benni looked at Charles as he said this, who nodded sagely and expensively. Was Benni testing him, or were these genuine concerns? Thought John.

"You are of course quite right," John remembered that it was always best to agree in an argument, "and that is why we will look to partner with big companies for some applications and maybe sell or licence the technology to them.

"Again a patent is important for this as the patent is the legal asset that is sold to or made available to the company through a licence." John hoped this didn't go too much further as he was reaching the edge of his knowledge, but didn't want to look like he was ducking difficult questions."

"OK, I get that, the patent is important. You ask for investment into your company EarStream. Does EarStream own the patent?"

John had been dreading this one. "No, the university owns the patent, but is working with us to commercialise the technology. So the University will enter into an agreement to exclusively licence the technology to EarStream and ..."

"... So licence, not own or assign, you don't actually own anything," Charles leapt in again, John could have throttled him.

"Yes that's true at the moment. Currently our agreement with the University is to have exclusive use of the technology to work up the applications, but we also have an agreement to move to an exclusive commercial licence once we have an investor on board or our first customer. There is then an option to assign the IP in exchange for equity if we reach scale in terms of sales or investment."

"What is this *assign*? You either own it or not," pressed Benni.

"If all goes well, we will own it." John tried to reassure him. "For this stage of the development it was safer, and cheaper for the company, if the University manages the patenting process. Also it is easier for the company to access government grants and support if the University is not a big shareholder in the business. Finally, with a licence, if the business, for some reason was to go bust then the IP would go back to the university, with an assignment it would not." John was really feeling uncomfortable now, this was at the edge of his knowledge of intellectual property matters. "If you wish I will introduce you to the Intellectual Property Manager at the university and he can explain the process and the agreements."

"Yes, yes, maybe, maybe later. For now, I just want to be clear - if I invest money now and you do badly and lose money, I don't own the technology?"

Charles interjected, with a grim face, "That's right. Not unless the IP is assigned to the company and you have that arrangement with the company."

Benni nodded, he didn't look happy, but at least he understood. "I will need to consider this further," he said with some finality. With that he rose, nodding to Charles to do likewise. There were handshakes, but the atmosphere was definitely less bullish. John wasn't quite sure if he had done or said something wrong, he had been as honest and as straight forward as he could be. They were a silent procession, as they walked down the narrow corridor from the meeting room back to the reception area. As they entered the light airy atrium Benni turned to John.

"John, I like what I see and I would like to see your plan and to understand better your patents. When I have considered, I will make you an offer." Benni finished with a slight bow of the head.

Maybe an offer I can't refuse, thought John, he found the Italian's manner and accent slightly menacing. "Thank you. I will send you the information and look forward to your offer. Thank you for coming out to see me."

With that and further perfunctory handshakes, including a limp one from Charles, they were gone. John stood for moment, still and alone, not quite sure what to make of it.

He felt a presence next to him. It was Simon.

"How did it go? They seemed happy enough as they left. Did they leave you with the big bag of cash, or are they dropping it off later?" Simon added with a grin.

"God knows. That was a weird meeting. Everything seemed to be going fine, until we got onto the subject of patents."

"Never a simple topic. What's the issue?" Simon asked. John relayed the discussion as best he could. Simon nodded, "There can be a lot of confusion around licensing and assignments. People feel they have to own everything, when really all they need is the right to use it. You can still have exclusivity and all the other associated protections. But as with all these things, unless you work with it regularly the legal terminology can intimidate and confuse rather than make things clearer. And the more that people don't understand the situation, the riskier it feels.

"I'm sure his lawyers can make sense of it for him. But heh, he wants to make you an offer. Atta-boy, your first pitch and you've hooked an investor." Simon's positive attitude helped to lighten the mood, and he smiled back, allowing himself to be just a little bit pleased with himself.

***

"Good news, I think." Simon had arranged to meet Laura from the University Technology Transfer Office (TTO) for a catch-up coffee. The Cafe in the Engineering School was quiet this time at the end of the afternoon, must be either lectures or ... did students still watch Countdown? Was Countdown still on?

"We may have got an investor for EarStream - Dr Lowe's audio technology."

"Oh, right, that's John Miller isn't it. Seemed a nice enough chap, though I wasn’t sure if he has the steel to make it through with defence related technology. Seemed distracted."

"Yes, he has a notion that the technology could help his autistic son. You never know, he might be right. Entrepreneurs have many motivations, it's all about channelling them. He's building some good advisors around him."

"That's right, I remember now, he was quite passionate about it ..." Her mind wandered, a man passionate about his family always appealed to her maternal, if not necessarily, her carnal senses. "An investor, sounds good," she looked quizzically at Simon's face, "you're not so sure?"

"Well, from what John's told me, I'm not sure the investor is that experienced in technology businesses and he's asking a lot of questions around the treatment of the patents - who owns what and when."

"It's a fair question, but as long as the investment is big enough that the IP protection is secured and they give confidence that the University gets its return, we can be flexible."

"That's a little harsh on the company, what about John's interests? What about 'making a societal impact with the University's research outputs'?"

Laura smiled at Simon's quoting from the University's Strategic Plan. "Absolutely, but it would be nice if just now and again the University actually made some money on this stuff. What do they think we are, a charity?" she said with a chuckle, it was always difficult to resolve the sometimes conflicting objectives of a university - economic, social, educational, commercial.

"Actually, this is particularly apposite. Dr Lowe's patent is coming up for the PCT national stage, and we'll have to decide in which countries we're going to go for protection."

"You mean when the real costs start mounting up."

"Absolutely, now we get into the tens of thousands, especially if we're going for China and Japan, the translation costs alone are a killer. Don't suppose EarStream can afford to take over the patent costs yet?"

"No, not without investment."

"Touché! And so the circle is complete. Let me know if I can give any input to the investor's IP questions."

Laura breezed out of the cafe, her mind quickly turning to her next academic-commercial conundrum. Simon remained seated, feeling distinctly uneasy. He had a feeling that Laura must be under increased pressure within the university to report some success for all the money they had spent in protecting their technology. This didn't necessarily have to be a big financial return, sometimes a good PR piece, presenting the university as being entrepreneurial or generating social impact could be seen as equally as valuable. He would have to do some digging.

CHAPTER TWENTY-SIX

"He wouldn't even look at me, let alone the other children, the entertainer, the party food. Just ignored everybody, and then when I tried to bring him back, he just went weird. I couldn't comfort him, he just screamed, so I just picked him up and left ... God knows what they all thought. The other children they looked shocked, frightened even. And the other mothers, they weren't much better. They gathered their children away from Daniel, like he was infectious, a leper!"

Lucy was in tears; it hadn't been a good day. It was Saturday and she had taken Daniel over to the home of one of her old teacher friends, it was their son's third birthday, and Lucy thought it would be a great way of catching up with old friends as well as giving Daniel a chance to socialise. Lucy had been out at the office so much in the last few weeks that she had forgotten just how *different* Daniel could be in these situations. The routine that had been established at home and at the nursery had lulled them into a false sense of security. Life had felt, if not normal, then at least settled, and that was as close to normal as they were likely to get. Lucy felt that her new found self-confidence could extend beyond the office and into their home and social life as well. She was wrong. No one had told Daniel that he was now *normal,* just because Lucy felt more in control. The experience brought Lucy down hard. She was as angry and upset about her own feelings of discomfort and embarrassment amongst the other mothers as she was about the lack of tolerance and acceptance of the other mothers.

"Oh John, it was awful," she dissolved into tears again. Her face in her hands, her whole body shuddering uncontrollably.

John stood awkwardly watching her helplessly. He knew that he should have taken her in his arms. He would have done automatically just a few months ago, but even the moment's hesitation now was grasped upon by Lucy. As John went to approach her, tentatively, she looked up at him, her red eyes glaring.

"But what do you care. He's just a bloody experiment to you. A subject for your *trials,*" she almost spat it out.

"What? Are you serious? Daniel is everything to me. He's the reason why I'm doing this." John was stunned by her reaction, the bitterness and her personal animosity was so strong. "Perhaps we've both been too distracted by work the last few weeks. Haven't given him the family time he needs."

"So it's all my fault is it? I'm a bad mother. I don't need you to tell me I'm a bad mother."

He sat down opposite her. Placed his hands over hers. Touching but restrained. "Oh Lucy, you're a wonderful mother and together we'll get through this. Sometimes it just gets too much and it wells up inside. We've both been through it. We both love Daniel. We do our best. There is no right way ...," John kept talking quietly and calmly, repeating words of comfort, gently stroking her hands as she stared at him, eyes streaming with tears. They sat there together for minutes, until Lucy started to regain her self-control. Eventually she removed her hands, roughly wiped her eyes and nose with a tissue and then pushed her chair back and got up.

"Right. I'd better get the tea on. Daniel will be hungry."

John remained seated and continued to stare at where she had been sitting. They had been here many times before. One of them distraught the other working to calm them down. This was the strength of being a couple. He got up now and approached Lucy and took her in his arms and they stood there together gently rocking.

They hadn't heard Daniel come in. Weren't sure how much he had heard, or if he had, understood. Daniel walked up and joined them, lifting his arms as he looked up.

"Cuddle," he said.

John and Lucy looked at each-other and smiled tearful smiles. John reached down and lifted Daniel up and as Lucy put her arms around both of them they all squeezed and said, "Cuddle," together.

This was the strength they had together, if only they could switch off the external factors, turn back the clock. But no they couldn't wish that. They had both grown personally through their new business ventures. They were different people now, they must find a way for their relationship to embrace their increased independence and confidence, to allow it to add to their marriage rather than to threaten it. This wasn't going to work by one of them giving in to allow the other to have their new life, while they drifted back into their old one, it would just lead to resentment. This needed just the right amount of selfishness as well as an overwhelming amount of love to put their family back together. At that moment they both wanted that, but how long would the feeling last?

CHAPTER TWENTY-SEVEN

"Where the hell have you been?" Lucy glared as Jason made his way through the tables, the diners and the impatient waiters. The same restaurant, even the same spot by the window, where they had shared confidences just a few weeks before. But now the tables were turned. Lucy was the one in control, Jason had become more timid, lacking his usual confidence and resolve.

"I just couldn't face them," replied Jason, shame faced, "those people, my team, I've let them down."

"Oh stop feeling so bloody sorry for yourself. Pull yourself together. You will be letting them down now if you don't fight for the business and for them. They're still backing *your* business, pulling out the stops and fighting to keep *your business* afloat. Backing you - though God knows why, at the moment you really don't deserve it, or them."

"I know, I really appreciate it, but they don't understand, they don't see the whole picture. It's not just about me and the business and our customers, which would be simple, there are others involved, other people who are trying to bring the business down. To get back at me," said Jason plaintively.

"Is this your girlfriends' father again, is he behind this?"

"She's not my girlfriend, but yes it's Benni, he's pulling the strings."

"For Christ's sake Jason, you've got to get this sorted, get this Benni guy off your back. This is real people's lives you're affecting here. People who have got rent and mortgages to pay, mouths to feed, families to support. What are you doing about it?"

"I know, I'll talk to Benni again, try and get him to cut me some slack over the cash I owe him."

"I've been going through the books with Janet — "

"— Janet? She's still talking to us?"

"Yes, despite you firing her, and calling her a, 'money grabbing capitalist whore', how could you?"

"Oh God, I did, didn't I?"

"Yes. You bloody fool, Janet, me your staff, we're the people that can help you through this and all you do is to hide or worse push us away. You need to face up to this and call upon the strength and loyalty of the people around you, the people that want to help you. "

"I don't deserve their, your, loyalty."

"Stop whining. Anyway, from what Janet could see the underlying business, or the *business fundamentals,* as she put it, seem good. It's just this cash issue. You've got no flexibility to operate the business. Look I've brought some of the paperwork with me. We could go through here, now?"

"Oh Lucy. I can't start going through the accounts now."

"Why not. It seems the best way of starting to make a plan to try and save the business. If we've got a solid plan maybe that would get this Benni chap to help us out of our cash-flow strangle-hold."

"Don't you understand? He's the one doing the strangling. He wants us to fail!"

"What? Why would the investor want us to fail? I know you explained it once, but it just doesn't make any sense to me. What can we do to make him change his mind?" Lucy sounded exasperated.

"That's the thing, if we fail this way, he gets me out and can wind the company down and get his money out."

"So this is all a waste of time then?"

"Actually there may be something *you* could do to get Benni off my back and so help save the company."

"Me? What can I do? What's it got to do with me?"

There was a significant pause while Jason stared intently at Lucy, uncertainty in his eyes. Then he wiped his face with his hands, sat back as if he had reached a decision and then leaned forward again and took Lucy's hands in his.

"What?" Lucy looked down at his and her hands and then looked back up at him. "Oh no," she exclaimed as if having a dreadful realisation. She pulled her hands away in disgust, “Oh no, I'm not doing anything like that!"

"No, what? Oh of course not. I didn't mean anything like that."

"Well, what then?"

"You could speak to John."

"John? What's it got to do with John?"

"It's Benni, he's interested in John's business, EarStream isn't it?"

"EarStream! What's EarStream or John got to do with...? How does he know ...?" She blustered, then she paused, as she tried to process this new development. Then she looked more intently at Jason, "Jason, what have you done?"

“Done, me?” Jason sounded defensive, innocent, almost offended by the accusation. "I've just made a connection. John needs money, Benni has money. So a logical connection. I'm just trying to be helpful, to everyone.”

Lucy's anger started to rise, "Jason. You've already told me that this guy is a crook. And now you pass him on to John. What are you playing at?"

"Oh he's not so bad. He’s just a businessman. I scratch his back —"

"— And he stabs John's. Oh that's just great."

"Come on Lucy, Benni is just another investor. John's a big boy now, he can look after himself."

"You bastard Jason. You stupid bastard. Call him off. Call Benni now and tell him that John's not interested, or that you've heard it's a bum deal. Anything, just keep that man away from John.”

"That's not the way it works Lucy. He's already met John. Likes the look of the technology, if he can get the right deal."

"Benni! Benni's the investor that John's so fired up about?" The realisation stunned Lucy, she slumped back in her chair. "Oh poor John," she almost whispered.

But Jason still ploughed on. "He's not going to listen to me ... but John will listen to you."

"Listen to me about what Jason?" she was talking very quietly now, "I'm not part of this decision."

"Oh but you are Lucy, or you can be. If John says yes to Benni, then apparently he can arrange it that his investment in DMM money is used to invest in EarStream. Benni will be very happy and a happy Benni will ease up on DMM. The business will have a future, and you can be a big part of that future Lucy."

"What are you talking about Jason, I'm just the PA."

"Oh, but you could be so much more. I need a partner Lucy, someone to help me grow the business."

"Partner! Stop this Jason, you're going too fast. Call off Benni or I am going to have to warn John about him."

"No you can't!" Jason almost pleaded, looking alarmed. People in the restaurant were starting to turn towards the drama. Jason paused as he noticed the people staring, he got himself back under control. "No we can't do anything to jeopardise the deal. I want you to support it. Think of the staff. Charlie and his student loans, Becky saving for her house deposit, Gary, Anne?"

"Oh don't lay that guilt shit on me Jason. I'm not responsible for DMM going down, for your bad decisions."

"No you're not. But you *can* be responsible for saving the company and their jobs. Think about it Lucy, think how much good you could do, plus John gets the money he needs."

"From a crook."

"That's John's decision, he's got advisors. His decisions are definitely not your responsibility."

"But my family is, I should warn him."

"You can't. Benni would close me down straight away if he got wind of it. Anyway, he may not even make an offer, then you would be creating trouble for no reason. This could be a win-win for everybody."

Lucy thought about that. She didn't like it, but it did make a certain amount of sense. "Let me think about it. And let me see where things sit between this Benni and John."

"You can't say anything Lucy."

"Don't you dare tell me what I can and cannot do! I can ask him how it's going with the investment - I'm not an idiot you know."

"Oh I know Lucy, that's why I want you as a partner."

"You bastard Jason. Leave me alone. Go and play your mind games on someone else."

He left, perhaps he felt guilty, maybe even a little ashamed, but he also knew that he had sown a seed with Lucy. A seed that had a good chance of growing, of gnawing away at Lucy. She could do some good, help Jason, without deliberately causing harm for John. Good intentions versus unintended consequences. Jason thought that was a fair bet. He wasn't proud of his actions, but he could live with himself if it got Benni off his back.

To become Jason's business partner. Under any other circumstances it would have been a golden opportunity. She felt like she belonged in the business. Felt that she had so much to give. Felt that she was part of the team. And she wanted to contribute more, give more of herself to this team, to this business, her business. But now Jason was offering to make her a partner, but more like a partner in crime.

But at least she was a part of this business. She contributed something to it and she got something back. What did she give or get from EarStream? EarStream had pushed her, and Daniel, out of John's life and however much she doubted the underlying motives, Jason wanted her in his business. Why was she fighting so hard to protect John, what was he doing to protect her? Everything in her life and in Daniel's, had been put at risk, or at least put on hold, by John. Jason was offering a potential future, a future where she could take control, be responsible for their future. It wasn't doing anything against John. Jason was right, John had his advisors, his precious Simon and Giles, who seemed to be playing a more important role in John's life than his own wife and his son.

***

There had been a few months when John had almost enjoyed doing the budgets and forecasts. A little like programming, the spreadsheets had a certain logic and predictability that suited him. He liked to develop smart little routines for Excel, to create flashy graphics, bar charts, time lines, sensitivity analysis, pie charts, not really because it gave him useful information, more to see what the programme could do. He knew he could, and maybe should, have handed this over to the TECHub team, but just for the moment he wanted to feel in control of something while everything else was in turmoil. But that was when he had had cash sitting in the bank, the main problem to face was managing the R&D Grant payments, which were often paid as much as three months in arrears, so the trick was to juggle the costs, to let others share the cash-flow issues. Fortunately, the University wasn't too much of a problem, as they were used to working with government grants, so there was less pressure to pay them, before the money had had been paid to him by the Government.

So every few days he would gather all the paperwork together, enter the University development costs and other expenses from the invoices and receipts, mainly the office costs, into his spreadsheet ready to generate his quarterly claim. He managed his cash flow pretty simplistically, but with lots of outgoings and only one incoming and that paid many weeks in arrears, it was like watching the sand fall through a timer, an inexorable fall to zero. All he could try and do was to make sure that he could make his cash last until the claim was paid and secondly that he would have sufficient money left to survive on after the University costs were paid.

But the money was definitely running out now. His spreadsheets and graphs weren't helping, they didn't stop the falling bank balance, just presented it in a whole variety of colourful ways. He reckoned that he might have enough cash for another few months' work before he would be running on empty. He wouldn't have spent all the grant by then, but he just wouldn't have any cash left to keep the business going.

This was one problem that he found working with the University guys, they weren't very budget conscious. Björn was great, he really liked him and Dr Lowe was all right if they kept their meetings to simple project updates. John wasn't sure that he and David Lowe were ever likely to become bosom pals, he didn't think that he would ever be forgiven for being more interested in *using*, what David thought was one of the simpler theoretical elements of his work, rather than *funding* the more cutting edge areas of the research. Björn, by contrast, loved to see how he could perfect the techniques and the algorithms, to make them robust, not just theoretically, but practically. But one thing their background at the University hadn't prepared them for was looking for cost savings or ways to accelerate the results of their research.

They weren't doing anything wrong, Björn was following a twelve-month programme of work and he was employed on a twelve-month contract. Apparently this was the usual work practice with post-docs. John was amazed that any contracts got finished, in his world anyone on a short-term contract would be concentrating on finding another job for the last few months. They were just not used to anyone saying that the money might run out after only ten months, rather than the scheduled twelve, so could they work a bit quicker please. For them the research money, once committed, was always there, Research Councils and Big Corporates didn't have cash-flow problems.

So he needed to find some more money. Could he go back to his mother for more? He honestly didn't think so. For her this had been an emotional release, not a financial investment. She wouldn't be interested in his market reports, competition analysis, technical progress or letters of support from the Ministry of Defence. John was sure that she wished him well, but probably more likely wished that he'd get over it quickly and get back to having a sensible job. She had released some of his inheritance early, to assuage herself of the guilt of not supporting his father's own entrepreneurial ambitions. He really couldn't see her investing more and to be honest he had no way of knowing if she had more that she could invest. His mother and father had always been very canny with money, never ostentatious, but always comfortable. No big purchases that they couldn't really afford, everything planned, saved for, budgeted. So she would have planned out her retirement meticulously, comfortably with minimum risk. John couldn't see her making a further risky investment in a technology start-up.

In many ways he suspected that that first investment wasn't an investment at all, it was a gift, she didn't expect it back. But by *investing* the money, it had made him to accept it as a business, accept that it came with legal and financial responsibilities. It also gave her some influence over the business, and she could never turn down influence could she? While he knew that Lucy would always resent her having any influence, he had begun to appreciate the subtle effect that the 'investment' had made on the set-up and early running of EarStream and he had developed some grudging respect for the way his mother had handled this. Even respect for Martyn Pearce-Mountford, yes he could go as far as respect, but little further for the lawyer.

Even if it were an act of charity rather than a business investment, that didn't make it any more likely that she could, or would, give him more. And anyway to even ask felt like a betrayal, it would diminish the significance of her original gift. He had felt that something in their mother-son relationship had changed when she had entrusted him with her investment. She was treating him like an adult, allowing him to take more control over his own future. To ask, would return him to the status of a child, the dependent, always asking for more. No he couldn't ask her.

Where else? The University? He had broached the idea with Simon about whether the University would put up some cash. Now that the technology was moving forward they could hopefully see the value growing. Simon hadn't said no, the University had a fund, but it was set-up to support academic spinouts rather than external companies, even if they were using University IP. University investment was a possibility, but not a straightforward solution, and certainly not one that could work quickly. Simon had also warned that he should avoid showing a business weakness, even though the University was committed to working with early stage companies and start-ups, their financial processes were still very risk averse.

Where else? The bank was no use unless he put the house on the line and that felt like it would be a final nail in the coffin of his marriage. Other types of personal loans could maybe keep the company going for another week or two, but that wasn't sustainable and he wasn't quite desperate enough yet for the pay-day loan companies.

And so, despite all the warnings from Simon and Giles, in his mind he was starting to rely on Benni making him an offer. He found himself dreaming the clearing off his personal debts and moving the R&D forward with Benni's investment. He had tried and failed to push the idea of the investment to the back of his mind, he mustn't, couldn't rely on it. The meeting had gone well, but how could you tell if it would lead anywhere?

CHAPTER TWENTY-EIGHT

It had become John's habit to try and bump into Simon on the days when he was working at the TECHub. It was these informal catch-ups, these *ad hoc* meetings, which were the root of the support culture at the Hub. Here there was no need to follow agendas, measure metrics, or review plans, here it was just two guys bumping into each other for a chat. A few words of encouragement, chuck in an idea, challenge an assumption, give a bit of advice, share an anecdote or pass on a contact. Potential gems.

But today was different. After days of fretful anticipation, John had finally heard from Mr Benni's lawyers, Byall, Byall and Woods, they had said that he should receive an 'Offer Document' later that day. John had called ahead and asked if Simon could be free for a meeting late that afternoon. A second call had secured some time with Giles early the following morning - he wasn't available to come in, but could join by conference call. John would email them the offer documents when they arrived. He knew that no-one would have a chance to go through the documents fully, but he wanted to get their initial impression of the offer.

Simon had explained that typically the offer would be outlined in the 'Heads', the rest of the paperwork would be the standard stuff that all lawyers seemed to put in to pad out the envelope and their bill. The 'Heads' or the 'Heads of Terms' should outline how much Mr Benni was prepared to invest and what percentage of

EarStream he wanted in return. The 'Heads' should also cover any other key aspects of the offer, which were critical to the deal. The purpose of the 'Heads' was to get an 'Agreement in Principle' of the primary terms before involving lawyers to go through the details.

John needed this deal, the lab work, whilst going great, wasn't cheap, even with the support of the university. The R&D Grant and the investment from his mother were all but gone. While he hadn't said anything to Lucy, they were basically surviving on her income from DMM and as far as he could ascertain from offhand comments from Lucy, that income was by no means certain, as it sounded like DMM were having cash problems as well. Shame, he'd liked Jason and Lucy seemed to be doing well there. But for him and EarStream another injection of cash was needed to keep the lab and the office going and perhaps pay himself something to help with his own living expenses. He needed to generate some personal income and not have all the money going into the research and development. He'd discussed this with Simon previously, but his answer hadn't been that promising.

"To be honest John new investors don't like to see the founders taking money out before the business is financially viable or at least generating revenue."

"That's fine for them to say. But what am I and my family supposed to live on? We've put everything we have into this."

"I understand that John. I really do, but that's not the way they think. They want their cash to move the company forward, to pay for more development, more marketing, more sales. In fact, anything that helps the business achieve the potential that they're investing in. If the cash goes straight out of the door to pay debts or straight into the founder's pockets, then it's not adding any value to the business."

"There's not much value if I have to quit and get a proper job, is there?" John was getting frustrated and angry with his situation, not with Simon.

"Of course I understand. But that isn't necessarily how an investor sees it. You have three roles in this, as an employee, in this case as the Managing Director, as a Board Director and as a Shareholder. These roles can be quite distinct, especially as the business grows. If you take a salary, then you do that as an employee, you should have a contract that defines your employment terms, agreed by the Board and the Shareholders. Since the business isn't generating revenue to pay a salary, any new investor will need to agree to it, as he or she is going to have to pay for it. And as I say most investors will want to avoid doing that."

"What about dividends, I thought that was how entrepreneurs got paid? You pay less tax as well, don't you?"

"Yep, that's quite right, but dividends are a share of the profits made, and you have made any revenue yet, let alone profit, so that's a no-go."

"So how am I supposed to get any money out then?"

"The only real choice left is to sell some of your shares."

"I thought that was what I was doing with the new investors?" John sounded confused.

"No, what you are doing is selling *new* shares in the company that go to the investor. You end up with the same number of shares, but you own a smaller percentage of the company – it's called *dilution.* But hopefully each share is worth more."

"I don't get it, why is it worth more?"

"Put simply, with the investor's money in its bank account – the company is worth more. But also the investor is valuing the business, more on its potential than its actual value - which for a start-up like yours, is virtually nil, just a few bits of furniture —."

"— Hang on," interrupted John, "What about the IP. I've invested all this money in the technology, surely that must be worth something."

"Yes, it is. But at the moment you don't own it. You have an agreement to use it and develop it and in the future hopefully to licence it. But at the moment the University still owns all the intellectual property."

"So what is the investor investing in then?" John was getting exasperated.

"They are investing in the potential of the business. How well you can build the value through the technology and launch new products."

"But isn't the whole point that we are going to spend their money to do that."

"The idea is that you spend the money to increase the value in the business. If you just spend it on paying yourself, then you are not creating more value."

"So if I take money out ...?"

"You are reducing the value of the business."

“And if I pay myself a salary ...?”

“You are reducing the value of the business.”

"So how do I ever get my money out then?"

"You *sell* your shares."

"So, I should sell my shares rather than dilute them?"

"Yes, though the problem with that is you still need investment to move the company forward. The investor doesn't usually want you to sell as they want you to be hungry to make money for all the shareholders, not just for yourself. And they want their money to help generate the value within the business."

"They don't make this easy do they?"

"The problem is that they are focused on the value of their investment. You taking money out doesn't achieve that."

"But surely me having no money to live on doesn't help the business either?"

"No, you're right. But showing that you are desperate isn't the best way of getting a good valuation."

"Oh God, it sounds like the banks again. They only lend you money when you don't need it."

"Well, they will only lend you money cheaply if it doesn't look like you need it or if you have the 'security' to cover it. It's all about the perceived risk."

"But the company doesn't have anything to put up as security."

"No. But you do."

"What do you mean?"

"Your house. You could always put up your house as security."

"No I can't. We’ve been through that before. I promised Lucy."

"Unfortunately that's not the concern of the investors, or the bank for that matter."

"They can't ask me to risk my, our, house, our home?"

“They can, because you are asking them to risk their money. Look John I'm not saying it’s right, I'm not even saying it's fair.

What I am saying is that you need to look at it from the investors' point of view. If *you* are unwilling to risk your house as security, why should *they* risk their money?"

"But —". John tried to protest.

"— No John, if you are not prepared to share the risk in that way, you need to be prepared to explain why. The founder's commitment to the business is often seen as a key factor for business success and taking a risk is one simple way of demonstrating it.

"I know that's over simplistic, but simple is easy to manage and simple is cheap to administer. So if you are willing to share the risk through some form of personal security or putting up your own funds, then that ticks a box. You have 'skin in the game'. If not, the fund manager has to make a bigger decision which increases the time and cost of the deal and opens up the fund manager to potential criticism of his judgement."

"It's different for them, they're not risking their homes. They're just investing other people's money."

"I know John. Everybody understands that, but the risk and the confidence that you show in the project is one factor that they will take into account. Their job is to be seen to be acting prudently with other people's money. Our job is to present the business case in such a way that it helps investors make a positive decision to invest, and to do that we need to understand what they are looking for.

"In this case you're dealing with a private investor, investing his own money, rather than a fund manager investing somebody else's. A private investor is more likely to take a more subjective view, as he doesn't have to justify his decision to anybody else. A private investor may well invest because he likes the person, or because he knows the sector well, or sees an opportunity for the technology, he doesn't have to rely upon the business' investment plan to explain the market or prove the model, he may well be looking beyond or outside the business plan based on his own judgement and experience."

"But how can I find out? Mr Benni didn't say anything about this when he visited, he just went on and on about the IP assignment."

"Well, with our usual investors I spend the time getting to know them, to help match them to appropriate opportunities. But with Mr Benni, I've not met him, so I don't know. How did you find him?"

"I didn't, he found me. His lawyers just called up out of the blue."

"Hmm. He didn't say how he had heard about the project?"

"No, he just said it was through, 'a mutual acquaintance'. I didn't think it was important, so I didn't ask anymore. Is that a problem?"

"No, it just gives us less to go on. What I can suggest, if you don't mind, is that you let me have his details and I'll give him a call and invite him to have a tour of the Hub and maybe see some of the other opportunities, hopefully I'll get him talking that way."

"Heh. But he's my investor, I don't want to lose him. I really need this deal Simon."

"Don't worry, it's just a way of getting him into a conversation. I'm not trying to steal him," Simon reassured John.

***

Jason had sent the staff home. He had made it sound like a reward, a bonus half-day holiday, but they were under no illusions as they trooped out. Now Jason and Lucy had the office to themselves and had been working throughout the afternoon, it was now getting late. Lucy had finally managed to get Jason to face up to the paperwork and go through the business accounts and project updates by opening a bottle of wine and pouring him a large glass of red. They had the papers spread out over the Board Room table, intermingled with biscuit wrappers and spent coffee cups, it had been an energy sapping session, but made better by the fact they were working together. This was personal for Jason as well as business, and the emotion of it was draining his energy. It was like going through a post-mortem while the patient was still just about breathing. But Lucy tried to make it lighter by pretending that she was Donald Trump and Alan Sugar interrogating his every business decision. But to be honest her impersonations wouldn't have got her very far on 'Britain's Got Talent'.

"Pizza," she announced, "we should have pizza, that's what they always do in the movies. The late night business vigil is always accompanied by pizza."

"But I haven't had a takeaway pizza for years. All that lukewarm, cloying, processed cheese —."

"— This isn't optional," insisted Lucy. "This is after hours, we've sent the office staff home, we've got the lights low, rolled up our sleeves. We've got paper strewn, even an overflowing bin of discarded ideas. This scene needs takeaway boxes and ideally, full ashtrays, but we don't have to go that far. So sod your *low carb* diet, we need pizza, get me pizza now. And coffee, and wine, we need more coffee and more wine."

Jason laughed, raising his hands in surrender. "OK. Pizza it is, but its extra pepperoni on mine and extra chilies on yours. You're going to pay for this over-stereotypical binge." He headed off to make the call.

Lucy laughed as she heard Jason putting on a bad New York accent as he placed the order. This felt like being a partner, she thought to herself.

***

The previous week Simon had been as good as his word and contacted Benni to invite him for a tour around the TECHub.

"Mr Benni, it's good to meet you again," Simon was at his most effusive. "I'm so pleased you have been able to come over, I always welcome the opportunity to meet potential new investors and give them a feel of what we do and the types of investment opportunities we have here. Let me introduce Giles Lansbury, also one of our prospective investors. I hope you don't mind that he joins us?"

"Simon, the pleasure is all mine. And Giles, of course it will make the visit even more interesting to get the perspective of another investor, especially as I do not have a scientific background. Do you understand these technology companies?"

"Well, I understand some of the technology, especially around electronics. But the companies themselves, who knows, that's people isn't it, not as simple to understand as circuits and capacitors and resistors?" Giles replied with a smile.

Simon agreed, "Yes, if the tech companies were run by machines, then life would be much simpler, or at least more predictable."

Benni looked more intently at Simon, "So Simon, is that your role then, to understand the people behind the technology?"

"In some ways yes. It would be easy to say that this is all about understanding the technology, the market, the money and the business model for each business, but in reality it's about understanding the individuals involved. A company's potential for success is very much a function of the individual entrepreneur." Simon started to move them off to get the tour started.

"I can believe it. Very interesting work," added Benni enthusiastically. "When I last visited I was fascinated by the place and I am keen to learn more. I had no idea that such a facility existed."

"That's not a very good endorsement for our marketing is it?" Simon joked.

"Ah, but I was not looking," replied Benni seriously. Giles nodded in agreement.

The pleasantries over, they moved on to Simon's office for a background chat with coffee, then started the building tour with quick thumbnail sketches of each business.

"This company is working mainly with App development, they had some early success with a *Utility App*, to do with secure storage of passwords, but are now focusing on mobile games. They have had some Seed Investment from their three 'Fs', but could be looking for more, especially where it comes with games industry contacts," Simon was in full flow.

"The three '*Fs*', said Benni, "what is this?"

"Ah, that stands for 'friends, family and fools," Simon smiled at the old industry joke.

"OK, so that does not sound so encouraging. These new companies, so many Apps, so many games, how can you know which one will take off?" commented Benni.

"That is literally the million-dollar question. It seems to be impossible to predict. Often it's down to the viral nature of the marketing rather than the quality of the product. And with the current trend for *Freemium* business models —"

"— *Freemium*, what is this?" Benni again interrupted, looking perplexed.

"*Freemium*, is where the software is *free* and the business relies of the customers to make small payments 'in-app-purchases', It's an alternative to selling advertising within the App. But in most cases very few customers ever make a purchase."

"Seems a crazy idea for a business, where most of your customers get the product for free!" Benni seemed even more perturbed. "Me, I'm only interested in investing in real products that people see the value of and are prepared to pay for."

"I'm with you on that," chipped in Giles, "difficult to plan when forecasting demand is so uncertain. I would always prefer to work with a product that you can test with customers and build sales channels for it."

Simon nodded in agreement, "And that's important for us to know so that we can help you find opportunities that might interest you. It's not that we are saying that they are good investments, we can't and won't do that, but we can steer you towards the type of businesses that you feel most comfortable with."

Simon moved on along the corridor, and coming to another door opened it to reveal a garishly decorated office, with the customary table-football machine in the corner. "This is 'Blue Monkey', they are developing products for Digital Marketing, which is another sector that sometimes divides investors."

"Divides, how so? I have some interest in Digital Marketing," Benni admitted.

"I think it's because the market is so dominated by Google company. Most of digital marketing is about second-guessing how the search algorithms work. A digital marketing business tells their customers that *they* know how Google works, but there's always the risk that Google will change the rules. As I say, it works for many, but some investors steer clear."

"I have some experience with such an agency locally, DMM they are called, it seems to be a business that's becoming less profitable."

"Certainly it's an area sector that's getting very crowded as more and more agencies start-up, forcing the prices down."

"Yes, I am reviewing how I proceed with my investment," Benni said negatively.

They moved down the corridor and stopped in front of EarStream's office, Benni's mood visibly lightened, “Ah EarStream, now we have a proper company."

"Yes, of course Mr Benni, I believe you've had some talks with EarStream. An interesting technology, I wondered how your assessment of the company is going? Is there anything that I can help with?”

"Yes, a real product and good patents based on University Research. This is of great interest to me."

"That's good. Can I ask, how did you heard about this EarStream?" Simon asks innocently.

"Oh, just through my accountant, they often mention opportunities to me."

No help there then, thought Simon.

***

Now it was the moment of truth. John had Benni's offer document as a rather perfunctory email containing a whole series of document attachments, it had been sent by his lawyers. He would have preferred a crisp, white, large envelope with seals to open, thick with important legal papers, looking more expensive more formal, more of the moment. But no, modern communication had again lessened the drama of a transaction. He stared at the innocuous looking document, it potentially meant so much, but appeared as nothing special in his inbox which was crowded with junk mail, personal messages and offers he would never succumb to. He was lucky that the email hadn't gone straight through to his Junk Folder.

***

Jason was getting depressed again. They were dissecting the company's projects, looking for savings, looking for corners to cut, it had never been the way that Jason had worked. He liked to think of himself at the quality end of the market, aiming to deliver over and above his client's expectations. He had wanted to give his staff time to express themselves, find new ways to excel, to create an extraordinary service. Now here he was scrabbling around with the low cost providers trying to find the minimum he had to do to meet their contractual commitments. Worse, trying to select which members of his team to keep, not on the basis of how technically brilliant they were or their future potential, but on how cost efficient they would be delivering the current projects, was against everything he had tried to create in the business.

"I don't know Lucy," he said despondently, "what we're doing, is it really worth it? We may be working to save a company, but it's not the company that I built, not the one that represents me. What we will end up with, after all the cuts and savings, is it worth saving?"

It had been like this all evening, an emotional cycle, each turn shorter than the last. She would perk him up with a piece of good news from the business, an opportunity that they could grasp, rather than a problem to cut, or maybe just distract him with a joke or a funny story. Then the harsh reality of what they were doing would gradually drown any good humour and he would start getting depressed again.

"Come on Jason, we've just got to get down to the core of the business, something that can operate within the cash limits imposed by Benni, while you find a way to get out from under him. Then you'll have a base from which to rebuild the business you want."

"I don't know Lucy. I don't know if can, or even if I want to go through this again."

But Lucy was tiring of his whining, she had never responded well to people wallowing in their own self-pity. If she had, she and John would never have coped with Daniel and all the life changes that that had imposed. She believed simply that you had to take what life throws at you and fight back.

"Oh get a grip Jason. Even if you don't want to rebuild it, let's sort this out so that we let as few people down as possible. If we go down, let's go down with our heads held high."

***

Two hours later and John still hadn't opened the attachments, he had stared at the email on and off all afternoon. In his own mind he had justified this by telling himself he was waiting until

Simon was available to provide an immediate interpretation of any legalese or other aspects of the offer that he didn't fully understand. Throughout this process he had been struck just how complex lawyers could make the simplest of deals, and this was too important to him to be ambiguous. If he waited for Simon, he could check anything that wasn't clear straight-away, otherwise he would spend the whole day fretting about it.

That was a good reason, but was it the real one? In reality his reasons for holding back were more emotional, possibly irrational. He should be able to view this offer objectively, just one person's view. This wasn't a test of him, this was a simple business transaction a rather subjective assessment of his business by a potential investor who knew little about their technology or the markets that EarStream was aimed at?

He knew that made sense, he had listened and agreed wholeheartedly when Simon had made the same point. Simon had explained that you could present the same early stage business proposition to a room-full of investors and get an incredibly wide range of responses. This wasn't an objective exercise, so you therefore shouldn't take it too personally. But it was still someone else's judgement on your business, your abilities and your future. You had to have extreme self-confidence to throw yourself into the investor's courtroom and not take their judgement personally.

John envied those smart, tech, usually American, entrepreneurs that you read about in the magazines, all brains, glossy hair and white teeth. They seemed to move effortlessly from the garage to the boardroom with such self-confidence that if an investor didn't like their business plan, then it was the investor that "didn't get it". And that, John guessed, was how the 'tech-bubbles' started, investors investing in technology businesses that they didn't understand, but didn't want to be seen to be behind the curve. John would dearly love to be in at the start of a tech bubble right now.

But John didn't have that self-confidence. He did take this personally. In part because this was proper new exciting but unproven technology, with applications in difficult and complex markets, rather than a trend-following App. As such it was more reliant on his abilities as an entrepreneur. It was up to him to understand the markets and get the best out of the science.

In his mind the science was proven, he had seen it work in the lab. Björn and Dr Lowe had done their bit, they had shown it working and they had been validated by the peer reviews and through the academic journals. If the technology didn't get to the market now, it wasn't the scientists' fault, it was his. And if the investor didn't make a favourable proposal, then it was a damming indictment of him and his abilities, not the science and not the scientists. John understood the arguments, knew he was taking this too much on himself, but it was not so easy to tell yourself not to feel a certain way, it was personal, it was emotional, it may even be irrational, but that was the way he felt.

He had fifteen minutes before his meeting with Simon. He opened the email and clicked open the attachment titled 'Investment Proposal - Heads of Terms'.

***

"DMM, he actually mentioned DMM." John was aghast.

"Yes, it was the only company he mentioned where he has an interest. I don't know them, but I take it they're in Digital Marketing," Simon explained, uncertain of why John's reaction was so strong.

"They are. It's where Lucy works, my wife Lucy works there. What's going on Simon?"

"Beats me, could just be a coincidence, a sequence of disconnected conversations."

"Could be. But like they say in the spy movies, 'there ain't no such things as coincidences', so somehow I don't think so. It just sounds like something is not right here. I'm going to have to talk to Lucy ..."

"But he's made the offer John?" Simon attempted to bring John back to the point of the meeting, but John remained distracted. "John, the investment offer. How does it look?"

"Oh yeah. It's good. Decent valuation, certainly more than our low estimate, but lots of conditions, especially over the IP. And guess what, he's even offered me a loan, which would really help, I don't know how he knew, but that could be a life-saver."

"A loan? That's unusual. Don't get me wrong, I can see how it helps your situation, but this loan what sort of terms has he offered?"

"Oh I haven't really looked, there seemed to be lots of conditions, but what the hell, it looks like a good deal. Two fifty for thirty percent, that's over three quarters of a million valuation and hundred thousand loan for me. It just sorts everything out."

"Sounds really good John," Simon sounded sceptical, "but let's wait to see what Giles thinks."

"What's to think? I can get the bank off my back. Get the University working on new applications. Get my family and my life back. Giles would need to have a bloody good reason *not* to like this deal."

***

After another half an hour spent pouring over the numbers, the project progress sheets and the forecast hours, Lucy and Jason's enthusiasm for the task was wearing thin and the bottle of red was nearly out. Jason leant back in his chair and stretched his arms and back. "Making a living didn't used to be this hard," he groaned.

"Come on," replied Lucy rubbing her eyes, as if a headache was starting to take hold, "another half an hour and we'll be —" She was interrupted by the outside door intercom on her desk buzzing.

"Ahh, saved by the buzzer," said Jason with a relieved sigh, "that'll be the pizza. I can smell the pepperoni from here and feel the heat off those chillies." He got up from the chair stretching again and made his way out through the Board Room door to Lucy's desk, where the intercom buzzed again. "Hang on Pizza man, ayza coming."

Lucy laughed as she gathered the papers together into neat piles to make way for the pizza boxes. She poured the last of the wine into the two glasses, more for him, she'd had enough on an empty stomach and was starting to feel a little squiffy. She heard the office doorbell chime, then the office door opening and Jason negotiating in a jokey way with the delivery man. She was confident that for all the dire financial straits of the business, Jason would still tip well. And then he was back in the doorway triumphantly holding the steaming cardboard boxes plus a bulging carrier bag of sides. "Dinner is served," he announced in his best butler's voice, reminding Lucy of Parker from Thunderbirds.

"Lay me on the table, Parker," she giggled as Lady Penelope.

"Yes, m'Lady."

The doorbell chimed again, and Jason struggled to put the large awkward boxes down on the table and swore, still in character, "Bugger m'Lady, the door, I must return."

Lucy fussed over the dinner, she arranged the pizza boxes and sides and got the serviettes out as Jason returned across the office. Pizza guy must have forgotten something, she thought.

Suddenly there was a crash and Jason shouted out, "What the fuck —!" She heard a slap and then a thump as Jason cried out in pain. She crept to the door, scared stiff but had to try and see what was happening. She strained her eyes to see through the crack in the door jamb. She saw a figure, must be Jason, sprawled, writhing on the floor, holding his face. A heavily built man loomed over him, his clothes dark and anonymous, his fists clenched. Jason moaned, part from pain, part from shock. About to scream, Lucy was silenced by the intimidating scene in the office. She felt helpless and vulnerable.

"Shut-it and keep it shut," a gruff voice said, unemotionally, like this was regular business.

"What d'yo —?" Jason's plaintive voice was cut-off by another thump as a boot landed in Jason's midriff. He groaned again.

"Are you alone?" the assailant growled, "who else is here?" Lucy shrank back against the wall behind the door.

"I'm alone," Jason's voice was muffled by his hands over his face. He started to rise, looking at his hands. "Christ I'm bleeding. What the hell …?" Jason's voice trailed off as he saw the man pull something from his belt, a short, stick, a cosh. "No, no!" he cried out. "Why?"

"A message, that's why. A message from your Landlord. You ain't paid up, so he wants you to remember how important it is that his other little investment goes smoothly." He brought down the cosh with a thwack on Jason's outstretched arm. Jason screamed.

Lucy could take it no longer, she ran through the door and screamed, "STOP IT! Stop it you bastard." She picked up a stapler and flung it at the man.

The attacker looked up at the sound and flinched slightly as the stapler hit the wall to his right and clattered to the floor. He turned on her grinning malevolently, "I should've known, too much pizza for one. Got a little love nest up here av'yer?"

She continued to run towards him, she grabbed anything heavy that came to hand from the desks as she passed and threw them blindly towards the man. "You bastard, you bastard, get out you bastard and leave him alone."

As she got closer, the man balanced his weight on the balls of his feet, a fighter's stance, and raised his right arm holding the cosh, "Come on girlie, your turn now, before I'm on me way."

She screamed as she got near to him, the intruders' eyes stared her down coldly. Jason was curled on the floor, clutching his injured arm, but could see what was happening and with a last effort screamed, "Noooo Lucy," he swung his right leg with all his energy, the movement making his whole body twist on the floor. His boot caught the man's back leg hard on the shin, just below the knee, and knocked him off balance. The attacker cursed as he dropped the cosh, and Lucy was on him, flailing her arms, kicking out with her legs, not looking, not seeing what she was hitting. Just hitting. The man swore again as he rose and regained his balance, seemingly oblivious to Lucy's blows. He raised his left arm, fending off her pounding fists, so that he could get a clear view of his attacker, and then with one swing of his right hand he slapped her hard, a backhander across the face. Her swinging limbs seemed to stop in freeze frame and her face showed pure shock as her forward momentum stopped and she was flung backwards by the force of the blow. She fell back and crashed into the sales girls' desks in the centre of the room. She landed in a crumpled heap on the floor and groaned.

The man turned to leave, satisfied that she was no longer a threat, he straightened his jacket and then looked down on the still writhing Jason. He aimed a boot at his body, which connected with a dull thump and a further expelation of air from Jason. "And don't forget, Mr Benni says there'll be no more warnings. He expects you to deliver on your little investment deal."

And then he was gone. Just the sound of his heavy footsteps down the stairs and the bang as the street door slammed. And then it was near silence, just Jason's whimpers and Lucy's tears.

CHAPTER TWENTY-NINE

It was late when John got home. The good news of the investment offer had got around the TECHub grape-vine and he'd had a succession of cheery heads popping through his door to wish him congratulations. A couple of the guys from other companies at the Hub had dragged him off to the pub to celebrate. He hadn't got round to calling Lucy, just a curt text - 'I'll be late'. There was some communication these days, not much, but at least not just the loud silences. He was surprised then, when he poured himself out of the taxi that had brought him home, to see that all the downstairs house lights were on.

He should have sensed something was wrong as he entered the house. The lounge and kitchen lights were blazing, but there was no sign of Lucy. Normally when she went to bed when he was out, she just left a small lamp in the hall on. He staggered round switching off the overhead lights, trying to keep quiet. Strange, Lucy hardly ever put the main lights on, always the lamps, she hated the stark, bright ceiling lights which stripped the room of its character, its homeliness. Overhead lights made her think of classrooms, or hospitals, they institutionalised the home. So this just didn't feel right.

It was the same on the stairs. All the lights were on, not the usual gentle glow of the Daniel's night-light. He switched off the main landing light as he peeked into Daniel's room. He was fast asleep, on his back, breathing deeply, not a care in the world. He washed and undressed down to his boxers in the bathroom, not wanting to wake Lucy. But as he entered their bedroom, at least they still shared a bedroom, he heard her sobs. He hated to hear her cry, he could feel a dull ache deep in his stomach, why couldn't they comfort each other anymore? He reached over as he got into bed, careful not to breathe his beer breath over her, he squeezed her shoulder. Her body shuddered and she moved even further to her edge of the bed. He heard a muffled, "Goodnight." between her sobs, which he knew meant 'leave me alone'. He rolled over onto his back, maybe with the prospect of the investment and the loan he could have a worry free sleep.

Oh God, why hadn't she told him? What barrier held her back? This had been one of the worst, most frightening nights of her life, and still she couldn't turn to him. She was hurt. Her face still stung from the blow she had received earlier and she could feel the swelling and the bruising coming out, and still she couldn't tell him. She was more concerned with hiding it or making excuses. But why?

After the attack, Jason was in a bad way. A broken arm she had thought, maybe even some ribs. She had called a cab to get Jason home, neither of them were in a fit state to drive. Jason refused point blank to call an ambulance or the police. Lucy couldn't understand why. This was an unprovoked attack, this was intimidation, this was serious stuff. But Jason refused to listen, said it would only make things worse, it was only cuts and bruises he said. And so he had let her tidy the place up, right the furniture, while he sat hunched over on Charlie's chair, feeling sorry for himself. The really odd thing was that Jason wouldn't look at her. It was almost like he wouldn't admit that she had got hurt. He didn't mention her swollen face, didn't ask how she felt, ask if she was all right. He sat there waiting for the taxi, moaning to himself and insisting that they mustn't call the police.

***

Five am. Lucy hadn't slept well. The events of the previous night had filled her waking thoughts and disturbed her dreams, in the end she got up around five, better to deal with her thoughts, which she could try and control, rather than her dreams, which she could not. Lying in bed awake, next to a boozy, snoring John had not helped. She grabbed yesterday's clothes from the chair and crept downstairs, careful not to disturb her sleeping family, this was more to avoid facing them and their questions, rather than her being considerate. While, in her heart she craved for John's support, sympathy and understanding, she felt she had moved too far away to expect it or to demand it. She knew that it was a journey back that she had to start, but not today, not today black-eyed and with bruised pride. Not today.

In the kitchen, she closed the door to shut her noise in and her family out. She checked her phone. There was a text from Jason. She scanned it quickly, but was disappointed that he still seemed more concerned with keeping the incident quiet from the rest of the team and the police, than he did with her welfare or explaining what had happened. She made a cup of tea and thought through the evening again. The attacker had said that this was a message from his landlord and he mentioned Benni by name. While she had understood that Jason was in a financial mess she had not expected that he'd get a visit from the *heavies*. Maybe this was just getting too risky, perhaps she should walk away now. But somehow this Benni was now linked to John and EarStream as well as Jason, so she couldn't just turn her back on it. She needed to protect them both if she could, at least that would put off making a decision between them.

She sent a group email out to the DMM staff, telling them to have the morning off and then she sent a text to Jason, saying that she needed to see him at nine thirty at the office. She felt better having done something, but it was still before six, so out of a kind of desperation she started cleaning. She had never been what her mother would have called *house proud*, but this morning she would have made any mother proud, surfaces were wiped, sink scrubbed, drainer scoured. The floor was next, mopped, though it had taken her a while to find the mop. She was on her second window, when she heard Daniel stirring, it was eight o'clock, two hours had flown by in a blur of bleach. That was it, she told herself, if this all goes wrong, she could drop out and become a bleach bum, which at least made her smile. She put her cleaning cloths away and went to see to Daniel. As she passed the mirror in the hall she caught sight of herself, which wiped the smile off her face. Oh God, what would people say, they'd think that John had been knocking her about. Hopefully Daniel wouldn't notice. He'd been in bed when she had eventually got home, and Lucy had managed to avoid a face-to-face meeting with the sitter. But today people were bound to comment, she'd have to come up with a story. Maybe it just looked worse to her, perhaps people wouldn't notice it.

She entered Daniel's bedroom with a cheery, "Good morning Daniel."

Daniel turned to see her and straightaway his jaw dropped and his arm came up pointing directly at her face. "What ...? What.....?" He stammered.

So much for people not noticing, Lucy thought. "Mummy had a little accident darling, but I'm all right now. Let's get you dressed and ready to go shall we? Playgroup this morning, but I don't think daddy will be up for taking you? He was out late. So we'll go together."

Daniel just stared at his mother's face, still pointing.

Later, Daniel sat at the kitchen table drinking his milk and eating toast, he liked toast. Lucy was in the downstairs loo, trying to see just how many layers of make-up you could apply to a bruise before it started peeling off like damp plaster. It didn't really hurt that much where she had been hit, the back of her head was far tenderer from when she had fallen backwards into the table. But you couldn't see the back of the head, what you could see was a pearler of a black eye, well more like a yellow and browning eye. She was definitely going to attract looks, and not admiring ones.

As she tried to work the magic with the foundation, she started to think again about Jason and the shock of the attack. But as much as she felt sorry for Jason, this was pushed aside by a sense of impending doom about John. What had happened to Jason had a certain inevitability about it, it was almost as if Jason accepted it, was resigned to it. He was in a mess and he couldn't see a way out of it without hurting others. But now those others included John and herself, and she had no confidence that Jason wouldn't sacrifice them to save himself. She had to talk to John, to warn him, but first she had to talk to Jason and get the truth out of him.

***

John awoke with a thick head and an empty space next to him in the bed. He hadn't heard Lucy get up, shame, he would have liked to have shared the good news about the investment offer, especially the linked loan, as that would make their money worries go away. He rolled over and checked the bedside clock, he fumbled for his glasses. His head hurt as he raised it off the pillow and his mouth had the taste of cat litter. He really should have drunk more water last night. Christ, it was after nine, no wonder Lucy was gone, she would have taken Daniel to the nursery. Damn, it was his turn to do it today as well, he'd probably get the silent treatment tonight, another responsibility missed.

He'd better make a move, while there was no one watching his time keeping these days, one benefit of being your own boss, Giles was due to call in at 10.30 and John was conscious that he still hadn't read the full offer document, just gleaned the key elements of the deal. He smiled as he remembered the quarter of a 'mill' for the company and a hundred grand for him, life was definitely looking up. He headed for the shower, he may need a long soak, and maybe a cold water blast, to get his mind and his body back functioning.

***

By ten o'clock, John was in the TECHub cafe with strong black coffee and a bacon roll, when Simon caught up with him.

"Heavy night was it?" he called sarcastically.

"Oh don't. Remind me never go drinking with engineers again, they take it so seriously."

"Hah, yes they certainly know how to down a few. Have you read it yet? Let's just hope you've got something to celebrate." John had his laptop open on the table, but he still hadn't been able to focus his eyes, let alone his brain, on the close typeset legalese contained within the email attachments that had accompanied the offer.

John was caught off guard by Simon's apparent negativity, "No, not all of it. What is it? Is there a problem?"

"Let's wait to get Giles' take on it, he should be calling in in a few minutes, bring your coffee through to my office once you've finished your butty, I'm not keen on the smell of another man's bacon."

"Giles. Good morning. I'm here with John and we've got you on the speaker phone." Simon and John were gathered around the meeting table in Simon's office, they were both leaning in to a futuristic looking conference phone in the middle of the table.

Giles' voice came through clear and crisp on the speaker, loud enough to make John and Simon sit back in their chairs. "Morning Simon, John, hope all is well with you guys."

"Morning Giles," John replied gruffly.

"I'm afraid that John is a little the worse for wear this morning Giles, one too many celebratory beers."

"Well let's hope there's something to celebrate."

John was struck again by the wary comment. "I thought it was a good valuation," ventured John, "at the high end of our expectations."

"Absolutely," agreed Giles, "but there are a few buried conditions. What did you think Simon?"

"Yes. There are terms in there that I'm certainly not familiar with. Not sure I could really follow it. Normally these things are pretty up front in the 'Heads', but here there seem to be special conditions buried all over the documentation."

"What do you mean? The quarter of a million investment and a hundred grand loan seem pretty clear and with Benni only asking for a thirty percent stake it still leaves me with a clear majority, not even taking account of my mother's twenty percent share."

"Yes, John," replied Giles patiently, "on the surface it looks like a good deal. But there are some interesting things in the Shareholder's Agreement and the Loan Agreement."

"Isn't that stuff just standard boiler plate, I haven't had a chance to read through it all yet, and when I do, I don't suppose it will make much sense."

"Unfortunately that's exactly why people try to hide stuff there. I'm not saying any one thing is suspicious in itself, but taken together, it raises concerns. For example, with the loan, it's secured against your EarStream shares, any problems with the repayments and you could lose a chunk of your equity."

"Better that than secured against my home!" John said defiantly.

"I'm not here to give you personal finance advice John, that's for others to do, I'm here to look at your position in the company. Under these loan terms you could easily move into a minority position in terms of the company shares if you have trouble keeping up with the payments. And remember John, there's no salary here, so those repayments could prove a stretch. And even if you do make those, the loan is set-up as a convertible bond that Benni can transfer into shares at any time unless you can pay it off in full. In some ways, the structure of the loan, with low cost at the start and capital repayments being delayed for a couple of years, looks really helpful to your personal cash position, but it also leaves you vulnerable to losing your majority position in the company."

"But why Giles, why would he do that? Is it legal?"

"Sure it's legal, it's a high risk personal loan secured against your assets, the EarStream shares. And as to why, well I can only surmise that he wants to be in a position to take control of the business."

"Control!" John shot back, "how can he have control when he only has thirty percent of the shares and I'm the Managing Director?"

"That's just it, if you default on the loan or if he triggers the convertible stock option, then he moves up to a forty percent shareholding, which given the University stake and your mother's, would make him the largest shareholder."

"Yes I suppose so, but not with a majority of the shares, and I'd still be the MD. I'd still be running the company," John was getting defensive.

"John, that's where things start getting interesting. He's also insisting that you, as MD, move onto a Director's employment contract —."

"— Yes, which is great, I get a salary."

"Indeed, once the company is cash positive, but as an employee you can be fired, if you don't meet some pretty tough 'Key Performance Criteria'."

"Oh those. They were just some rather fanciful projections of the revenue, additional investment and profits, just to show the potential for growth. No-one really believes them do they? All the books I read said that investors want to see a 'hockey-stick' graph of revenue, so I provided one, the growth might happen."

"Well now it's written in stone, and if it doesn't happen you could lose more shares under the performance criteria or you could be dismissed by the Board, which he will control."

"Dismissed? Why would he dismiss me? It's my idea, my company?"

"Because if you are dismissed, you forfeit your shares, that's what is proposed in the Shareholder's Agreement."

"But. But ... Why ...?"

"Why, because if the technology is proven and the markets identified, he doesn't need you."

"Christ, and that's what he's going to do is it?"

"Honestly John I don't know, it's just one reading of what could happen under the terms of the offer. There's nothing here that declares his intentions. He may not exercise any of these options. And then there's this Jason Collins chap, we don't know what his role might be."

"Jason?" John sounded suspicious.

Simon stepped in now. "Yes, I was intrigued by that. Apparently the investment offer is being made through a company that Benni has interests in, DMM Ltd, and Jason Collins is named as the nominated director appointed by the investor. Unusually though, this director isn't a non-executive position, but here, this Jason will have a commercial management role in the business."

"Jason. But I know Jason, he's my wife's boss, what has he got to do with this?" John now sounded confused and crestfallen, his life-saving deal seemed to be falling apart.

"We don't know John. And that's what makes this whole deal so complicated, we don't know why these conditions have been included. And I suspect there's more that we haven't spotted yet. You are really going to have to get a legal opinion on this John." John had never heard Giles sound so serious.

"I can't afford a lawyer."

"You can't afford not to." The foreboding in Giles' words seems amplified by the speaker phone, like a warning from the heavens.

"Thanks Giles." Simon stepped in to wrap things up. "I know you have to go on to another meeting now, thanks for your time, it was invaluable."

"Thanks guys, let's speak again soon. Don't sign anything without a lawyer."

John grunted, his head is in his hands. His hangover just got worse.

***

"So the investment offer on Dr Lowe's technology is in then?" Laura looked keenly at Simon over their coffee. This had become quite a regular catch-up meeting for them in the engineering coffee shop.

"Yes indeed, but it's not as straightforward as one would like." Simon went on to explain some of the more unusual aspects of the offer.

"OK, so difficult for John, but how does it look for the University?"

"Are you kidding? You'd support a deal that's not in the interests of the entrepreneur."

"We have to look at it Simon. John may have spotted the opportunity, but it's the University's IP, and we have to see how to secure value for it. This investor might offer a better route to the market than John does. Don't get me wrong, I like John, and we can look at ways of protecting him to some extent, but in the end this has to be a commercial decision. What does the offer have to say about the IP?"

"Full assignment of the IP once the full two fifty has been invested. The investment is phased on research outcomes."

"OK. I can understand that. Presumably it has the standard University rights to continue to use the technology for research purposes."

"Yes, that at least seems straightforward."

"Anything about royalty rates?"

"No they still stand as per the original agreement with John. But there are tag-along options for him to buy out the University and other shareholders at the current valuation."

"Hah, cheeky bugger, the investor can't honestly expect us to fall for that one. That will have to come out. Of course we can discuss future buy-out options and valuations, but we are definitely not going to tie it to this valuation."

"Sure. And to be clear, you don't think the University will stand behind John in this negotiation?"

"Only so far as it doesn't unduly prejudice the University's commercial interests. You've got to remember Simon that the people making these decisions don't know John and have no history in this development. They just want to see some commercial return from the fortune we spend on patents."

"I understand. Though I don't think I'll try explaining it to John, not at the moment anyway."

"One bit of possible good news for John is that we are getting positive noises about that Research Council bid we submitted ages ago. May come to nothing, but as far as I remember we had some good industrial partners tied in, so that will push the value up." Laura delivered this with a smile as she breezed out of the cafe.

***

Jason was already in the office when Lucy arrived. He looked awful. He was slumped over in his office chair just staring blankly out into space. His face wasn't just pale, it had that grey pallor of pork that's past its date, beads of sweat stood out on his forehead and his usually lustrous hair lay lank.

"God, you look awful," Lucy observed helpfully.

"Thanks, that's not your best look either," his voice barely more than a whisper, his expression strained.

Lucy raised her hand to her bruised face, seeing the condition of Jason had made her forget her own injury. "Walked into a door," she smiled at the cliché. "How's the ...," but then as he shifted in his chair, she saw it and the pain in his face as he moved. He had fashioned a sling from a tie and she could see from the way that it hung that it was broken. She stepped towards him, real concern of her face, "...We've got to get you to a hospital. That doesn't look good at all."

"Leave it," he hissed, part pain, part annoyance, "what have you said to John?"

"What! That's not important now. We need to get you sorted out."

"No. I need to know what you've said. What you've done."

"Oh for Christ's sake Jason, don't you know when to stop? I've said nothing to John. I hid and ignored him. Anyway he didn't come in 'till late, probably celebrating this great new investor. God knows why I'm protecting you, I should be protecting both of you from this bastard Benni? He should be locked up. We need to call the police."

"No we can't. I'm in too deep."

"You'll be six feet under too deep soon. We can't just let this man go round intimidating people, beating them up. What's he going to do next, to you, to John, to me? No Jason, this has gone far ..."

As she spoke, her resolve for action was growing, Jason rose in his chair to remonstrate. He wobbled as he got to his feet, he hit his injured arm on the chair and cried out with the pain, his balance continued to fail him and he fell, first onto the desk and then slid to the floor. His silence was even more disturbing than his cry. Lucy ran round to him, but his body was wedged between the desk and the chair facing away from her. She thought he must have fainted with the pain, but she daren't move him, not wanting to damage his arm still further.

At least the first decision had been made for her, and Jason was in no position to object, she pulled out her mobile and dialled nine, nine, nine.

***

"I'm not available to take your call at the moment. At the tone, well you know what to do…" John frowned at Lucy's recorded message.

"Lucy, it's me, where are you? I need to talk to you. I've got an offer of investment but somehow your company DMM is involved and it says that Jason is to be their Director in EarStream. What's going on? Call me!"

Where the hell was she? John was pacing round his office at the TECHub, his mobile clamped to his ear. He hadn't seen her in the morning and there was no note or anything when he had eventually got up, just no Daniel, so he assumed she had taken him to the nursery. Now no answer on her mobile and stranger still, no answer on the main DMM number.

Giles had given him plenty to think about with his comments on the investment offer, but as Simon had said after the call, this could just be a negotiating tactic. So he needed to work through a strategy as to how he should respond. Plus, he had to find the money to pay for legal advice. All that would have been plenty to concern him, but this mention of Jason and DMM put a completely different slant on things. Was this something that Lucy had done to help him? Surely she would have mentioned it? He had liked Jason, but had never considered him getting involved in the business. He would like to think that this was a positive development, but he had a real nagging doubt that there was more to this than met the eye.

He called the DMM office number again, nothing. He tried Lucy. "I'm not available to take —," with annoyance he cancelled the call.

***

"... What's going on Lucy? Call me."

Lucy stared at her phone. Jason as a Director for EarStream? Now what was that all about? It was one thing trying to help Jason get his business out from under Benni's control. But now Jason seemed to be part of Benni's plan to get his hands on EarStream. His man? That put a completely different complexion on things. But she couldn't talk to John now. She could hear the confusion, the suspicion, the anger in John's voice. But what could she tell him? She needed to have it out with Jason, but he was now in surgery and she was sitting in this very sterile waiting room, feeling very vulnerable and alone.

The ambulance had come quickly once she had said that Jason was unconscious. The paramedics had been efficient in getting Jason onto a stretcher and out of the building. Jason had groaned, but not woken up. She had travelled with him in the ambulance. A 'colleague' she had said, when questioned by the paramedic, and she was very vague when he questioned her about Jason's injuries as they sped to the hospital. He clearly noticed her own black eye and asked if *she* was all right. He probably thought that they had had a fight and she had beaten Jason up, she just might when he woke up. They hadn't mentioned the police and Lucy wasn't sure if they would be informed automatically when they got to the hospital. In some ways she hoped that they would, at least that would take another decision away from her.

Ping. Another text from John. 'Where are you? Call me'. She couldn't just ignore him, he deserved an explanation, it was just that she didn't know what it was. She would have to talk to Jason first, maybe to the police as well. Oh God, how had she got herself into this?

'I'm at the hospital. Jason had an accident. Will tell you all about it tonight', she texted back. She knew it wasn't enough but it was all she could do for now, she had to wait for Jason to wake up.

***

The mobile had rung, but John didn't recognise the number, another mobile. John answered hoping it was Lucy.

"John? Is that John Miller? It's Phil, Phil from Enterprise IT, remember me, your old boss."

"Phil, of course how are you doing? You haven't finally found a bug in my coding have you?" John laughed. It was nice to have a distraction.

"No," he replied chuckling, "though God knows we've tried. You were very good until you went off the Ruby Rails. That's why I'm calling actually."

"Why, what's on your mind, are you having an epiphany?"

"So to speak. You could say that the Angels have been speaking to me. My management team at Enterprise are looking to do a management buy-out, thought I'd get out while I'm still young enough to enjoy it, and let them have a chance to take the business on to the next level."

"Wow, big decision! Don't tell me, the lads wouldn't take it on unless I come back to lead them?"

"Hardly. No the discussions with their backers led to me meeting a small group of private investors, and one mentioned your project —"

"— Oh God, his name wasn't Benni, was it?"

"No. Don't know a Benni. Should I?"

"No. Don't worry, it's a long story."

"Anyway, as you know I was always interested in what you were doing, so when I mentioned that I knew you, they suggested that I catch-up and do a bit of a recce for them. They do that, get one of the group to do the initial leg work, hope you don't mind?"

"Mind? No of course not. In fact, to be honest I would welcome a bit of friendly advice anyway."

"Sure, what's up?"

"Probably too complicated to go into over the phone. It would be great if you could come over to the TECHub, then you can see the technology, and I can pick your business brains over a coffee."

"Sounds like a deal. My diary is a lot emptier these days, as I let the other lads take the reins."

"The sooner the better."

***

Lucy was alone, dozing in one of the institutional hospital armchairs in the hospital waiting room. A nurse gently shook her shoulder.

"You're here for Jason Collins aren't you? He's coming round now if you want to see him."

Lucy nodded her thanks to the nurse and then got up stiffly, trying to shake some feeling back into her limbs. She followed her into the ward, Jason was in a private recovery room off to the side. "We'll move him back onto the ward tomorrow, when he's properly recovered from the op. His arm break was quite messy, plus he had a couple of broken ribs. He really should have come in straight away, you always get a better bone-set if it's dealt with immediately."

Lucy just nodded and waited for her to leave, but the nurse fussed around the bed checking her patient.

Jason was semi-propped up against the pillows, but his eyes were closed, his face was still very pale, but less grey than before. There were plenty of bandages, tubes and leads. Despite her anger, Lucy was at least relieved that he had received proper medical treatment.

Though there was a visitor's chair at the side of the bed, Lucy chose to stand staring down at him. She made no attempt to take his hand or have any physical contact with him. She just stood, cold faced, arms folded, willing him to wake up, she needed to have this out with him.

Jason must have sensed her stare, his eyes flickered open, took one look then closed again. He tried to speak, but his mouth was still very dry from the anaesthetic, "Water," he croaked. Lucy stood, while the nurse came around and poured him a glass from the jug on the bed-side table and handed it to him. His hand shook as he sipped.

She looked at him and he nodded. She checked Lucy again, retrieved the glass from his hand and replaced it on the table. "Just a few minutes then, he's still coming round." She left the room, leaving the door ajar.

"Your bedside manner could with some work," Jason said with some effort.

"You're lucky I don't break your other arm," Lucy seethed, "I hear you're joining the EarStream Board. What, are you Benni's monkey now?"

Jason closed his eyes. "I'm feeling very tired," he said weakly, "perhaps you should call the nurse."

"Oh you're not getting away with it that easily, no wonder you didn't want the police involved, you're up to your neck in it. And what is this ...," she waved vaguely to his hospital bed, "... some stupid plan to gain my sympathy. So that I would support you over my husband."

Jason held up his good arm trying to stop her, she paused, but still glared at him. "Hey I'm a victim here too —" he said plaintively.

"— A victim? Maybe I could have accepted that before, but now you seem to be lining yourself up to take some hot-shot position in EarStream. What am I supposed to think?"

"No," his voice was getting more strained as he tried to interrupt her flow, "I didn't know I was going to be named in the investment offer, really I didn't. I guess it just makes sense to Benni as he's using the cash out of DMM to make the investment, so I suppose he thought I was the obvious person to nominate. I honestly don't know what he has put in the offer, I never saw it, I just brought him the opportunity."

"Oh, that's plenty, believe me." But Lucy's anger was dissipating, he looked so helpless and vulnerable in the hospital gown and bandages. He started to cough, he really shouldn't be talking this much. She passed him the water and turned to leave. "I don't know Jason; I just don't know. I have to talk to John now, I have to tell him everything. I owe it to him."

"Don't you owe anything to me?" asked Jason weakly.

"Don't push it Jason," she said as she left, without looking back, not sure if she would ever see him again.

***

John returned home early. His mind was in turmoil, he couldn't concentrate on his work and he was achieving very little staying at the office. With Lucy at the hospital he also needed to collect Daniel from the playgroup. The investment offer and loan, that had seemed so attractive yesterday, now was mired in legal terms and confusion over just who this investor was and what his plans were for EarStream. Why had Benni apparently hidden all these legal traps in the offer and the agreements? And what was the involvement of DMM and Jason and Lucy?

Lucy got the taxi to drop her off at the end of the road. She wasn't absolutely sure that she was ready to face John yet. She walked slowly down the road towards their house. The house that she shared with her husband and son. Their home. Home was your security, your castle against the big bad world, you shouldn't be scared to go home. As she got nearer she could see that the downstairs lights were on. There was a bluish flicker through the lounge window, must be Daniel with the television on or a favourite DVD. Where would John be? Maybe in the lounge as well, staring unseeing at the TV, believing that he was keeping Daniel company, but really his mind would be elsewhere, in another place entirely. Or maybe in the kitchen making Daniel's tea. Or upstairs getting changed from his work clothes. Would he be over his hangover now? Would he still feel like celebrating?

She shivered, it was getting chilly now as the night drew in, but more than that, she felt cold inside and she needed the warmth of her family, her home, to fix that. She put her hands in her pockets, put her head down with determination and pushed herself to walk straight to their drive, their house, their front door. Without hesitating she pushed open the door, they often left it on the latch for each other, and entered the hall, shaking off her coat. She called a "Hello," to Daniel through the lounge door, but as expected, got no response from him. As she continued down the hall she saw John sitting at the table in the kitchen, his back was to the doorway, so she couldn't see his face, he made no effort to acknowledge her. She entered the kitchen, leant down and put her arms around John's shoulders and kissed the top of his head. "We've got some talking to do," she said affectionately.

John's body remained stiff as he turned towards her, his was face impassive until he saw hers.

"My God, what happened to your face?" He stood, breaking free of her hold, but then turned fully and took her in his arms. "Who did this to you? What's happening to us?" The more he asked, the tighter he held her. The tears came to her then, and she wept in his arms, such deep emotional sobs, that she was powerless to speak. They held each other close for a long time.

Later still at the kitchen table, Daniel was seated having his tea, seemingly happy that both his mum and his dad were in the same place at the same time. John and Lucy sat, still holding hands, as she explained what had happened with DMM, and Jason and Benni over the last few weeks. She told the story calmly and without emotion so as not to alarm Daniel. She felt that it was important that they were all together as a family right now. As she described the attack at the DMM offices, John reached up and touched her bruised cheek. "Oh you poor baby," he said gently, "why couldn't you have told me?"

"It was all so confused, I didn't want to hurt anybody and didn't want to let anybody down. In the end I've hurt everybody and let everybody down," she started to cry again, but tried to hide it for Daniel's sake.

"Don't be daft, you've just been caught in the middle of somebody else's war. Jason had no right to involve you, or me for that matter."

"He was desperate I suppose. Is the offer from Benni that bad? I know that you, I mean we, need to find more investment for the business."

"Well it's made to look good, but both Giles and Simon think it stinks, not for the initial deal, but how the terms can be manipulated to get me out and leave me with nothing at some point in the future. Then I guess that would leave your beloved Jason as MD."

Lucy was shocked by John's change in tone. "He's not my beloved anything. He just gave me a job and gave me the confidence to do it well. All this came later, I'm not even sure he really knew what Benni was doing. Benni is strangling Jason's company as well."

"Sorry. It's still pretty raw. I so needed that deal to work."

"What will you do?"

"Giles says I must get a legal opinion, but I really haven't got the cash and anyway it hardly seems worth it, I can't take the money now, not after what's happened to you."

"Couldn't you negotiate a fairer deal, take his money, but get rid of all the tricks. Presumably he wouldn't have done this if he didn't think the company was valuable."

"Maybe. I'm going to talk to some other people, like Phil, you remember Phil, my old boss from Enterprise IT. He got in touch yesterday and wanted a catch-up, I'd value his opinion. But basically without the investment, the company's in trouble."

"Heh," Lucy said reassuringly, "we can always get new jobs. Sell the house. Start again. Just the three of us."

"Sure, I guess we can give up and start again." John went silent then, thoughtful, watching Daniel as he ate.

***

The next day Phil visited John at the Hub. They met in reception, and John appreciated the enthusiasm of his greeting.

"Wow John this is quite a set-up," Phil said as he looked round, impressed with the facilities, "do you fill the whole place?"

John laughed, he welcomed this distraction from the current uncertainties, "Of course Phil, it's all smoke and mirrors. Shall we grab a coffee before we head down to the lab?"

It took John longer than he expected to tell the story of the last nine months since he left Enterprise IT and last saw Phil, it made him realise just how much had changed in his life, how he had changed as a person and how his whole life now revolved around EarStream.

"Quite the 'emotional roller coaster'." Phil emphasised the cliché with air quotes. "This Benni sounds like quite a character, I'm surprised I haven't come across him through the local business networks, if he has that kind of reputation."

"That's part of the problem, you meet the guy and he seems fine, as genuine as you would expect within this investment world. All this dodgy stuff is sort of third hand that I've either heard from my wife, or it's my advisor's interpretation of what his lawyer put together in their offer, and to be honest Giles is pretty conservative and risk averse. I'm worried that I might be about to write off the opportunity to really move the business forward, especially when I don't have an alternative plan."

"Tell you what, I'm not busy for the next few hours, after we've been to the lab why don't you leave me with the offer documents for an hour or so and I can hopefully provide another view. I'm not a lawyer, but I have seen my fair share of contracts and investment terms. And I've never been regarded as risk averse"

"Really," John tried to sound cool and professional, but his relief got the better of him, "that would be great. I know I should hire a lawyer, but that would cost money that I don't have, and would probably give me a great long list of reasons not to do things, what I need is some ideas on what I could do."

"It's a deal. Now let's go and see the interesting stuff in the lab."

It had been a few days since John had been in the lab, what with all the distractions over the investment discussion. It felt good to be back, this was, after all, the real reason for the company, to get the technology working and hopefully to prove that it could help Daniel. Björn was pleased to see him, it would give him a chance to show off what he'd achieved with the technology. John made the introductions and then they got down to the demonstrations.

Björn switched the speakers on and this time, while you could definitely tell that there were voices, not one of them was distinguishable. Björn started the explanation.

"Following the initial spec from the MOD, I've added a lot more extraneous noise to the soundtracks, in this case heavy road noise and a train. I think they would have liked battle noise, but I didn't have any sound files for that. They were also interested in the effectiveness of the algorithms for different languages, so I've been experimenting there. The algorithms work fine across all the Latin and Greek based languages and I'm starting on the Arabic ones now."

John and Phil watched the screen as Björn selected different traces and they heard distinct individual voices become clearly audible.

"That's really impressive," said Phil, "are the voice signatures unique?"

"Pretty much. Though with biometric data like finger prints you don't get people deliberately mimicking, like you can do with voices. We need to look at whether there is any research on comparing the underlying voice signature between skilled impersonators and the original. There is also the question of how well an individual's signature carries when they speak in different languages. For example, if a native French speaker is talking in Arabic, is the signature still consistent?"

"Fascinating, but I guess that's a whole other area of research that goes well beyond the electronics?"

"You're right. But this is not an area for us to research, only to understand the current thinking as it applies to the applications we are looking at. If the research says that the voice signatures are unique and do carry across different languages and other conditions, then that is an added benefit to our technology, if not then that limits the claims we can make. Currently we are confident that the technology will work in most circumstances."

"Björn, this is great news, I'm glad we met today. Have the MOD said anymore about the funding for the trials?" John was struck that what Björn was saying was news to him, he really must get a daily update from Björn as this contract seemed to be moving very quickly.

"The MOD say they want to talk to you this week. I was just writing the email."

"Excellent. In the future Björn it would be good if you could find me straight away with this sort of news, it could be very important for the investment talks. Great, let's get back to the demonstration."

Phil was intrigued as Björn showed the technology working in different noise environments: football crowds; train stations and jungles, in different languages and lastly through walls of different thickness and construction. Even without a detailed knowledge of the defence industry it was clear why this could be an important new technology for the security services.

"How does the measurement work over longer distances?" Phil asked.

John stepped in on this one, he wanted to show that he did know his own technology. "It's very dependent on environmental conditions and the types of microphone technology used to capture the signal, but while the accuracy and reliability certainly drops below ninety percent, it's still at a level that is of definite interest to the clients we've spoken to."

"Hmm, have you looked at all at broadcasting?"

"No," said John, "what are you thinking of?"

"I have a friend that works in sports broadcasting and I know that in some particularly loud environments like Formula 1 and some football stadia, they have a problem being able to pick-up and broadcast the commentator's voice distinctly."

"OK, that's interesting, someone has mentioned on-body microphones for the police and even rugby referees, but I would imagine the broadcasters' have really high quality thresholds, maybe integrating the technology directly into the microphones could work."

"Looks like no end of possibilities. I could spend all day here going through the technology, but we probably ought to get back while I still have time to go through the documents we discussed?"

In the end it was a good couple of hours before Phil and John sat down again to talk through the offer. Phil rubbed his eyes, tired after some serious reading time. "Jesus, these guys have got small print in the small print. Let me go through what seems to be the high, or maybe more appropriately, the low lights." He had made a bulleted list of points on a pad. He starts ticking them off.

“So Benni takes thirty percent of the shares for the initial investment of two fifty.

"This values the company at a little over eight hundred thousand.

"This dilutes the original investors so that your mother and the University go from twenty percent each to fourteen, Giles and Björn's share goes down from two percent each to one point four and the TECHub's drops to nought point seven percent. Altogether that leaves you with thirty-eight point five percent.”

Phil looks up and John nods, to show that he’s following.

"However, Benni is offering you a hundred thousand as a personal loan on good terms. He’s doing it as a ‘convertible loan’, which means he can convert the loan into shares, *your* shares at any time. into equity, by taking ten percent of the equity in the form of your shares at any time, unless you repay in full. So if he exercises this, then this is would be a straight transfer of ten percent of the shares from you to him; he would end up with forty percent and you are down to twenty percent.”

“Yes but there’s still the other shareholders.” John protested.

“Of course, but while I assume your mother would always support you, you can't always assume that the University will always be on your side.”

“But …” John started to argue, but then thought better of it, Simon had told him that the University was under pressure to get a quicker return on the technology.

Phil continued, "The balance of the shares could become very important when it comes down to how the Board looks at the company’s performance against the targets. As the MD you will be held responsible. Under *these* terms, *you* could be forced to forfeit some of *your* shares if the company fails to meet the targets or KPIs that have been set in the plan. And as the largest shareholder he has the right to purchase those shares.”

John is starting to go pale as he sees his company slipping away. But Phil hasn't finished. "If things get really tough, then he, or rather the Board, which he controls, could even fire you and any shares you still hold would be returned to the company for him to buy. And If he holds more than sixty percent of the shares he could trigger Clause thirty-seven, which enabled him to buy-out the remaining shareholders and take complete control of the company relatively cheaply."

"Oh shit!" John exclaimed, "Giles said it looked bad, but this is crazy – he's trying to steal my business from right under me."

"Now it could be that his lawyer is just being overly cautious, and there is a good business reason for each one of these conditions, but together I believe it gives him too much power. The question remains, do you trust him not to use these powers, apart from in exceptional circumstances?"

John frowned, "From what I've heard that's a definite no, I have no reason to trust him and plenty of reasons not to. He got my wife and her boss beaten up at another company he has shares in."

"Doesn't sound like the sort of guy you want to negotiate with."

"No, you're right. Oh God Phil what am I going to do? I need that cash. Do I just give up, let the dream die? I'm sure that's what Lucy wants me to do."

"No one can tell you what to do. You have achieved a lot and that advancement of the knowledge will not be lost, it gets retained by the University and may still get taken forward —"

"— But not by me."

"No John, not by you. You have to decide how important it is to you. To be honest you are in a funny position, from the demonstration we've just seen and the likely interest from the MOD, there is the potential that the value of the IP and the company could rise substantially if you can afford to wait. That would make the Benni offer a bad deal purely in financial terms. However, you will find it hard now to attract another investor, they don't like coming in when the cash has run out. The technology has clearly got potential and there is market interest, if only you can hang on a bit longer."

"Thanks Phil," John sounded despondent, "I really appreciate you going through things, it's clearer now, but no simpler in terms of my options."

"I know John, let me have a chat with my contacts, this is certainly too big for me on my own, but let me look at some options. I really don't want you to have to rush into a decision that you may regret."

***

Lucy was at the DMM office when her phone rang, it was John, but she was not ready to talk to him yet, she pressed *ignore* on the small screen, the phone was silenced. There had been a subdued atmosphere all morning, the whole team was in, but there was a sense of foreboding, some would be leaving that night and not returning. Even the Sales Team, Jules and Tina, were in, though Lucy had not expected them back, there was an "all for one and one for all" feel that had drawn them in. All that was, except Jason. He had been released from hospital, arm plastered, bandaged ribs, bruised kidneys, but he would live. And he should have been there, Lucy thought. There had been plenty of gasps from the team when they had first seen Lucy's black eye, and she knew that with Jason's injuries she had to come up with some sort of explanation. So she had said there had been a drunken intruder that night, that there had been a scuffle in the office, punches were thrown and Jason had been pushed down the stairs in the melee, resulting in his injuries. The drunk had run off, nothing had been stolen or broken and so Jason had decided not to involve the police. Lucy wasn't convinced that the team believed her story, but it didn't really matter now.

She stepped out of the main office and into the Conference Room and shut the door. She took a deep breath and returned John's call. John answered straight away.

"Lucy, how are you, how's your eye? You shouldn't have gone in," he garbled.

"I'm fine John," she hoped that she sounded better than she felt, "I had to come in." There was a pause, neither knew quite where to go next. Lucy broke the silence. "Did you see Phil, did he come in this morning?"

"Yes. He's only just gone. He went through the documents and confirmed pretty much what Giles had picked up from the offer. It looks like Benni is trying to trick me out of the company, to take the IP and get me out of the way. I can't let that happen Lucy, I'm going to have to tell him *no*."

"Oh thank God, I'm so relieved John. I don't really know what this means for the company or for us or where we go now, but I really didn't want that man in our life. I've never even met him, but he seems to haunt me. We'll work it out John. Together we'll work it out."

"I know. But we were so close. I really felt that we were nearly there with the technology. That we had got something that would make a difference." Lucy could hear the emotion in his voice, but this hardened her.

"John, I don't care about the technology, this was hurting people, real people."

"I know but ..."

"— I don't want to talk about it now John, I've got to go."

She hung up.

***

Later that day John got another call on his mobile. "Phil, I hadn't expected to hear from you so soon, I thought your investment group didn't meet until later in the month?"

"No John, you're right, I haven't talked to them yet. Have you responded to the investment offer yet?"

"I have, but after talking to Simon here at the Hub, I decided to send a holding email for now. 'We're evaluating... Lots of interest... comparing offers…' You know the sort of thing. You never know, he might come back with something more straightforward, but to be honest ..."

"I know, you'd probably still have to say no. Once the trust has been broken it's difficult to contemplate going into partnership with someone who has tried one on. If it was a straight sale at a decent price, then that would be different, but under an investment offer you have to work with them and that really requires a positive chemistry... And well, with this guy, that chemistry seems, pretty toxic. But that's not really why I called."

"OK, what's on your mind? And if I didn't say so properly before, I really appreciate your input and advice earlier."

"No problem. I was thinking about your cash position. I don't do lending, it's too easy to fall out, but when you worked for me, before your head was turned, you were a damned good project manager. How do you fancy some contract work? We've still got a lot on, and I'm sure the management team would welcome an extra pair of hands, it can be part time and pays well."

"That's a really good idea Phil, thanks for thinking of me."

"No problem, you don't have to decide straight away, take a few days to work out your time commitments over the next few months then give me a call, I'll have a word back at Enterprise."

"That's great Phil, appreciate it, I'll get back to you in a couple of days, and I'll let you know if anything develops with Benni."

***

It was late morning when Jason eventually arrived at the offices of DMM, he did not have his customary swagger, he moved quietly, his confidence physically diminished, partly by his injuries, but more than that, by his own reduced sense of self-worth. At first the staff didn't notice him as he edged round the desks, careful to avoid knocking his injured arm. When they did see him they sensed the difference in him and responded in kind, a nod, a wave rather than a call-out or a high-five. Lucy stood as he approached and acknowledged his weak smile, she moved across to the Board Room and held the door open for him. They needed to talk.

"Coffee?" she offered as he passed her. Would this be the last time she offered?

"Sure." he replied. Would this be the last time he accepted?

She went over to the coffee machine and, as she prepared two cups, she watched him through the open doorway as he struggled to remove his satchel-type bag and his jacket with his immobilised arm. It was a pathetic sight, this man that only a few weeks ago would have held the attention of all in the room merely with his presence, was reduced to this. Was she was going to knock him further? She hated to kick a man while he was down, but she had made her decision and it was time for her to go.

She returned to the Board Room with the coffee, placed his in front of him and her own across the table, no longer side-by-side. She closed the door and sat down. He looked at the coffee and then looked up at her. "I'm sorry ..." he started.

"— No, I'm sorry Jason. Sorry, that it's come to this and sorry that I can no longer trust you to act responsibly or honourably." Honour? Where had that come from, Lucy wondered, she hadn't planned to say that, but honouring your position with your staff, honouring your friends, that was a big part of this wasn't it? She had lost respect for him, not just as a businessman but as a person, because he had betrayed those who had supported him. It was wrong she thought when people said that it was not personal, that it was just business, you couldn't separate the two, how could you live your life differently from how you run your business? It was about who you are. No matter what the circumstances, she knew she wouldn't have betrayed those who had supported her over the years.

"I've talked with John and *we* will be turning down the investment offer from your Benni."

Jason's head sagged, but it was with resignation rather than surprise. "Of course," he said quietly, "then this is over." He looked around the Board Room, the framed business award certificates on the wall alongside the case-study posters of successful campaigns. "It was fun while it lasted."

Lucy was not sure quite what she had expected from him, but abject defeatism kind of summed him up at the moment. "So what shall I tell the staff?"

"Oh what does it matter, just tell them to go home."

Lucy shook her head, disappointed in his reaction. "Thanks for that, I'll just go and share the good news with then then." She pushed her chair back angrily and left the room leaving Jason slumped in his chair staring at his coffee.

***

"OK, so what's the plan going forward?" Simon said cheerily, he was good at maintaining the forward momentum of the companies at the TECHub, not allowing them to dwell, or sometimes wallow, in disappointments.

"Find another investor I suppose. The problem I have is keeping the research going in the meantime."

"I guess we've still got some of the grant money left?"

"We have, but I can only draw it down if I can show the matched spend from the company. The University has been good about not chasing payment from us too aggressively, but the invoices still keep coming and I'm out of cash."

"Being bankrupt won't help discussions with investors."

"No, of course I understand that, but what can I do? I'm also worried about keeping Björn on the project. He's the one pushing the technology forward, but if his job security starts looking risky, he's bound to start looking around for other opportunities."

"Sure. The good news is that we're starting to get positive vibes about some of the university-industry research projects, which should be good news for potential investors as well as the academic staff."

"That's great, I can use any good news I can get at the moment."

"Heh, if it wasn't a challenge, it wouldn't be worth doing."

"I'll tell that to the bank manager."

***

Lucy took a deep breath. "OK guys, listen up." She waited while the muted conversations were concluded, work was saved, and chairs scraped as they were turned towards her. Finally, there was silence and she was faced by a room of expectant faces. She sat on the edge of her desk, all their eyes were on her, she was once again filled with the rush of taking responsibility, being in control. Whatever happened now, whatever she did next, she knew that she had found a new inner-strength, knew she could motivate people. She knew she didn't want to lose the thrill of leading a team.

"Right, you all know that things haven't been going well for the last few months. They have now come to a head and it looks like the company won't be able to continue in its current form," she paused, gauging the reaction, some of the younger faces were crestfallen, but there was little real surprise, an unexpected sob from Anne in accounts.

"As you know we've got a small number of projects in progress, which I'd like to wrap up as best we can, but we won't be taking on any new work. Basically, I can't guarantee that the company will be able to pay you going forward, unfortunately the cash position is out of my hands ..."

Charlie stood and Lucy paused to let him speak. "Lucy, we appreciate you being upfront with us, and really we've all been expecting this for a few weeks. A few of us have been talking, and me and Gary have put together a bit of a plan to do our own thing. We didn't want to do anything to hurt DMM, but now seems a good time to try and save some of the business, or at least the clients, for ourselves and try and make a go of it." He looked round at the other staff. "We can't promise all of you a job, but we feel like we've got a good team here, one we want to preserve if we can. So we would like the chance to talk to our existing clients and see if they will come with us so that we can maintain some continuity."

Lucy was stunned into silence. She hadn't known that these conversations had been going on, but she was really proud of the team for pulling together and trying to find their own way out. She realised that Charlie was waiting for her to respond.

"That's fantastic Charlie," she said with some uncertainty, "I don't know quite what to say. I need to talk to some people about how this might work err ..." At that moment the Board Room opened and Jason came out, standing straighter and looking far more assured than when he had gone in.

"Charlie, Gary," Jason stood next to Lucy, commanding their attention, "I couldn't help overhearing, but I'm really pleased that I did. To hear that you want to take this on and keep working together makes me so proud. I have let you down in the past, but I won't let you down now." Lucy could feel the atmosphere change, the staff were sitting up a little straighter, they watched Jason with rapt interest. Lucy moved to the side and sat quiet, happy to let Jason take centre stage.

Jason continued, "Building this company, this team, has been one of my most satisfying achievements, and to hear that the team that has worked so well as DMM may continue makes this current set-back for me easier to bear. Because you must know that this has been my failure, not yours. This business has performed superbly well, every element from sales, tech, graphics," he looked to each of staff members in turn, and each bathed in his approval, "client management and finance, has performed like a well-oiled machine and delivered a first class service and product. You have been let down in leadership and bad decisions made by me. I want you to learn from my mistakes, to be better through my faults, to succeed more through my failure, to gather strength from my weakness.

"Whatever it takes, I will do what I can to help you, if you will let me. I will personally contact each of our top clients and recommend that they continue to work with you. I make a promise to each and every one of you that you will get all money owed to you in terms of your notice periods, final salaries, expenses and commissions, even if I have to make the money up personally. You deserve to be rewarded for what you have achieved and I am only sorry that it can't be more. Finally, DMM is shutting down as soon as practical, circumstances outside my control have made it impossible for me to continue, so I have no need of the desks, the chairs, the computers, the screens, even the plants. Take whatever will help you get started. Let the closing acts of my business be the opening of doors and opportunities for you."

Jason's closing remarks were vintage Jason, there was an initial pause as his words sunk in and then the staff team started to applaud, gently at first but rising in sound and in enthusiasm. Tina and Jules were definitely crying now, but they weren't alone, everyone had a lump in their throat and a tear in their eye. One by one they had come up to either shake the hand or to hug their boss. Lucy smiled, she hadn't been at the company long, but she felt the mutual affection and respect that this diverse group of individuals had built up as a team. Even though she could see that Jason was only just holding things together, she knew that this was a much more fitting end to what had clearly been a good business.

Jason extricated himself from the unexpected close embrace of Anne, "Now clear your desks and head down to the Crown, the drinks are on me."

Lucy was the last to stand. She watched Jason as he watched his team leave his company, probably for the last time.

She put her arm around his shoulder, "Well done, you did the right thing in the end. That was the old Jason, the one they were proud to work for, the one they followed."

His body sagged from the emotion of the moment. "I wanted this to finish on my terms, my timing, rather than Benni's. If I'm not going to run this company, neither is he."

She turned towards him and hugged him hard. "You can start again, you've got the talent, the charisma." She stepped away from him and looked into his face. "You can build another team."

He looked at her hopefully, "Would you ...?"

"I don't think so Jason, I've got my own rebuilding to do."

She was conscious of another presence in the room, she turned round and saw Gary and Charlie hovering by the doorway, Gary beckoned her over.

"Can we have a word?"

"Sure," She turned and looked back at Jason, who was looking around the office forlornly, "but let's step outside."

They made their way down the stairs in silence until they got to the red door and then out onto the street. "Was he serious about us taking the stuff?" Gary asked sheepishly, embarrassed that the question might appear insensitive.

"Sure," replied Lucy, "he certainly meant it. Though I don't really know where we stand legally." She thought - I guess at the moment, he stills owns the company, he hasn't gone bankrupt, and so he can do what he wants. But she had better play it safe. "Let me check with the accountant, just to be sure."

"Thanks that would be great," said Gary, the two of them fidgeted nervously.

"Was there something else?"

Charlie and Gary exchanged looks, as if they were egging each other on. In the end Charlie took the lead. "Yes," he cleared his throat, "we'd completely understand if this isn't suitable, and we can be flexible, what with you having a kid and all."

Lucy looked confused. "What are you asking?"

"Oh right, we'd like you to join us, our new company, to manage us, so to speak. We think you're, well, really organised and good at keeping us in line. We don't what you'd be called exactly."

"Mother, by the sound of it," she laughed.

"No, right, we didn't mean that. You're really good with the clients as well, and the money side."

Lucy was quite taken aback, and realised that they must have found it difficult to ask her. Probably thought that she was too close to Jason. And the way that they were looking at her expectantly made her realise just how far she had come in the last nine months. They wanted her to run their business.

"Charlie, Gary, I really am so flattered to be asked and I'm excited by the prospect of building a new business with you, but to be honest I really don't know if I could jump straight into it."

The lads looked a little crestfallen. "We could pay you. Probably not what you're getting here, at least not at first, and we can give you shares. I suppose you'd be a Partner."

Partner? Lucy smiled. "It's not the money," she said, though she hadn't even thought about what she and John were going to live off. "I just feel that I need to help Jason wind the company up. What I can do is help you with the company set-up and introduce you to a good accountant and push Jason to organise the discussions with the current DMM clients. And then, in a few weeks, when things have settled down, we can talk again. I don't want you to rush in to taking me on before you've even got going."

"We appreciate that Lucy, and your help in the setup will be really useful." Charlie replied. "On the management side, we've been thinking and planning this for a while. We think that you've got the right organisational ability to coordinate and pull together the different strands of the business, as well as being confident to be able to talk with clients. If we don't have you, then we can't manage the smart, lean structure that we're after. So take the time you need Lucy, but when you're ready we need you."

Lucy was finding it hard to believe that this was the same Charlie that last week was playing juvenile practical jokes on the sales girls, he'd suddenly matured and was taking his responsibilities seriously. But more than that, Lucy realised that Charlie wasn't making a panicky decision to employ someone to do the work that they didn't want to do, this was more strategic, more planned. She knew that she should treat Charlie and the offer with the respect it deserved.

"Thank you Charlie. I really value the offer, it would be great to sit down with you and Gary and go through your plans and see where I can contribute. Just give me a few weeks to sort out Jason and my home life."

"Done. That's great." Charlie and Gary beamed at each other and shared a high-five. The serious business faces were gone, the surfer and the Goth were back."

CHAPTER THIRTY

John kicked himself that he hadn't attended with Björn. It had seemed such an academically orientated conference. Reading through the abstracts of the papers to be presented, he could find little that he could understand, let alone that interested him. That was the problem with the medical applications, despite his interest in autism, John found it difficult to follow the scientific discussions as the terminology was completely alien to him. The security applications of the EarStream technology were so much simpler for him to comprehend and address, it was just a case of *hearing the bad guys* better. With the medics, there was a greater need to present the underlying theory and to show how the electronic output from the technology would interact with the human auditory system and the brain. Of course the *how* it worked was important, but John was far more interested in the *what* it could do. So Björn had attended the conference in Berne with Dr Lowe. It would be the first formal presentation of Björn's paper aimed at the medical applications of the technology.

On their return Björn had looked particularly pleased with himself and even Dr Lowe was quite effusive about the response the paper had received from rival academics. He particularly liked it when one of his protégés presented *his* work, it made him look magnanimous when it went well and shielded his reputation when not. "Professor Leopold from Vienna referred to it as the 'Holy Grail' of auditory science," he proclaimed to all who would listen in the Engineering School Departmental Meeting. "Apparently we will have problems holding on to our young star," he said as he shone his own limelight on to a flustered Björn. "'Quite the catch', they say." Dr Lowe beamed at his young apprentice, "But I think that our Björn knows where his future lies." Björn smiled, he enjoyed the attention, but he definitely didn't look that sure that he knew when his future lay.

There was quite a market amongst the universities for poaching researchers from one institution to another, especially where an academic appeared to be on the cusp of an interesting new field of research, or looked likely to attract funding. While, like with every job, salaries were a key element, the incentives for an academic to move were often more related to the offer of bigger and better facilities, more research staff and technicians, and most important of all, the freedom to continue and to concentrate on their own research.

"Wow, that must have been quite a presentation," John congratulated Björn after he had heard the story of the paper and the reaction of the audience afterwards. "Do you sing and dance as well?" John hoped that the remark didn't appear ungracious, he realised he was in danger of getting overly possessive about any attention the technology received that didn't include him. Fortunately, either Björn didn't pick up on the sarcasm, or he just ignored John's flippant remarks, as he normally did.

"No. Yes?" Björn wasn't sure what the right response was, "but there is more, much more."

"More? What do you mean more?"

"Lots of academics liked the paper, clinicians too, so David got very excited, but all the companies, they all want to talk to us, to you." Björn held out a fan of business cards. John could see the names of Philips, GEC, Medtronics, as well as many smaller, less well-known companies, some of which John recognised from the market research, but also new names.

"And not just for hearing problems, there was interest for ADHD, dementia as well as autism. John, they were all over it, asking about our stage of development, licensing, patents."

Later that morning, as Simon walked through the Hub, he came across John leaning against the wall by his office door. He looked lost in thought. As Simon opened the door for him, John's trance was broken. He spoke as if he had just woken from a deep sleep, "I feel like I'm standing on the edge of a precipice Simon," he said shaking his head. "I can see the other side. See the market potential, the business partnerships, the products. But how do I cross that chasm? Don't get me wrong, it's great that Björn's paper has attracted such interest from the medical companies, just as it's great that the security businesses are starting to knock on the door. But it still doesn't help me. They all want to see *more* development; they all want *time* to evaluate the technology. But how do I pay for it, how can I buy us more time.

"I really believed that Benni was the answer to my prayers, but now I feel like I'm in a worse position than I was before met him."

"Heh," said Simon trying to be positive, "there will be other investors out there. Benni may have been a pratt, but he was a pratt with a good eye for a business opportunity. Not all investors are going to try and screw you"

"That's as maybe," John was not so easily cheered. "But it will take time to find another investor, time I haven't got. Everyone is slapping Björn on the back, banging on about the great potential of the technology, of the company, meanwhile I'm running out of cash, both for the business and for me personally."

Simon could understand John's dilemma; he wouldn't be the first promising company in the TECHub to run out of cash before the technology got to investment or revenue. As the cash position worsened, so the entrepreneur was all the more likely to make rash decisions which could undervalue the business and the technology or bring in the wrong partners.

Simon didn't want to rub salt in to John's wounds, but felt he must be honest. "Not to forget John, the IP doesn't legally transfer into the business until the current R&D funding programme has been completed."

John looked up at Simon sharply, almost suspiciously, "What happens if all this industry attention leads to a licensing offer for the IP before the programme has finished?"

"Well, it depends on the University, but an offer for the IP *now* would be an offer to the University, you don't own it. How much is still left of the grant?"

"About fifty grand I think, but what's the point if I can't spend it. I can only draw it down if I can provide the matched funding."

"OK, yes you're right. But at least the new industry interest will give potential investors more confidence. There's nothing an investor likes more than a customer chomping at the bit to get hold of the product.

"Look, we have another investor event at the end of the month, I can probably squeeze you in to have a pitching slot, if you're up for it." John looked more hopeful, "But, as you know," warned Simon, "we can't guarantee a quick result. The due diligence and legals on these deals always take time, even if the investor is keen."

"I know, I know. There are no quick fixes in the investment game. Thanks Simon, can you pencil me in and I can start on the presentation?" John walked slowly to his desk. As Simon turned to leave, John looked up to him again and said, "I guess in the meantime it all comes down to the patience of the University."

Simon nodded to John, but as he walked away he thought to himself - *and that's not something you necessarily want to rely right now. Especially when the research is attracting so much academic and commercial interes*t.

***

It felt odd for Lucy not to have anywhere to go, no work projects to fret over, no staff to cajole or clients to schmooze. Well, she thought, as she snuggled under the warm duvet, I could dedicate myself to my family for a while, be a loving wife and doting mother, or should it be the other way round? She threw off the covers with renewed energy, ready to embrace her role as home-maker. After a quick shower, she felt alive. She was singing as she went into Daniel's room, she drew back the curtains letting the weak morning sun fill the bedroom. Daniel's head buried deeper under the cover. "Pancakes, I think this morning; it would be nice to have pancakes for a change."

"Toast," came the muffled reply.

She busied herself with laying out Daniel's clothes for play-school, she picked brighter ones than usual. Then she turned to Daniel, who was still cocooned in bed. "Right you, monkey," she grabbed the edge of the duvet and started to pull, Daniel hung on, he shrieked with laughter, but in the end mum won as she wrestled it away with one hand while she tickled Daniel with the other. As she left a breathless and laughing Daniel, "Pancakes," she announced triumphantly.

"Toast," he shouted back.

Downstairs she happily cleared away John's breakfast plate and cup, not even moaning that it wouldn't have hurt him to put them in the dishwasher. They didn't have enough meals together she thought, she would stop off at the shops on her way home from play-school and pick up something proper for tea, maybe braising steak or lamb stew. Something warming, with gravy and mash. Something homely. As she prepared the pancake batter she looked around the kitchen, they hadn't really decorated properly since they had moved in, just *made-do-for-now*. That attitude had pervaded the whole house and while they had plenty of possessions and pictures that made their house their home, they were underlain by somebody else's decor. It was like renting a flat, you knew it wasn't yours, just a temporary fill. No, she thought they should decorate, brighten the place up, they might not be able to afford new carpets, but hell, they could manage a few pots of emulsion. She would use the few weeks she had before she had to decide whether to start work again to spruce the place up, clear out the junk that they had allowed into their house and into their lives.

Lucy beamed at Daniel as he came into the kitchen, she chatted to him abstractly, not really saying anything, just interacting. She could see that her good mood was having a positive effect on him. He seemed more aware of her and his surroundings. She made a big thing of tossing the pancakes and Daniel gasped at the skill and danger of it all. She laid the plate of pancakes on the table next to the toast and was delighted when Daniel reached for the pancake.

That's what we all need, John, Daniel, herself and the house, time and attention. Time and attention to rebuild the family and to properly make this place their home.

***

The TECHub 'Investor Pitch Day" was set to start at five. Simon always felt nervous, not for himself, he had run many such events, but nervous for his businesses. Pitching your idea to a room-full of strangers was a daunting process. And not any room-full of strangers, these were *investors*, mythical beings that potentially had the future of these business in their hands.

How do you play it? Should you hype it up? Play the big, confident entrepreneur? Act as though your business would be the 'next big thing', move over Uber, step aside Deliveroo, there's a new kid on the block. But Simon had seen so many crash and burn. The big sell had to be backed up. Investors were an understandably cynical lot – they're putting up their own money after all.

"Play it straight" was always his advice. If you give the investors the right product and market information, and the idea is good enough, then they will see the opportunity. Investors like to follow their gut instincts, so give them enough to entice them – make them feel that they have discovered a gem. Don't bang them over the head with it. The bigger the sell, the harder they will look to pick holes in it.

Two pitches down and three to go, the investors were refilling their coffees and chatting about the two presentations they had seen. The 'Look Local' App for finding reliable tradesmen had attracted the most interest, a neat twist on the usual business model. The 'Kapputt' match-three game had got short shrift from the room – the game was not even at alpha stage and had no real market data to back it up. Simon was certain that the two young aspiring games designers would think that these old farts just *didn't get it*, but in reality it wasn't a great pitch.

Simon approach John at the edge of the room. John looked edgy, while he was seated his whole body looked taut, his feet were shuffling. This was *too* important to him.

"Ok John, you're up next," Simon said calmly. "Just play it straight, like we went through in practice sessions."

The presentation had gone well, John thought, their R&D had produced enough positive results to show real progress and, as Simon had predicted, the direct industry interest from potential customers had driven a lively question and answer session from the audience. The worst thing, he had heard, was to get no questions –

it definitely wasn't a vote of confidence that you had covered the subject comprehensively.

So now was the clincher, could he convert those questioners into investors. The pitching session was run so that all the entrepreneurs were invited back at the end to mingle and chat with the investors. Active discussions at this stage were a very positive sign, assured Simon. So John was genuinely pleased when two of the investors made a beeline for him when he entered the room.

"It's John isn't it," started the first, an intelligent looking lady in her mid-forties, she was dressed in smart business attire as if she had come straight from a Corporate office. "I'm Carol, Carol Moore. I was very interested in the EarStream technology." She looked so intensely at John that he was concerned that he wouldn't be able to hold her gaze. "I represent my family's investment fund; we are quite active in the field. We have ..." She trailed off as another person joined them.

"Can I join you," John looked around towards the voice, quite relieved, it was an older gentleman, quite scruffy in comparison, he looked like he'd just wandered in from a walk in the park. "I'm Andrew, I also liked the look of your technology. I've done a fair bit of electronics myself."

Carol looked a little peeved to be interrupted. She fished into her bag and pulled out an expensively embossed business card, which she proffered to John. "Give me a call John," she looked daggers at the older man, "when we can have a *private* conversation." With that she was gone, out of the conversation and then out of the room.

"Well," said Andrew with a smile, "I guess my interjection wasn't welcome. Let's hope I can make our conversation worthwhile."

John instantly felt quite comfortable with Andrew. He had a practical and personable manner about him. As the conversation deepened John realised that it was because he was approaching EarStream more as an engineer than as an investor. John allowed himself to be monopolised by Andrew, who seemed to be more intent on presenting his own experience to John than in asking more in-depth business questions about EarStream.

It was only when Simon came over tapping his watch, "Last orders gents," that John realised that everyone else had gone and that he and Andrew had been talking intently for the best part of an hour.

"I'll be in touch soon," assured Andrew as he struggled back into his jacket. "Very soon." And with that he was gone.

"That looked promising?" Simon said as he collected up the last of the coffee cups. "Andrew is usually quite quiet at when I've seen him before, I've never seen him take such an interest."

"Yes," said John, "I like him. Do you know his background?"

"Had his own electronics business, I believe, sold it ages ago. I guess he's been kicking his heels ever since. He's turned up to these events a few times, but I haven't known him make an actual investment as yet. Did I see you talking to Carol as well?"

"Hmm yes. I liked Andrew, got on with him. Not sure about Carol, she seemed a bit aloof."

"Beggars can't be choosers, or so they say. Let's see what transpires shall we." Simon finished his tidying and heads for the door. "Some of us have got homes to go to."

***

Lamb shanks, mashed potatoes and sprouts. OK the shanks were part of an M&S ready meal, and it was microwave mash rather than cooked from scratch. But it would still be warming and homely and oozing with rich gravy. She'd done Daniel's meal earlier; she'd wanted this time alone with John. She'd laid the table, napkins and everything, and opened a bottle of red, just cheap stuff, part of an offer, but still wine. Still special. And she waited for John to come home.

She knew that he was 'pitching' tonight, though she wasn't exactly sure what that meant. But she had hoped that he would be home by eight. He hadn't phoned or sent a text, but he was busy, she knew that. By nine, the sprouts were looking a little stewed, but heh, they would still taste good in the gravy. She heard the key in the door. She pushed any disappointment down, there was still time for this.

She rushed out to the hall and helped him out of his coat. "How did it go? The pitch? How did it go?" She took his arm and ushered him into the kitchen.

"It was good. Went well. Better than I expected." John looked around, taking in the laid kitchen table, the wine, the candle. "Have I missed something? Are we celebrating?"

"Just the fact that we're all together and we've got our home and our health. All the important things," she said as she served the shanks, mash and sprouts onto two plates. "You pour the wine."

John obeyed, he poured two large glasses and then sat, looking at Lucy through the candle light. "Daniel?"

"He's in bed. He's fine. You'll never believe it; he chose pancakes this morning over toast. Pancakes!" She placed his plate in front of him. "The sprouts may be a bit soggy, but you can never overcook a shank," she said with her best smile as she joined him at the table.

"Cheers," John raised his glass, "to Ear—"

"—To us," she interrupted.

"To us," he clinked his glass to hers. "And talking of EarStream …"

"We weren't." She continued to smile up at him. "I think we should decorate the lounge. Red and gold, I think."

"I met this really interesting chap tonight, Andrew, had his own electronics business, which he sold."

"At least with those colours, we can just about get away without changing the carpet or the sofa. Maybe just some new cushions to tone in."

"Red yes, sounds good. Anyway this Andrew, I think he may invest. He sounded really interested."

"John, just tonight, leave it. Let's talk about something else. Talk about us for a change."

They ate the rest of their meal in silence.

***

"John. John is that you? It's Andrew from the Pitch event." John's head was heavy, he'd stayed up last night and finished the wine. Lucy had gone to bed, early, hadn't even washed up.

"Oh Andrew. Yes of course. Thanks for getting back to me so quickly." John shook his head, trying to clear his brain. "How are you?"

"I'm good. Couldn't stop thinking about the EarStream project last night. What we could do to accelerate things."

John's heart leapt, he had said 'we', he had said 'accelerate', these were the type of words he needed to hear. "That's great Andrew, really great." He wondered how hard to push the conversation. He wished Simon or Giles were here to guide him. "We should get together. Go through the plans."

"Sounds good John. Can't wait to get started."

He sounded so keen, John had to ask. "So Andrew. Just so I can prepare an updated project timetable. How much money are you thinking of putting in?"

"Money? On no money John. What *I've* got money can't buy. *Experience*, that's what this project needs. Add my years on the front line with all this University stuff you've got going on and I really believe we can make something happen …"

John was stunned. "But we need money Andrew. I was pitching for investment, equity investment."

"I can promise you my hard and soul John. Sweat equity, isn't that what they call it. You don't even have to pay me, not at first anyway. Just expenses."

"You don't understand Andrew. I need money. Money to keep the lab work going. Money to prove the technology. I have to have investment."

"You and me together John. A team like us, we'll find the money."

"I'll get back to you Andrew." John turned off the phone, not waiting for the reply. Sweat equity, he couldn't even afford his own sweat equity.

***

Simon caught up with John in the café. "How's it going? Looked like you certainly attracted some interest last night."

"You wouldn't believe it. That Andrew guy. The one I spend hours talking to."

"The electronics guy. Could be a good fit," said Simon positively.

"Sure great bloody fit he is. I thought you vetted these investors?"

"What do you mean *vet*? Successful businessman. Sold up a few years back. What's to vet …"

"He's got no money Simon. No fucking money. He expects me to pay him!"

"Oh shit. I'm sorry John. We don't personal financial checks. He seemed kosher."

"Kosher. But no cash. Who'd have believed it."

***

They crossed in the hallway. Lucy was just collecting her bits together as John came through the door. "God, I'm glad you've got here. Gary and Charlie have an issue with one of the old DMM clients. Well one of my old clients, actually. I'm going to do some schmoozing. Hopefully I haven't forgotten how."

"What? OK, sure. Daniel?"

"He's in the lounge. He's had his tea. Cheesy jackets tonight for us – I didn't get to the shops. See you later." She was gone.

John sighed. He didn't resent Lucy going. Funny he thought, she'd earn more in a few hours this evening helping the boys out than he'd earned in months. Hardly the breadwinner, was he?

He took off his coat and stowed his bag. He hadn't brought any work home tonight. Couldn't see the point. The call with Andrew had really knocked him sideways. How could the guy have no money?

He went through to the lounge.

"Daniel. DANIEL, daddy's home." No reaction. Daniel sat, as he so often sat, in front of the telly, but not apparently watching it. His cars were lined up on the table next to him. Today's chosen one, a green Volkswagen Beetle, was undergoing a thorough examination as Daniel turned it slowly in front of his eyes, squinting at the curves and contours.

John decided to leave him be. He slumped down in the armchair in the corner and watched his son. Not with anger, or disappointment, just helplessness.

***

“John, I shouldn’t really be telling you this,” said Simon conspiratorially.

“What is it Simon. I could really do with good news right now.”

“Not sure this counts. You remember Carol, the lady investor at the Pitch event.”

“Sure,” John looks up hopefully. “I meant to call her, but the Andrew thing threw me. Has she been in touch.”

“Actually yes. She called me yesterday, after you’d gone home for the night –.”

“You could have called me Simon. I’d have spoken to her.”

“That’s just it John, she wasn’t calling for you. She was asking for a contact in the University to talk to about the patents. Apparently one of their other investments …” Simon trailed off, seeing the look on John’s face.

“Give me some time Simon. Can you do that? Find me some time to find the money.”

“I’ll try John, but this time, time is not within my gift.”

***

John knew that he had already made the decision, despite the list of pros and cons he had been writing distractedly on the pad in front of him. He knew he couldn't turn back now, whatever the consequences. He reached for the phone.

"Good afternoon. I'd like to talk to someone about a business loan secured against my house."

CHAPTER THIRTY-ONE

John and Lucy had often talked about moving back to Brighton. But not like this.

For them it had become aspirational, somewhere to live out an affluent family life when their careers had matured to provide a level of comfort. A place where they could potter round the quirky, independent shops in the Laines, or the seafront, or the theatre. Where weekends would be spent in idle leisure, sunshine filled, sipping cappuccinos in a street cafe while a busker played cool jazz on a mellow saxophone and the beautiful but often eccentric locals walked on by. They would read the papers in the knowledge that there was little in the headlines that would disturb their comfortable existence. Even in their musings, they hadn't assumed wealth, they'd never expected that, and indeed up until a few months ago, they hadn't been doing anything that could have led to wealth. They didn't dream of lottery wins or unexpected windfalls just that their life was on a course to comfort. Their dream was simply not having to worry that much about money, just to have enough to get by. But not like this.

The City had its extremes, from the celebrity rich in their seafront apartments to the abject homeless poor looking for shelter in the shop and office doorways. From the mass of students living, partying, studying along the Lewes Road leading to the campus to the hope-sapping estates. Much was made of the vibrancy and colour of the large community of creatives, designers, artists, film and TV producers, directors, actors and writers. But what made this such a positive place was that so many people came to live here as a lifestyle choice. They hadn't moved here because their work was here, they had come because they could *get* to their work from here or that they could *do* their work from here. There were many who worked from home, self-employed or freelancers. They'd chosen to be here for the lifestyle, for the people, for the culture. But not like this.

He had come because he had nowhere else to go. This was not how he had imagined it. And worse he had never imagined coming back alone.

The slick, be-suited letting agent, little more than a boy himself, left him alone to look around the cramped, dingy space. It wouldn't take John long, there was little more than a tiny galley kitchen which formed part of what was optimistically called the *living room*, but that was at least a contrast to the previous property they had visited where the tiny single bedroom looked like it had seen its fair share of death. He didn't even look for the bathroom, confident that it was unlikely to contain a walk-in wet room or sunken bath, John was prepared to assume the worst. Christ, he thought to himself, had he really sunk this low? Strange, when you thought of an entrepreneurial lifestyle, you thought of attic studios and riverside apartments, this wasn't what came to mind. As bad as it was for him, at least he could keep it to himself, he knew he could never, would never, bring Lucy or Daniel here. He had lived more comfortably when he had been a student, at least then he had had friends to share his digs with. But in those carefree days he hadn't had another house to pay for, plus the extra mortgage for the business. Here he was utterly alone in his squalor, his debt and his feeling of abject failure.

The young agent returned, his nose twitched with distaste at the squalid living quarters. He looked on John with pity. He probably assumed that John was one of the many separated or newly divorced men slipping down the housing ladder. Or perhaps it was only a ladder when you were climbing, it was definitely a snake when you started to fall.

"I'll take it," John said with resignation. There was no point looking round or even questioning the details, that would mean that he was considering this as an option long-term, and John could never accept that and carry on with any confidence in the future. "What's the shortest period I can take it for?"

***

Lucy couldn't believe it had come to this, she was alone in their double bed. Sure John had been away many times before, but this felt different, was different. The bed felt cold, empty, devoid of love. Even when they had been at their lowest together, when they had each retreated to their edge of the bed, he had still been there, their warmth had mingled under the duvet even if their bodies were separate.

John hadn't moved out as such. He just wasn't there. Most of his clothes were still in the wardrobe, his shoes in the cupboard, his books and DVDs on the shelves. He had left with just a holdall of clothes. He hadn't been back for more. Where was he washing them? The thought of him alone in a launderette made her quiver, it seemed so sad, so desolate. Maybe he was taking his washing to his mother's. Oh she'd love that wouldn't she? Back looking after her precious son while his wife neglected him. Lucy could almost hear the whispers of malcontent she would be feeding him. How she, his wife, wasn't supporting him, wasn't caring for him, wasn't loving him.

But that wasn't right, she was supporting, caring and loving him, she just wasn't talking to him, and he not to her. After a while the not talking turned into not listening and now into not seeing. He was now temporarily living somewhere else because he felt that, just for the moment, she and Daniel would be better off without him, better without the atmosphere. And the reason - he had gone back on his word. He had reneged on their agreement, the line they had drawn in the sand, the 'red-line'. He had put their house, their home at risk, for the sake of the company. He had promised, that early morning many months ago now, 'Not the house', and it wasn't a light, idle promise, they both knew and understood that it was a defining promise. The one that separated the financial business risk, from risking the family. The one that said, that above all else, the family was sacrosanct and that they would, should, fight to protect it, to preserve it.

And he had crossed that line, broken the promise. He had come to her with that pre-prepared sheet of paper, that simple request. "Could you just sign here, love, just a bit of admin around the mortgage." Admin my arse, she had thought, he was putting the house up as security for the business. He hadn't asked her. Hadn't tried to explain the position, the problem, the dilemma that had pushed him to disavow himself of his responsibility to his family. No, he had tried to slip it past her, to trick her into signing away their home.

"It's not a problem love, just a short-term cash flow issue, just to tide us over until the investment comes in."

"Investment? Like from Benni you mean? Now I feel so much better," she had said angrily.

She had every right to be angry, every justification. He had crossed the line. And she had reacted as she thought she should. She had shouted, she had sworn, she had called him names. And he had left. But not before she had signed that bloody piece of paper.

But really she hadn't been that angry, not deep down, not about the money anyway. When it came down to it, the red-line wasn't the money, wasn't the house, it was them. She was hurt that he hadn't come to her to share the problem, to ask for her help. Sad that he hadn't realised, known that she would want to help, to understand the problem and share it. But while they were at the red line, they hadn't crossed it yet. They were close, but she believed that they would stop short of crossing that line, of completely giving up on each other.

Her reaction to him had been pre-programmed. She should be angry because he had gone back on his word and betrayed her trust. It was right that he had left, whether she had pushed him out or if it was of his own volition, driven by guilt. And it was right that he should suffer for a while, have a chance to feel his guilt. God she thought, she could hear her mother's words. "Go to your room and think about what you have done." It hadn't worked beyond age fourteen had it? But this was different, this was a grown-up betrayal of trust. She deserved to be able to wallow in self-righteous indignation. It was just that she didn't really feel it. She missed him. She worried about him. She didn't want him to go to his mother's because then he wouldn't need her as much. It was important that they all need each other, she, John and Daniel, they were tied by mutual love and mutual need.

So how long should she make him suffer? More to the point, how long should she make herself suffer? She could only surmise his pain, she felt her own. He might be out there rediscovering his bachelor days, having a whale of a time. Perhaps he was out every night on the University Campus, seducing young students with his sophisticated ways. She laughed to herself, John didn't have sophisticated ways. Maybe not, but compared to her they were young and exciting, not tired and jaded, worn down by life and, she felt her face, battered. And they might be impressed by his passion for his project, his entrepreneurial zeal, his desire to do something for his son. Yes, they might be attracted to that. It was funny, in the movies, a single man with a kid was attractive, somehow made the man seem more sensitive, but for a woman a child was just a tie, baggage. Yes, she could see that, John talking passionately about his son and his desire to develop technology to help him would impress idealistic students. Funny, she thought, he wouldn't even know he was doing it. Wouldn't know that he was attractive, he was naive like that, thank God. She didn't think he would go looking for solace. He was more likely to heap blame on himself and torture himself about what he had done.

No, she doubted that he found any pleasure in this. John was a good man, a good husband, a good father. She knew deep down that he was doing EarStream for all the right reasons, she just hoped that the destination was worth what they were going through on the journey.

***

John stood alone at the ready-meal aisle in the garage. 'Pot Noodle'? Did people actually eat these things?

It had been quite a few days in the bedsit and John thought it really was about time he had something hot to eat in the evening. The family evening meal had been such a simple highlight with Lucy and Daniel, one that he had not appreciated enough. Not that there was anything wrong with his now, habitual, cheese and apple and ham. It was the 'three-for-two' offers on the deli items that always seemed to be running in his local supermarket, that had sucked him in. It lured you in to buying more than you needed for a single meal. Then whatever he ate, he always had something left over for the next day, but not enough for a complete meal. Whether it was a spare apple, or maybe ham nearing its date, there was always something remaining that prompted you to replenish your supplies rather than abandoning food and setting off in a new culinary direction. So it seemed that three for two was no good for one. It made life so complicated, he longed for the simple solution of takeaways, but the health messages that bombarded the simple consumer had had their effect.

Then another of the great consumer trends had hit him, 'just-in-time-shopping', he didn't have planned meals in the cupboard and the fridge, he had convenience stores that he could pass on the way home. It was just that today, they hadn't been on his way home, and so they had become an inconvenience. A quick stop at an independent garage revealed a plethora of fizzy drinks, snacks, crisps and chocolate bars, but not much in the healthy-eating aisle. Hence the 'Pot Noodle'.

He looked again at the white plastic tub, the dehydrated noodles ready to de-congeal within. He thought of his one remaining apple and the small carton of orange juice on the part broken shelf in the dirty old fridge at the flat. Mmmm tempting, a 'still-life' worthy of a Turner prize, if not a Michelin Star. At least there was one, maybe two of his five a day. He wondered if, along with 'Teflon' and the microwave, the 'Pot Noodle' was one of man's great innovative discoveries resulting from putting a man on the moon. His mind was definitely wandering now, his brain trying to distract his stomach from the unappealing food in front of him. Would it make a good advertising slogan, three for two make five for one?

"Sod it," he said out loud and left the garage to find a Chinese takeaway.

***

Lucy realised that she had become a slob. No work, no husband, no hope. Evenings and sometimes even days, were spent slumped in front of the telly, not caring what she watched, not really watching. Meals were a bare minimum, eaten alone, Daniel pushed off to munch away in front of the telly. She hated herself for being like this. Knew she ought to talk someone, see a doctor or something, this was probably depression. But she couldn't see the point. She blamed herself as much as she blamed John, so she deserved what she got.

Her phone pinged, a text message, probably John trying yet again to get her to meet him, but what was the point. It pinged again, it always pinged twice, must be a setting somewhere on the phone, the persistent sound made it seem urgent, pressing. She reached for the phone.

I need to meet with you, sort a few things out. I'll be there at 8.00. Switching my phone off now, so you can't say no. xx.

Eight, she looked at her watch, she stood and walked out into the hall, she looked in the mirror, she didn't want him to see her like this, not looking needy. The bruising and the black eye had nearly gone, but she looked tired and drawn. No he wasn't going to see her like this. Last time he had seen her she had been in control of a business, of a family and, most importantly, of herself. How quickly she had sunk. She had nearly an hour to transform herself back into a superwoman, she trudged up the stairs like a dawdling bullet.

***

John was working late at the office at the TECHub. He was doing some contracting work for Phil, which took up most of the nine-to-fives, so he was catching up on the EarStream work in the evenings. Phil had been good to his word, and the project work was well paid, interesting and fairly flexible. It did feel good to be part of an IT team again, this was work where he felt confident, knowledgeable and in control, he was respected for his experience, for the projects he had taken on and completed because he'd been there and got the T-shirt - all the things that he didn't feel at EarStream, where he was still finding his way and often felt out of his depth. He was also pleasantly surprised by the reaction of both his former colleagues and new members of the team, to what he had been doing with EarStream. He was suddenly interesting, he had a different type of experience to share, unusual stories to tell, especially of his dealings with unscrupulous investors. They applauded him, even envied him, for having a go. He hadn't appreciated just how far his life had departed from the norm over the last nine months, colleagues listened in awe. He realised that like him, most of them had thought or even dreamt at one time or another of setting up their own business, not just freelancing, but a real business. And he had done it. There was no jealousy from them, just genuine interest and respect.

EarStream was ticking along. The income from the contracting work, had enabled him to get the additional loan on the house to keep the research going with the University. Which was great as long as he didn't think about the personal sacrifice that he had had to make to get the money. He had betrayed Lucy, he knew that, and no matter how well he could justify his actions, or how confident he was that there was little no real risk to the house, that didn't alter the fact that he had gone back on a promise.

But he couldn't dwell on that, it was done and no amount of moping was going to change it or get Lucy and Daniel back. He had to push on and make the business a success and hopefully Lucy would see that the sacrifices had been worthwhile and maybe, one day, she would forgive him. He missed them terribly. He had no sense of freedom or release, he had not re-gained his bachelor life, he had lost his life as a husband and a father. The grungy bedsit, the pathetic meals, these were his punishment.

The talks with both the medical and security companies were proceeding well. Some of the security companies were showing a real commitment by funding additional applied research to test the technology for their particular application of interest. But in working with them, *they* were dictating the research agenda, and what, with the pressure always being applied by Dr Lowe to achieve publishable research results, Björn was being pulled in every direction apart from the one that John wanted. Björn hadn't worked on the autism application for months.

John and Simon had talked about how technology development seldom went in straight lines. Often the most commercial application had to be favoured over the one that drove the passion. You had to prove a commercial market to cover the costs of the R&D. In their case it was the electronic miniaturisation costs. How to move the technology from the surface mounted electronics of the laboratory, with individual components, like resistors and capacitors, mounted on to a circuit board, to an integrated circuit design, with the technology on a tiny silicon chip. While the cost of miniaturisation was way too expensive for a start-up like EarStream, and even for the University, it would result in much smaller components and lower the production cost. This would make many more uses of the technology commercially and practically viable.

For some applications, such as security surveillance, it was the unit size and the reliability factors that were key to the development. Circuit boards were cumbersome in comparison, plus were less reliable in field conditions. So if the security market was to be addressed, someone had to cover the large investment needed to produce the 'technology on a chip'. But once done, it could open up the other markets. Anything wearable in the medical field would need the miniaturisation, but they would then need to go through expensive clinical trials to get the certification as a medical device. So even though Björn's work was proving that the technology could work, the road to actually producing and selling a product was still looking pretty long. John didn't have the resources for this. He needed help.

John checked his watch, it was getting on for seven thirty and he had plans for this evening. He made a rudimentary attempt to tidy the papers on his desk, but in the end just shuffled them into one big uneven pile and shoved them in a drawer and locked it – his version of a 'clean desk policy'. He shrugged into his coat, he had no real idea if it was warm or cold outside. He checked his watch again, quarter to, plenty of time as the traffic should be light now.

***

The doorbell rang shortly before eight, Lucy was showered and changed and felt renewed. She opened the door and looked out expectantly. Jason was standing back from the doorway, respectful of her space as this was the first time he had visited her home. They stood, quiet for a moment as they took each other in. So much had happened in the short time they had known each other. They really weren’t the same people that had held that clumsy interview those nine short months ago. He was looking so much better than when she had last seen him. As his injuries had healed, so he had regained some of his self-confidence. He was standing straighter, filling out his stylish but casual clothes. She noticed a glint of white from his sleeve, so guessed there was still a cast on his arm, but apart from that he looked good. He did, however, appear somewhat reticent of her, as if not sure what to expect. She smiled a welcome and his face lit up. Her hair was still damp from the shower and she was barefoot in her faded skinny jeans.

"Wow, you scrub down well," he said tentatively.

She smiled self-consciously, her hand going up to her damp hair. "You're looking a lot better too. Come in."

"I probably couldn't look a lot worse," he grimaced remembering those unhappy weeks following the attack, "is John here?"

"No I should think he's still at work. He's doing some IT subbing during the day, back with his old firm, so has to do his EarStream work in the evenings." She wasn't sure why she didn't want to say that he'd moved out, but she didn't. She stood back to let him pass into the hallway. She smelt his scent as he passed her, a rich almost oaky perfume, it suited him. John never wore scent, except at Christmas when some relative would misguidedly think that aftershave was a suitable gift for a man who had worn a beard for the last ten years. She closed her eyes as she breathed him in.

"First on the left is the lounge," she said, "do you want a drink?" she offered.

He followed her into the kitchen. "Beer if you have one."

"Sure, but nothing fancy, John likes his traditional northern bitters. Is a Boddies OK?"

"Perfect. How is John?"

"Oh, he's fine, working too hard I suspect, too absorbed in the business. He's still getting plenty of interest in the technology, but they always seem to want him to prove something else before they commit to any money."

It was the way she said it, the way she talked about him, the sadness in her voice, he knew. "He'll come back," he said quietly.

And that was all it took. Her face crumpled as the tears came. "He broke his promise," she managed through her sobs.

"I'm sure he had good reason." He stood helpless watching her, then held out his arms and she collapsed into them as the tears streamed down her face. He smelt her wet hair as he held her, it smelt of apple. "He'll come back," he said again.

It was at that moment, as she was held in the arms of the lover she had never had, but often coveted, that she knew for certain.

***

They held the EarStream Shareholders Meeting in the TECHub's Board room. John was feeling fairly confident, the company's position was difficult rather than desperate, and the money was at least stable. They had the market interest, especially for the medical device applications, but just needed time to do all the extra tests that companies wanted, to answer the technical questions, and do a deal. Giles was in the Chair today and around the table were John, Simon, Dr Lowe and Laura. Björn was at the front of the room giving a technical update.

"So the MOD have agreed to the funding for the multi-language testing —"

"— I suppose they have put a publishing restriction on this work as well," grumbled Dr Lowe. The military had been providing small funding grants to prove that the EarStream technology performed in a variety of environments. And while the results weren't necessarily secret data, the MOD were understandably very sensitive to others knowing what technology they were looking at, and there were often reporting and publishing restrictions imposed. "How is Björn ever going to get his academic recognition, if he can't publish his work?"

"At least it proves that they are still interested, and at some point we will be able to market the results of the tests to others in the security sector which will put us in a great position," Simon interjected. "Giles could you help us draw up some targets for this?" Giles nodded, sagely.

Laura who had been sitting quietly, seemingly distracted, perked up at Simon's comment. "We don't want to do anything that compromises the confidentiality of the University's relationship with the MOD," she said forcibly.

"Oh course not," replied Simon surprised by her reaction, "we're only using it as implied market intelligence, we won't do anything to compromise our confidentiality agreements," said Simon smoothly.

"And don't you dare publish results of the tests you performed for them." Laura stared at Dr Lowe to emphasise her point.

"God forbid an academic publishes anything!" mused the Doctor.

"I just wish they'd make up their minds and make a proper order," John said in frustration.

"So, Björn," Giles tried to get the meeting back on track, "it looks like we're at least meeting all the MOD's requirements."

"Yes, I think so. They seem very pleased. We shall see what they ask for next."

Laura intervened again, this time more positively. "Giles. If the MOD like a technology like this, are they likely to fund it directly through to a final product?"

Giles paused for a moment, giving Laura's question due consideration. "No, the MOD these days try to avoid getting too directly involved in the 'Development' part of the R&D. They are more likely to introduce one of the 'Tier One' suppliers to take it on, one that has a history of successful delivery."

"So how does that move us forward? Do we have to wait for one of these Tier One's to approach us?" John was impatient to see progress. "Or can we go straight to them?" Everyone turned to Giles, it was good to have an expert round the table.

"No, we can be proactive in approaching them, and we can say that we have been talking with the MOD, our contracts with them may well already be a matter of public record, but not the specifics of what we are talking about."

"That sounds more interesting," said Simon enthusiastically, "maybe better to get a few interested. Who knows we could start a bidding war."

"Exactly. I'll talk to some of my contacts, see who is in favour these days amongst the suppliers. Of course there are options with intermediaries as well, companies that will invest in the technology and take it closer to market, either to sell further up the line to the Tier Ones, or to move up the supply chain themselves."

"Great," said Simon, "sounds like the Chair is creating *actions* for himself. That's quite a breakthrough for one of these meetings." There was a chuckle around the table, Giles did have a habit of leaving every meeting having allocated work to everyone else, but no actions for himself.

Giles smiled, as if he had been caught out, "Yes well, I guess I had better get moving on it then."

The meeting broke up on that positive note. Dr Lowe bustled out first, he always seemed anxious to get back to the safety of his lab. Giles remained seated as he made himself some notes in clear bullet points on his pad – must be his military training. Simon caught John's eye and nodded, "Alright?" he prompted, "I know it's slow, but at least it's moving in the right direction."

"Yeah I know," sighed John, "but I could really do with something a bit firmer, just to give me a bit more confidence in the future and something positive to tell Lucy."

"I know," Simon said sympathetically, "but these things take their own time." He looked up and saw that Björn had finished packing up his laptop and papers and was heaving his backpack over his shoulder. Simon waved to him. "Good presentation Björn, see you back in the lab."

"Excuse me, coming through." Laura pushed past Simon, seemingly anxious to catch-up with Björn. "Bye guys," she called over her shoulder. She reached Björn, they shared a look and he took her hand.

"Seems that EarStream is not the only breakthrough that Björn's made recently," he laughed as the couple left the room, but John was now more pensive and had a distant look in his eyes as he watched them.

***

Lucy wasn't getting used to being on her own with Daniel. In the practicalities it was fine. She wasn't working at the moment and Daniel seemed quite settled at the playgroup. To be honest, when John was at home he created more mess than he cleared, so the house was cleaner and tidier without him. Financially things had improved as well. While she would never admit that the loan on the house had been a good idea, that plus the money from

John's contract work and the rather generous redundancy that Jason had paid (from his own pocket she suspected), she and Daniel were comfortable. But comfort didn't fill the hole in her life. She wasn't prepared yet to write off their marriage. Yes, she could manage as a single mum, but life with Daniel was likely to get harder not easier, and while he didn't show it much, she could tell that Daniel missed his father, or maybe she missed Daniel being with his father, or maybe *she* just missed *him*.

She had done what she could to tidy up the projects with DMM, in many ways it was simpler with Charlie and Gary setting up on their own, it offered a way of providing some continuity to their clients, while helping the lads get started. Jason had been good as his word and had handed over far too much office furniture and equipment for the new company to cope, with as they struggled to get set-up in the spare room of Charlie's parents' home. Lucy even suggested that they contact the TECHub about some early virtual office support. Though Lucy didn't know how she would have coped working for them a few doors down from John and EarStream.

No, she still had that decision to make. Charlie and Gary were doing well, but at times their immaturity slipped through. She had had to intervene when she saw their Companies House registration form, The *Surfing Warlock* was not a business name that promised longevity and Charlie's idea of a company logo was something else. So they had settled for 'SEO Simple', which Lucy felt could work. She was going in to see them a couple of times a week, so she may as well have been working, but she wasn't quite ready to make that commitment yet. She knew that she would go back, that she had found something that she was genuinely good at, managing people and projects. She enjoyed the responsibility. But there was no rush.

And Jason, poor Jason thought Lucy. Doing the right thing by Charlie and Gary may have assuaged his guilt, but it had started more unpleasantness with Benni. It was looking increasingly unlikely that Jason would be able to escape Benni and keep his company intact, or his body for that matter.

CHAPTER THIRTY-TWO

The rain poured down, dripping off his already soaked hair and down onto his sodden shirt collar and light jacket. In his defence, he was pretty sure they hadn't forecast rain when he had heard the radio weatherman drone on this morning at his dingy bedsit, and so carrying an umbrella or coat had seemed a needless extravagance. However, he found that radio weather forecasts were one of those things that you think you are listening to, but afterwards, you could not recall a single word that was said. Now the rain and his lack of preparation for it would be yet one more thing that made his standing here feel like such an ignominious failure. Here he was, a supposedly mature married man, a father with responsibilities, a budding tech entrepreneur, standing dripping on his mother's doorstep looking for a comfy bed and a decent hot meal. He hadn't called ahead, wanted it to appear like a spontaneous surprise visit, rather than a desperate plea for help. But now his *popping in* had turned into a slopping *in* of a drenched desolate son returning home because his wife had kicked him out and he had nowhere else to go.

And still he stood, loathe to ring the bell or knock on the door for fear of the inevitable look and sigh of disappointment he would get from his mother. He looked behind him, the taxi that had delivered him had moved off. He was stranded. But he couldn't just stand here on the doorstep in the pouring rain. He shifted the weight of the holdall that was slung over his shoulder and turned to leave. Well he couldn't get any wetter, he would walk back into town. As he trudged back up the garden path the door behind him opened.

"Oh for goodness sake, come in and get dry." Her voice was surprisingly light and friendly, not the caustic sarcasm he was expecting.

"Mum, I ..."

"I know son, I know. Don't worry about it now. Let's just get dry and warm and we can talk later. There are dry, warm towels in the airing cupboard and clean sheets on your bed. Why don't you go and have a nice relaxing bath and I'll make you something to eat?"

John felt himself welling up, but he said nothing, just wiped his feet under his mother's watchful eye as he passed her in the doorway and headed up to his old bedroom.

***

It was late afternoon and a weak sun was breaking through the clouds as Lucy entered the cafe where she had arranged to meet them. She and Jason were both avoiding going to the old DMM office. What had once been a place that emanated energy and business creativity was now just a set of abandoned, desolate rooms. Where the once framed Award Certificates had hung, were now just stain marks on the wall. There were still odd bits of unwanted office furniture lying around, like the big Board Room table that had been too big for Charlie and Gary to use. Their office was a place to move on from rather than to return to.

Lucy was first to arrive and had chosen a table big enough to accommodate them all. She ordered her Cappuccino and got out her red and black active file. She had been working on and off for SEO Simple, she was enjoying having the freedom to develop and implement her own ideas for the business rather than always seeking approval from Jason. Charlie and Gary arrived just as Lucy started to sort out her schedule for the next few weeks. Just seeing the two lads together made her smile, they made such an incongruous pair, Charlie with his mane of surfer bleached blonde hair and boarder casual clothes, Gary still the Goth, all pale skin and black clothes. But together they formed a powerful fusion of creativity and technical knowledge.

"How's it going?" she opened as the lads got themselves settled. She hadn't been to their office much for the last few days as Daniel had been at home with a temperature. While they had shared telephone calls and emails, it's wasn't the same as picking up the body language from a face-to-face meeting.

"It's OK, I guess," replied Gary, looking sideways to Charlie for support.

"Come on then, out with it, is it the staff, are Loo and Stacey playing up again?" It was one thing that the lads couldn't cope with, managing the sales girls. They were too close to their own age and too much like the girls they fancied for them to manage with any conviction.

"No they're fine. It's not the staff."

"Well what then?"

"It's some of Jason's old clients …" Gary looked over at Charlie, as if he feared he was breaking a confidence.

"What? What is it Gary, are they messing you around?"

"No, well yes, it's just that Jason has been back in touch with them."

"Jason? Why would Jason be contacting them?"

"It's like he's trying to get them back."

"Get them back? What on earth —?" She was interrupted as Jason noisily entered the cafe.

"There they are, the old team." He was clearly drunk, his face florid and his dark eyes slightly glazed. He swayed as he walked over to their table. He wrapped his arms comradely over Gary's and Charlie's shoulders, "How are you boys? How's my A-Team? We'll soon have us all back together, the A-Team will be back on the streets."

Charlie and Gary tried to shrug off Jason's unwelcome physicality. "Hi Jason," Gary managed limply, "good to see you."

"You'll be seeing a lot more of me as soon as I can get a new office sorted. We'll need to get my furniture moved back."

Gary and Charlie looked more and more alarmed. Lucy knew she needed to step in. 'What do you mean Jason? The A-Team? The furniture? And have you been contacting our old clients?"

"Of course. That's just it, they're *my* clients," said Jason expansively, "they're all *my* clients and you're *my* team."

"Not any more Jason. You've closed the —"

"— Temporary set-back. Nothing more," Jason interrupted. Then lowered his voice as he addressed his ex-employees, "Didn't think you could manage without me, did you?"

Gary stood up, his anger and frustration showed on his face and he almost hissed back, "We were managing just fine Jason, until you ..."

"Gary, Charlie why don't you head back to the office," Lucy intervened, "Jason and I need to have a chat, and I'll call you later."

"That's it. You kids run along, let the grown-ups sort it out." Jason shooed them out with his fingers as if they were naughty five-year olds. The lads walked away, shaking their heads in dismay. As they got to the door Charlie looked back and caught Lucy's eye, he mouthed, "Please," to her and then they left.

Jason turned woozily to Lucy, "And now we're alone." He planted his hand unsteadily on her thigh. "Just the two of us."

She saw that he was having a problem focusing his eyes on her. She removed his hand, firmly placed it on his own thigh and looked him hard in the eye. "What the hell is this Jason?"

"Me? What?" He looked affronted. "Just happy getting the team back together."

"They're not *your* team anymore Jason," she said forcefully, "you let them go. DMM is finished."

"Oh I can replace them," he waved his arm dismissively. "Those junior tech and graphics guys are 'ten-a-penny'. You and me, we can rebuild it. I've got the clients —"

"— You haven't Jason, you gave up the clients —"

"— I can get them back, we can, get them all back, you and me, we're what makes the business –"

"No Jason," she said firmly, "there's no business, and no you and me."

"But there can be." He tried to move to sit next to her, forcing his arm around her. "You've felt it. You and me. We're right for each-other." He leaned his head towards her as if to kiss her. His breathe reeked of red wine. She was suddenly hit by her disgust and disappointment in him.

"Get your hands off me," She said loudly and firmly as she stood. Heads in the cafe turned towards them.

Jason stood up as well, holding up his hands as if in surrender. "Heh, hold your horses, I'm not doing anything. Let's just sit here and calm down." He looked around at the onlookers in the cafe, he sneered at them, "Wind your necks in, you lot, there's nothing going on here." He reached for Lucy, but she shrugged him off. "Come on Luce, let's sit back down. Have another drink."

"No leave me Jason and you definitely don't need another drink. You're pissed, or at least I hope you are, given that you're acting like a complete prat. I thought you wanted those boys to respect you, well you're not going the right way about it. Keep your word, leave them alone and leave your old clients alone."

Now, with the look of a shamed toddler, Jason reached again for Lucy and said mournfully, "I'm sorry Luce, forgive me, come on sit down with me, like old times."

"Oh for God's sake Jason, go home, sober up and grow up." She stormed out, leaving Jason swaying drunkenly and standing forlornly at the abandoned table.

***

If nothing else, staying at his mother's had brought order to John's eating habits. Patsy insisted that if he was to eat dinner at her house, then it would be together and at six o'clock. John accepted his mother's terms with equanimity. He now left the house regularly at eight in the morning, following a good sleep and a healthy multi-grain breakfast, his body felt better than it had for weeks. Three days a week he was doing contract work for Enterprise IT, giving him plenty of time to keep on track with Björn in the lab. The much heralded Research Council grant had come in, promising an up-scaled research and development programme with high profile industrial partners. His mother placed few demands on him and made surprisingly few comments about his business or family affairs. She seemed to enjoy having him home and sharing his company, not wanting to push him away and so she held her tongue. In so many ways life for both of them was organised, effective and good.

That was unless John considered how much he missed as a husband and father.

It wasn't just that he missed Lucy and Daniel, he felt the loneliness as a deep hurt inside, a hurt that wasn't assuaged by Daniel's fleeting visits to his grand-mother's house. Lucy seemed to resent him even more since he had moved in with his mother, maybe that was it, his move seemed too easy as if he didn't need his real home anymore. And with the Enterprise IT contract work and the increased intensity of the EarStream research programme, he was hardly ever there when Daniel did visit. Sure, that was nice for his mum, but it did nothing to fill the gaping hole in his own life and did nothing to move him any closer to getting back with Lucy. He had to find a way of getting his family life back on track.

***

Björn had always been happiest when he was working in the lab. He liked John, and liked the freedom that John gave him to explore the potential of the new technology. John was so unlike Dr Lowe, who always seemed to have one eye over his shoulder, looking for aspects of the research that might further his own academic position and might be publishable. While Björn fully understood the importance of publishing and of gaining academic credibility within the university setting, other priorities had entered his life. The problem was that university postdoc positions just didn't pay very well and they gave you precious little job security, which had been fine, he hadn't needed much money to live on. Shared digs, simple meals and a few cheap beers in the University bars with the other student labour had suited him, as long as he could work on something that he found intellectually challenging.

Things had improved with the increased level of interest from industry. It had really started after the medical conference where he had so successfully delivered his paper. Companies started contacting him in the weeks after with questions, so many questions about the technology, about the sensitivities, the specifications, the applications. Initially he passed them on to John, but so often, as these were detailed technical research questions rather than business ones, John had referred them back. And so at Simon's suggestion they had got Laura involved. She had quickly taken over the conversations with the businesses, established protocols where enquiries could be turned into small application research projects. "If a company wants to know if the technology can be used to meet their specific needs, they can pay for us to test it." She had decided, quite reasonably. And with that, many of the enquiries turned into proposals prepared by him and Laura. She had even managed to persuade the Engineering School to hire additional staff to help with the work, only short-term contracts, but even so it was better than nothing. And she had got Björn a promotion, much to Dr Lowe's chagrin, as Team Leader of the new 'Applications Group'.

"A monkey could organise these experiments," complained Dr Lowe, "Björn should be pushing back the frontiers of science with his work, not cow-towing for the corporate shilling."

And for Björn that was how it had started with Laura, a drink with John in one of the better campus bars, to celebrate yet another contract secured by him and Laura. "Quite the team," was how John had described them, and they had smiled at each-other and then they had stayed on after John had left for his mother's at five thirty. "She gets grumpy for the whole evening if I change plans at the last minute and miss dinner." John had explained, sounding like a naughty teenager. But left alone, Björn and Laura had felt comfortable together and as their conversation had moved from work to life, it had seemed oh so natural when Laura had suggested they go into town and get something to eat.

Laura drove in her small, sporty hatchback, Björn couldn't afford a car on his postdoc salary, and she chose the restaurant, a small Italian pizzeria, which Björn hoped wouldn't be too expensive. Laura knew somewhere to park where she could leave the car overnight so that she could have more wine. Laura seemed to take the lead with everything and Björn was happy to follow. Over a rustic pizza and a few glasses each of Chianti, their eyes had sparkled in the candlelight and their lips were reddened by the wine. They shared a Tiramisu with their coffees. It was when the bill came and Björn tried to insist on paying, that they first touched, Laura laid her hand on his and looked deep into his eyes. "Tonight Björn it is my chance to treat you." From that moment on and for the rest of the night they remained touching.

So for Björn now everything had changed, now there was Laura, beautiful, intelligent, sophisticated Laura, who was used to a real life outside the campus. Laura that he wanted to take to the best restaurants, the theatre, to travel to the great cities, to experience the better things in life with. Now the simple postdoc level of living wasn't enough. He needed to move on, get a proper job with a decent salary, if he was to keep his Laura.

***

Jason was becoming a pain. Ever since the scene in the cafe he had been pestering her with texts and calls. Some plaintively apologetic, others protestations of his innocence, still more just demanding her attention. After a few days of patiently listening, trying to tell Jason to move on, Lucy had taken to just ignoring the texts and leaving his calls to go to voicemail, forever to fall on deaf ears. Lucy realised that this was personal, not really to do with the business, Jason was hurting and disillusioned and reaching out, but she knew that what he was reaching for, she was never going to give him. She wasn't going to be the consolation prize for him losing his business.

The silent treatment seemed to be working, there had been no calls for a few days now and the volume of texts had slowed to a trickle, just one or two a day. Lucy was relieved, but knew in her gut that this wasn't the end. She busied herself with Daniel, who sadly seemed to have adapted well to the changed family circumstances, seldom asking where his daddy was. Lucy didn't like this, not wanting them to accept that John gone was now the new norm. She wanted them to fight for the return of John to their home, for Daniel to scream and shout for his father to be there. But life wasn't like that, the family evolved, adapted, Lucy filled the gaps in Daniel's life, she wasn't working too much and so she was there for him, Daniel probably had more parental attention now that it was just the two of them - not that Daniel demanded much attention. In many ways autism creates self-containment, it was those on the outside that assumed that they must break in.

So Lucy was busy, she was busy filling gaps at home for Daniel and even more so for Charlie and Gary at work, but she had long nights of sad self-contemplation wondering if anyone would ever fill the gaps in her life again.

***

John had taken to going for long walks in the evening. The streets were quiet, most of the rush-hour cars had reached their destination, the groups of children on the pavements had been called in and replaced with solitary dog walkers. The walks gave him time and mind-space to think, it allowed the events of the day to settle in place, plans to be made for the next day. The walks also allowed him to get away from his mother's house, not that she had said anything or made things difficult. It was the relentless kindness, the unquestioning consideration, the blind motherly love. His mother had never been emotionally demonstrative and always cuttingly critical, so her quiet acceptance of his returning to her created an unreleased tension in him. He wanted someone to shout at him, tell him how stupid he was being. Why couldn't she tell him to grow up and go home? And so he walked.

Always his mind would return to Lucy and Daniel, what would they be doing? How had their day been without him? As he passed the windows lit by TV he thought of the mums, dads, kids, couples gathering for meals and family time. It was funny as you walked past the houses, you always imagined happy families inside, never lonely people. As he walked, his route unconsciously led him towards his home area, his street, his house. Led him towards Lucy and Daniel.

***

Daniel was bathed and ready for bed, quiet now in his room with his favourite cars and a much loved audio book on the CD. He could lie there for an hour or more, seemingly content, but Lucy could never settle until she knew he was asleep. She was in the kitchen, having finished her own meal, a sad solo affair which she still insisted on eating at the table, feeling that resorting to a tray in front of the telly would be a slovenly step too far. She washed up her single plate, glass and knife and fork. Not enough to trouble the dishwasher. Only when everything was tidied away and Daniel asleep would she attempt to relax on her own in the lounge, always on her own.

Her phone pinged, signalling an incoming text, maybe it was Charlie reporting in on his latest client pitch, she smiled at his new-found business seriousness, wrapped up in his surfer-dude style. He had that sort of easy-going charm that drew people to him, he attracted work just because people liked having him around. That's not to say that he wasn't a talented designer, he was, he was also an extraordinarily likeable, talented designer. She picked up the phone, and her smile dropped from her face.

'I need to see you', the text said, 'I'm coming round now'. It was just signed with a J. She knew who it was.

No, she thought, I don't need this, not now, not tonight, not ever now. Maybe she could switch all the lights out, pretend she was away. No, she couldn't plunge Daniel into darkness, not while he was awake, and his bedroom was in the front, and so you could see his bedroom light from the street. No, she just had to tell him no. Make him understand, make him realise she didn't want anything more to do with him, make him go away. She may have felt something for him before, fantasised more like. But that was it, a fantasy, it was never supposed to become real. Why wouldn't he just leave her alone? And then she heard the doorbell. God, he must have been right outside when he sent the text. She wasn't ready for this. She needed to compose herself.

***

As John entered his street, he could just see his house in the distance, he started imagining the scene inside. He could see Daniel's lit bedroom window from quite a distance down the road. In his mind he could see him lying on his bed, gently rolling from side-to-side as he examined a car. Would it still be the yellow Porsche? John hoped so. He could hear the story CD, a Postman Pat, he suspected, Daniel had played it so many times that John and Lucy could say the words along with it. John smiled, for all his communication issues, Daniel's world was comfortingly predictable and familiar. What would John give to be lying, comfortable in familiar surroundings, with his favourite objects, listening to his favourite stories, knowing that he was safe and secure and that his favourite person was downstairs if he needed her? As he thought of Lucy downstairs in their house, their home, he smiled again, though it was tinged with sadness. Could he stop, knock on the door, just to see her.

As he neared the house, his pace quickened as his resolve hardened. It would be so good to see her and maybe he could pop in and just be with Daniel for a little while. He didn't want to make a scene or disrupt their evening, he just wanted to see them, in their, his and their, home, and see that they were safe and comfortable.

The road curved round to the left, he was across the road from his house, just a few more houses and then he would cross between the cars parked along the roadside. He could see Lucy's small battered Renault. And then he stopped. The door to his house opened, the light spilled out from their hall light into the porch, illuminating a figure waiting outside. It was him, it was Jason. He ducked down behind a car. He felt caught, he felt stupid, he didn't want her to know he was here. He didn't want her and Jason to laugh at him as they drunk his wine, sat in his lounge, on his sofa. He didn't want to be here. He turned and without looking back retraced his steps, his head bowed, his shoulders hunched and walked away.

***

She couldn't just leave him out there. He knew she was in. As she opened the front door, the light shone on him outside the porch. A movement across the street caught her eye, but she couldn't really see, probably just a dog walker. Jason was standing there, he swayed slightly, he held up a bottle and grinned childishly.

"I thought we could have a little talk, maybe a little drink and a little talk," his words were slurred.

She didn't open the porch door, just folded her arms and shook her head. "You've drunk quite enough and we've got nothing to talk about," she said, quite sharply. This had to stop.

"But I can make it alright again Luce. Make it like it was before. We can be a team, partners." He waved the bottle to emphasise his point, almost smashing into the porch wall.

"Just go home Jason. I don't need this. Just go home." She shook her head again as she retreated back into the house and closed the door.

Jason stood for a moment and stared at the door, as if not believing that she had been there and now she was gone. Then he backed unsteadily away from the house and as he got to the street he sat down on a low garden wall. It was quiet now, not another soul on the street, he heard distant footsteps walking away. He sat quietly, he knew that he had probably had enough, but shrugged, 'what the hell', he unscrewed the top and had a drink from the bottle that he had meant to share with Lucy. Probably just a bad time to catch her he thought, not in the mood, never mind, perhaps she would want to see him tomorrow. Jason weaved his way back towards town, leaving the street outside the house silent and empty.

CHAPTER THIRTY-THREE

They were seated together at the kitchen table. There were mats and serviettes and proper place settings of cutlery. Patsy liked to maintain her standards. John had his head down, tucking hungrily into braised steak and mash, a meal often promised by Lucy, but seldom delivered. He couldn't complain at the quality of the food back at home. Patsy looked at him a little sadly and put her knife and fork down, it was time she said something.

"John, I've kept my peace since you've moved back in, but I really think you have to start planning on the basis of you and Lucy not getting back together —"

John held up his hand to silence her. "— Not now mum, I can't think about this right now. I haven't given up on this marriage yet, but I couldn't honestly tell you why or how it's going to come right. So let's just leave it, OK?"

Patsy knew better than to argue too hard with John. She had almost driven his father away by constantly questioning or undermining his decisions, she didn't want to push John away. She couldn't deny that she enjoyed having John at home, caring gave a purpose to her life and however much effort she could put into charity shops and good causes, nothing could replace the simple pleasure and satisfaction of caring for one of your own family. And it wasn't that she didn't care for Lucy, more that she felt that Lucy could, should have supported her husband more (do as I say, not as what I do, she thought to herself with a grimace). After all, John hadn't betrayed the marriage in her eyes, he was faithful and supportive as a husband and a father, if anything his fault was trying to do too much to help Daniel. So why had she kicked him out, though John had said that he had left the house before she had the chance, but even if that were true, why hadn't she accepted him back? John said that he hadn't earned the right to ask for her forgiveness. 'Codswallop', she thought to herself.

"OK John, I'm not having a go. I'm just thinking that you do need to start establishing ground-rules in case it doesn't work out. Like access to Daniel. What if she finds someone else, you need to make sure that you have equal access to Daniel?"

John looked up at her. She saw that that had struck home. She sensed that something new had happened between him and Lucy, though she didn't know what.

"I'm just saying," she said, "you need to consider these things."

John slowly lowered his head and concentrated back on his dinner and considered.

"I think it's time we set up a more definite arrangement."

"But you can see Daniel whenever you want," Lucy sounded exasperated, John's call had been out of the blue, he was suddenly making demands as if they were in a battle. "Honestly John I thought we were keeping this flexible for your benefit."

"Maybe that was fine before, but now I think we should formalise things, get it agreed which days I can see Daniel. Perhaps we should get a lawyer to draw something up."

"A lawyer! Who can afford a lawyer? Is this your mother talking? We only need a lawyer if we're in dispute. I'm not disputing. When do you want Daniel?"

"Right, well, err..." John realised he probably should have thought this one through before he made the call. Having Daniel this week wasn't factored into his diary. But he couldn't step back now. "Right. I want Daniel on Thursday." He winced as he remembered that his mum was going away and so she wouldn't be around to look after him. This was going to cause him all sorts of problems.

"What *this* Thursday?"

"Yes. Is that a problem?"

"You know we had plans for this Thursday. My sister, remember, I did tell you?"

She was right, she had told him, he couldn't keep this up. "Alright then, what time on Thursday night can I have him?"

"He's not a thing to be passed around John. If he has a full day with my sister and her two on Thursday, he'll be tired by the time we get back, he won't want to start packing up and going off to you."

"So you're saying I can't see him on Thursday?"

"Oh John, what is this? Why is Thursday suddenly so important?"

"It isn't. I just think we should regularise it." "Regularise?" she was starting to lose her patience, "are you quoting from the 'Divorce for Dummies' book or something? Regularise? Who regularly feeds him, bathes him, wipes his bum, sits and cries when he completely ignores me. But you just want it regular, but when it suits you. Fine you can have him on Friday, and then two days a week starting next week, but you state which days you regularly want him."

"Friday. But I'm busy ..." He heard her sharp intake of breath over the phone, a sure signal that she was about to lose her temper. "No Friday's fine. We'll make it Friday," just in time, he thought, as he heard her breathing normalise, "we'll do something nice on Friday."

Lucy sighed, "Good. I'm sure he'll enjoy that, and if you can get him back to me lunchtime on Saturday, there's a parade in town, you know he likes watching the parades. Unless you want to take him that is?"

"No, of course not, he knows he's going with you, I don't want to upset his plans." Daniel didn't respond well to changed plans, wherever possible changes needed to be fed in gently with lots of positive affirmations. He knew that Daniel coming to him on Friday would be alright, he had been coming over quite frequently to stay with Patsy on some of the days when Lucy worked.

"Right, Friday then. Will you inform the lawyers or shall I?" The sarcasm in her voice hurt him. "Or is that every Friday, do you want to regularise it?"

"No. No it's not that. It's just if your circumstances change, you move on ..."

"What are you talking about? I haven't gone anywhere. You're the one that left."

"Yeah, but someone else might move in."

"What? Who? What is this about?"

"What if Jason —?"

"Of for Christ's sake John, grow up." She cut the call off without another word. Jason? What on earth did John know, or rather not know, or perhaps thought he knew, about Jason? She couldn't believe it, maybe she *should* run off with him, he certainly seemed willing.

CHAPTER THIRTY-FOUR

God, why had he made it this Friday, of all days? His mum was away and he had a VC investor coming to the lab to look over the technology. And not just any VC, this was the one that Giles had been courting, the one he thought would be a perfect fit for EarStream. And here he was lumbered with Daniel.

Lumbered? No never lumbered, he chastised himself as he looked in the rear-view mirror to see Daniel absorbed with his car, this time a racing green Jaguar. John had to admit, Daniel had good taste in cars. He smiled to himself. "Nice car," he called into the mirror to Daniel, "a Jaguar, one of my favourites." Daniel turned the car in his hands, watching the morning sunlight glint off the beautiful curved lines of the model car. "We'll go to the cafe when we get to work," he called again. "We can have some cake," he almost shouted, even though he knew that there was nothing wrong with Daniel's hearing. "CAKE! You like cake," he tried again, but with little expectation of a response. He switched the radio on to the local news channel.

"Toast." He didn't hear.

Giles had been as good as his word in using his many industry, military and investment contacts to first profile potential development partners and then to establish first contacts. It was the great advantage of using Giles, not just as 'grey hair', to give the business more credibility, but more importantly, he was well known within the right circles. Giles' front runners were Advanced Surveillance Systems, ASS, and Red Rock Ventures.

ASS was a technology business that had started up ten years ago in Israel based on new night-vision system. They had grown quickly, on the back of government contracts and significant investment, and had established themselves as favoured suppliers to the military and security services in the US and across Europe. Their business model ticked lots of boxes because they had created a well-respected R&D facility near Cambridge and had gained a reputation for acquiring other early stage technology businesses in their market area and fast-tracking new products to market. Most of all Giles liked them because they were engineers first and foremost.

On paper Red Rock Ventures was a very different type of business, an American Venture Capital business that had started as a spin-off from Merrill Lynch in the Dot Com days, but had ridden the crash and benefited from some shrewd investments in the chip design and manufacture and in mobile technologies. They had led several high profile Initial Public Offerings, IPOs, where they had taken some relatively early stage businesses into multi-million dollar companies. But what really impressed Giles was the management and development of their technology business portfolio. While backing the right horses was key to the success of any investment business, Red Rock went a step further by creating their own businesses by identifying key new technologies, making acquisitions or investments, and then working across the management teams to re-combine and bring together complimentary technologies to create stronger businesses. Like Simon Cowell creating a successful boy band by putting individual singers together as a group, they had a reputation of being able to see a winning combination, where the whole would be greater than the sum of the parts.

Giles had brought ASS over to the University the previous week. The meetings had seemed to go well, but John had felt he was almost redundant to the exercise, the term 'spare prick at a wedding' came to mind, the ASS guys were only interested in the technology and its applications to solve specific known technical audio problems for their clients in the defence and security sector. They had loved Björn, but even he was quite intimidated by the technical level of the interrogation, sure they were covered by patents and NDAs, but even so it felt like being technically raped.

Giles had been disappointed by the visit, saying if they only talked tech, rather than business opportunities, then he was concerned that their valuation of the business would be on the low side. They may see it as another product to sell to their existing clients, rather than a way of opening up new opportunities. He said he would need to have another conversation with their commercial team and get their first impressions. However, as Giles maintained, on the positive side, it further confirmed that there were problems in the surveillance market that EarStream could potentially fix.

Today would be the first opportunity for the team from Red Rock to get a good look at the technology. Following the ASS visit Giles was quite equivocal about it, "It all depends who they send," he opined, "if it's purely a technical team again, then we might be looking at a low valuation based on incremental sales. What I'm hoping is that we meet someone with a bit more commercial flair."

John believed that he had thought the logistics through. In this instance Daniel's autism potentially worked in John's favour, as long as Daniel felt comfortable then he was quite happy entertaining himself with his cars, he didn't really need a lot of adult attention or supervision. As long as John was close and kept an eye on him, things would be fine. It was just a matter of finding somewhere nearby to where John was meeting where Daniel could sit and wait. He had explained all this to Daniel, but it was difficult to tell how much of it had gone in. Things were not helped by John's increased stress caused by the importance of this meeting. He really didn't want to resent having to have Daniel here, or Lucy's insistence that he have Daniel today, but...

Giles had picked-up the Red Rock party up at Gatwick Airport. Not that they had flown in, it was a convenient point to meet the London trains. There were two of them. Brian was a relatively, to Giles, young English electronics engineer in his early thirties, he had the intense manner and Hipster look that in today's corporate world probably declared him as brilliant. At the car, he headed straight to the back seat, never taking his eyes from his latest model tablet computer. Tom was clearly the more senior of the two, confident and highly personable, he immediately engaged

Giles in that charming Boston American way that managed to convey real personal interest and sincerity.

In the pre-meeting conference calls, Brian had led the discussion, often more like an interrogation, always focused on the technical, the theory behind the electronics, the performance of the algorithms, the progress with the intellectual property protection. But now they were here with Giles, Brian kept quiet in the back while Tom led the conversation focused on the people side in the business, asking about the inventor, Dr Lowe, the development engineer, Björn, but most of all he wanted to know about John, his background, his style, his motivation, his support. Giles' answers were vague, not wanting to weaken EarStream's negotiating position, but he was still surprised by Tom's approach.

John was confident that things would be alright in the TECHub's cafe. Daniel had been there many times before, so he was familiar with the surroundings and John had his settled him on a corner sofa with his cars and books and a CD player with headphones. Simon was stationed in the cafe, as he always seemed to be when John had key visits, and John knew that he would keep an eye out for Daniel as well.

Giles arrived with the Red Rock Ventures pair. John had Laura with him, which gave him more confidence, as well as Giles being there and Simon close-by. Giles had suggested that they start in the cafe, to get the introductions out of the way and to create a more informal atmosphere, this apparently better suited the Red Rock style, though Brian seemed keener to head straight out to the lab.

As they settled over the coffees, John kept a watchful eye over Daniel, but he seemed happy with his cars. He had primed Jenny and the other the cafe staff to keep Daniel topped up with toast and cake.

"So John," Tom started in his soft American accent, "what brings you to this point in your life?" When John looked quizzical, Tom expanded, "I've seen your CV John, I know that you've got a decent education and that you've proved yourself a competent software guy, but that's not what got you here.

"I've known enough entrepreneurs to know that they are either born or made, and by that I don't just mean the old argument of 'nurture versus nature", I mean that for many they are made into entrepreneurs by necessity not volition. They take on the role of entrepreneur to get something done, to build something that would otherwise not get built. Their businesses tend to be very different from the classic serial entrepreneur who does it because they love the challenge of creating the business? I've only just met you John, so forgive me if I'm wrong, and this is in no way a criticism, but you don't come across as a natural entrepreneur. "So what brings you here?"

John was worried that what was the right answer for him, would be the wrong answer for Tom. Did Tom and Red Rock Ventures want that type of thrusting ambitious entrepreneur that would only be happy when he had taken over the market, or did they want the real John that was doing this because he believed that it would help his son? But also, while the reason for starting the business was all about Daniel, the more he had immersed himself in the business the more he enjoyed it. He did want EarStream to realise its potential and he did want to be a part of that success. So what answer did Tom want to hear?

If it was one thing that John had learned from being at the TECHub, both from Simon and from meeting other businesses, it was that if you tried to present yourself or your business as something that you were not, to potential partners or investors, then you would most likely get found out, either sooner where it could scupper the deal or later when it could undermine the trust in the relationship. John decided to stick as close to the truth as he dared.

"Well Tom, I have to admit that when I first started down this path it felt like an unrealistic dream. Had I found some new technology that could help people with social communication problems, like ADHD and autism, and could I create a business that could develop and commercialise that technology? I had neither the experience nor the training to start such a venture, but start it I did and though I say it myself I believe that I have taken the project a long way, both in developing the technology itself and in creating the market opportunities around it. I have learnt a huge amount about myself and have changed in my attitude towards business.

"So by your definition, I am probably nurtured rather a stereotypical natural entrepreneur, but I believe that I have proved both myself and the ..." John had caught sight of Daniel, who was fidgeting and had started to look agitated as he looked around anxiously for his dad. "Excuse me a moment." John got up and headed over to Daniel.

John knew this was hardly the right time to break-off from declaring his single-minded commitment and devotion of time to his business, but what could he do?

"Daniel, what is it?" Daniel wouldn't look at him, but continued to wriggle and resist him, John got hold of his shoulders and physically turned Daniel to face him. "Daniel," his voice was not sharp, there was no anger there, John had learnt from hard experience that anger achieved nothing with Daniel, but his voice was quite firm and forceful, "Daniel, what is it?" People in the cafe, including the Red Rock party, turned to look.

Eventually Daniel's eyes passed across John's face and focused on his left shoulder. "Pee pee," he said quietly. John mumbled an apology to his visitors as he lifted up Daniel and left the cafe for the loos.

Seeing the surprised looks from Brian and Tom, Giles quickly stepped in. "His son," Giles said, by way of explanation, "he's autistic and John needs to bring him in to the office sometimes."

"It's no problem," reassured Tom, "I get family." Brian looked less sympathetic.

Giles held the conversation on the general business climate for the security sector, while John was away. When he returned, he ordered another drink and more toast for Daniel at the cafe counter and got him back settled in the settee area.

"I apologise." John retook his seat, "he's not used to the toilets here, he'll be fine now." But John had spoken too soon, as they could hear Daniel as he started to get upset at the other table. The cafe staff had kindly brought Daniel's food over, but something was not right. John sighed, it was probably the triangles again he thought. "I'm sorry," he said as he rose from his chair again, he knew that this wasn't going well. "I'm sure he'll settle in a moment."

Tom nodded in understanding, probably a family man himself, Brian though looked increasingly impatient. Again Giles picked up on the situation. "Tell you what, looks like we've pretty much finished here. Why don't I take you down to the lab to meet Björn? John can join us later when he's got Daniel settled," he looked around for agreement.

"Ah yes, Björn," Brian perked up. "I've read his paper, seems like a bright lad." He got up to leave.

This definitely wasn't in the plan that John and Giles had agreed, but then again, neither was Daniel. As the Red Rock guys got their stuff together, Giles stepped across and whispered in John's ear in a less than sympathetic tone, "We can only expect so much patience from these guys. I appreciate the situation, but get this sorted. Why did you bring him today of all days?"

John shrugged. "It wasn't planned," he said quietly to Giles. Then he noticed Tom and Brian standing with their bags in their hands. "Makes sense, I'll join you at the lab in a few minutes." As they headed out with Giles, John went back over to Daniel, who had pushed the offending toast onto the floor and was back with his cars. "Hi big guy," he said, as he tried not to let the frustration seep into his voice, "Was the toast not up to scratch?" He sat down on the settee next to him, but Daniel didn't respond positively to his father, and he unconsciously turned his body away. John sighed again as he watched as Giles and the visitors walked past the window on their way down the hill towards to labs. "Why today?" he said again to himself.

Simon wandered over. "Looks like you've got your hands full," he said with a concerned expression. "Anything I can do to help?"

"Not really," answered John, "when he's in this mood he won't settle with anybody but Lucy or me."

"Yeah, we were lucky with ours, when they were younger, anyone could just have pushed them round the block in the buggy, and they would have been asleep in no time."

"I wish," John said with a sigh.

By the time that John arrived at the lab with Daniel in tow, after a walk, a swing, a play on a swivel chair, and a short game of hide and seek, Tom and Brian were in the middle of an intense technical session with Björn. Giles looked on from the side-lines, like a proud father.

The EarStream demonstration lab had evolved over the months. Björn's control desk now faced an array of different speakers at different distances and heights from which a wide selection of sounds and voices could be programmed to be broadcast.

Björn was pulling out all the stops, with multiple voices, multiple languages and multiple changes in the ambient noise levels. EarStream was performing well, with Björn the conductor drawing the best out of his technology through subtle shifts in how the audio technology was displayed. He allowed his guests to create the most complex array of sound puzzles for his magical technology to distinguish the one selected voice perfectly every time. Tom watched to see Brian's reaction, this was why Brian was here after all. If he was impressed, then Tom was impressed. Tom was the deal maker, but more than that, he was the mind reader, a psychologist who could play peoples' motivations and emotions just as well as Björn could play his box of tricks.

"That's fantastic Björn, really impressive," Brian admitted begrudgingly. "But, it is your test data set? Can we try it with some new voices?"

If Brian thought that he'd played a winning card, Björn quickly trumped it. "Actually I recorded your voices while you've been watching, we can feed these into the sample whenever you like. With that Björn made some adjustments at his terminal and then they could clearly hear Tom and Brian's distinctive voices through the far speakers. They both laughed, recognising not just the skill behind the demonstration, but the complete confidence that Björn had in *his* technology.

As John watched from the side-lines holding hands with Daniel, he again felt a tinge of envy over Björn's ease with the technology but more acutely the simplicity of his life. Björn could work all night in the lab if he wanted to or go off to a conference at a moment's notice. While John didn't resent the complications in his life, in many ways it was the complications that make your life, he was acutely aware of them.

John looked around the lab for somewhere to leave Daniel for a few minutes while he joined the demonstration. There was a reasonably clear desk and chair at the far side, one of the write-up tables used by the laboratory staff. He led Daniel over, and checked that there was no equipment there that could be a danger to Daniel, or conversely that could be damaged by Daniel. Laughter broke out in Björn's group as Björn mixed and then distinguished Tom's gentle Bostonian accent from a pack of hyenas. The better the demo went, the more John felt left out, isolated. He rushed Daniel into the swivel desk-chair and quickly emptied Daniel's cars from his backpack while he kept one eye on the backs of Tom and Brian, who were engrossed in the demonstration. "There Daniel, will you be OK here for a few minutes? Will you be good for daddy while he goes and talks to those men over there? It's important for daddy's work."

As John started to move away to join the group. Daniel looked round from the desk anxiously, "Drink?" he said. John looked round impatiently, it was only going to be a few minutes he thought to himself, but then relented and returned to the desk and retrieved Daniel's juice bottle and a packet of crisps from the bag. Daniel seemed appeased, as he took a long pull on his drink. With a sigh John turned again and tried to walk nonchalantly over to the group, which had now been joined by Giles, huddled around Björn's workstation.

"How's it going, Björn?" John asked, looking to re-establish his rightful place in these discussions.

"Oh, Björn's been giving us a fascinating demonstration of what he has achieved with his technology," intervened Brian.

His technology, thought John, he really needed to take control here. He eased himself to the front of the group, and subtly tried to put himself between Björn and the Red Rock guys. "So has Björn taken you through some of the other market applications, not just surveillance?" John knew that Björn would always focus on surveillance, because that was where he had done the most testing and was therefore most confident in the results. When Tom and Brian shook their heads, John launched in to the early stage enquiries that EarStream had received from the medical and broadcasting sectors. Tom especially looked intrigued, though Giles looked at John with some alarm. This was not their agreed strategy. They had discussed that their best approach would be to demonstrate where the technology had been proven to work and then to let Red Rock make the mental leap to the other markets. In this way they couldn't be accused of overselling EarStream or over-promising on the technology, but Red Rock could make their own evaluation of the other potential markets. But John had ignored this to get himself back at the centre of the discussions. To show that he had the business head, the entrepreneurial leadership, that he was in charge.

John held forth for a good fifteen minutes. He focused mainly on the areas of medical application, where there had been interest from clinicians and the medical device development companies, in the possible use of the technology for breaking communication barriers for patients suffering from attention disorders and autism. John reeled off the statistics of how many people suffered from the various conditions, the medical and social cost of care. He had their attention, John knew.

Björn sat back from his terminal, there was nothing that he could show to demonstrate the applications that John was extolling to the visitors, because they hadn't any proven technical models, or proven clinical outcomes, just a theoretical idea that the technology could help improve social communication. Of course Björn knew the reasons behind EarStream, why John had started the business, his original ideas around autism, but the research, the technology, the market had moved well beyond that now. Now they were talking about real world problems and solutions, real customers in the defence and security industry. Now they were talking about real money.

As John spoke, he felt his confidence growing, his stature rebuilding in the eyes of these money men. He was selling more than just a business, he was selling a dream, an opportunity to do some real good, to change people's lives. He was selling ... and then he noticed, he could see over Tom's shoulder, see the desk where Daniel was playing, should be playing. Daniel wasn't there.

To John the room fell silent, movements around him seemed in slow motion. He just stared at the empty chair where Daniel should have been. He started walking towards the desk, oblivious to the words and stares from Tom and Brian and Björn.

"John are you all right?"

"Is something wrong John?"

"What's the matter John?"

"Daniel," John's voice started quite softly, "Daniel," but grew in intensity as he repeated the name. Finally, he was shouting, "DANIEL." The people around him looked round in alarm, firstly at John, then as they realised what was happening, they started looking around the lab. "DANIEL," John's voice was getting more strident, more desperate, "DANIEL."

"Don't worry John he can't have gone far."

"DANIEL."

"When did you last see him?"

"DANIEL."

John couldn't think rationally; he could only imagine worst case scenarios. What hideous and dangerous environments do you find in a University Engineering lab? John imagined lasers, lathes, circular saws, drills, blow torches. How do you think logically where a small child would go, faced with that array of calamitous consequences? So John just stood, rooted to the spot, wide-eyed with panic, imagining the worse.

Giles, with good military training, took control, organising command control, search parties and call-throughs to all exits. The University still maintained the quaint practice of having Porters, which somehow gave more logistical confidence than receptionists. So with the main exits covered, they concentrated the search on the immediate environs. Following a word from Giles, Björn made some calls and summoned search support from a small army of lab technicians, who made the lab-to-lab, and door-to-door enquiries. But there was no quick resolution. The earlier easily shared platitudes were silenced as it became clear that Daniel clearly *had* gone far and there *was* something to worry about.

John had been ordered to sit, to calm down and to leave things to others. But that wasn't working. He wanted to be everywhere. Most of all he wanted to be where Daniel was. Giles said it made absolute sense for him to stay where he was so that they knew where to find him, when they found Daniel. He felt his phone, silenced for the meeting, vibrate in his pocket. Hoping for good news, he pulled it out and answered it without checking the caller ID. It was Lucy.

"Oh hi John, I didn't expect you to pick up, I was going to leave a message about arrangements for tomorrow."

"What? Tomorrow?"

"Yes, you know, tomorrow, dropping Daniel off in time for the parade. It's just that I might not be at home, better we meet in town."

"Daniel?"

"What's the matter? You sound odd. Has something happened? Where is Daniel?"

"Oh God I'm so sorry."

"Sorry? For what? What's happened to Daniel, John?" Her voice tightened as the realisation that something was wrong sunk in.

"I only left him for a moment. He seemed fine with his cars. I just had to talk with someone ..."

"Left him? Where are you John? Are you at the TECHub?"

"No. The lab. We've got people looking. He can't have gone far." His voice wasn't that reassuring.

"Oh God," exclaimed Lucy, then she went quiet, as she considered the situation. "The lifts. Have you checked the lifts? I remember the last time I came with you to the lab, Daniel was fascinated with the lifts."

"Of course, yes, the lifts." John cancelled the call as he leapt to his feet, the lifts. "The lifts, have you checked the lifts?" he shouted as he pushed his way through the people milling around the lab, attracted by the drama. His phone was vibrating again in his hand, he looked down and saw it was Lucy calling again. Not now, he had to get to the lifts.

He ran down the corridor, past the blue doors, past people sticking their heads into rooms and calling out his son's name. The corridor turned to the left, and into a small lobby area, a glass panelled door led off to the right to the emergency stairs and there on the left, were the bank of lifts, three of them evenly spaced along the wall. He remembered that Daniel had liked watching the scrolling red digital numbers at the side of each silvery lift door, which showed the current location of the lift and its direction. Daniel had loved predicting which lift would arrive next. He had kept Lucy waiting there for ages.

John pushed the call button, then he stood in front of the middle lift willing them all to arrive and for one of them to be holding Daniel. His eyes scanned the three lifts, where were they now? The building had five floors and he was currently on the second. The first lift was heading down to the ground floor, well hopefully the Porter would grab him if he came out there. He was more concerned about the basement floors, where the more heavy duty workshops and laboratories were. The red numbers showed that the second and third lifts were both up on the high floors, which were mainly offices and meeting rooms. The phone in his hand kept vibrating, Lucy, of course it was Lucy, but while he knew she would be worried sick, there was no value in talking to her now.

And then he heard something, crying, was it a child crying? He could hear it through the lift shaft, but which one, and was it up or down. He put his ear to the gap between the two lift doors on the middle lift. He could definitely hear it, it sounded like a child. 'DING', the third lift arrived, having come down from the fifth floor, he stepped back to check the inside of the lift. Nothing. Should he take it? He could definitely hear crying, it seemed to be getting louder, and so his instinct was to go and try and find Daniel. He started to move towards it, but felt a hand on his arm. It was Giles.

"If that sound is Daniel then it's definitely getting closer, so best you wait here," he said calmly, making John wait and watch despairingly as the doors to the third lift started closing. Then Giles strode quickly to the lift doors and just got his hand in to the diminishing gap to trigger the safety mechanism, the doors juddered to a stop and then opened again. "Maybe best if we keep the lifts here as they arrive."

The crying was definitely getting louder now. "Sounds like your boy is coming down in the middle lift."

John could feel the sweat running down his back, he felt so helpless. The phone vibrated again. He looked down quickly and seeing Lucy's picture, swiped the phone and then lifted it to his ear. He ignored Lucy's shouting as he said into the phone. "We think we can hear him," that silenced Lucy. "We think he's in the middle lift coming back down, we're just waiting for the lift now, it's on floor four... three..." The numbers seemed to change so slowly, but the sound of crying, while calming a little, was getting louder. "Two… Nearly here now."

"Oh God John, what if he's not in there? What if it's not him?"

"We've still got loads of people looking. We'll find him," John sounded more confident than he felt. But the need to reassure Lucy helped him to calm himself.

"OK the lift is arriving." He could hear whimpering from inside as the old lift clunked to a halt. The doors started to open. John held his breath.

"There's daddy. See I told you he'd be there, waiting for us."

John's heart leapt and his stomach fell as he saw Daniel looking small and fragile standing next to Tom, holding his hand. Daniel looked up at him, his face tear-stained, he pulled his hand free and he stepped forward towards John.

"It's him," he said to Lucy, "Oh Daniel. Thank God." John swept him up into his arms dropping his phone. "Don't ever run off like that again." He hugged him and Daniel squirmed.

"Lift," he said simply.

"I know, you like the lift." While John could have hugged him for hours, he could feel Daniel's discomfort, so he set him down and retrieved his phone from the floor. He looked across at Tom, who was standing there, looking on, smiling. "Thank you," John said warmly.

"Sure, no problem. When I came out here, two of the elevators were down in the lobby with one going up. The lights showed the elevator stop on the fifth, so I took a punt that that might be him. Kids do like flashing lights."

John gasped his relief. "Good call," was all he could say.

"Given his hollering, I'm not sure he appreciated being found," Tom laughed.

"He's not good with strangers," John explained.

"I think you'd better get that." Tom indicated John's phone, which was still on and they could both just hear Lucy's increasingly distraught voice.

John smiled and turned away, talking gently to Daniel as he did. "I need to have a word with mummy now, let her know you are all right." He lifted the phone to his ear. "Hi, yes sorry, he's fine, just went for a little walk... Yeah, Tom found him. The American guy I was meeting, up on the fifth floor would you believe... Yes, I have thanked him.... Yes, I'll bring him home now.... I'll see." He leant down to talk with Daniel and offered him the phone. "Do you want to speak to mummy?" Daniel shook his head. John stood back up and raised the phone back to his ear. "No, I don't think he's feeling very talkative at the moment... Yes, I'll bring him home now." He hung up.

John turned back to Tom. "My wife, Lucy, says thanks."

Tom smiled again. "It's fine. Now get that young man home, I'm sure he could do with a nice slice of cake."

"Toast," said Daniel quietly. Both Tom and John laughed.

John started to walk away, but then stopped and looked back. "But what about our meeting. We need to talk about EarStream ..."

"It can wait," said Tom kindly.

As they walked back into the lab, there was a cheer and some applause from the small crowd of searchers who had drifted back to the lab. Daniel shied away, hiding behind John's leg. Giles and Simon came over and Giles placed a father-like hand on John's shoulder.

"Good ending," he said.

"Yes. But Giles, we need to ..."

"We've got it covered," Giles assured him, "now go home."

Smiling, John thanked them all, then gathered up Daniel's things and headed back to the TECHub, taking the stairs this time.

The small crowd dispersed and Brian pulled Tom away into a quiet corner.

"Hey, the technology looks sound and I like this Björn lad a lot, but John looks pretty flaky."

Tom laughed, "Brian, you're a real people person."

CHAPTER THIRTY-FIVE

Lucy was waiting in the front porch of the house. When she saw John's car pulling up to the kerb and Daniel's small face peering out of the back window she didn't know whether to laugh or cry, to hug Daniel or to hit John. In the end it was easy, she ran to open the car's back door and hugged Daniel in his car-seat, tears running down her cheeks. Daniel wriggled and squirmed against the physicality of her attention. In the end she relented, and focused on undoing his buckles and helping him out of the car. Released and standing on the pavement, Daniel looked up at his mother and asked, "House?" she nodded and Daniel retrieved his bag from the back seat and walked towards the house.

John was out of the car now and standing on the pavement waiting for Daniel to walk away. Lucy looked up at him, she knew there was no value in blame or recriminations, these things happened.

"God that was awful," John started, "I've never known a feeling of panic like that before."

The anger and worry and pain bubbled up inside her. She yelled at him. "John, how could you leave him? To put our son in danger, just for a poxy business meeting." She turned on her heel and followed Daniel into the house, leaving John standing, stunned, on the pavement.

***

John welcomed the tea and sympathy he got at his mum's. She listened to the whole story in silence, allowing John to talk through the events, and also his feelings and emotions. She realised that he was in shock as well. While she could understand Lucy's reaction, it was only natural for the maternal protectiveness to show through in emotional ways, it was telling that they couldn't bring themselves to comfort each-other, to recognise the need for mutual support. Sure you can shout, but then you should support. It sounded like the only one to come through this unscathed was Daniel. But who could fathom what he thought or felt.

"I feel like jacking it in mum, just walking away, it's not worth it."

Patsy had been expecting this. "No hasty decisions John, you've invested a lot in this, it's far more than a job you can resign from, it's more complicated than that."

"It's not complicated. I just don't go back. The technology goes back to the University. Daniel goes back to Lucy, and me, hopefully I get my old life back."

"But there are others involved John."

"Oh, yes of course, you. I'll find a way of repaying your money mum."

"I don't mean me! It's never been about the money for me John, you must know that? No, other people, like Björn for example and Giles, they have invested their time, their energy in the project. I'm not saying that they expect something in return, but don't they deserve your consideration?"

"But what about Daniel? I put EarStream ahead of him. I resented him and it ended up putting him in danger."

"John, you took your eyes off him for a minute. As parents, we've all done it. We juggle priorities, try and do too much and sometimes things go awry. In the end there was no harm done. There was no wilful neglect, nothing done on purpose. You perhaps made an innocent mistake while you were under a lot of pressure. What mother or father hasn't?

"You love Daniel, and your motivation for the business is to help him. So stop beating yourself up. An accident happened and thankfully nobody got hurt."

"I don't know, mum, everything I've done with EarStream seems to have taken me further away from my family."

***

Giles was sitting at his customary place at the head of the table, he looked serious as he spoke, "The good news is that they liked the technology and they see a value and a fit with a number of their business areas."

"And the bad news?" Said John, it was his first day back at the TECHub since the Red Rock Ventures visit, and Giles was in with Simon and John to review where they were with the investment discussions. "Were they put-off by the hysterical father who lost his child while they were here?"

"Well, it was a novel pitch, but no not at all," Giles replied with a smile. "Tom was just happy that it all ended well."

Giles then turned more serious, "As always, these discussions are complicated, every business investment is different. Are they investing in the business itself, the technology or the people?"

"Surely it's got to be all three," insisted John.

"Not necessarily," Simon joined the conversation, "it depends where they see the value. The technology or management can be stripped out and used with their existing businesses."

"What? Isn't that asset stripping? I thought that was illegal."

"As with most of these things, it's the way it's done, rather than the process itself. Some companies are far more valuable broken up than they are in their current form."

"Well it doesn't sound too good for EarStream."

"It so depends on the deal and their motivation. Let's say, for example, that they saw you as the next Head of Red Rock Ventures and so wanted to buy the company as a way of getting you."

"Have they said that?" John had a moment of unwarranted excitement.

"No, it's just an illustration. Perhaps a bad one. But if they did, would that be a good deal?"

"Well it sounds like a good deal for me, but what about the rest of the company and its shareholders."

"So they have to be looked after, maybe with shares in Red Rock or one of its companies. The point is that everybody can be happy, but EarStream the company changes."

"But what about the technology, what do they want to do with that, you said they liked it?"

"Like I said, they do. But an important aspect is what do you want to do with it? The University obviously want to see it used as widely as possible, but they have already done a deal to go through you. So what *you* want is critical."

"Well I ... What I mean to say is ... The key point is ...," John realised he didn't haven't an answer, or at least not one that felt right.

Giles saw that he was struggling. "Look no-one is looking for an answer straight away. They haven't even asked the question yet. But I am warning that the question will be coming, whether it's asked by Red Rock or someone else, it will be asked."

***

Björn met with Simon in the TECHub's cafe. "I don't know what to do or who to ask for advice. I don't want to let anyone down, the University and John they have been good to me."

"Look Björn, in the end you have to do what's best for you, EarStream and the University will find a way to replace you if you leave. What have they offered you?"

"Nothing specific as yet, Brian said that he could see opportunities for me at Red Rock even if they didn't manage to do a deal on EarStream."

Alarm bells started ringing for Simon. While he believed firmly in what he had told Björn, and he would help him where he could, he was also conscious that EarStream had little technical credibility without Björn and that John needed to find a partner as soon as possible.

"Look Björn, what would be your ideal solution?"

Björn looked back innocently, "I like what I'm doing in the lab, I want to continue, but I need to be paid properly and not to have to worry about my next contract. I want to move on from being a student, to start thinking about others, to settle down."

"Laura?" Simon asked with a smile.

"You know?" Björn looked astonished, "I thought we'd kept it secret."

"Oh Björn, it's been obvious for weeks. Not even you look that happy just from working in the lab. Everybody is really happy for the both of you. You deserve it."

"Ahh, she is wonderful. But I want to buy her things and take her places, and it's no good on a University salary."

"I can imagine. But if you do join Red Rock Ventures, there's no guarantee that the job will be based anywhere near here. They have business interests all over the world."

"I know, but Laura and me, we talk about this and we try and make the new opportunities work for us."

"I understand Björn, there comes a time when you have to move out from under the wing of the University and maybe Red Rock's interest in you and EarStream gives everybody a good opportunity."

"I think so," Björn looked relieved. "Will you talk to John?"

"I will Björn, I definitely will."

***

Giles had sensed that the time had come to try and bring things to a head. He had invited John and Simon out for dinner at a small Italian restaurant where Giles knew they wouldn't be disturbed.

After small talk over the starters, Giles opened with the surprise news that Advanced Surveillance Systems had made an offer directly to the University, rather than to John, to acquire the EarStream patents. The offer was to purchase the patents outright, which involved all the rights being assigned to them. The price offered, while not insubstantial, was low, considering that there would be no ongoing royalties. "They're even placing restrictions on the University retaining rights to use the intellectual property in ongoing research projects, which is very unusual."

"How can they just cut me out?" complained John.

"Well they're not exactly. They're relying on the University to talk you round. For the University, a large capital sum up-front is good for them, an uncertain royalty stream is a much higher risk."

"But why would they do that? We've made such good progress on the security applications."

Giles had heard through some of his military contacts that ASS had been hawking round an advanced audio capture system of their own over the last year, and Giles was concerned that their interest in the EarStream technology might be more of a patent-blocking move, to stop the development of a potential competing technology to their own. While the EarStream solution may be superior, ASS had already invested huge amounts of research and development in their own system. But Giles didn't want to upset John with what really only amounted to industry rumours at this stage.

"Who knows?" He replied vaguely. "There are so many factors which can affect the strategy of a company like ASS. Mind you, a decent cash exit wouldn't be such a bad result for you would it? And your mother would make a decent return on her investment."

"But what about their plans? Do they say how they would develop the technology for other sectors like medical?"

"You mean for your ideas of using it with children with autism? While they don't say anything for certain, I wouldn't hold out much hope for applications that they would see as non-core."

"Non-core? What do they mean, non-core, it could help people? We've had some good test results showing that it might help people. Surely they can't stop that?" John was getting increasingly agitated.

"John. Calm down, they haven't said anything. It's just if they want to acquire all the rights, they obviously want to control and probably restrict, all the application development."

"Are you thinking that they want to kill it?" Simon interjected.

John was horrified. "Kill it? What do you mean kill it?"

Simon looked at him kindly. "Come on John, don't be naive, sometimes companies gain more by making sure that a new technology doesn't get developed, rather than if it is. We've all heard of stories of oil companies buying up and killing off promising new fuel technologies. Well, this could be the same sort of thing."

"So just drop it, so all this, everything we've done, everything we've been through, it's just thrown away."

"Well you would get a sizeable cheque for your troubles." Giles reminded him.

John couldn't believe it, the conversation paused while the waiters arrived with their main courses, steaks all round. They ate in silence, but John had lost his appetite. "But it's not just about the money ..." He shook his head sadly.

"Well it is for some," Simon said without enthusiasm, "and for others the money is taking on a greater importance."

John looked up at him sharply. "What do you mean? Do you mean the University; do they want this deal?"

"I don't know John; this is the first I've heard about the offer. No I was thinking about Björn, his infatuation with Laura has now turned to love. And love these days is expensive. You can't be in love on a postdoc's salary."

"He's leaving?" John couldn't believe it, everything was falling apart.

"Nothing is decided," Simon reassured him, "but he's certainly having to think about it."

"He can't! He can't leave, we haven't finished the work ..." John got up from the table, "Jesus, I need some air." He pushed his way through the tables and headed out through the front door. Giles watched on in surprise.

"He'll be back."

"You reckon?" Said Giles looking sceptically at Simon. "You think you know him better than me?"

"No. He's left his coat," Simon replied with a smile.

They both returned to their steaks.

John was back at the table ten minutes later, just as Giles and Simon finished their meals. The fresh night air had cooled his temper and he apologised as he retook his seat.

"I'm sorry. It just seems like everything is falling apart."

"No John, as things move on, people's motivations change or become clearer." Giles paused and looked seriously at John. "It's time for you to be clear about your own motivations. What is it you want out of this John? And what is your walk-line?"

"Walk-line?"

"It's the point that you will not cross in a negotiation. The one thing that you won't give in on."

"You mean in the valuation? The minimum valuation that we would accept?"

"It could be John, but in this case I'm not sure that the valuation is the final driver for you. But I do need to know *what is,* if I'm going to help you negotiate a deal."

CHAPTER THIRTY-SIX

Two months later, it was another conference room, at another lawyer's office. This time in the City, the venerable Dunholm and Mills, acting on behalf of Red Rock Ventures.

John had come to rely more and more on Giles as his business advisor and mentor. With Simon, it had become something more personal, part confidant but perhaps more simply a friend. As he and Lucy had become more and more estranged, he had welcomed the chance to have someone he could just talk honestly to. The experience with Benni and Jason had really shattered his faith in human nature. It had come as quite a shock to realise that he had such a naive expectation of fairness from other people. Of course you read the stories, of crooks and rogue traders, but these were smart professional people, with their lawyers and advisors, he hadn't expected them to want to steal and defraud him. It had made him suspicious and distrustful of everyone around him. Did that include Lucy? He didn't know, she had after-all introduced Jason into EarStream. Who could he trust?

And so it had been Simon that he had come to rely on. It had helped that Simon had turned down his offer of having personal shares in EarStream. He had explained that he didn't want anything to suggest that his and the TECHub's advice could be driven by his personal interest or gain. It was fine, Simon explained for the TECHub itself to hold equity or take success fees, as any returns would be invested back in support for the next generation of entrepreneurs. John appreciated this approach, liked the idea of giving something back. But he had assured John, in his usual light-hearted way, that while he couldn't guarantee that he would always give the best advice, it would always be in John's best interests. And, as he always maintained, if John really wanted to cock it all up, there was nothing that he, or anybody else, could do to stop him.

The relationship with Giles was different. Giles had been introduced through his mother and he was there for his industry knowledge and the deals that he had led in the past. Simon had counselled John to be wary of Giles telling him how *he* would run *his* business, but John had always found him fair and very open to John's own ideas. Both Giles and Simon were at pains to keep reminding John that it was *his* business, not *theirs*.

Proper technology, Giles liked to say, used proper engineers that made real things that worked. In recent years the Tech-world had once again become dominated by the software companies, this time the emphasis was on the App designers and social gaming companies. And, Giles had to admit, if a handful of developers could come up with the next viral success in picture or music sharing, and be bought for a few billion, then why bother with the years of research and development, consumer or clinical trials and regulations needed to actually get a physical product onto the market. That seemed to be the main business driver these days, not how to sell more products, but how to get bought by Google, Facebook or Amazon? For these behemoths it was not necessarily about the additional profit that the new business acquisition could bring, it was about retaining their own virtual monopoly positions in the market place. It was sad, Giles had mused in one of their 'Chairman chats', that so much of the talent was wasted on the seemingly trivial and unproductive.

So Giles had enjoyed the prospect of finding a home for a proper new technology, he had spent a lot of time researching the investment market and using his many commercial and military contacts to investigate various venture capital companies and also the corporate venturing arms of major engineering companies like GE and British Aerospace. And the deeper Giles dug, the more the reputation of Red Rock Ventures came across positively, it seemed to be a real investment company, which clearly did like to venture, to take a risk on an idea rather taking the risk on the rise and fall of the stock markets. It was known for building companies, rather than breaking them up. To build real value in the IP through generating products rather than just looking for the fastest turnaround on re-licensing the patents to Corporates that just wanted to protect their position. And that to John, certainly compared to the seemingly underhand approach taken by Advance Surveillance Systems, was perfect.

So it was important to John that he was accompanied to this final meeting by Giles, his Chairman who, with the help of a lawyer friend, had led the negotiation, which as Simon had intimated and John had quickly realised, was a very specialist skill. John had refused to use Pearce, Pearce and Mountford. This was to be his deal, on his terms, not his mother's. John would have liked Simon to have been there, he had, after all, been a part of every major step and decision that John had made with EarStream. But no, Simon had maintained that this step was for the real owners alone, not the people behind the scenes. John had promised that they would have their own celebration, maybe invite some of the other companies at the TECHub. It was important that they share their success. When he had first joined the Hub, John had drawn great comfort and confidence from the war stories of the other companies, whether they be fanfares or failures, it brought them together as a community. Yes, it would good for John to stand for a few bottles of bubbly and raise a few glasses with his fellow entrepreneurial travellers.

It was late, after eleven, by the time all the paperwork had been finalised and Giles and the lawyers had had a last chance to check the dotted i's and crossed t's. But they assured him that it was always like this, late night signings. Must be the equivalent to the *Macho-City* desire for early starts. That if any deal is worth doing, it is worth doing at some ungodly hour. Or perhaps it was for the lawyers, when you're signing, everyone must see you doing sixteen hour days to justify the bill.

There were three suits there from Red Rock, as well as Tom, they were as indistinguishable as their suits. Deal makers, John thought, did he really want to hand over his company to them? All that he had worked for, all that he and his family had given up, sacrificed. Was this what it all came down to, just money? But no, Giles had assured him, sometimes, in some industries, you needed the big boys, with the big bucks, to get the product to market. And with Red Rock at least they had Tom, who gave some confidence that the technology would be progressed. So this was it, in the end they had had to choose an investor, find the least bad option. John was understandably mistrustful of so called investors. He had nearly lost everything with Benni, and worse, they had tried to use Lucy against him, unforgivable. So what made Red Rock different, were they out to screw him too?

"Look," said Giles, as he had shown him a stack of news articles, nice stories in glossy magazines, shiny pictures of young entrepreneurs with model looks, he assumed they must be American, he hadn't seen many model types at the TECHub. "They have a good record of delivering final products." Perhaps it was OK, thought John.

Giles had invited Tom, the Technical Director of Red Rock Ventures back over to the UK to talk with John more personally. While it hadn't come across so much on his first visit, Tom, a little like Giles, was an old school engineer, used to solving problems and making products. He eulogised about CAD models and 3D printing, about how they would get their demonstrator models out there, to get the future customers really on board with what was possible. John knew that all this was to give him confidence in handing his dream over to them, and they were right, Tom was the sort of engineer that John knew the technology needed. But more than that, Tom understood and empathised with John's passion. You didn't make things for the sake of it, you did it with a purpose and Tom had got to understand and respect John's purpose. He had asked many questions about Daniel and about how John thought that the technology could help.

The University had done their due diligence. Red Rock Ventures had done previous deals with both Imperial and Southampton, so they were happy. It would be a significant result for them, one the biggest technology patent deals they had ever done and it could end up making them millions. Dr Lowe was delighted as well, he had agreed to put the money back into his department's research group, to give them some much wanted extra resource and the freedom to follow their own research ideas, even sponsoring their own PhD's. There was to be a new Red Rock Chair of Audio Electronics. John was pleased for the academics. Even though in the early days the commercial success was almost achieved despite the actions of the academics, the University had backed him and granted him access to the technology. They had all played their role.

Even Björn would receive his share from the licence fees paid to the University, plus John had made sure that he had some of his own shares in EarStream. And Björn would also be leaving the University. Tom and Brian had recognised that practical spark in Björn, sure he would make a *good* academic, but they believed that he would make a *great* development engineer. They had offered him a special position to oversee the introduction of EarStream technologies through several of Red Rock's subsidiary companies. He would also act as a liaison back with both this University and others to spot new technology targets. The salary was more than Björn could have hoped for and because he would be away working at offices in Boston and San Francisco as well three or four sites in Europe and Asia, it didn't really matter where he was based, so an initial office at one of their subsidiary companies in Guildford was offered, allowing Björn to stay close to his new found love Laura. They were both there to see the culmination of this deal that they had had such a big part in bringing to fruition, they stood arm-in-arm, clearly the happy pair much to the surprise of Dr Lowe who hadn't noticed their relationship at all.

And now for John it would all be over, well at least different. He wasn't even sure that EarStream would continue as an independent company or even a product or brand name. Tom had talked of merging the technology into one or two of their other subsidiary companies. They talked of portfolio technologies and using the power of their vertical integration and Björn's technical know-how to speed up the route to market.

But did it matter what happened to the defence and security technology? In the end did he care about the surveillance market? He didn't even really care about the money. Sure it would make their life comfortable. But that wasn't why he had done it and that was why he wouldn't, couldn't take the deal they offered. It was a relatively standard arrangement Giles had told him, even the University thought it was a normal request. An 'earn-out' it was termed. He would get his money, all his money eventually, but in return he would be expected to stay on with EarStream and Red Rock Ventures for the next three years, then if the technology and commercial milestones were met, he would make far more in share options and milestone bonus payments. But why would he want to do that? He didn't want to run a technology business, even a well-funded technology business. He wasn't even sure that he would really be any good at it. He wanted his life back, his family life back.

So that was when the negotiations really started. This wasn't a standard deal now. What if his projections, his forecasts didn't pan out, Red Rock's lawyers had argued? He surely couldn't expect to get paid on the basis of the same valuation if he wasn't sharing in the risk. No, he couldn't, he had told them. All he wanted was something fair, he fully recognised, well Giles had told him, how much risk and how much further investment would be required to develop the technology. So John had understood, had been sympathetic, he just wanted a fair valuation for him and all his shareholders, including his mother and Lucy and Daniel, with just a few conditions. Tom intervened, perhaps, John thought, he didn't want an inexperienced rookie messing up his neat corporate strategies, but more likely John had thought, Tom had understood him and wanted to give him back the opportunity to rebuild his life. And so a deal was done, a compromise from all sides, as a compromise should be and John had walked away, a little bit richer, but a lot happier with a few special conditions agreed on the side.

As they entered the room, it was hushed. Just the whispering of the lawyers who had gathered in their opposing legal teams, soon to be joined together as one. The university commercialisation team, rather less suave than the Red Rock guys, seemed more nervous, agitated at being away from their usual turf. This was late night in the City where the investment lawyers stalked. But there was little need for chatter, the deal had been agreed and Giles had assured him that it was a good deal, in the circumstances.

It was particularly late for Daniel, but John and Lucy had agreed that he should be there for the signing, but now he worried that Daniel would be agitated by the strange surroundings. But no, there seemed to be something about the cool boardroom, the dark oak furniture, the many men in suits that spoke in hushed tones, which relaxed him. John smiled at Lucy and Lucy smiled back. It had been a long road, but he had got there, proved his idea could work. Did it matter to her that he had been proved right, that he had gained so much, or did she only think about what had been lost? But no, thought John, that was tomorrow, or another day, today was a good day, a deal-signing day. He saw his mother, as seemed usual these days, on the other side of a lawyer's table. She stood with Martyn, talking quietly, they seemed close in the way they interacted with each other. She and Martyn were even standing close together, surely closer than normal, no - surely not. John pushed that thought away. She smiled at John, had backing him cleared her guilt of not supporting his father? John hoped so.

On the table, two thick piles of legal documents sat laid out in front of two signing chairs complete with special pens and blotting pads. They were there for show, nobody would be reading them tonight, they showed that the lawyers had done their work and earned their fees.

Waiters were ready with the obligatory Champagne. But they held back, standing around the edge of the room, it would be unseemly to drink before the deal was signed.

The conversation was hushed by the expensive chink, chink of a silver spoon striking a cut-glass Champaign flute. It was Giles. He, as Chairman of EarStream and introducer of Red Rock, was the natural Master of Ceremonies.

"Ladies, gentlemen, friends and colleagues." There was silence in the room, even Daniel was struck silent by the solemnity of the occasion. "There are few things more vital in the world of business than the coming together of a new partnership, particularly, as in this case, when it is based on Engineering, Enterprise and Entrepreneurship. These three 'E's' are as important in driving our economy, our world forward as the three 'R's' are in education, and at least ours are phonetically correct." He paused for the expected laugh and was rewarded with a chuckle that rippled through the room.

"I have been working with the John and EarStream since I was introduced by his mother, who thought that her son could use a few grey hairs to guide him. And after the roller coaster of the last few months any hair that I had that wasn't grey has finally succumbed." Another chuckle.

"Engineering has always been my passion, real solutions for real problems, and with EarStream, John and his academic team have developed a platform technology providing multiple applications across a number of important sectors, including health and security. It was with this in mind that I believed that an entrepreneur like John needed the resources of a bigger partner to fully realise the potential of the technology. In that regard, Red Rock Ventures fitted the bill perfectly, with existing products in both the security and health sectors, they bring the technology development resource and the market presence to take forward the fine entrepreneurial work that EarStream has initiated. So we can see a great future for this still young technology to reach its potential.

"I'm also delighted to announce that as part of this deal, Red Rock Ventures has established a new EarStream Charitable Trust to develop new technologies to support children and adults with social communication disorders. I would like to invite the new Head of the Trustees, Tom Turner, to say a few words."

Tom stood, he was clearly a man used to speaking to a room full of people, he smiled at the familiar faces around the room, and then his eyes focused on Daniel.

"It was some months ago that I was first introduced to this young man over here, Daniel Miller. Daniel, more than anyone else, including John and Björn and Andrew, has been responsible for us all being together in this room. It was Daniel that inspired his father to give up his job and the life that he had known to set off on an entrepreneurial journey that would, in the end change many people's lives. And it was Daniel, who I first met in a lift on the fifth floor of the Engineering labs at the University, who inspired me to structure my first ever deal designed to generate something other than wealth. It is an honour to have been asked to head up this trust, which has been formed from John Miller's share of the proceeds of the sale of EarStream, matched by a charitable donation from Red Rock Ventures, plus one percent of the future royalties received by the University. Finally, we pledge the exclusive rights of the EarStream patented technology in the treatment of autism and other social communication disorders to the trust in perpetuity.

"I believe that the EarStream technology and the technical expertise behind it will lead to commercial success for my company Red Rock Ventures, but in doing so I am proud that we will also be exploring new medical interventions as believed possible by John.

"In conclusion I would ask you to raise your glasses and to drink to the completion of this deal and to the future of EarStream and finally to toast our inspiration, Daniel."

"To Daniel," echoed the crowd of people together, raising their glasses.

"Toast," said Daniel.

CHAPTER THIRTY-SEVEN

He could have posted the cheque. That would have been the normal way, or he could even have arranged a bank transfer, that would probably have been more secure and certainly quicker. But no, John wanted to hand it over personally as a final affirmation that he had done the right thing. But now he wasn't so sure. He had always maintained that it wasn't about the money, and here he was trying to use money to show that it had all been worth it. Was he just trying to assuage his guilt? Would she respect it, or resent it?

They had agreed to meet at Daniel's favourite cafe. They made good toast there. Daniel liked toast.

John had arrived early, well not just early, a good hour before they had arranged to meet. He had just been so fidgety, couldn't settle, nervous energy. Why was he so nervous? He was just meeting his wife and son. They hadn't been separated for that long, just a few months when the pressure of the business had got too much. It had really been about protecting his family, especially Daniel from his dad's mood swings and the stress of the situation both at home and at work. But all that was over now. They could get back together as a real family. Couldn't they?

He knew for certain now that there had been nothing going on between Lucy and Jason. Jason was just a desperate man doing whatever he could to save his business. John could at least understand that, even if he hated what Jason had done to Lucy. He didn't know, and didn't really care what had become of Jason, or for that matter Benni. He had never been able to ask Lucy what she felt.

By the time it was time for Lucy and Daniel to arrive, he was on his third strong, black coffee and had read, but not taken in, the Mail, the Mirror and most of the Telegraph. He should have been the most informed man in the town, but if asked, he would probably struggle to tell you a single headline of the day. His mouth was bitter from all the coffee and he felt slightly queasy from the fried bacon sandwich that he had eaten too quickly. Basically he was a wreck, a caffeine soused, nervous wreck.

He was sitting at their favourite window table. How many times had he sat with Daniel in the early days of EarStream? He working or reading the paper, Daniel lining his cars up or just eating his toast. They had been silent bonding times. Father and son together, no need for words or conversation, just father and son comfortable together, in companionable silence, bonding. You couldn't break bonds like that. Could you?

He should be able to see them as they walked down the road that ran alongside the park leading from their house, their home, to the parade of shops where the cafe was. John wondered if they would be excited, knowing that the life would be getting back to normal? Would they be laughing, or holding hands, or playing a game? He wondered if Lucy had told Daniel that daddy would be coming home soon?

The window kept steaming up. It must be cold outside. John hadn't noticed when he had walked down to the cafe. He couldn't have told you if the sun had been shining, or if the roads had been quiet, or even if the cafe had been busy when he had arrived. He was just here to meet Lucy and Daniel, and that was all that mattered. He wiped the steamy window with his sleeve, making a porthole through the steam and stared out at the streets and the park. It was raining, he could see that now. The pavements were glistening wet. People had umbrellas. Cars had their side lights on and the windscreen wipers running. Maybe it had just started? Surely he would have remembered if it had been raining when he had walked here? He rather self-consciously began to feel his jeans, his t-shirt, his hair, were they wet? Maybe damp, but he had been sitting here a long time, they could have dried. Couldn't they?

So intent was he on watching the road, the park, the pavement where they would walk down, he didn't notice the bell of the cafe door opening. Didn't notice the sounds as people made their way across the now crowded cafe. Didn't notice them until they were there, at the table, dripping and wet, hoods up, raincoats sodden. He turned, confused. He had been watching for them. He couldn't have missed them, not while he was watching so intently. But they were here now. Daniel and Lucy. Lucy and Daniel. They were here. He didn't how they had got here, but they were here.

He stood up, too quickly, clumsily, banging the table with his knee. The coffee cups rattled, but as they only contained coffee dregs, there was nothing to spill. His knee hurt, he felt the urge to rub it, to make it better, but for some reason this didn't seem appropriate. He manoeuvred himself from behind the table, careful not to bang or knock any more things. "I got our favourite table," he said to Daniel, who looked up blankly, but didn't respond. John felt his heart ache. He looked at Lucy for a reaction, her eyes smiled for him. "That was thoughtful," she said. But John felt momentary anger grow inside him, *thoughtful*, made him sound like a distant relative or maybe a kindly neighbour. He was Daniel's father. He swallowed the feeling down as Lucy helped Daniel into his favourite seat by the window. Daniel reached for his backpack that Lucy had been carrying and pulled out his cars. He was settled.

"How've you been?" John ventured.

"Fine. It's only been a few days since we saw you at the signing. But yes we've been fine." As John saw Lucy fishing around in her handbag for her purse, he intervened.

"Here let me. Do you want a coffee? Still a Latte is it? And Daniel toast I assume?"

"Yes John. Latte and toast, same as always." Lucy sounded annoyed, an edge to her voice. John didn't know why, he thought he was being nice. As John made his way to the counter, Lucy had a moment to herself. Why was John acting this way, she thought, as if this was some big reunion? They'd met like this a hundred times before, met here, had coffees, had toast. What was so special about this time?

John returned with the drinks. "Here you go," he said to Lucy, "the toast will be along in a minute," he said to Daniel.

Daniel nodded, but didn't look up. "Toast," he said.

"How's it going?" he asked, "any more trouble with Jason?"

"He still texts occasionally, but I think he's got the message. He's got his hands full with Benni."

"He went after him then?"

"Yes, through the civil courts. Benni seems to take these things personally, not a man to slight in business apparently."

"There but for the grace of God go I," John mused.

"Exactly, but perhaps more, 'there but for the advice of Giles and Phil'."

"Well 'all's well that ends well'," they both smiled, it was game they had played many times, 'Platitude Snap'.

"Such is life."

"C'est la vie."

"Enough already." They both laughed, a shared moment.

John leant across and laid his hand on Lucy's. "I've missed you," he said softly.

She leant back, pulling away her hand, but not aggressively. "How's your mother?"

"You sure know how to change the subject," John winced, “she's the same, unbearable to live with as ever. At least she's got me fitter, I go for very long runs now."

"Yes, I thought you were looking trim. Still working with Phil?"

"Well, yes, with Enterprise IT, there’s no end of contract work there, a man could earn a decent living."

"Yes, thanks for the extra money." John had been generous to a fault in passing on most of his earnings to Lucy. "But really, we were doing fine, the boys have been paying me regularly now, so there's no need."

"I have nothing better to spend money on," he said meaningfully.

"I know. But you have to build a new life outside work."

"I don't want a new life. I want my old life back."

Lucy sighed, "Not this again John, not now. Maybe we'll get to that, but just not yet. Let's let things settle shall we."

"But the reason we split, it's all resolved now."

"You know that's not it John, it was what you did and how you did it. The end didn't justify the means."

"I don't know what else I can do." John looked despondent. "If all I'm good for is to provide an income, then I can do that better by going away. Phil has offered me a contract out in India, supervising the development of a new software product he's invested in. Good money and nothing for me to spend it on. Perhaps I'll do that."

Lucy was taken aback. She might not be ready to take him back yet, but she was certainly not ready to see him leave. She decided to soften her position. "We need to find a way to reconnect John, to get to know each-other again, to trust each-other. I was reading this thing in a magazine about 'date nights'."

"Date nights?" John burst out laughing, "So it'll be back to Weatherspoon's and a quick kiss and a fumble behind the bike-sheds." He shook his head in disbelief.

"No John. It means dating like grown-ups. Making time for each-other, time to really talk."

John now regretted his outburst. "Yes, of course. I would love to date you. Whatever you want. Whenever you want."

"Good. So will you go? To India I mean."

"I've got a few weeks to make up my mind. So plenty of time for dating. When do we start?"

"Hold your horses. The whole point is to take it slow. I'll send you a text with a date and a time." She turned to Daniel. "Have you finished your toast darling, time to head home?"

"Sorry, no, can you wait a minute? I haven't got to the reason I wanted to meet." John removed an envelope from his coat pocket. He laid it on the table in front of her. "This is for you."

"What is it John?" Lucy looked uncertain and made no attempt to take it.

"Open it."

"No John, tell me what it is first."

John sighed. "It's the proceeds from the sale. I had transferred half of my shares to you and Daniel. So this is for you." He pushed the envelope toward her. "Maybe not as much as I'd first thought, but it'll pay off the bulk of the mortgage, or whatever you want to do with it. It's not for me to say."

Lucy took the envelope and slowly opened it as John watched her face intently. "You know it was never about the money John."

"I know. But in the end the money may help."

She opened the envelope and her eyes widened as she looked at the cheque. "It's too much John, this was your company."

"It was ours."

"But what about you?"

"My share goes straight into the trust to help develop the technology. Red Rock has already commissioned some work on that."

"Oh John thank you. I know you are trying to make everything right. And it is appreciated. I won't touch the money until we've discussed it more."

"Whatever you decide. It's yours to do with as you wish, for you and Daniel."

"OK, but no hasty decisions." She reached across and touched his hand, he quivers. "I'm looking forward to our date John." She got up to leave. "Goodbye John, say goodbye Daniel."

John turned to Daniel. "Here, before you go, I've got something for you. Something you can try for daddy." John pulled a neat looking device from his pocket, a little like a tiny hearing aid. "It's just an early prototype," he said as he bent down to Daniel and fitted the device around Daniel's ear. Daniel wriggled at the touch of something he wasn't used to. "It's OK Daniel, it's like a special toy, special because I made it just for you." He stood up and then reached into his bag and retrieved what looked like a mobile phone. "Daniel. Look, see this special phone, this lets you see and hear who's talking." John bent down again and showed the screen of the device to Daniel. The screen looked blank, but when John started talking you could see a voice trace tracking across the screen. John touched the trace on the screen and a label appeared, 'John Miller'. "That's my voice, see it says John Miller, that's me. Shall we record your voice?" Daniel nodded, for the moment his attention focused on the device. John took a moment to set up the device and then said to Daniel, "OK, Daniel, now talk into the 'phone'. Just say anything, anything at all."

"Hello," he said uncertainly.

John nodded encouragement, "How old are you Daniel."

"Four," answered Daniel more confidently.

John pointed to the voice trace on the screen and said, "That's your voice there Daniel." He touched a menu and added Daniel's name to a comment box on the screen, "Let's try mummy now."

Lucy got up from her seat and moved over to where John was crouched down with Daniel and bent down to be at the same height. "Hello, my name's Lucy." She spoke into the phone. I am Daniel's mummy and I am thirty-four." John, smiled up at her and pointed to the voice trace for Lucy. He noted Lucy's name on the device and made sure that the traces were correctly stored under their names.

"Now," he explained, "if we are all talking together, we can choose who we want to listen to. Let's sit back down and try it." He placed the device in the middle of the table and helped Daniel back into his seat. He and Lucy sat down at opposite sides of the table, either side of Daniel. John checked the device again, pressed some keys to adjust the volume. "Let's make sure we can hear it shall we? Right now everyone has to talk at once. Say anything you like"

Lucy joined in reciting a nursery rhyme that she knew Daniel liked, while John started a make-believe jokey football commentary. The screen showed a mass of sound waves which then quickly narrowed down to two clear traces, one labelled Lucy, the other John. John alternated between them on the touch-screen, firstly as he selected Lucy's trace, her voice could be heard through the speakers built into the device even though John was talking over her. "Wow," she said, though not sounding overly impressed. "It actually works real-time, that's fantastic. Come on Daniel you talk as well." But Daniel struggled to talk over the others, essentially Lucy and John had trained him not to talk over people - great for politeness, lousy for this demonstration.

John could see that Daniel was losing interest, his eyes drifted away from the device and back to his cars that were lined up neatly on the table. John looked a little deflated, he realised now that the demonstration was never going to work as well here as it did in the lab where they could simultaneous broadcast numerous voices and pick out selected voices with a high degree of confidence. Picking between two voices was just too easy to be impressive, but he wasn't confident that he could get Lucy and Daniel to come into the lab at the moment.

"That really is great John," said Lucy, trying to sound supportive. "But it really is time for us to go now. Time to put the oven on for tea." If John was hoping for any last minute reprieve, an invitation to come back with them, for tea or forever, he was disappointed. It would take time Lucy had said, but how much time?

Daniel started to gather up his cars, he had got so much better at this over the last few months, John thought, months when he hadn't been around to notice the small changes. Daniel could now accept that it was now time for a change in activity, in this case leaving, and the need to pack up his things without a fuss. Lucy reached over to Daniel, making as if to remove the ear-piece that Daniel was still wearing.

"No, leave it on," said John softly, "it would be good if he could get used to wearing it."

"But, we won't be with anybody ..." She looked sympathetically into John's face and relented, "sure, he can keep it on for now. It doesn't seem to be bothering him at all."

John nodded a thank you. He reached and picked up the device from the table. "It works on Bluetooth," he explained to no-one in particular. "The headset will connect anywhere within ten to fifteen feet of the base-station." He looked at the screen, but didn't switch it off, left it tuned to his own voice.

"Wow. Ten to Fifteen?" Lucy said over-enthusiastically, but without conviction, as she struggled to get Daniel's arms into his coat. When she had successfully re-dressed Daniel, she took the proffered device from John and placed it into her handbag, without looking at it.

The cafe was now entering its lunchtime rush. There was a bustling queue at the counter with people calling out orders over the increasing din of patrons chatting, laughing, scraping their knives and forks on the cheap white plates. People eyed their table as John and Lucy separately gathered their things together, there would soon be a competing scramble to claim the prize - a window seat. Lucy took Daniel by the hand and she offered her cheek to John for a perfunctory farewell kiss.

"I'm really glad the sale worked out and the technology looks like it's moving forward. But give me some time John, I, we, need some time to put this behind us." She looked down at Daniel, say good-bye to daddy, Daniel, we'll see him again soon." Daniel stared straight ahead, not responding to his mother's voice at all.

"Daniel." She tried again. "DANIEL." She shook her head, not a flicker of a response from Daniel, or even recognition. It wasn't that he was deliberately ignoring her, he just didn't seem to hear her voice. She looked back at John and smiled a sad smile. "I'm sorry, you know what he's like when he's like this, especially when it's noisy and crowded, nothing gets through. He's probably just tired,"

John nodded and touched firstly Lucy's shoulder, which he squeezed and then Daniel's hair, which he ruffled. Lucy turned and taking his hand, started leading Daniel through the bustle of people in the cafe, stepping out of the way of a couple of pensioners who were fighting their way determinedly to their table. John strained to watch Lucy and Daniel as they were gradually lost to the crowd.

"Excuse me, is this yours?" a voice said behind him.

"Err, what?" John was still distracted by the sight of his family leaving.

"This?" An elderly man, one of the couple who had successfully claimed the table was holding out a small yellow, plastic, sports car, a Porsche. John knew it was one of Daniel's favourites, he loved yellow sports cars. "Yes, thanks," he said as he almost snatched it from the man's hand, "thank you so much."

He stepped into the seething crowd, holding out the car, bumping into people as he tried to follow. Someone pushed back their chair as he made to leave, banging into John's knees.

"Daniel," he voiced hopelessly, "your car."

"Oh sorry'" the man said.

"You're so clumsy." his companion said.

"Daniel."

"Watch your back love," a waitress pushed past him, "number sixty-nine, egg and chips twice."

"Over-ere love. Sixty-nine that's me."

"You wish!" a cackle of laughter.

"DANIEL!" John was beginning to feel panicky.

And then he saw him, saw Daniel pulling an astonished Lucy back through the crowd, "DADDY!" Daniel yelled.

"Daniel?" John muttered in wonderment.

And then Daniel saw John's biggest smile....

THE END

ABOUT THE AUTHOR

For the last 20 years Michael has been running a Centre for supporting new technology businesses. He has personally assisted hundreds of entrepreneurs to launch new products and grow their tech companies.

He has won many awards for his work, culminating in the Queen's Award for Enterprise Promotion in 2013.

Supporting an entrepreneur to start and build a successful business is as much about building their self-confidence and business mind-set as it is about helping them to better understand sales, finance and marketing. It has been the experience of working with so many "reluctant entrepreneurs", that has led him to want to tell their stories.

Prior to the Innovation Centre, he had a successful career in the oil industry where he worked around the world as a rock physicist. He now lives on the Sussex coast with his wife, family and pets.

Made in the USA
Charleston, SC
14 December 2016